THE REBEL IN VIOLET

Book One of the Freedom for Rhethos Series

HANNAH R. LYON

THE REBEL IN VIOLET
Book One of the Freedom for Rhethos Series

Inspired Legacy Publishing is a division of (DBA) Inspired Legacy, LLC
PO Box 900816
Sandy UT 84090-0816.

ISBN 979-8-9877883-0-1 (paperback)
ISBN 979-8-9877883-1-8 (hardcover)

Printed in the United States of America.

WHAT PEOPLE ARE SAYING

"A beautiful tapestry of adventure and intrigue. A debut novel that you can't put down."
–Finn O'Malley, Bestselling Author of "Keeper of the Elements" Series and More

"I couldn't put the book down! It pulled me into a world of intrigue and wonderment."
–Deborah Wiener, Senior Board Member of the Quickscrews International Corporation

"This story shines brightly in the fantasy realm!"
–Woody Woodward, Author, International Speaker and Coach

"Reading *The Rebel in Violet* was like a voyage for my mind."
–Sophie Roumeas, Mindful Therapist, Bestselling Anthology Author

"This book a powerful escape from reality."
–Jacob Cooper, LCSW, CH, RMT

"I was delighted to find a combination of engrossing worldbuilding and amazing female empowerment in this book."
–Nancy Mills, Energy Artist, <u>SpiritedWoman.com</u>

"Full of surprising twists and turns, it kept me guessing until the very end."
–Tiffani Freckleton, Bestselling Author of "My NICU Story: Written with Love" and "Letters to a Future Nurse"

"In a time when many people are searching for meaning and purpose, 'The Rebel in Violet' offers a powerful message of hope and inspiration."
–Jeffery Olsen, Bestselling Author of "Knowing" and "Where Are You?"

"It is an epic adventure with heartfelt connection that is worth diving right into."
–Trevor Farnes, CEO and Co-Founder of MTNOPS

"Exquisitely written, Hannah Lyon is a master storyteller."
–Maureen Ryan Blake, TV host at Maureen Ryan Blake Media Productions, International Bestselling Author of "Step Into Your Brilliant Purpose"

DEDICATION

For the "real" Angelyn, my fellow conspirator.
Also my husband, for being all the inspiration I need.

CONTENTS

CHAPTER ONE

BAD WEATHER AND WORSE NEWS

Will spat a mouthful of blood into a nearby rain puddle, a chip of a tooth bouncing off the cracked cobblestones. His cheek started to swell, but he was used to the fights, the throb of pain, the burn of a bruise.

"Is that the best you can manage, Ross?" Will said, smirking. "I bet your wife could hit harder!"

He hadn't seen the first cheap punch coming, but this time Will dodged sideways, grabbed his enemy's outstretched wrist, and twisted. Ross' cry of pain echoed off the dark alley walls, back to the stables where Will had thought they were meeting amicably.

These dilapidated pathways near the docks of Kaylyn Towne were old enough and dangerous enough that not many frequented them, making this a reliable place to meet potential allies for the rebellion . . . till tonight.

Will had to use his free hand to wipe away the fat, cold drops of water that endlessly smacked the top of his head and leaked into his field of vision. The thick leather of his worn trench coat shielded him some, but no matter where one went in Kaylyn, getting soaked to the bone was unavoidable.

Ross fought against Will's hold, the top of his head barely reaching Will's shoulders. He tried to tear his wrist free and Will bent it sharply till it snapped. Ross shrieked and Will flinched at the unpleasant feeling, but Will held his ground. *He told me with his help this central piece of Kaylyn would follow me easily. So why attack me instead?*

"Please, Will," Ross cried, clutching his left arm to his chest. He lowered his voice, both of them knowing that the rain only masked so much sound in an alley that, by law, should be silent this time of night. "I thought I could help you, but I was wrong. It's hopeless. I'm sorry."

He took several staggered steps backward till his shoulders hit the alley wall behind him. The layers of moss and stinking filth that clung to the rough-cut stone stained Ross' cloak green, and Will observed that the shorter man's face now held the same pallor.

Will glared back, still refusing to show mercy to someone clearly full of cowardice he hadn't seen before. "Hopeless?" he hissed, and his right arm darted out to grab Ross' throat. "You're *sorry*? Do you have any idea how little that means to me?" Ross opened his mouth to protest, his good hand grasping at the one around his windpipe to no avail. "How about you tell me what you've done before I have to kill you?"

Ross gasped for air, the bottom of his boots kicking wildly at the wall, chunks of crusted dirt turning to mud when they fell to the flooded ground. Will loosened his grip, waiting. Ross had made a promise to give him the names of loyal Rhethosian families who would stand for the growing rebel cause, but now that clearly wasn't going to happen.

"You know what you've done to this towne. Thanks to Lieutenant Sarrett's constant patrols for rebels, he's got us all caged in our homes," Ross croaked. His voice trembled with fear when he said the military leader's name, just as any other sensible citizen in Kaylyn would. "Have you seen the bodies hanging from Towne Centre? That never happened before you arrived! I can't run my business. My wife blames me for it, and—"

"Ah. I see now. So what did your Katie tell the lieutenant?" Will said, his throat constricting when he began to understand where Ross was coming from. "If she said anything or wrote something down, this will be the death of the cause."

"The cause," Ross mimicked, then coughed as Will squeezed tighter on his throat, digging in his nails.

"I'll have to find her now, Ross," Will threatened. "You know that."

Anger filled Ross' eyes, but Will stared blankly at him till the fire faded to only the fear that lay underneath.

"No," Ross insisted. "She didn't tell Sarrett anything. I wrote to the lieutenant myself. One of my sons is carrying the information to Towne Centre tonight. Sarrett will let my family live when he gets my confession about you and your people. I thought knocking you out here tonight would be a nice bonus to ensure our safety."

Will cursed under his breath. If what Ross said was true, Will maybe had half an hour, probably less, to find that information and destroy it before it reached Kaylyn's military representative.

Doesn't he have any idea how many rebel hidden families he's putting at risk? How many of his neighbors and friends secretly support the cause who will be implicated by his actions tonight? he thought. *If everyone dared to speak, like they have in the northern townes . . . but it can't be helped now.*

His fingers twitched toward the old scar of a prayer rune on his arm, instinct telling him to give blood, cast a spell, to make this right. But the magic he could once use to help others was long gone. The Goddess' Touch only belonged to those who stayed faithful, and he was anything but.

Will's practiced rebuttal for this kind of situation was on the tip of his tongue when new voices abruptly echoed off the wet walls. Deep tones of authority reached his ears and grew stronger with each beat of his chilled heart.

Both Will and Ross froze, and Will had to tighten his hold on Ross, who tried to cry out and draw attention to them a moment later. The narrow space between two towering Kaylyn shipping warehouses led to a dead end at the stables, but in the opposite direction, the alley opened out onto the main road that ran along the docks.

One sharp voice from the main thoroughfare carried into the alley's shadows: "Don't put up a fight or it'll be worse for her."

Will didn't need to see the man speaking to know he was one of Sarrett's guardsmen patrolling the main road to enforce the latest stringent curfew. Will grimaced as Ross sputtered against his hold, trying to flee toward the men he'd clearly sided with.

A quavering voice, smaller than the first, coated in fear, echoed down the alley: "I've done nothing wrong! Lara, go home. I'll speak with these men. The children are waiting—"

"Not so fast," cut in the guardsman's voice. Will could hear a smirk in the man's tone. "You both are in possession of illegal Sahma wine, and out beyond Lieutenant Sarrett's curfew. Take them." The guardsman's voice lowered and Will grit his teeth from his hiding spot.

Several shouts bounced off the surrounding buildings, coupled with the crunching of fists and flesh, and the sharp sound of swords ringing from their sheaths.

Will's free hand twitched toward the hilt of his own weapon. He wanted nothing more than to drop Ross in the filth and help the innocent couple being arrested not fifteen steps away. But they would recognize him, and everything he had built for the last ten years would be lost.

As always, when he was drawn between what was right and what needed to be done, Will's mother's voice whispered softly in his mind: *You cannot save them all, darling. The people of Rhethos have hardened themselves out of fear of their leader who claims to protect them, but if they learn the true potential of a free life, miracles could happen.*

Lara's screams escalated into shrieks of pain, then subsided into sobs as the guardsman's irons rattled. Will knew the couple would be taken back to Kaylyn's Towne Centre and down into the dungeons below the government building where Sarrett kept his victims. Whether the citizens had truly possessed anything illegal, neither would see the light of tomorrow's sunrise, and their children would wake alone.

As the noises on the main road faded, Ross renewed his struggle against Will's grip. Will had to hold him steady, his trained intuition telling him if he let Ross go now, he'd run after the retreating guardsmen, hoping to save his own skin by revealing the rebellion's wanted leader: Master Will Tarran.

"You know that it's *not* my fault that the people of Kaylyn live in caged fear?" he tried, hoping there was some piece of belief in his cause still left in Ross. "It's because of The Bradford and military tyrants like Sarrett that you cannot breathe without fearing for your lives. The lieutenant will show you and your family no mercy, Ross. You have to stand strong with me against monsters like him."

"Don't you understand? I . . ." Ross started now, his voice rasping, ". . . they'll know soon enough, Will. We never would've broken free of The Bradford. He keeps us safe from the Blood Goddess. It's not worth risking life without his protection."

Will couldn't help lessening his hold at these disparaging words. Ross took a deep, shaky inhale. "It was a dream," he insisted. "They would have taken my Katie, as simply as they got those two bastards. They'll burn my home if they find out I've worked with you. Sarrett shares The Bradford's love for death by fire."

Will exhaled, shutting his eyes. *The reward of a kingdom free of fear of The Bradford's misinformation is worth the danger. I can't do this alone, not after what happened to her, dying without seeing her dream realized. Give me strength, Mother, and I will make this kingdom right again.*

Will's hand darted to his right arm where a ragged, violet cloth was tied over his coat's sleeve. He yanked hard on the fabric till it tore in pieces. Several scraps fell into the nearest puddle. Will held the fabric up to Ross' face. The man's eyes grew wide, rain water leaking along the wrinkles under his eyes and the lines around his mouth.

"What does this mean to you?" Will demanded softly, his tone icier than the rain that continued to pour into the pathway. "Please, tell me."

He only waited a breath for a response, but Ross seemed at a loss for words.

Will shook the drenched violet rag in Ross' face. "This is freedom, Master Ross, for you, your wife, and your children. I *will* find a place here to build against The Bradford, no thanks to you. This violet color represents the ability to choose right from wrong for ourselves, to *not* blindly follow corrupt leaders who would have us eating shit in gutters like this for their amusement!"

"Master Will, it's a lost cause—"

Will shoved the violet rag into Ross' mouth, cutting off his words. Ross struggled, but Will landed a solid punch to the side of Ross' face, cracking his skull back against the stone wall. His head bounced forward again with a sharp snap.

"I thought you were on my side, ready to fight and die for Rhethos," Will said, his voice blended with the impact of the rain and the sound of crashing waves as they stormed against the nearby docks. "But I need loyal rebels, not traitors."

Ross tried to escape, but Will held him pinned. He began to panic, squealing protests against the violet cloth in his mouth, waving his intact wrist frantically. Will hesitated only for a heartbeat before pulling a dagger from the folds of his trench coat.

He placed the point on Ross' windpipe. "Say a prayer to the Lord in the south or the Goddess across the sea, I don't care which. I'm sorry, brother."

Will shoved the blade through the traitor's throat, a small grunt of effort escaping his lips when he felt the tip of the dagger scrape against the stone wall. Ross' eyes widened even further, then closed. Blood from the mortal wound soaked down into his coat, mingling with the rain.

Ross' corpse fell limply forward and Will caught him awkwardly before lowering the body to the cobblestones. He retrieved his blade and wiped it clean on the dead man's jacket. He knew he didn't have the time to hide Ross as he should.

Will needed to find that confession Ross had sent before it was delivered to Towne Centre. His eyes fell on the violet rag bulging from Ross' lips, and he quickly stooped to yank the fabric free. If a body was going to be found by Kaylyn's guardsmen, he didn't need his rebels' colors between its teeth.

As he retreated deeper into the shadows, Will thought about his people and his mother's dream, and deeply buried the sorrow he couldn't feel for his dead fellow conspirator.

I will suffer no traitors.

CHAPTER TWO

BLASPHEMOUS RUMORS

Joshua McKinlee could see the black stretch of the unsettled ocean from the fogged window. Strong waves churned and gagged over the docks and boats along the Kaylyn shore. Nights like this, he felt grateful for the sturdy, old walls of the Hamond Inn, both his family's business and his home.

The iron lamps that lit the street corners swung violently, rain pouring down their glass that protected such small flames. Joshua grumbled under his breath, listening to the gales sharing a mournful tale of the tempest outside. Behind the common room's bar, at the very end, was his favorite spot in a comfortable corner where he would spend most evenings listening to people gossip with the sailors.

Fewer ships came into port the last few years, though, bringing harsher times for the entire towne. He'd even heard some people whisper that Kaylyn wasn't what it used to be; the old, seaside port could be dying, with more lucrative trade points like Lorington nearby.

"Hey, little McKinlee! Fill this up, will ya?"

Joshua glanced across the bar into the very red, drunken face of one of the Hamond's regulars. Master Leerstrom, the local tanner, was a large man who always wore a layer of furs despite the heat inside the hall. He shoved his empty glass forward.

Joshua took a moment to stretch before refilling the man's glass. Master Leerstrom clutched at the bar's smooth edge as he swayed, and Joshua figured he was drunk enough to need an escort home . . . or to say something he shouldn't.

"So," Joshua began, wiping foam from the edge of the glass, "those men you're sitting with over there . . . they were talking about some interesting rumors last night."

"Oh really?" Leerstrom slurred and rotated his broad shoulders to glance back at his table. He reached toward his glass, but Josh pulled it back.

"They mentioned folk in towne from the north," Joshua whispered. "I heard some of them may be—" But he choked back the last word, not daring to say it aloud: *rebels.*

Master Leerstrom got a hold of his glass and headed back to his table, oblivious to Joshua's unfinished thoughts. Joshua looked around in case he spotted any Rhethosian guardsmen nearby, somehow thinking, however absurd, that they could finish his thought and arrest him.

He casually made his way through the crowded hall, gathering empty glasses and listening hard. Usually, there was only one main story being agreed upon:

The Lord Bradford keeps us safe, like the very First Bradford did, hundreds of years ago. Without his protection, however harsh it may seem, we would be vulnerable to the Blood Goddess' magic. Being enslaved by Her and her pagan ways would be worse than anything a local guardsman could do on the streets with no consequences.

Now, however, Joshua had heard a different version being spoken by those who dared to imagine life without their southern Lord:

The Bradford lies about threats from the ancient deity. If we broke free of him, we'd have the power to choose for ourselves who to worship and how to live without misinformation, oppression, or fear. The rebellion is real and its leader is ready to fight.

Joshua set down his armful of dirty ale cups and stepped over to where Master Leerstrom had retaken his seat amongst his two companions. The young man across from the large tanner was clearly a sea trader, from the looks of his salt-stained, ragged clothing. His speech was lowered and fast, and Joshua knew he wanted to hear every word.

"What was that you were saying?" Joshua asked, taking a seat on the edge of the table. He tried to keep the desperation for real news out of his voice. He hated being stuck in these four walls for over a year now, too afraid to step outside and be conscripted into the military or imprisoned for looking at one of Sarrett's guardsmen wrong.

The trader smirked dryly at Joshua. "It's about the war. There's talk about the rebellion comin' here. People all over towne are sayin' they ain't wanting The Bradford dictatin' no more—"

"What could we have a problem with?" interrupted the man across from the sea trader. His eyes were red and glazed over just like Master Leerstrom, yet he drained the last of his tankard with a steady hand. "We need our Lord to keep us safe from the Blood Goddess across the sea. She chains up her followers and makes em bleed for her. I say we live well enough here!"

Joshua recognized Master Danamark who lived close to the Hamond and rarely missed breakfast or supper here. There was a pointed tone in his voice. Locals like Danamark were well-practiced in the art of paranoia.

"Yeah . . . yeah, o' course," the sea trader agreed, catching on. He lowered his voice, and Joshua had to lean down to hear him continue: "But . . . there are people who want to make their own choices for Rhethos. You may be too young to know it, boy, but the current Bradford treats us all like cattle, worse than any other before him, and that ain't right."

"But those that do speak up aren't around anymore," Joshua countered in a whisper. "Just last week one of the girls who worked here was complaining about the late hours her guardsman of a husband had to work. She talked about moving north to a towne that bore rebel colors. I haven't seen her or her husband since."

"I hope she made it," muttered the sea trader, shaking his head. "Though she needn't have bothered traveling through the shitty weather up there. The rebels have finally reached Kaylyn. Haven't ya wondered why Bradford's left hand, Sarrett, is up here from the south? It's a serious threat if they've got a man like him crushing this place."

"Is it true that the brother townes Patten *and* Morely have changed their colors to follow that rebel leader?" questioned Master Danamark softly.

The salt-stained sea trader and Master Leerstrom nodded as if this were old news.

"But . . . both of those places are just a day north of us!" Joshua said in awe. Two loyal Rhethosian townes full of law-abiding folk had turned against their Lord?

"I dunno what those crazy mountain townes were thinking," muttered Leerstrom. "There's no redemption for traitors, only the noose or the pyre."

"I've read books about—" Joshua started, then frowned when all three of the men laughed hard.

"Books, eh?" one roared, slamming the table and sending ale sloshing from their cups. "How old are you, boy?"

Joshua cleared his throat. "Old enough. I heard that Patten and Morely suffer from a sickness because they're close to the Goddess' Woods. But even when they were loyal to our Lord, they kept dying. Those trees creep right down to my backyard, and we never get sick. We don't pray to the pagan Goddess to keep us safe . . . so why are some of us fine and some of us dead, whether we wear Rhethosian Blue or rebel violet?"

The sea trader's expression sobered when he met Joshua's eyes. "Makes ya think, huh? All I know is Armellans can get sick across the sea, too, despite their 'Loving Mother' watching over them. Young ones fall ill during winter and are dead by spring in both kingdoms, and neither Bradford nor the foreign Goddess cared."

"Oh, praise the Lord and all he gives us," sighed Master Leerstrom, and Joshua's jaw dropped when he heard the sarcasm, no, the pure *hatred* in his tone. If any military guardsman heard a bit of this conversation . . .

The sea trader cleared his throat and leaned even closer to Joshua. "Look, boy. You should be allowed to grow up askin' questions because none of us could. 'Fear is the enemy of freedom.' That's what the rebel leader tells all his people."

Joshua nodded. He could smell sweat, ale, and salt emanating from the man's skin and clothes.

"If you wanna find the supporters," the young man continued, "just look for a show of violet on em, like a scarf or armband, though that's becoming rarer with the lieutenant around. You've gotta know the right people if you wanna keep your mum here safe. These men are ready to fight for the freedom they want and we all deserve."

A hand clamped down on Joshua's shoulder and he nearly slid off the table in surprise. With his heart in his throat, he glanced up to see one of their barmaids, Ada, giving him a strained smile. Right behind the pretty, young girl stood his mother, and Joshua's heart plummeted from his throat to his stomach.

"Joshua!" his mother snapped. "It's ten past nine! You're supposed to tell me ten minutes *before* the curfew bell rings to empty this place. That's your job!"

Joshua whipped his head to the clock above the bar and grimaced. He'd been so caught up in the conversation that he didn't even think of the time. When nights were actually busy, his mother was caught up booking rooms, cleaning tables, and sorting laundry.

"Yes, Mum." He gave this response to everything she said regarding their home and family business. Lately, however, he'd found it harder to agree as he'd done as a child. A lot of tension had soaked Kaylyn, and he was old enough to see it on their patrons' faces and feel it in the freezing wet air that rushed in every time the front door opened.

In his mind, he didn't see what the problem was anyway; they weren't doing anything wrong, and more coin for the inn meant more coin in the lieutenant's pocket come tax day. But Joshua had no possibility to voice such concerns, even to his mother behind closed doors.

Ada leaned forward and messed his dirty blond hair into his eyes. "Too much responsibility for you, huh, Josh?"

Joshua shoved her hand away, frowning as intense heat bloomed on his face. She'd been teasing him since she started working in the common hall a couple years ago, and Joshua didn't mind, since the inn's staff was part of his small collection of friends he could see with the lieutenant's new laws in effect.

"I'm sorry," Joshua added to his mother, who merely gave him a short nod. She pulled her long hair back and tied it with a deep blue ribbon, one that matched the color of her working dress she always wore under her thick apron. "Rhethosian Blue," the locals liked to call that shade of azure, and most wore it daily to show their loyalty to their Lord Bradford.

"Time to send these folk home," Angelyn muttered, and climbed on top of the nearest table. The cramped hall was still mostly full of bodies milling about the high-ceilinged room. The local musicians had already wound down their last tune for the evening and were hurriedly packing up.

Joshua winced as his mother put her fingers in her mouth, preparing for the shrill whistle that rang high above all other sounds. Everyone stopped to glance at her, and the kind but stern grin she held well on her lips.

His mother put on her best smile and politest voice. "Thank the Lord you're all listening!" she exclaimed. "I'm afraid it's after nine, and that's when I have to close. If you want me to keep up and running and *not* be shut down by the guardsmen down the street, you'd best move out!"

Several groans peppered the room, though they only came from the sea traders and their crew members; the local patrons stared wide-eyed at those that were being defiant. Faces became frantic as cups were set down and chairs were pushed back.

Joshua watched his mother, knowing how much she feared the military force that held such a tight sway over their little home. He glanced over and noticed his mother's hands shaking. Her hands quavered like that more and more lately, and Joshua knew she wasn't aware that he noticed.

Only a few inarticulate complaints were left as the common hall quickly emptied, and his mother said nothing in response, letting everyone blow their steam inside her walls instead of out on the streets. Sad but true, Master Harling down the High Road would be happy to make a report at Towne Centre that the McKinlees couldn't keep their people under control.

And Lieutenant Sarrett will listen to him, Joshua thought bitterly. *His family name has Loyal status. He's earned The Bradford's ultimate title of respect in Rhethos.*

Even after Master Leerstrom was helped by his companions out the door, Joshua followed his mother' gaze to one particular group that stubbornly remained, raising wine glasses that spilled fresh, red stains on the floorboards.

"I think that particular group has taken quite a liking to the Armellan wine," Ada observed as she helped Angelyn down off the table. When she mentioned the free kingdom across the sea, Joshua heard contempt in the barmaid's tone. Trade with such a place was strict, especially with how The Bradford unearthed new threats from Armelle's Blood Goddess this season. They had to be careful or the foreign deity's attention would be called back to Rhethos, like the ancient times when every human was enslaved to the Goddess' whims.

"We've got to stop serving that stuff." Angelyn shook her head. "It's not worth the shipping costs, and it's clearly causing trouble."

"Oh, I don't think it's *your* wine that's the problem, Miss," Ada explained.

"That lot brings in bottles under their cloaks from Master Harling's. I think that he does something to it, infusing it with the Sahma herb from—"

"I know. I'll take care of it next time we catch them drinking it. And don't mention that nasty drug in front of Josh," Angelyn said, glancing in Joshua's direction.

He raised his eyebrows at his mother. "Really, Mum?" Joshua muttered. "As if I don't hear worse every night. . ."

"I wish I could do more," Ada insisted, hands on her hips. "With Sarrett here, I can barely lift my head and say a word for fear of—"

"Nonsense, Ada. Our Lord gives us strength and safety through the storms," Angelyn finished.

"Yes," Ada said, though Joshua noticed she paused before agreeing dutifully. "We are thankful for his love."

Such was the common phrase used when folk in Kaylyn complained about one thing or another. Joshua must have heard it uttered a hundred times tonight alone, always with the proper, required devotion.

Angelyn took a step toward the remaining drunken group, but an older man strode up to them first. "Now, that's enough, brother," he began, his frail voice full of soft tolerance as he touched one of the men's shoulders. "Let's get you and your friends home."

CHAPTER THREE

HIDDEN SCARS AND TWISTED JUSTICE

Joshua watched how the older man motioned for Ada the barmaid to come over to him. After murmuring a few words to her, she nodded and respectfully replied, "Yes, Master Chapman."

Thank the Lord for family names like his that still demand respect around here, Joshua thought.

Ada opened the front doors for the last group of patrons to exit into the rainy night, then the older man turned toward the McKinlees.

"Thank you, Gabriel," Angelyn sighed, putting a hand to her forehead. "They get worse every night."

"I've known you since you were . . . well, Josh's age." He patted her arm, and Joshua watched with concern as she clung to her friend. He continued, "You can handle yourself and your home, Angel."

"Why did you call that man 'brother'?" she asked.

Gabriel chuckled and winked. "'Tis a saying, dear, nothing more."

He placed a worn hat over his thin, white hair. Gabriel wore a fine vest over his dark green tunic, and he straightened it before reaching for the last cloak by the door. It was thicker and more well-kept than all those Joshua had seen tonight.

Joshua rushed forward to open the door for him, and a fresh wave of rain and icy wind tore inside. Gabriel bid them both goodnight, but Joshua stepped out with him under the awning.

"What is it, Josh?" Gabriel asked. He had to raise his feeble voice to be heard above the screaming wind. All the light and warmth of the Hamond had dimmed down to the one lamp that hung outside the inn that shone down the length of the covered porch.

"I . . ." Joshua started, then shook himself. The air, despite its invading chill, was so refreshing. "I've got to take in the banner."

This little bit of time he had just outside his home every night was, sadly, the favorite part of his day. Joshua reached up to the horizontal iron pole just outside the entrance. The sopping fabric clung stubbornly, and Gabriel reached out a hand.

"Let me help," the old man insisted, and rolled back his sleeves. Together they managed to work the banner free and Joshua fanned the navy cloth to reveal a brilliant golden sun stitched in the center, curved flames of yellow and black emanating from its core. Soaring proudly through the sun's orb was a dark raven, wings spread in an expansive proclamation of power.

"Thanks," Joshua said. He should go back inside, but instead he tried to think of something, anything, that would let him breathe this fresh air for a few more minutes. Gabriel eyed him suspiciously, as if he knew exactly what Joshua was doing.

Joshua found his gaze rested on the one word emblazoned in white letters across the raven's wings on Rhethos' sigil: justice. "Tell me why we have to have this word on the banner again?"

Gabriel, who looked quite ready to make his way to the warmth of his own home, sighed and glanced down as well. "It's been ten years since that addition," he spoke patiently. "When the current Bradford came into power, guardsmen marched down the streets and told us we needed to renew our displays of loyalty or be punished."

"It really means 'Rhethosian Justice', right?" Joshua mused. "People use that phrase a lot, saying one cut throat deserves another. Is that really justice, or revenge?"

"It's all just a load of rubbish, Josh. But don't tell your mother I said so."

Joshua smiled and did not push the subject. Instead, he noticed a marking on Gabriel's arm, just below his elbow where he'd rolled up his sleeve in the lamp's light. It looked like an intricate scar, similar to the ones marked on the barrels of Armellan wine his mother ordered.

"What is that?" Joshua asked, nodding at Gabriel's forearm.

The old man started and shoved his sleeve back down. "Nothing important. At least . . . not anymore."

"But I really—"

"Was there something else you needed, Joshua?" Gabriel cut in. His pale blue eyes, surrounded by dozens of wrinkles, were inquisitive under the brim of his hat.

"Master Chapman . . ." Joshua started after taking several deep breaths. "I just want you to know Mum is getting worse. She doesn't sleep much, and her hands . . ." He had trouble speaking plainly about Angelyn and her ailments.

Gabriel frowned, his attention shifting again to the banner over Joshua's arm, dripping rainwater onto both of their boots. "Look, Joshua," he said, narrowing his eyebrows. "Since your father left, your mother has been running this place and raising you on her own. Even with a husband, life here isn't easy. As always, I'm more than happy to help with the money, but there are many worries hanging over her."

The Chapmans were one of the wealthiest families in Kaylyn, which wasn't saying much in Rhethosian standards, but Joshua wasn't concerned with coin right now. "I just want answers," Joshua said. "Some explanations so I can understand what's happening in Kaylyn."

"You need to support her, Josh," Gabriel replied. A harsh wave of wind tore underneath the Hamond's awning, and the old man slapped his hand on his head to keep from losing his hat. "That means do what she says. If she doesn't want you talking to sea traders, don't do it. If she doesn't want you leaving the Inn, don't do that either."

"But," Joshua insisted, "you've no idea what it's like to be stuck in there, day after—!"

"Don't argue," Gabriel cut in. He smiled and stepped out into the rain. His hat instantly plastered to his head. "And remember you have something to look forward to. I have a special present for your sixteenth birthday tomorrow!" he called above the storm. "You're going to love it!"

Joshua was about to shout a reply, but the old man had already shifted toward home and disappeared into the rain seconds later.

Joshua stepped back inside and slammed the dark blue door shut behind him. He shivered as the cold was cut off. His mother was finishing her usual routine around the hall, turning down the oil lamps. She locked the back door leading to the stables, the kitchen door leading to the side alley, and the front door in the main hall, then double-checked them all. Joshua saw fresh, dark circles under her eyes, and a wave of pity washed over him.

"I hope Gabriel didn't tell you anything inappropriate," she said, dropping her heavy key ring into the front pocket of her apron. "The Lord knows

I love him dearly, but I've seen him talking with those men spewing their dangerous rumors."

"He's fine, Mum," Joshua said. "He just said he knows it's been tough for you. . .especially since my father left us."

"Neither of you should worry about that," his mother dismissed. She put a hand up to his cheek, staring hard into his eyes with her dark blue ones. Her touch was warm and soothing against his chilled skin. "Your eyes are like your father's," she said. "That deep brown . . ."

"Why don't you ask about him?" Joshua asked tentatively.

Angelyn stepped away, toward the nearest dirty table to collect empty plates and glasses. She deliberately put her back to him.

"It's been such a long time, with no word or reason as to why he's just *gone*," Josh pressed on.

"I'm not the only one who lost someone back then," Angelyn pointed out. "Lots of able-bodied men went missing, not long after the current Bradford came into power. There were whispers of secret, high-paying military jobs that caught the attention of unhappy, violent men like Travok."

Joshua nodded solemnly. Military life serving their Lord was the best thing any Rhethosian boy could dream of. But what kind of "job" could take a man willingly away from his family for over a decade? "I know we're not supposed to ask," Joshua began, "but don't you want to know if he's alive? With the lieutenant in towne, maybe we could both go and—"

"That is not how things are done," she cut in. "I am sorry, darling, but you must understand that we are here to do as we are told, and to keep our heads down. Yes, life is thin and dark, but manageable."

Joshua's fingers curled into frustrated fists. Somehow, despite Gabriel's warnings, his mother's explanation wasn't enough. In his heart, he was beginning to realize he *deserved* more. "But tomorrow, for my birthday, even if it rains, do you think I could go outside? It would be so nice to—"

"No," she snapped. "The lieutenant's men are becoming more abusive. If they get word that you're sixteen, I'll never see you again. I'm sorry, little Josh, but I can't lose you, too."

He recoiled and grimaced, biting his tongue against the irritation that rose in his stomach at that child's nickname.

"It's best if you stay here with me," his mother continued. "I'll try to make the common hall as nice as I can for the whole day."

He wanted to shout that being stuck inside this building till he died was terrifying, that he wasn't her "little Josh" anymore. But he lowered his head. "Yes, Mum." Stepping over to her, he took the stack of dishes from her hands. "You go ahead and go up. I'll take care of clearing the tables. You look tired."

She leaned in and kissed his forehead. "Thank you, darling."

Joshua let his smile drop as soon as his mother climbed the staircase that wrapped as a balcony around the inn's second level. She headed down the farthest hallway, her steps heavy on the old floorboards. She lived in a back bedroom, raised slightly on its own level for privacy. He knew his mother would collapse immediately and (hopefully) fall asleep.

But first she'll stare at the painting, Joshua thought as he hauled an armful of dishes and cups into the kitchen. *That huge oil painting of her parents holding her when she was a baby is her prized possession. And nothing can stop Mum from sticking to her safe, isolated routine.*

Joshua sighed. He wasn't sure what "freedom" meant, let alone a rebellion. Hopefully those men would come back tomorrow and he could ask a few more questions.

Would any of the rebels know where his father could have gone and how Josh could find him? And if he could, would he want to know the man who abandoned him or demand why he'd hurt his mother so badly by deserting her?

And could someone explain to him the truth about how "safe" they were under their Lord, or what a deity who wanted blood from humans could possibly want from the people of Rhethos?

He fell asleep thinking of the scars he'd seen on Gabriel's hands, ones that looked like they belonged in a story about magic runes long buried under their ruler's oppressive eye. *Tomorrow,* he thought, *I will get answers.*

CHAPTER FOUR

ONE MAN'S AMBITION

Lieutenant Jonathan Sarrett retrieved his uniform jacket from the floor. He smoothed the stiff shoulders and repositioned the line of gemstones, then glanced over his naked, broad shoulder. He flashed what he hoped was a convincing grin at the bed behind him.

"Find my boots," he ordered, shaking his brown, sweaty hair from his eyes, "before your sister gets back from the market, preferably."

The pretty mess of blonde curls and bare skin stretched, smiled back at him, and pushed off the loose bundle of blankets and furs. She followed the instruction without much modesty, bending over and ducking on her hands and knees to search around the mattress for the lieutenant's shoes.

Part of him wanted to turn away, the part of him that knew this whole charade was just a necessary part of his plan to get Kaylyn Towne under his thumb. His thoughts went to his mistress Mayra in southern Rhethos, caring for their children many miles away from him. Would she understand, or would she hate him if she knew?

Esvele finally found his boot and tossed it at him. Even though he had barely finished fastening the buttons on his trousers, Sarrett caught it with a practiced reflex.

"What difference does it make if Lyara comes home early?" Esvele asked. She sat up near the edge of the bed and loosely gathered a blanket around her front. "Are you worried we'll fight over you?"

Sarrett swung his foot next to her and laced up his boot, dusting off the leather that ran up to his knee. "I'd welcome the challenge," he laughed. He hoped the confidence in his voice sounded more genuine than it felt; he didn't actually care about either of the girls.

Esvele bent to retrieve his second boot and held it out toward him. Sarrett placed his other foot up beside her on the bed and waited till she got the hint to slide the polished leather onto his foot and lace it herself.

"Don't waste your time with Lyara, lieutenant," she said, weaving the strings through their gold-studded holes till she reached the top. Tying the laces in a bow, she playfully twirled the ends around her fingers, then slid her hand up the inside of his thigh, squeezing hard.

Sarrett had had enough and brushed away her touch before setting his foot down with a dominant thump. "My time is never wasted, Miss Harling." He resumed his inspection of his lieutenant's jacket before donning it. "Don't you northern girls know at least that much about the Sarrett family?"

"I never heard of your family name before you came to Kaylyn, lieutenant," she said innocently. "Do you have a *big* family in the south? Loyal status? Lots of brothers and sisters?"

Sarrett paused, caught unaware by her last question. "I had one sister," he confessed. "She drowned a long time ago."

"I–I am sorry, lieutenant. I would miss my sister if I lost her. Though . . ." Esvele faded off, winked, and her sincerity washed away like a shallow wave, ". . . I'm much more fun than her."

Sarrett closed his eyes so she wouldn't see him roll them. He straightened the hem of his jacket so it lay perfectly above his belt buckle. "I'm sure. Family is clearly important to you Harlings. Your father can confirm how . . . useful his two girls are."

"You mean he knows that we—?" Esvele said with a hint of shock.

"Damn right he does." Sarrett didn't look at her; every time he glanced her way now he saw Mayra's face instead, and the guilt was eating at him more prominently than before.

To steady himself, he carefully fastened his gold buttons into place. As the uniform enclosed his torso, his sense of authority heightened, and his nerves settled. This was what he was sacrificing his conscience for. Common folk in the street avoided his gaze and stumbled out of his path. He knew how to command their fear, how to exploit their fragile emotions, and within a moment, they would never forget who he was because of how his captain trained him.

The uniform amplified the tools of success he'd honed to a sharpened edge in the south, and once the command was given for him to clean out the treasonous stench of rebellion from Kaylyn's sea-watered streets, he knew this was his chance to make a true name for himself in the Rhethosian military. If he could keep Kaylyn safe, he could earn respect, make his mistress happy, and create a real, happy home for his children.

Sarrett glanced at a rounded, gilded mirror on the Harling girl's wall and straightened his sleeves. He set back his shoulders and rolled his neck from side to side.

Finish what you started, he thought resolutely. *She's hanging onto you because she knows what good it could do her, but say what you came here to say before she took off her dress. Then it'll all be worth it.*

"Do you know what else your father is aware of, sweetheart?" Sarrett continued in the silence, plastering on a sweet smile when he pivoted on his boot heel to face her. Esvele shook her head. "Master Harling sells his 'special creation' to sad locals, deadbeats, and criminals, but he knows now that the extra gold has to go somewhere if he wants to continue this work."

The lieutenant raised his arms, as if indicating the rest of the situation was obvious. His blonde friend only smiled unsurely, and Sarrett sighed. He knew Esvele was dull but finished his thought anyway.

"Your father knows that for him to keep up his side-work, I pocket half for my kindness and silence. He knows the consequences if he tries to double-cross me, and he *knows* I'm sleeping with you and your sister. So why don't you be a good girl and get me a free bottle of that wine for the road?"

"Yes, lieutenant," Esvele said, as if she truly understood it all. He doubted it. She scrambled from her bed and threw on a thin, fur-lined robe before scurrying from the bedroom.

The middle class in Kaylyn were used to their positions being the highest social rank, with few wealthy folk willing to live in such a dying, weather-strewn towne close to the sea. Despite the dishonorable stink of the entire situation, putting this family of lazy Loyals in their place gave Sarrett a small sense of justice.

The Harlings got the idea that their elevation above the poor dock workers and sea traders made them special. But it had taken only a few steps to gain the grounds he had now. It had started with one dinner with the wealthier tradesmen, then a quiet conversation with Master Harling about the hidden supply of illegal Armellan Sahma herb in his inn's basement. Followed up with a simple threat on his daughters' lives, and a couple easy smiles toward Esvele and Lyara, and Sarrett now had a good sum of extra gold in his pocket and more authority under his belt.

Esvele came back with a tall wine bottle. Sarrett took it, only acknowledging the girl with a quick nod before he left. He was already thinking about the next letter he wanted to write to Mayra, asking how the children were and inviting her to join him in Kaylyn soon. The towne was almost presentable despite recent rumors, and he wanted to show her what he could make: not just a safe towne, but a safe kingdom free of rebels.

By threatening Kaylyn, they've officially crossed into Southern Rhethos, close enough to The Bradford that he's taken notice and wants them officially stamped out. I'm sure I'll get some resistance, but nothing I can't handle without my Captain.

The streets were dark and wet when he stepped out onto them, yet only a small amount of rain fell. He had arrived nearly a month ago, but the gloominess of the coastal towne during the storm season put him in a horrible mood every morning.

The southern cities, so much larger and prosperous, were always full of warmth and color and light. He could close his eyes, as he sauntered through Kaylyn's narrow pathways, and imagine his old home in Clancy.

He imagined the roaring river and blossoming fields he'd grown up next to, within walking distance of the towering stone battlements that enclosed The Bradford's city. Those rich, marble hallways, savory meals served by beautiful women, bright music played by talented musicians, and debates with witty scholars drew his attention throughout his teenage years.

And The Academy. . .the place where unknown people in power would train the worthiest young man to become the next Bradford. He had dreamed of being accepted there as any young boy would. Such ambitions could possibly come true in Clancy, yet the best he'd managed so far here in soggy Kaylyn were a couple of willing sisters and their unlawful father.

He crested a small hill on the main street, which curved with the natural line of the coast, and Kaylyn's Towne Centre appeared before him. The building was the largest in towne, a formidable block of stone painted midnight blue, its center a tower that rose high into the congested, gray sky. A pointed spire gleamed at the highest point, an old copper likeness of a past Lord Bradford standing atop it.

To the lieutenant, every Bradford looked the same, taking on the continual dictator's name and reigning with as much suppression as the last. The amount of power held by The Bradford was so consistent through the centuries that no one questioned the way the kingdom worked. After all, The First Bradford had broken Rhethos away from the religious oppression of the Armellan Goddess and banished her people across the sea. Who could doubt the absolution of a ruler who created a stronger, better place for them to live?

Sarrett eyed the bottle in his hand with caution. The reason behind Harling's wealth was not hard to discern. Sarrett had been told by the officers most eager to curry favor with him to seek out this particular tradesman, the vague statement of "ask for the special bottle," being given to him on a piece of paper.

After some golden persuasion, Harling had retrieved a bottle from his cellar and grudgingly explained how he infused the Sahma herb into the contents of Armellan wine barrels.

The effect of the tampered foreign substance was euphoric, and Sarrett found that sipping the beverage in measured amounts was equal to an amazing waking dream. Three mouthfuls put him on a cloud of bliss, making his heart race and colors more prominent in his sharpened vision. Half the bottle produced a state of ecstatic confidence that, if he focused hard enough, seemed to make him more perceptive and manipulative than his sober self.

He had been warned, however, against drinking an entire bottle of the Sahma wine, with or without food. Most of those criminals he easily arrested and condemned were guilty of abusing Master Harling's creation. Sarrett had seen their red faces go blank, their reasoning capabilities leave them, and had to restrain them when they began to hallucinate and scream.

The double doors that led into the Towne Centre were flanked by two guardsmen Sarrett knew well. They straightened and saluted as he approached.

The towering slabs of ancient oak were hinged on old brass pieces that took time to open and close for every person entering or leaving the building.

All the lieutenant had to do was clear his throat and the men worked to open the thick, heavy doors.

"Lieutenant, sir," one of the guardsmen spoke up as Sarrett stepped forward. "You've been requested downstairs. They're having trouble with several rebels that were caught tonight."

"Trouble?" Sarrett repeated, brows raised. "How hard can it be to make a few dogs confess where the lead bitch is?"

"They don't crack easy," the guard responded. "They're . . . very loyal to their leader. If you persuade them yourself, I'm sure we'll learn something."

"I see," Sarrett said, a sour taste rising in his mouth at the idea of torturing the latest captives. His captain was the one who adored torture, not him. But how could he tell Mayra and the children to come north and see what a loyal towne he'd made of Kaylyn if he couldn't root out a few rebels?

Sarrett paused to swallow another mouthful of wine. His body heated to a pleasant temperature and his heartbeat slowed to a more manageable speed.

A flash of heat ran across his palms. It was as if the places where his hands had touched the bottle were suddenly warm and dry, like desert sand. A feminine voice full of power touched his mind:

Use caution, dear lieutenant, when using an herb like Sahma. It will numb your guilt, but only until it eats you alive.

Sarrett shuddered and handed the wine bottle immediately to one of the men before him. Harling never mentioned such side effects happening so quickly. The Sahma infusion in the wine would have to be something he used with great caution. And superstition about the Goddess who could be reached by using such herbs? He didn't think it was truly possible.

After straightening his shoulders and forcing himself to forget the words spoken into his head, Sarrett gave the guardsmen a flawless grin. "If those rebels won't talk, then get the captive's families. Bring them downstairs, and I'll make them *all* sing of Rhethos' greatness."

CHAPTER FIVE

MAGIC INSCRIBED IN GOLD

Joshua knew his mother would try to make his day something special. All he expected was the usual assortment of his favorite foods and perhaps a few modest gifts. He knew it would just feel like another day where he struggled to breathe within the confines of the inn.

When he descended the stairs just after dawn, a dozen people in the common hall greeted him with shouts and hugs. Colorful cloths and ribbons hung from the rafters, shining in the morning light. Varying banners, all woven and hand-stitched with intricate designs, covered the walls, adjacent to the flowing navy representations of Rhethos' sigil. He loved the way the common hall always looked, but somehow these simple, added bits of color made him grin.

As a boy who could barely wear his clothes for a month before he grew out of them, he more than appreciated the huge breakfast that the inn's cooks kept piling in front of him not long after the front doors opened for business. The Hamond seemed half-full of locals he knew well, and certainly their friends who made life worth living. He finally pushed his plate away from his engorged stomach.

Gabriel, who was one of the first to arrive, was dressed in layers of fine Rhethosian wool. Of course, he led the swarms to the bar, as what seemed like the entire towne streamed in to wish Joshua a happy birthday.

By midday, it felt like Joshua had entertained at least a hundred people, as they came up to his decorated seat at one of the largest tables. Everyone wished him well and some, whose faces he knew but names he couldn't place, set gifts down in front of him.

When his mother bustled around to his seat and their eyes met, he realized that she felt just as surprised by the generosity. *Maybe that's why she made my birthday into such a feast for everyone; they needed an excuse to smile.*

His favorite games were played, the best songs were sung, and the hours whirled by with more joy than Joshua thought he'd ever felt. Angelyn finally collapsed next to Joshua as the sun was setting. She sighed happily after her best cook, Bertram, had presented Joshua with a gigantic dinner he could hardly eat.

He hugged his mother, then glanced toward the darkening windows to see that rain still fell even as the sun descended below the ocean's uneasy surface. The common hall had grown stuffy and hot with the number of people, especially as folk continued to pour inside, shaking beads of water from their cloaks and hoods. Both of The Hamond's large fireplaces were fully aflame now that the evening had fallen, and warm light filled the entire room from floor to high ceiling.

As Joshua watched, several men cleared a good space of the floor for dancing now that the evening's set of musicians had arrived. Ada had told him earlier that her betrothed knew the band of traveling players, and they had agreed to play for free for the party.

It was one of the few kind things she had said about her husband-to-be. Joshua had chosen to ignore the disdain in her voice when she mentioned him. He didn't know much about the man, but Joshua was aware he chose to drink at Master Harling's tavern down the road, and that spoke more loudly than anything Ada might say.

Joshua returned his gaze to his mother and watched her face light up as partygoers approached the table to bid him congratulations and pat him on the back. She frowned, however, when they walked away.

"They're all pretty happy for you, aren't they?" she whispered in his ear, and gestured to the table full of gift boxes, as well as plates both empty and full of food.

Joshua nodded. "It's kind of odd, and a bit overwhelming, actually," he muttered back, picking up on her suspicious energy. "But I'm not complaining." He gave her another hug, happily surprised to find she wasn't shaking in the slightest. "Mum, I can't believe you did all this for me. This is the biggest party you've ever had at The Hamond!"

Angelyn frowned. "Well, that's sweet, darling, but it really wasn't my doing at all. According to the girls, Gabriel gave them the idea. Then Ada got a little over-excited and it turned into all of this."

They both glanced over at Gabriel, who was deep in conversation with several locals. Joshua's throat tightened when he recognized the sea trader and his friend he'd spoken with last night. He also noticed the way Gabriel held his lower back when he moved, leaning close to anyone speaking in order to hear their replies.

When Gabriel made his way over to Joshua's table, Angelyn rose to offer him her seat, and he collapsed into it gratefully. "Good Lord," Gabriel groaned, massaging his knees. "It seems I'm not made for these social events anymore. I can barely stand long enough to hold a decent conversation!"

"Yet you somehow managed to orchestrate all of this," Angelyn pointed out with a thin smile.

Gabriel waved away her words. "Now, my boy, let me see if I can find that present of yours. . ."

Even though Joshua knew full well that the old man had the gift on-hand, he waited patiently as Gabriel tucked his hand into the folds of his fine cloak. He pulled out a small, brown box tied shut with a length of violet string. Joshua noticed his mother stare at the color that was supposed to represent Rhethos' rebellion, but he happily took the gift from Gabriel.

An odd feeling overcame him when he accepted the box and held it between his hands. He needed to pause, run his thumbs over the box's surface, and catch his breath.

Joshua could not explain it, but whatever was in the box, even though it was still wrapped, felt *right* in his possession.

"What is it?" Joshua asked, and was surprised that the question came out as a hoarse whisper.

The old man's face broke into a grin. He reached out to put his gloved hands over Joshua's, tightening his already strong grip on the box. He leaned forward till his lips were inches from Josh's ear and replied in a tone too soft for Angelyn to hear: "It's your destiny."

Joshua leaned back, eyes wide. "I'm— I'm not quite sure what that means."

Gabriel let out a laugh, then glanced at Angelyn, who was clearly concerned. "Like I said," he continued at a normal volume, "you'll love it. Happy birthday, Joshua."

As soon as Joshua took the violet ribbon off the box, his mother snatched it up and tucked it away in her apron. But Joshua could hardly look at her. The entire common hall seemed far away as he stared at the small, wooden box, held shut by a single hinge on its top. His fingers hesitated under the lid for one breath, then two, and he flipped it open. Inside, on a folded swatch of white silk, was a brass compass.

"Gabriel!" Angelyn gasped, her eyes wide. "Why would you get him something so. . .?"

Her question faded off, but Joshua knew exactly what she meant to say: *Why would he get me something so expensive? It's . . . amazing. I've certainly never owned anything like this before.*

"I didn't get it for him," Gabriel replied smoothly. "It's been in my family for a long time, yes, but now it's Joshua's. It was always meant to be his."

Joshua shot a look at his mother, whose expression softened a little. He knew, too, that Gabriel didn't have any family of his own left. It was a heart-warming gesture that he'd pass on a piece of his heritage to Joshua on his birthday.

Joshua picked up the compass, his fingers trembling. It looked extremely old, but the brass surface was smooth and polished, and only had one single scratch on it. When he opened the finely curved lid, the candlelight caught in its circle. He blinked and smiled when the needle quivered, then pointed perfectly north. As Joshua stared at it, he could imagine those townes up the coast, inland, that flew rebel violet banners.

His mother was gently admonishing Gabriel about the extravagance of his gift, but Joshua wasn't fully listening. He turned the compass over and found an inscription etched into the bottom curve of brass. It was finely done, several of the characters rubbed down till they were almost invisible.

Whatever it said, Joshua could not read it. The letters were odd, ancient runes, carved shapes that melted from geometric blocks to smooth loops and lines. *It's that language from Armelle, the one they use for prayers . . . and for magic.*

The marks on the compass suddenly glowed red, pulsing with shocking strength and clarity. Angelyn and Gabriel both whirled and looked down as Joshua sat transfixed, his face illuminated blood red.

"Good Lord!" Angelyn said, and shoved the compass down into Joshua's lap underneath the table. She glanced around nervously. "What is that thing, Gabe?"

"It's hot!" Joshua exclaimed, turning the compass over in his hand. The brass surface heated in his palm almost to a burning point, but he wasn't frightened; in fact, holding the present close made him feel safe and happy.

"Master Chapman," Joshua said uneasily. He had to clear his throat before continuing. "What do these markings mean? Does this compass have magic in it?"

Gabriel winked. "I've been waiting since I was your age to give you this. You see," he lowered his voice almost to a whisper, "when you're sixteen you can have your Blood Fortune read by someone of Armellan heritage. They can connect to the Goddess and learn part of your Fate's String to share with you."

"My *what?*" Joshua was thoroughly confused now.

"Gabe, he can't have something like that!" Angelyn insisted, grabbing Gabriel's arm. "Do you know how much trouble I could get in if someone saw what just happened? Or if they repeated anything you've said?"

Gabriel gave Angelyn a serious look, the wrinkles in his face hardening. "I don't have a choice, sweetheart. This is part of what She's asked me to do . . . on this very night. For your boy, and for the sake of Rhethos itself. Josh has to have that compass and decipher whatever the Goddess has written on it for only him to see."

Angelyn opened her mouth, no doubt to reprimand her old friend again, but Gabriel wasn't even looking at her anymore. He leaned sideways to glance around the many shoulders of those milling about the common hall. When his pale eyes focused on a particular group heading toward the private parlor on the east wall, Joshua saw his mother hone in on the movement, too.

She didn't miss a thing.

CHAPTER SIX

AN UNDENIABLY PERFECT SPOT

Angelyn knew the space of the common hall better than anyone. She could analyze each movement, sense each change in emotion, all from many years of experience. So, when her oldest friend's smile faltered and his attention shifted to something other than the seemingly magical present he'd just "fatefully" given her son, she stood from her seat.

"Gabriel," she began, "what's going on over there?"

"Nothing to worry about," he assured her, but she saw the worry lines around his eyes. For a man who was usually comforting and sunny in her dismal life, seeing him fret made Angelyn's throat go dry.

All day and night, something hadn't felt right to her, but she'd dismissed it every time she saw her son's shining face. Tonight, her private parlor had remained empty, simply because no one had asked to use it. Gabriel and the other wealthier families of Kaylyn often spent time there to avoid the noise of the common hall, but never had a group gravitated toward it together, at a certain time, without asking her first.

Angelyn took a step toward the parlor, but Gabriel grabbed her wrist. She gave him a stern look. "Either you let me go over there," she began, "or we can sit here and continue to discuss whatever pagan piece of magic you've just given Josh."

"Gabriel isn't a pagan, Mum!" Joshua hissed, a hint of disbelief in his lowered voice. Gabriel, however, clearly didn't want to discuss that subject and let go of Angelyn.

She wanted to march right over to the parlor's door, but knew better than to panic; maybe there was nothing wrong here. Maybe her gut had been lying to her all day. Instead, Angelyn walked slowly, pausing a couple of times to talk to patrons who milled about in every bit of space.

With each step she took, she caught glimpses of more men and women stepping into the isolated space, some of them glancing at the clock. Angelyn sidestepped a group of drunken revelers who decided to create their own dance space in the middle of the common hall and grabbed the edge of the parlor's door.

"Excuse me," she began. "Is there any particular reason why the lot of you need to use this room without asking permission?"

Inside the private room stood two dozen chairs, the finest the inn possessed, and all were occupied. The ornate drink cart on the far wall, below several windows looking out onto the stables, had been emptied already, though Angelyn noticed none of the filled glasses set on the long table had been touched.

"Miss McKinlee! What are you doing here?"

Angelyn spotted Ada amongst the group. Her gaze shifted over Angelyn's shoulder, and Angelyn turned to see Gabriel behind her, with Joshua close by.

"I thought you were keeping an eye on her," Ada said in Gabriel's direction. "He should be here soon!"

"Who?" Angelyn demanded. "Someone needs to tell me what's going on. Now."

Gabriel sighed and motioned for Angelyn to take a few steps into the parlor, though it was already crowded. "Do you know why they're having such a party out there?"

"Ada said that they wanted to make Joshua happy," she started slowly, "and the staff was right this morning when they said we need the business. You know how bad it's been lately."

Gabriel shook his head sadly. "It's much more than that." He paused, looking at her. "You've heard the rumors, just as Josh has, about the war. The rebellion's supporters, well . . . we need a place to speak in private and plan how to take the towne. There are groups like this all about Rhethos, men with the same beliefs, gathering to see how many of us there really are."

"*Us?*" Angelyn could only mouth the word silently, too shocked to speak.

"The Lord sent the lieutenant up here to put a stop to it, but he doesn't care enough to lift a finger himself," Ada added from the other side of the room. There was clear disdain in her voice. "The Hamond was suggested as a safe place to meet. You've never had any trouble with Rhethos' government before, but you've never been one to be too judgmental, either, Miss."

"Rebels?" Joshua spoke up, and Angelyn snapped her attention to where he stood in the parlor doorway. "Here? Tonight?"

"Not just rebels," Gabriel replied, though his attention was on Angelyn. "The rebel leader himself: Master Will. Ada is right; we should expect him any minute."

Angelyn took a step back toward the door, her legs numb with disbelief. She gave each person she saw even looks of disbelief; she didn't recognize her oldest friend, her staff members, or her neighbors that she saw before her.

"Don't worry, Angel," Gabriel began. "I don't know Master Will very well, but he's been a good friend to me the last week he's been in towne."

"Now this rebel leader is your *friend*?" Angelyn breathed unevenly.

"Yes," Gabriel insisted. "He has ties to the Goddess, like I do." He paused, staring at her intently.

Angelyn, however, found herself quickly glancing down at Gabriel's glove-covered hands, hiding the scars on his skin. Never, in her entire life, did he mention aloud that he had Armellan blood in his veins.

Except for the night Joshua was born . . . when Gabe saved his life.

"So," Gabriel continued earnestly, "I trust the rebel leader. Old, frightened people like me have waited our entire lives for a night like this. But Master Will doesn't want the lieutenant suspecting us of having this meeting. So how could we make it look as if there wasn't anything suspicious going on?"

Her heart sank at the nauseating feeling of betrayal. "And none of you planned to tell me. After all the false kindness you've shown me and my boy today?"

"Please, Miss McKinlee," Ada tried. "Just sit with us. You'll see that this is the right thing to do."

When Angelyn glanced at the rest of those present, she started to notice shows of violet under their cloaks . . . and the hilts of weapons, too. She took one more step back toward the door, putting herself solidly between the parlor's occupants and her son.

Her gaze fell on Gabriel, and it hurt to find that, for the first time, she was horribly upset with him. "What can I do?" She tried to keep the desperation and anger out of her voice. "If I can't physically stop this Master Will or his people, how do I keep Josh safe?"

"He won't be in danger here with us," Ada put in. "We're not monsters."

Angelyn, however, glared at her until the girl dropped her gaze. "You need to go upstairs, now."

Joshua shook his head, his right hand still clenched around the compass. "I'd rather stay here, Mum." He said it loudly, and many of the patrons around him glanced their way. Ada and several of the other bargirls present exchanged wary expressions.

Just then, the parlor's back door leading to the stables swung open. Despite the subtlety of the action, Angelyn clapped a hand over her mouth. All talking in the parlor stopped, and all heads shifted toward the doorway, letting in rain, wind, cold, and a man that could only be Master Will.

His long, black hair was covered by a wide, black hat, the brim just above shockingly bright green eyes. He wore a black tunic, a black leather coat, long black pants, and boots. Silver straps ran along his boots, weathered and travel worn.

He had a sword belted at his waist, a smaller blade on the same sheath just below it, as well as a dagger on the outside of each leg. He wore cracked, black gloves that were cut off at the fingers.

As he deftly pushed the door shut with a boot, everyone stayed silent. Will strode over to one of the men sitting at the table and shook his hand as though he knew him well. Angelyn watched as he whispered something, and the man pointed to her, taking in his funeral-like, dismal attire. Will, soaked in rainwater, looked at her, and grinned.

She knew in that one look that this man was no good.

He walked over to stand in front of her, still with that mysterious smile on his face. He was almost a foot taller than her, with strong, broad shoulders that took up all of her vision. As he took off his hat, Angelyn had to grip the parlor door's edge. He was much more handsome than she had expected, and she didn't like it.

"Are you Angelyn McKinlee?" he asked. His voice was deep and soothing, making her feel unwillingly comfortable.

"Why?" she snapped, straightening herself to her full height. She instinctively shouldered Joshua, who was staring open-mouthed at Will, farther behind her.

"Because I'd love to speak with the famous woman who runs this lovely place all by herself," Will replied, taking in his surroundings with an appreciative expression.

"This is my inn," Angelyn snapped.

"So you are Miss McKinlee," he said, observing the group and the cozy, private room. "And these—" he opened his arms, gesturing to all the people gathered there, "are my fellow conspirators." He finished with a rough laugh.

Several men rose to murmur words of welcome and hand him drinks, but Master Will waved them off with more smiles.

Angelyn stood rooted, her eyes glued on Will, her temper burning to a point that was almost unbearable. She was used to dowsing her fiery personality with fearful submission to authority. After all, there was no other way to survive in Kaylyn. How could this man walk into her home and suddenly make her so upset that she dared to speak up for herself?

Gabriel went up to Will, and Will wrapped one arm around the older man's shoulder in a tight hug. "I heard about the trouble with Ross," Gabriel whispered, though Angelyn could hear him from where she stood. "I vouched for the Master as well as his wife, so I still can't fathom why he and Katie would—"

"I handled it with the little time I had," Will voiced quietly. "When I went back for Ross' body, though, it was gone."

"His *body?*" Gabriel trembled when he replied. "Why, if you had to kill him, would you leave him where the lieutenant could—"

"Let it be for now," Will said strongly, then turned to help those moving their chairs to allow him more room. "We will speak about it together later."

"What do you think you're doing?" Angelyn tried to hide her panic now that she'd found her voice. Will stared at her with everyone else. She felt Joshua's tentative hand on her shoulder behind her. "This is *my* inn!"

"You've told me that already, Miss," Will said calmly. "And we have our business to attend to. You are welcome, of course. Unless you want to stay in the main hall and continue the party you have going. The noise level is perfect, and the back door into this room will serve as the perfect exit. But if you stay, lower your voice, if you don't mind. There are plenty of folk here that are passionate about my cause, but we all need to learn discretion as well."

"I will not let you do this!" she cried, glaring at her barmaids who were present, several of her cooks, and many of her friends. "And how dare all of you do this on my son's birthday? I thought you wanted to celebrate because you love him. Did you think you could do this behind my back? And with the lieutenant in towne?"

"Don't be so worried," Will said soothingly, taking a step toward her. She took an equal measure backward. "I promise I have everything set up for you. Men are at every street corner keeping watch, Sarrett's officers and their guardsmen are being kept busy at Towne Centre, and I've made sure you can't go anywhere to try and alert the local authorities." He paused, and a smirk rose on his face. "You just have to trust me. Isn't that right, brothers?"

A rumble of quiet approval issued from the gathered group.

Angelyn fumed further as she recognized the term "brother" Gabriel had used the previous night with the men she didn't know. And now Gabe had mentioned that Will was also connected to the Goddess, like her oldest friend was? That was enough to throw in his lot with this rebel leader because of a pagan, foreign deity they were raised to fear?

Despite Will's looks and Gabriel's proclamation of his courage, she already hated him. "Please, just get out," she hissed. "Now, before the bells ring for curfew."

"Mum, don't," Joshua said from behind her.

"I'm sorry, Miss McKinlee," Will said with a deep bow, "but we're already here, and I can't risk moving my men again. I'm asking you to let us stay. Not to mention that, if you send us all away now, there's no way you and your boy won't be implicated."

Angelyn eyed him, deep distrust running through her mind. "Fine," she conceded. "But I'll be right outside. At fifteen minutes to curfew you need to clear out, because after that the guardsmen *will* come. Stay in this room, and I swear, if anything happens"

"Don't worry, Angel," Gabriel interrupted softly. "We know what we're doing."

Angelyn ignored him and scowled at Will. "You know that you aren't allowed to bear any arms inside towne limits. You've got a lot of nerve coming in here, endangering my family with your weapons."

Will gave her a suggestive smile. "Would you like to disarm me, then?"

Titters rose from the group, and Angelyn blushed. She balled her hands into fists and grabbed Joshua's sleeve. When she stepped out of the room, however, he refused to move with her.

"Joshua, come with me," Angelyn commanded, her face still hot with color. "We cannot be seen with these rebels."

"I want to stay," Joshua said, and when Angelyn snapped her gaze to him, shocked, she found him glancing past her shoulder at Will. "I don't want to hide anymore."

Angelyn tightened her grip on Joshua's arm and forced him into the common hall at her side, away from the warmth of the parlor.

She glanced over her shoulder once more and saw Will taking a seat at the head of the narrow table. Everything intimidating about him seemed to diminish when he sat at the same level as the rest of the group and took off his wet hat. His expression softened, and this time, when he spoke, there was a soft urgency in his voice.

"I want each of you to take a moment," Will said, "and recognize everything it took for you to get here tonight. What doubt slowed your feet, what fear did you face, and what uncertainties still fill your minds?"

Shoulders relaxed, backs slumped into chairs, and every eye was locked on the rebel leader. Unwillingly, Angelyn felt herself let out a breath of tension she'd been holding in her chest.

"I'm here to tell you two things: those elements cannot last against a united front of clear intention, unity, and freedom from the ties that bind you now. The second thing you need to know is that any questions you have will be answered by me personally, until you have no doubt that what you currently suffer will be resolved within my cause."

Angelyn shook herself, breaking whatever peace Will's voice emanated. Before slamming the parlor door shut, she was surprised to see every man and woman's face full of hope. That was a sensation she had never felt before in her common hall.

CHAPTER SEVEN

QUESTIONABLE CONVERSATIONS

Angelyn spoke curt orders to her staff before hauling Joshua upstairs. Once they reached her large bedroom, Joshua spun to face his mother, and she could see thousands of questions and waves of excitement brimming in his eyes. "Those men last night were right!" he exclaimed. "The people who want to fight for freedom *are* in Kaylyn! And their leader, he looks so—"

"Enough!" Angelyn insisted before he could say another word. "Darling, those traitors lied to you all day to hide the truth from the guardsmen. They ruined your birthday. How could you say you want to stay down there with them?"

"They haven't done anything wrong. Maybe if I'd spent the day *outside* like I wanted, you wouldn't have this problem," Joshua countered. "For the Lord's sake, Mum, I'm getting sick of being trapped in here!"

"Do you realize how dangerous it is for you now?" Angelyn snapped. "If you catch the attention of local guardsmen, which you *will* with the attitude you've had lately, they will realize your age and take you away from me. I know it hasn't been a law for very long, but the lieutenant will turn you into one of those monsters who haunt the streets, burning homes and hanging traitors from rooftops!"

She stopped before her voice rose to a scream. Never before had her son argued with her like this, never in his life. He was curious, observant, and smart, yes, but in the last year, he had begun to resist the sheltered lifestyle she forced on him.

I cannot lose my boy, she thought. Terror crept up her spine and iced over her brain. She shivered and swallowed dryly. *I cannot have my parents die, my husband abandon me, and my son taken away. If we are quiet, if we stay obedient, nothing will happen to us and I can make sure he's still safe come sunrise.*

As if reading her mind, Joshua spoke up. "Mum, I'm not little anymore. I can decide what is best for me."

"No, Joshua," she replied. "You can't. Don't talk to that man, don't look at him, don't ever be in the same room as him! Do you understand?"

Joshua frowned and sat down on the edge of her bed, head hung, gazing on the compass in his hands. When his thumb passed over the inscription on the back, a faint red light issued from the brass surface.

She stood in front of the door in silence, the air taut with the rift between mother and child. Angelyn wanted to speak up and soothe her boy's temper, to somehow make him see that her decisions were for the best, but nothing that came to mind seemed to hold weight when she opened her mouth to say it.

Eventually, it appeared that Joshua had given up arguing as well. Angelyn was content to have him sulking up here, even on his birthday, if it meant he wasn't associating with the rebels downstairs. She let out a breath she didn't know she was holding.

Suddenly Joshua stood up and shoved his compass in his pocket. A defiance burned in his eyes that she'd never seen before, and it frightened her. "Mum," he said strongly. "Last night one of the sea traders said the rebellion is all about overcoming fear. I've been thinking about it all day, and I think he was talking about more than fearing the lieutenant, Lord Bradford, or even the Goddess. He said this Master Will stands for not fearing things we can't control because behaving that way will never make us happy. I think I understand what that means. Do you?"

"I . . ." Angelyn started uncertainly. "I'm not sure what you're trying to say, Josh."

"I'm saying I'm going downstairs to listen to their meeting. It's almost curfew now, anyway, so there can't be much more to be said. Come with me, Mum."

"Joshua, you can't!"

"Yes, I can! And I will. Are you going to stop me?"

Frustrated tears formed in Angelyn's eyes. Before she could say another word, Joshua shoved past her and left the room. She tried to stop him, but instead let out a sigh of defeat and followed him.

The common hall was empty of patrons when she and Joshua descended the stairs. Several of her barmaids were cleaning up, while other members of her staff made sure none of the remaining patrons wandered too close to the parlor's closed door. One of them winked and showed her a violet armband under his tunic's sleeve, and Angelyn felt her throat go dry.

Rebels, she thought. *Everyone left here follows* him.

Joshua gave his mother a look that said, "what were you so worried about?" Angelyn gave him a stern shake of her head when he started to make his way to the west parlor. Her own expression plainly said, "then let it be and don't draw attention."

Thankfully, Joshua conceded and walked over to the bar to take a seat.

Angelyn went into the kitchen to get her and her son some fresh tea, mostly to calm her own nerves. When she returned to the edge of the bar with the hot water, she heard light footfalls behind her and spun around.

"So you've decided to come down here and support the cause after all?"

Joshua rotated as well at the question. They both saw Master Will standing there, hat respectfully in his hand.

"Hello!" Joshua exclaimed excitedly.

Angelyn swallowed, then scowled at Will. She could tell that her son admired Will a great deal from the bit of conversation they'd heard before going upstairs, but she resisted the urge to grab Joshua's wrist and drag him away again.

"Josh, don't" Angelyn began, then stopped.

The door on the east wall suddenly opened, and Ada emerged from the cellar carrying a wooden crate. She closed the door deftly with her heel, but stumbled under the weight of the box that touched her jaw. Angelyn had assumed the girl was still in the parlor with the others, but before she could step forward to help, Will crossed the room and took the crate from Ada's hands.

"You should be more careful, Miss Ada," Will said with a kind smile. "Darren would not be pleased if you hurt yourself working alone so late at night."

Angelyn watched Ada's entire face light up with a confident grin. When Will returned her smile easily, the young girl blushed.

"I was just making sure everything was stocked up here so Miss McKinlee didn't have to worry," Ada explained.

"Aren't you sweet?" Will chuckled and set the crate down on the nearest table. "Miss McKinlee is lucky to have you, my dear."

Ada shook her head. "We're the lucky ones to have you, Master Will," she insisted. She spoke these words at her boots. "Thank you for bothering to remember my name."

"I remember everyone's names, Miss," Will said, and Ada glanced up at him. "And you and your betrothed are valued people in my eyes."

"He isn't the fastest nor the strongest man," Ada replied, "but I can pull my weight and his, I promise."

Angelyn cleared her throat loudly and gave Ada a pointed look when both she and Will glanced at her. It wasn't proper for a young girl to speak of her future husband in such a way, but something told Angelyn that Ada didn't believe in such rules. Whether she was excited or not about her engagement, Ada had no right to flirt with the rebel leader.

"Every one of us has value," Will said. "Now watch yourself going home. The guardsmen are out in numbers, looking for curfew violators."

"I know a safe way," Ada said, and Angelyn felt shock when she gave Will a sly wink. "I'm not afraid of the lieutenant's men."

"Good girl. Give Darren my best," Will said, and she left through the back door.

Angelyn tried to regain her composure, but found herself fuming. How could everyone love this man, despite all the dangerous rumors? *His suave smile and polite attitude might make Ada blush, and Gabriel may be readily devoted, but I cannot stand him!*

Will shifted so his warm smile fell on Joshua and made his way over to the bar where he and his mother sat. Angelyn didn't like that grin Will kept flashing. It was stunning and welcoming, but there was something else as well, some sly trickery that made her uneasy.

"How are you, my boy?" Will asked Joshua. "I heard you turned sixteen today."

"Yes, Master," Joshua replied proudly despite his mother's nervous hand on his shoulder. "I thought you had left, but I'm glad you're still here. Did you need something?"

Will glanced at Angelyn quickly. "Yes, Joshua. I actually wanted to talk to your mother."

"If this man wants to talk then you're going to bed," Angelyn told Joshua.

"This is ridiculous," Joshua muttered under his breath, then stood. He turned to Will and glanced up at him. "You're here to help us, aren't you? All the problems people have been talking about, you're here to solve them, right? Even though everyone's scared?"

Will glanced at Angelyn for a mere second before directing his gaze back to Joshua. "Yes," he replied. "I will try my best because Rhethos deserves freedom."

Angelyn almost burst out that his help wasn't needed, and he should never come back here again, but the shine of hope in her son's eyes stopped her. Then Joshua did something that Angelyn least expected and would never forget: he hugged Will.

The moment Joshua threw his arms around Will, red sparks erupted in the air and hung in bright shimmers. Joshua jumped back and Angelyn screamed. The bits of ruby-like twinkles drifted between Joshua and Will for a moment, coruscating in the pale lamplight, then showered down to the dirty floorboards.

"What just happened?" Joshua gasped.

"It's not possible," Angelyn interrupted.

"He's Goddess Touched, Miss McKinlee, just like myself," Will said, surprise in his tone. "That's what that magic means."

Angelyn shook her head. This was too much in one day, and she couldn't accept the fact that ancient, outlawed Armellan magic could burst into her common hall right between the rebel leader and her son. She'd taken measures to assure nothing like this would ever happen, right on the night her boy was born.

"I'm *what*?" Joshua prompted, his eyes darting questioningly between them.

As a child, Angelyn's grandmother had told her tales about those favored by the Armellan Goddess, and how they gave off traces of magic when their skin met. Those magic remnants were treasured and celebrated across the sea; yet, they meant death here to those who could potentially bring the Goddess' attention back to Rhethos. She hadn't thought of those stories in a long time, and yet somehow, she remembered them right now with frightening clarity.

"That's enough, Joshua. Go to bed," Angelyn said, and her voice cracked a little. Joshua peered at her curiously.

"You should probably listen to your mum for now," Will insisted gently, and, to Angelyn's relief and irritation, Joshua actually listened.

Even as Joshua ascended the stairs, as slowly as possible, Angelyn knew he wouldn't go back to his room. It was almost guaranteed he'd wait just around the corner and listen to whatever Will said.

Keeping this in mind, Angelyn spun sharply on her heel and strode around behind the bar. Keeping her gaze down, she grabbed a glass and a bottle of whiskey, poured an even measure, and slammed it on the bar in front of Will.

"Now what do you want?" She glared at him as furiously as she could manage.

Will sat down at the bar. She could smell his leather coat and the wetness of rain in his long hair. Every time he shifted she heard a muffled clink of metal, as if the man wore many more hidden weapons than the several already visible.

"To start," Will said calmly, "I'd love to hear what you know about The Goddess' Touch."

Angelyn blinked, a little taken aback. "I know that the Armellan faith is illegal, and that magic isn't real," she recited swiftly. "And I know you've just played some nasty trick on my son, you and Gabe, with that compass and that . . . whatever that was."

Will looked confused, then shook his head. "He's sixteen, born under the last Blood Moon. I want to know how you hid it from the guardsmen who test the blood of every baby unfortunate to join the world at that time."

Angelyn glared, but she could tell the emotion wasn't as ferocious as she wanted; helpless tears sprang up, reminding her of a night long past she had chosen to forget. "Lower your voice," she pleaded in a whisper, pointing at the stair's landing above them. "I'm begging you."

He eyed her for a moment, as if weighing his options carefully. "Fine," Will conceded, and held up his hands in a sign of surrender. "I won't push it anymore. What I actually meant to say to you right now was a simple apology."

Angelyn let out a sigh, then frowned. "What for, exactly?" she returned. "For ruining everything on a day that was supposed to be special, with no warning at all? Or is there something else?"

"Well," Will replied slowly, "for one, yes, choosing your inn as a place for my meetings. Though, I have to say, that apology is only halfhearted because no other place in Kaylyn is better. Secondly, I am sorry for speaking with your son when you are so anxious to keep him from me. I respect a mother's right to choose what is best for her child. And three, I must apologize for making you upset in any way."

Angelyn bit her bottom lip and glanced away. She wanted to accept his apologies as she would with any other person, but she did not think Will should be trusted so easily. Nevertheless, she asked, "Really now?"

He took a sip of the whiskey, then gave her a wounded expression. "Yes, really."

"Good," she replied, and let her eyes fall to her cooling tea.

To her surprise, Will laughed. "You don't like me, do you, Miss McKinlee?"

Angelyn was going to answer no right away, then thought about it. She knew Joshua was listening, and, better yet, her parents had taught her differently. Rhethosian Justice went both ways; if someone was trying to apologize, even halfheartedly, they deserved to be heard. One cut throat deserved another, but one bit of kindness could also grow into an unexpected gift.

"I don't know about 'not liking' you," she said, more honestly than she originally intended. They had spoken for five minutes and somehow he'd gotten her to tell him the truth. Who was this man? "But I don't trust you. Why would I?"

"You have every right not to," Will said smoothly. "I understand."

"No, you don't," she said. His casual complacency inexplicably set her temper afire as no one had in years. "I've run this inn by myself for almost two decades. I've raised Joshua alone since he was born, and now you and your lot come in here with ideas and magic that I don't want my son involved in! I've half a mind to walk down to the Towne Centre now with a written confession and report everyone! The next time you come here I could have a team of guardsmen and Lieutenant Sarrett himself waiting for you."

"So you'll turn in your friends and workers, yourself and your son, to a slow death of torture and public execution?" Will replied just as sharply.

Angelyn blinked, surprised by the sudden passion that lit his brilliant green eyes. His conversational tone had been replaced by one of a seasoned debater. She straightened her shoulders, trying not to notice how small she was in comparison to the broad man who sat before her.

"With my reputation, I could easily avoid losing my home, let alone my life," she countered, trying to show this man she was much more knowledgeable than he was implying. "I could close my doors to everyone, claim damage to the roof from the latest storm, and put you out on the exposed streets. A letter to the Towne Centre tonight would be simple enough as well."

Angelyn straightened her back, trying to seem more intimidating than she felt. "Or maybe you're not here to talk to me." The thought hit her like a nasty punch, and she gripped the edge of her bar tightly. "Maybe you stayed behind tonight to kill me."

Will snorted. "Goddess above, Miss McKinlee," he laughed. "I truly am sorry now. My presence here seems to have made you more paranoid than the Rhethosian lieutenant himself."

Angelyn frowned and raised one brow, as if he should give her a reason why she shouldn't be.

"You haven't yet seen what Sarrett is capable of," Will explained, his tone serious again. "The man was twisted by Bradford's captain, your Rhethosian military's head, into the power-hungry worm he is today. You won't be spared for being the one who raised the alarm, no matter how well you think you can do it. Mark my words, Miss, the lieutenant will burn this towne piece by bloody piece if he has a bad turn of luck, or enough pressure from Captain Caldrell. You know what they call Sarrett's superior in the south, yes?"

Angelyn swallowed and nodded. Her husband had always spoken highly of the military's violent leader. "The Insane Captain," she said.

Before she could add more, Will pressed on. "I won't say another word about Captain Caldrell and his despicable acts for your sake, Miss. But let me ask you this: would you rather stay as you are, compared to a better life? Things are changing, Miss McKinlee, whether you want to acknowledge or ignore them. I am merely attempting to make the change in a direction that will not end in flames and chaos."

Will picked up his whiskey glass again. He tilted it back and forth slowly, always moving his wrist right before the amber liquid could spill.

"Soon the southern Lord and his Loyals will get the idea in their rich, conceited heads that they don't want women running businesses, and what little rights you have will be taken. Such things have already begun to happen down in Clancy. Your Northern Masters will claim your home, your son, whatever they want. You might think you've made it well enough till now by following every rule, by bowing your head and reciting 'Yes, my Lord,' but the latest Bradford is different. Haven't you noticed? He's worse than any before him. If we don't make a stand, you'll soon have nothing to live for."

"I have something to live for!" she retorted, shakily. "My son is enough."

"Miss McKinlee—"

"No, that's enough. I need you to leave and don't come back to this place." Angelyn marched out from behind the bar and strode toward the door. Her knuckles were white when she clutched the knob.

Will sighed and finished his drink. He walked to the door and placed his hat on his head. "I'll be back tomorrow. Once this wheel starts turning, there's no stopping it."

Fuming, Angelyn slammed the door shut behind him and shoved the lock home. She made her way up the stairs and ignored the sound of Joshua quickly stumbling back to his room as fast as he could so she wouldn't see him just around the corner. Angelyn put out the lamp, lay in her bed, and stared straight at the wall.

Hours later, she still could not sleep. Will's words stuck in the forefront of her mind and she could not stop herself from thinking about what he'd said.

Fitfully, she tried to ward off memories of the day her parents had died. The previous Bradford, unhappy with declining trade numbers from Kaylyn, had brought in a brutal new group of guardsmen to threaten local business owners.

Father fought back. Mother dared to say no. After they were put in the dungeons, I never saw them again. Then it was Travok and me, him with no business knowledge and me with barely enough to stay afloat.

Angelyn flinched against her pillow. She turned over in bed harshly, but she couldn't stop thinking of the day she had begun running The Hamond alone. Her violent husband had taken out any failure on her physically, as if it was her family's home, her personal fault for not knowing how to balance books or rent rooms.

I didn't need them, she thought resolutely. *And I don't need the rebellion now. I will keep Joshua safe.*

CHAPTER EIGHT

FUTILE PLEAS FOR MERCY

"**K**atie, dear, if you won't answer me, I'll have to get your husband. Will his day-old corpse help you tell me the truth?"

Miss Ross' sobs echoed around the dungeon. The woman was old, overweight, and blubbering uncontrollably. She shook her manacled wrists and ankles against the cracked stone slab.

Below Towne Centre, Sarrett held a collection of suspected traitors, including loud-mouthed crewmen from recently docked ships. Rumors from up and down Rhethos' dismal coast added up very nicely with the proper persuasion. The torture techniques that his captain seemed to gain great pleasure from were methods Sarrett never cared for. His stomach always turned along with his guilty conscience.

Still, if they wouldn't talk . . .

Few torches were lit along the freezing stone walls, which were covered in filth and moss and old blood. Sarrett preferred to question his prisoners at night, when there was little activity and few guardsmen watching his every move.

"Please, Lieutenant," Katie wept. Her blonde hair stuck to her face in sweaty clumps. Her plain, brown dress was covered in dirt and torn at the sleeves from her struggles. "I've already told you everything. Master Ross didn't know—"

"Stop *lying*," Sarrett barked. He held his hands beneath the stone table, so neither Katie nor anyone else could see his trembling fingers. Sarrett clamped his jaw shut to further quell the shakes, and his eyes drifted to the bottle of wine next to him. He'd already had several drinks from it before starting this process, but he found his resolve weakening again.

Sarrett reached for the Sahma wine and tilted the bottle to swallow another mouthful. Almost immediately the entire dungeon exploded in bright, golden light, the corners illuminated in brilliant shades of pink and orange. The lines of cells over his shoulder gleamed like freshly polished silver as stars of color slid up and down their bars. He licked his lips and blinked several times to focus on Katie Ross.

"My guardsmen found your husband in an alley at the southern end of towne with his throat cut clean through," he said. The woman let out fresh tears at his words. Sarrett leaned forward till his mouth brushed her ear and he felt her entire body trembling. "There was a scrap of violet cloth found near his body. The brave men who keep this towne safe are out patrolling for more of your husband's violet-bearing friends, so tell me what Ross knew about the rebellion."

"I told you already," Katie insisted weakly, shaking her wrists desperately against their chains. "He spoke of Master Will favorably, but as soon as he did so in front of the children, I sent a confession letter to you. You should have gotten it! There's nothing more I can tell you!"

Sarrett sighed and rotated in his seat, his dilated eyes drifting over rows of tools he used to loosen tongues. He felt his guardsmen's eyes on him, waiting to see what he'd do next. Though torture made him ill, his instincts told him there was more that this woman was holding back.

"Do you know what the Armellans believe, across the sea?" he asked suddenly. "Those dark-skinned desert monks feel that freedom is a right each of us is born with because of some unseen Goddess who lives in the sky." He paused, his head spinning. Maybe he'd had too much of the wine . . . maybe.

"Their Goddess used to poison Rhethos with pointless scriptures, useless magic, and passive fragility," he rambled. "Till The Lord Bradford set us free. If the rebels upset the balance we've created, what's going to save us from Armelle's Goddess' wrath?"

"Lieutenant, please"

"Miss Ross, if you say 'please' one more time I will be forced to cut out your tongue and make you spit the answers to my questions with your blood."

The woman said nothing, only releasing another whimper of fright that almost sounded like her husband's name.

"Do you know what I think, dear?" he prodded further. "I don't think any of this is your fault. I pity you for your involvement with a traitor like your husband. You have a loving Lord, though, Miss Ross, and he will forgive your irresponsible actions *if* you tell me what Master Ross was doing out after curfew, with trashy rebel violet next to his body."

"I don't know why he was out, Lieutenant Sarrett. He didn't tell me why he left."

"I *knew* we'd have to bring him in here." Sarrett took another measured sip from his bottle; he was going to need it if this was the length he had to resort to. The entire chamber swayed happily in his vision, uncontrollable euphoria enveloping his mind in waves of bliss. He chuckled deep in his throat and set the glass down carefully. In his mind the process took ten minutes of expert placement, yet the action was realistically as simple as ever.

"Ross' corpse is just down the hall," he said. "My men could bring him over here to persuade you further. What do you think, Katie? Would it help if you touched his hand again, felt his skin on your face, his arms wrapped around you?"

Sarrett's stomach turned violently, but he managed to keep his face passive. "Unfortunately," he continued, "Ross is a bit of a heavy weight right now, so that wouldn't work very well, would it? Maybe we can make do with just his head."

He cleared his throat and leaned back in his seat so he could see where the closest officer stood. "Barton," he demanded. "Go fetch my sword so we can make quick work of her bastard of a husband and loosen Katie's tongue."

"Oh, Lord!" the woman whined, jerking harder on her bonds. "Don't—"

"Then tell me *now*," Sarrett snapped, and leaned forward to speak in her ear again. Tears had cleared away trails of dirt that traced from the corner of her eye. "Tell me the truth about the rebels and I will let you go home to your children, unharmed."

Katie shook her head and cried, the heels of her boots pounding the stone underneath her. "I—" she choked. Her breath came in short, labored gasps. "I told you everything. Ross was helping gather local men to change their views, but I knew what my husband was doing was wrong! I persuaded him to send that letter of confession! Lieutenant, don't hurt me anymore. I didn't even see his conspirators, I was never—"

"Shh," Sarrett soothed, reaching out a hand to brush a lock of hair off her round face. "It's all right now, dear. Thank you for telling me the truth. I have to know, though, where are they planning to meet? The Ross house isn't large enough to hide those violet-wearing blasphemers. Your words are useless unless you give me a family name or an establishment. Where are they?"

"I don't know," the woman insisted.

Sarrett, despite the effects of the wine, felt his heart sink. Why couldn't she just speak whatever she was holding back? He sat up straight and saw that half a dozen other guardsmen had joined Barton at the end of the dungeon's hallway. They were watching him intently, several with expressions of anticipation, others with more judgmental looks on their faces.

She really doesn't know anything else, he thought and picked up a thin knife from the table next to him. *I promised to let her go, but . . .* One glance back at the assembled guardsmen told him that would be a mistake.

"Master Barton," Sarrett said loudly, his voice projecting down the damp walls toward the guardsmen. This officer was a hardened veteran, one of the few useful tools Sarrett had found when arriving in Kaylyn. "Take Master Ross and his wife outside and string them up above the Towne Centre doors. Gather a few other traitors and do the same. Obviously, folk need to be reminded how the lives our Lord has given us are precious."

The officer nodded stiffly and headed to Ross' body, discarded at the back of the dungeon. A few of the others nodded with approval.

"Wait," Katie stammered. "I . . . remember something now! I . . . heard him mention a family name. People who could spread the word of the rebels' arrival and increase their numbers."

Sarrett raised his brows, waiting. He couldn't let the anticipation or hope show on his face. Katie's eyes darted from side to side as she spoke, as if straining to find salvation somewhere along the rows of cells. Horror spread in an ugly pallor across her face when Barton gathered several manacled prisoners and prepared to carry out the lieutenant's orders.

"The Luwenns, on the High Street," Katie stuttered, holding his gaze. "Their children play with mine. My husband said the Master of the house wanted to speak with Will himself. But he wouldn't tell me more. I'd written out the confession letter by then, and—"

"Very good." Sarrett motioned for Barton to continue. A moment later, the sounds from the other prisoners struggling rose to high squeals for mercy.

Chains clanked and several grunts and scuffing sounds reached the lieutenant's ears, but the series of noises were slowly silenced. Barton approached his lieutenant, bloody sword held casually in his hand.

"Thank you, Katie dear, for being honest in your last moments," Sarrett said.

"But . . .you said I could go home to my children," she whimpered, staring with wide eyes at Barton's weapon. "You said I wouldn't be harmed for my husband's mistakes."

"I *lied*," Sarrett whispered in her ear. "Your only concern right now should be whether you want to die before or after I hang you."

"Lieutenant, I know you have children, too. Please—"

Sarrett swung his arm up, then plunged the knife down into Katie's chest. She shrieked and arched her back, but the lieutenant shoved his other hand roughly over her mouth. She retched blood and bile into his palm till the warm liquid leaked between his fingers.

Moments later, Katie stopped twitching and fell silent, and the lieutenant jerked his blade free of her heart. Wiping the knife and his hand clean on the sleeve of her dress, Sarrett had to keep his head down. Nausea rolled through his body in waves, and he had to resist the urge to slap a hand over his mouth and swallow his dinner back down to his stomach.

Rhethosian Justice, he thought shakily, clinging to the twisted rule as if he truly believed in it. *My children's future for hers. Her husband's wrongs for my kingdom's safety. There's justice in it.*

After steadying his breath, Sarrett sat up and turned to see Master Barton staring at him with a blank expression. The other guardsmen were all smiling appreciatively.

"I told her not to say 'please' again," Sarrett said, and he shrugged as casually as possible.

Barton smirked.

"When you're done making an example of this trash," the lieutenant said, "call all the guardsmen and their officers who aren't on the streets down here. I want to make some surprise changes to the patrol schedules."

CHAPTER NINE

ACROSS THE SEA

*G*uide us with your light and love, Mother.
Empathy comes from the heart, and the heart holds happiness.
Happiness is freedom.

In the Valsara Temple, Devaki Tarran knelt with her eyes squeezed shut as prayers coursed through her mind. Black marble floors made her knees ache. Above her, in the middle of the large circular room, stood a towering statue of a stunning woman.

Her tall, naked form bent slightly with her arms extended and head inclined to those who prayed to her. Thick locks of hair, cast in perfect stony waves, trailed down her body to her ankles. Lines of red paint branched from her left breast down her arms, legs, and torso like veins full of blood. The Strings of Fate, the lines of destiny that Cybarys wove for all her human children.

Come to me and kneel, the Goddess' kind countenance seemed to say. *With a small offering of blood and sincere words, you will know peace.*

Armelle's largest Temple to Cybarys was mostly empty this late at night, but all the devotion candles remained lit, tended by the monks who lived within the towering sandstone structure. The desert heat of the day had cooled to a tolerable temperature, and moonlight streamed through the openings that let in peaceful, warm air.

Though only a few others knelt in the empty space for prayer and meditation, the teenage girl paid them no mind. They were here for the same reason as she, and watching others as they supplicated the Goddess was considered rude. Devaki still turned her head slightly to see that each person had a Goddess Touched individual, someone blessed with magic, at their side. Blood flowed from freshly cut Blessing Runes on the magical individual's skin, making offerings to Cybarys.

"Protection" was cut on one man's arm, "Guidance" on another's, and "Strength" on a woman nearby. Blood, a prayer for the desired result related to the rune's meaning . . .and hope that their Mother would hear. Maroon sparks of magic remnants flew out of the corners of her vision. Even though she was alone, no one ever came to Devaki to ask for *her* Touch.

She couldn't have that comfort.

"Dear Mother," Devaki murmured, her voice barely more than a whisper. Its tone carried no more than a few feet from her thin form, but she knew that the Goddess heard her. "Show me my Fate's String. Guide me where I can find purpose in this life."

Devaki's fingers began to tremble where they lay in her lap, clasped tight. The golden prayer bracelets on her wrists shook, playing an uneasy echo around the high ceilings. Devaki exhaled a controlled, steadied breath, then folded her fingers one over the other, creating an intricate knot. She raised her hands, palms out, and pressed them against her damp forehead.

Happiness is freedom, she prayed once more. The insides of her eyelids sparkled with spots the color of blood. *The Goddess knows I am not happy here. I have been punished my entire life for a crime committed before I was born. Cybarys, you must help me. Set me free.*

"Her name was Isaka Tarran. Weren't she and her sister beautiful? They were murdered by a Rhethosian man over ten years ago."

Devaki jumped at the words. Usually only desperate prayers and blood-soaked prophecies were uttered within the temple walls, but this was a subject that struck her to the core with guilt and sorrow.

She saw, amongst those kneeling with their eyes closed, an elderly woman with her granddaughter at her side. The child stared not at Cybarys' twenty-five-foot statue; instead, she squinted at a small shrine against the far curve of the wall.

Amidst the flicking red candles stood a large painting surrounded by jars of flowers, sticks of incense, and stacks of parchment sealed in wax and blood. The canvas depicted two beautiful women, both with deep almond-shaped eyes, flawless dark skin, and clad in the most luxurious silks and jewels.

Devaki could not gaze at their painted faces; it caused her too much pain. She hunched forward as much as possible, as if in deep meditation, and tried not to listen. Tendrils of unruly, curled brown hair tickled the sides of her neck, but she held still.

"But why do we pray to her and her sister?" the little girl asked, her voice lacking the restrained volume of her grandmother's. "What is a 'murder'?"

"We do not pray *to* them, we pray *for* them," the grandmother explained. "So we do not forget that their lives were taken from them so horribly. A compassionate monk took in two shipwrecked Rhethosians as children, and they repaid him with blasphemous violence. Another reason to never trust the people and their Lord across the sea."

Devaki tried to shut out the following explanation the grandmother gave, including a rather harsh definition of the word "murder." She knew why children in Armelle did not know the meaning of such a word. Any kind of violence, or any weapon for that matter, was outlawed by their Temple Leader. Cybarys made it clear the blood under her children's skin was sacred, and should only be shed in small amounts in devotion to her.

There was no reason that the tale of the only malicious act in Armellan history shouldn't be told. The shrine to Isaka Tarran and her older sister, the former Queen of the kingdom, had been covered in prayers for sixteen years now, a reminder of the evening that one man from Rhethos, their violent neighboring kingdom to the north, had put a bloody scar on their people forever.

If that woman and her grandchild glanced my way, would they even know who I am? Devaki wondered. *Would they apologize for speaking of that bloody night in my presence, or would they merely stare at me like everyone else does, with pity and a bit of disdain? They might even have the courage to tell me it's my fault.*

Her question was answered when the grandmother led the little girl away toward the exit; on the way, she skirted close to Devaki, close enough for her to land a solid kick to one of Devaki's knees where she sat on the floor. Devaki flinched, but she did not raise her head. Many had done worse in the past. She couldn't stop the flood of the usual whispered slurs from entering her mind:

"Disgraceful orphan." "Cursed bastard." "Unworthy bitch."

She unknotted her fingers and smoothed the cool silk of her sleeves, which never seemed to absorb any heat from the innumerable surrounding candles.

After glancing to see that no one was watching, she slipped one hand down the front of her leather bodice and pulled out a crumpled note.

This was the only thing that could drown out the conversation happening in the prayer room. This was the only bit of hope that she had to cling to. The parchment was one she had taken everywhere for the last week, held always in place over her heart.

> *Devaki:*
>
> *This is the last note I will write to you for a long time. I must ask you to speak to your cousin once more about my cause. I already know Sehran's feelings, and I'm sure you may anticipate his answer, but I must have it in writing to satisfy my followers.*
>
> *Deliver his sealed response to my friend Master Rowlann when he arrives in Valsara in one week. When the time is right, he will be the one I send to bring you home to Rhethos.*
>
> *I am trying my hardest to create a place where you can live happily, where you can feel truly important and valued. Your existence is only a shadow of what I know you deserve, and I promise that when you see Rhethos for the first time, it will be a free kingdom. We will meet soon.*
>
> *-Will*

Devaki read the paper once more, focusing on the last sentence, which seemed to resonate straight to her core. She folded the parchment and crumpled it in her fist. Glancing around, she noticed that the grandmother and her grandchild had gravitated to the far side of the temple's prayer room near the exit, lighting blood-red candles, their backs to her. Devaki drew a deep breath and strode to the shrine on the far wall, her soft slippers making no sound against the floor.

"Soon," he says. "When the time is right." But why do I have to sit here and do nothing? Am I that useless to this world?

Devaki kept her head bowed, scanning the arrangement of gifts and prayers. In an incense bowl lay a half-burned shred of a Sahma leaf, one with eight points and a rough, green coloring. Its smoke, when inhaled, helped the monks sink deep into a meditative state and contemplate their connections to Cybarys. The effect was even more powerful for those who were Goddess Touched.

She leaned forward reverently, drew a deep breath, and felt the instant calm wash over her. The colors of the temple amplified to brilliant clarity, and the edges of the prayer papers before her glowed with a golden effervescence.

Devaki placed the tip of her middle finger on the inside of her upper left arm, where a rune scar in the shape of "Guidance" had been cut many times. She traced it slowly, and heat suddenly filled the air around her until a sweat broke out on her brow.

Tell me where to go, Mother. Show me what to do, and I will do it in your name. Help me. Guide me.

"Be still, child."

The voice that replied was one Devaki knew well, a soft feminine echo in her head and heart full of ancient power and love. It would have terrified most, even shocked the most devout Armellan, but Devaki merely smiled. She shut her eyes and felt herself sway with the effects of the Sahma incense.

"You must always be aware and be calm, dear girl. The sea's strength can bring you toward your lost family or take you away from them forever. Weather this life's pains for me: you are the one who can help guide the world to true freedom.

"Now is the time to go home."

Devaki shuddered as she felt unseen hands rest on her shoulders, squeeze her tightly, then release like a gentle breeze. She knew better than to write down or memorize the prophetic riddle just given to her: the details were in her heart, and she had faith she would recall every word when she needed them most.

"It *is* time," she whispered.

Devaki was about to open her eyes when a sharp image started to rise out of a veil of thick smoke. She held her breath, and felt terror rise in her chest when the vision became clear: she saw a grey countryside, and in its center, a huge forest larger than any she'd ever seen. It was up in flames, and the fire devouring the trees grew endlessly up into the sky.

The Goddess' Woods . . .the ancient place across the sea where Cybarys' first temple was built.

Devaki opened her eyes and gripped the edge of the prayer altar for support. Her heart ached with loss and terror at the idea that, sometime in the future, such a sacred place could be destroyed. She shakily extended the hand that clasped Will's note, now crushed into a tiny ball. Rhethos' rebellion's leader said "soon", but her Goddess said "now."

Devaki let it go on top of the nearest red candle and watched the flame envelop and destroy the parchment.

It is time for me to go home.

CHAPTER TEN

DEATH ON THE HIGH STREET

Angelyn rarely took Joshua out when she made her weekly trip to the market. Usually, Gabriel was nearby and could keep an eye on her son, either at his home or inside The Hamond. Today, however, had blown by in a haze of worry for Angelyn. Nothing seemed to get done on time, and before she knew it, the sun was beginning to lower into the foggy surface of the unsettled ocean.

No, she thought, wringing her hands against her apron's hem. *There's still so much to do! What's wrong with my head today?*

"Gabriel!" she called out as she made her way down the stairs with an armful of dirty linens. "Wait!" The old man was headed out the inn's front door with his hat and cloak snugly in place, but she didn't want him to go; she still needed to go out to the market, despite the late hour, and someone had to keep an eye on her sulking, rebellious child.

The common hall was only half full, with few drifts of murmured conversation dispelling the silence. She glanced quickly around and immediately knew why. Several of the lieutenant's officers sat at the bar, and Ada topped off their drinks with a respectfully lowered head.

Of course, these men drank for free, and whenever they loitered around, depleting her ale, the locals were much more subdued. Talk amongst the officers was loud and casual, and Angelyn had heard at least one of them mention several rebels being caught last night. When they spoke a couple family names she knew well, her stomach turned.

Gabriel paused at the door as she made her way over, the late sun dyeing his wispy hair a sickly shade of orange. "What is it, Angel? You look flustered."

"I've been running from one corner to another since before dawn," she replied, holding in an exhausted sigh. She was about to tell him the truth, how since her conversation with Will the previous night, she felt more frightened than usual. She couldn't have slept more than an hour.

All day she'd made sure that every surface was clean, every glass and plate was in order, and every room organized, with each traveler documented properly. The constant movement had kept her hands from shaking and her mind clear, two things she needed after Will had spewed ancient Armellan ideals and impossible dreams in her lap.

Despite all her desperate tidiness, she couldn't get his damned words out of her head, nor the way they both excited and terrified her out of her heart.

"Well, busy is good," Gabriel replied, as if reading her mind.

"Yes. Yet," Angelyn said, and she lowered her voice further, "last night, in the parlor, you mentioned the family name Ross. Those officers were just speaking about Katie Ross, and it sounds like she isn't alive anymore. What's going on?"

Gabriel grimaced and shook his head. "Don't worry about that. You'd best run to the market now before the light's gone. Otherwise I'm sure Master Harling will have bought the last of the fresh produce, and there's not another ship due to port for several weeks. You know how the tradesmen favor the Loyals."

Angelyn groaned. She dreaded the idea of being out on the street after dark, all alone, and chastised herself for letting her nerves make her lose track of time. "Can you stay here for an hour and make sure Josh will be all right? He's in the kitchen helping with the bread. It looks like it'll be a slow night, and I won't be long."

Gabriel shook his head. "Unfortunately, I've got . . . business this evening, dear." When he paused, his eyes flicked to the men in Rhethosian Blue uniforms.

A lump formed in Angelyn's throat as she took his meaning of his involvement with the rebellion. Vaguely, she realized this was one of the first moments she couldn't speak her mind to Gabriel. They normally would talk openly about anything to one another since she was a child, yet now, things had changed and she had no control over them.

"Will *you* be all right?" Gabriel asked. "You know Josh is quite capable of handling himself, as well as the entire inn, while you're away."

"Yes, I suppose," Angelyn conceded, and caught the arm of a barmaid drifting past her with empty mugs. She handed off the laundry to her and grabbed her own cloak from its peg by the door. As Gabriel left, she called for Joshua. Her son emerged from the kitchen, cheeks flushed red from the heat of the ovens, flour dusted down the front of his shirt. For some reason, she didn't want to leave him alone right now.

"Darling, can you come out back and help me with the wagon?" She asked the question tentatively, and winced when his face sprang into an expression of pure delight. He had been sulking moodily all day, but this chore actually cheered him up. For the first time, Angelyn felt a nasty pinch of guilt.

"Am I coming with you up the High Street?" Joshua exclaimed. "Really? I can't remember the last time I got to go out with you! You know *yesterday* was my birthday, right?"

"It's getting late and I need to buy some things before they're gone," she explained and collected her son's cloak and handed it to him. "But remember, don't say anything while we're outside. Let me talk to the tradesmen. You keep your head down and your hand on the cart no matter what. Understand?"

"Of course, Mum," Joshua replied, and he headed straight toward the door.

Angelyn paused briefly to catch Ada's eye at the bar. She held up one finger and mouthed "Half an hour," and the young girl nodded.

The wind stung like a chilled blade as they stepped outside. Low clouds clung to the nearby docks in thick tendrils, softened by the golden glow of the retreating sun. Scents of luscious, baking bread behind her and the sting of the salty tide beyond the road clashed together. The main street between the Hamond and the water was already deserted, despite the fact that today's weather hadn't been that rainy.

Joshua led the way around the corner, down the narrow alley between their home and the neighboring businesses. Empty crates and trash lined the rough brick and stone, still moist in the late hour. The cart she used for her trips to the market was situated near the end of the alley, whose only opening led to the stables, where her animals and travelers' horses were housed. It seemed, as the day grew shorter, that even the beasts behind the worn doors knew better than to make much noise.

The cart was a sad, old thing, splintery and cracked along its sides from many years of ventures back and forth to the High Street Market. Joshua took the left handle with both his fists, staying true to his word to not speak aloud. As Angelyn grasped the right and they began to wheel it into the open, she remembered walking in this same fashion a long time ago, with her father holding the worn handle she held and her in Josh's spot.

"Your empty girl's head had better remember all I'm teaching you," he'd said, his tone always disappointed and upset. "Teaching a daughter a trade is useless. It's a good thing we'll marry you to a sensible man who can take over the inn before you ruin it."

She must have heard that insensitive declaration many times before she'd been sold to Travok at fifteen, but it had never truly bothered her. Now, as she and Josh pulled the cart up the road and she tried to nod kindly at those they passed, the words seemed harsher in her head.

At the time, her father's pain had been justified. What good was she, a small girl with no weight in Kaylyn, let alone Rhethos, to a business owner with a decent reputation? *Yet after he and Mother died, so close together when that cold winter blew through, I endured. Not yet sixteen, with a hurtful husband and a child in my belly, but The Hamond still stands as sturdily as ever.*

Angelyn cleared her head as they neared the split in the road. East of them, the cobbles faded to dirt muddled with hoofprints. The path continued toward worn-down homes and Kaylyn's eastern watchtower, manned by several dozen soldiers. They pulled the cart west along the High Street, named for its sharp incline. The market itself was nestled between the towne and the crest of the hill where Towne Centre stood, a formidable work of harsh stone towering above all else.

Joshua gasped and set his handle of the cart down abruptly. Angelyn stumbled at the impact, but before she said anything, she followed her son's gaze up the hill to the tall government building. Her heart jolted when she saw the five bodies hanging from the lower tier of the structure, fresh corpses on ropes that swung serenely in the strong wind. Even from this distance she vaguely recognized two of the bodies, and she narrowed her mouth into a fine, tight line.

"Don't stare, Josh. Keep moving," Angelyn whispered, and pulled the cart up on her own.

Joshua, however, didn't seem to be able to look away. His face had gone extremely pale, then took on a sickly blue color. Angelyn reached out to touch his shoulder and move him forward again, but he shook off her touch.

Swallowing, Joshua stood up straight and held his chin high. "That man's throat is all opened up," he muttered in awe. His eyes were wide, his voice edged with fright. "And that lady's got a hole in her chest where her heart should be. Do you think they were part of the—?"

"I said hush!" Angelyn insisted. Her son's voice gave her chills, the way he seemed drawn to the lieutenant's latest traitors. Even though the Rosses had lived on the other side of Kaylyn, Angelyn felt sick when she realized the rumors she'd heard had been true.

She hauled the cart with all her might up the incline, desperate to put the gory display out of her son's vision as soon as possible. Yet the way Towne Centre was located, everyone in Kaylyn could see the bodies. *That's what we're supposed to do. This is what happens to people who associate with Will, and this is why I keep my boy inside. If we're not careful, the next two corpses up there could be us.*

"Miss McKinlee!"

Angelyn nearly screamed when she heard her name spoken. She shook the gruesome image out of her mind to glance around.

They had made it to the enclosed circle off the High Street, though its round formation of stalls was mostly empty. A young man in a dark, gray cloak and poorly spun cloth waved at her from the cover of one booth. Master Nobeth, from whom she'd bought fresh produce and many chickens for nearly five years, smiled grimly.

"I was beginning to think you'd had a bad week and didn't need anything," he said as she and Josh pulled their cart over. Nobeth was a short fellow, skinnier and less well-off than most. Without a wife or children, he lived alone in the far eastern corner of Kaylyn on his farm, growing what he could in the damp, dark weather. Angelyn gave him her best smile and studied what was left of his stock for the day. The measly carrots, cabbages, and potatoes would have to do.

"I've been as busy as always, actually," she replied. She didn't mean to be rude, but the sun was getting lower by the second and she wanted Joshua away from the grisly sights at Towne Centre. "I just had a late start today and the time caught up with me."

"Good Lord, is that your little Joshua?" Nobeth exclaimed, staring. "It's amazing how big he is. It's been forever since I've seen 'im. Keep growing like that, boy, and the lieutenant will have you in a nice guardsman's uniform before you know it!"

Joshua opened his mouth but Angelyn grasped his shoulder tightly till he closed it. "We've got to get back soon. My common hall's full," she insisted.

"Well, there's not much," Nobeth said rather sadly. He gestured at his stall with a defeated sigh. "It's not even that I don't have much to offer. The more I bring into towne, the more the guardsmen take."

Angelyn nodded almost imperceptibly, keeping a polite smile on her lips. She knew Nobeth suffered like the rest of them, but his disdainful comments were louder than usual. Was it Will's presence in the towne that was making poor farmers like this one brave enough to speak to others about their hardships?

"I'm glad I have enough to fill 'bout half your cart. With my folks getting on in age, and these men comin' for taxes more often each month, it's been horribly—"

He broke off, however, when the tradesman with the stall next to his returned. The man eyed Nobeth nastily. She was glad Nobeth had stopped talking. Even conversational complaints weren't worth the potential danger. Plenty of people hid what they owned lately when the guardsmen searched for funds or items equal in value to pay Sarrett's rising taxes, but the last thing Angelyn wanted was someone to tell the nearest officer that her home needed to be searched, due to her publicly complaining with this tradesman.

"I'll take what's left," she said as she dug coins from her apron. Joshua silently helped her pile Nobeth's goods into their cart. "And maybe Master Harling will be kind enough to lend me anything I'm missing, Lord willing."

Before he could reply, Angelyn handed over the payment and worked the cart around. Perhaps it was time to try and find someone else to trade with who would keep their mouth closed on the open road. The hazy orange ball had sunk below the watery horizon now, its glow fading rapidly. Joshua silently took up his handle and helped lead their supplies down the hill.

"Keep up, dear," Angelyn said as they went. She almost told Joshua to get in so she could wheel them home more quickly, but a glance at her boy told her his days of riding in the wagon were long gone. Instead, she shrugged to let her cloak fall closer around her and kept her eyes on the cobbles before her feet. Joshua, however, held his head up and stared everywhere, as if he loved the feeling of the evening breeze in his dirty blond hair and the last of the sun on his face.

As they rounded the corner to the level road, a sudden uproar of marching feet and shouting voices bore down on them. Spinning shakily, Angelyn saw two dozen guardsmen descending the High Street at an alarming pace, almost running in their direction. One man stood out before the others, tall and bulky in his thick jacket and cloak. Several held torches, and they passed one lit brand amongst themselves till the evening air filled with a bright heat.

"You!" the officer in the lead thundered as they approached, covering the entire road with a cacophony of metal and authority. "Yes, you! Miss!"

This is it, Angelyn thought. She reached numbly across the cart and grabbed Joshua's shoulder, the rest of her body rooted to the spot. *They've found something at the inn while I was gone, or someone spoke out of turn and those officers heard mention of The Hamond. They'll drag us back and lock us in before they set the place afire.*

Angelyn shut her eyes and waited for the mass of blue uniforms and flames to take her and her son away.

CHAPTER ELEVEN

A FORCED HANDFUL OF FLAMES

Joshua knew the moment his mother froze that he needed to do something. Last night he'd heard Will talk about freedom, and not letting fear stop someone from doing what they thought was right. Instead of worrying, Joshua stepped in front of his mother as the guardsmen rushed down the road toward them. If they were going to arrest them, let it be him first. Although he didn't know the first thing about fighting, he still wouldn't make it easy for them.

The officer in the lead put out a rough hand to Joshua, shoved him back, and grabbed the handle of their cart. Without any effort, the officer hauled the small, wooden wagon out of the way of his men, who seemed bent on moving as quickly as possible, oblivious to Joshua and his mother.

"Are you blind, boy?" the officer snapped. "You best move off the street when my men are pushing by." He towered above Joshua, his pale face darkened by the shadows of the retreating sun. His mouth was set in a hard grimace as he regarded Joshua and his mother. "When the lieutenant gives an order for a burning, most are smart enough to stay out of the road."

"Yes, Master," Angelyn replied quickly. "Sorry, sir." Josh heard the strain in her voice behind him and kept his stance in front of her.

The officer ignored her and looked to his men who were surrounding a nearby home. It seemed like any other on Kaylyn's main roads, with rough shingles and drooping old archways. As Joshua watched the lieutenant's men approach the front door and knock on it playfully, he couldn't see anything about the meager home that shouted conspiracy or rebellion. When the reflection of a woman stepped forward to open the door, the officer in front kicked it back into place. Several cries of distress sounded from inside.

Joshua tried to take their cart's handle and move forward again, but the officer blocked his path. Joshua felt his mother's tight grip on his shoulder, bidding him to stay silent. He squirmed at the pain of her grasp, but reached up and squeezed her hand, his eyes glued on the house as the guardsmen teased it with lit torches.

The officer suddenly shouted past Joshua at his men, making him flinch. "Hurry it up, before it rains! Lock the door already and step back! I don't need any of you idiots blistered."

Those with torches shattered the windows and threw the flames inside as the rest stood guard on the front stoop. One man lit a rolled cigar with his companion's torch before stepping back and hurling the flaming stick onto the home's roof. The next shriek echoed down from the second story, a high-pitched sound that unmistakably belonged to a child.

"I swear," the huge man muttered right in front of Joshua, and Josh dared to glance up at him. "This part's the easiest job in Rhethos, but some of these boys can't throw straight. The lieutenant does the hard work of finding those who betray The Bradford's trust, like the Luwenn family here. But this bit is pretty simple."

He chuckled, marched over to one of his men, yanked a blazing brand from his hands, and stepped back to Joshua and his mother. He grinned wickedly. "Here ya go, son," he said amiably, offering Joshua the fire. "Throw a torch at the traitor's home!"

Joshua gaped at the flames so close to his face, sweat breaking on his brow. His first instinct, as it had always been, was to look at his mother. One glance, however, told him she had no idea what to do.

Will this man imprison both of us if I say no? he thought, swallowing hard. *How can I agree when just last night Rhethos' rebel leader sat in my home and had tea with my mum?*

"I . . . can't," Joshua said, and the big man's eyes narrowed dangerously. "I'm . . . afraid of fire," he added quickly, and squeezed his mother's hand on his shoulder as if telling her to back up the lie.

"He had an accident at the inn when he was little, Master," Angelyn put in smoothly, tingeing her voice with sadness.

"Ah! You own the Hamond, yes?" the tall man asked. "My boys love your place."

He turned his full attention to Joshua, his bulking form towering over the boy. Joshua couldn't help leaning away from the torch the man still held close to his face. "You'd better get over that fear soon, boy," he said seriously, his tone darkening. His face was shadowed again, this time by the growing fire over his shoulder instead of the setting sun. "If you're going to serve your southern Lord well up here, and protect your mother, one day pretty soon you've gotta learn to *love* flames like this. The lieutenant says they get rid of rebel rumors faster and more permanently than anything else. You know that's true, don't you?"

Joshua nodded, but that wasn't enough; the officer reached out and grabbed his wrist. He tried to pull back, but the man held Joshua without any effort. Grinning, he pressed the flaming brand into Joshua's hand and yanked him away from his mother. The officer's huge fist closed around Joshua's and forced the boy's arm back in a wide arc. Unable to stop himself, Joshua threw the torch at the already blazing home.

He stifled a cry as the torch landed on the roof. The raging conflagration accepted the new flames greedily, and the high wall of thick smoke rose higher.

"That's much better!" the tall man cheered. He slapped Joshua on the back. "You've got a good arm, boy. Why don't you come by Towne Centre tomorrow and we'll see if the lieutenant has room for a strong lad like you."

Joshua balked as several more shouts of pain and terror issued from the home's shattered windows. The guardsmen on the porch laughed and passed around an open bottle of wine with one of Harling's signature Rhethosian Blue ribbons at the neck.

Joshua wanted to speak, to demand what the family burning alive in the home had done to deserve such a fate, to rush forward and stop the squeals of agony coming from inside. Instead, all he could do was blink away tears as his mother drew him back toward their cart.

The officer seemed to lose interest and waved them along, returning his full attention to his men. His mother yanked the cart forward before the officer's shoulders had even rotated all the way around, and Joshua numbly followed her down the High Street.

Why? How could those people deserve to die like that? There were children in there. And those men were laughing, laughing while they burned.

His mother said something, but Joshua did not hear her. When they had placed the cart in its spot in the Hamond's side alley, several of the evening's staff came out to help unload its contents. Joshua helped Bertram haul a heavy sack of potatoes through the side door to the kitchen. If the cook said anything to him, Joshua did not hear it. He headed back out to the alley, head down so he could not see the tower of smoke rising above the rooftops. The firelight brightened the night sky.

"Come on in, Josh," Ada called from the doorway a moment later. "We've already gathered everything, and it looks as if it's about to rain again."

Joshua stood at the empty cart, a hand clasped tightly around one of its handles. The smooth wood felt so similar to the torch, and he could practically feel that officer's fist around his, forcing him to squeeze the flaming brand.

"Just a minute," Joshua murmured, barely hearing his own voice. He did not see the cart in front of him, only a blaze of heat and brilliant orange that wouldn't go away each time he blinked.

Ada glanced up at the ascending pillar of smoke. "Oh Lord," she gasped, putting a hand to her heart. "Is that the Luwenn house?"

Joshua turned toward her, his eyes wide. "Did you know them?"

Ada nodded sadly. "They were friends of my betrothed," she replied, her voice falling to a whisper. "I . . . they had three little girls. Damn it! I wish we could have done something."

Joshua felt his heart stop for a moment as he recalled the high-pitched screams from the second floor of the burning home. He opened his mouth to say something, but Ada had gone inside.

Crossing his arms over his chest, Joshua leaned against the Hamond's wall, trying not to cry. The tears he could dismiss, yes, but the hot anger growing inside of him seemed unstoppable. It rose in his stomach, stronger than the flames he'd been forced to throw, until it reached a boiling point in his throat.

He didn't hear his mother open the side door and come out to stand beside him. When she reached out for his arm, Joshua spun away, knocking over several empty crates. "Don't touch me!"

She backed up a step, raising both her arms. Joshua couldn't apologize, however. He could see in his mother's eyes exactly what she would say. *"This is why you cannot go outside, little Josh. This is why I force you to live your life within the same four walls every day. This is why we have to march down to Towne Centre first thing tomorrow, turn in the rebels that have taken over the inn, and put you in a brand new guardsman's jacket, so you can help kill more children."*

A voice suddenly echoed from the back alley, a burst of low, male words that ran from the east down to the stables. Joshua froze, as did his mother, and he listened hard. He could tell she wanted to bolt back inside, but Joshua reached out and grabbed her hand. Together, they tentatively crept forward to the edge of the Hamond's rear wall. Peering around a high stack of crates, Joshua held his breath and watched.

He could see three men hunched forward and covered in heavy cloaks moving slowly down the alley toward them. This pathway was narrow, used only by those who lived along the seaside or owned an establishment like the Hamond. One man held his arm gingerly, and Joshua saw a collection of fresh burns along his shoulder. His cloak smoldered, and Joshua's eyes narrowed. Surely no one had escaped the guardsmen' flames down the road.

The other two figures moved slower than the first, and Joshua saw why. Between them were two children, little girls with soot and blood on their clothes and faces.

Joshua heard his mother gasp beside him when she recognized the dark coat of the man helping one of the girls walk: Will's green eyes were unmistakable.

"Hush, little one." His voice traveled to their hiding place, and Joshua found himself straining to hear him over the rustling of their movement. Will sounded different; last night, he was full of authority and a quiet, commanding charisma everyone responded to. Now, Joshua detected a soothing kindness, a touch of pitiful love even in the words he spoke. "I know you're frightened, but you're safe now. Tell me where it hurts."

The trembling child clutched at Will's coat with one hand, the other clasping her sister's. As she touched a spot on her head, her fingers came away red. The child pointed at her shins next, which were scraped.

Will glanced around the alley, then knelt in front of the girls while his men stood watch. He brushed a strand of hair off the little girl's face as she sobbed.

"You're very brave, you know," Will said quietly. His voice echoed off the nearby buildings. Joshua swallowed hard, but the stone of guilt and anger in his throat would not go away. "Since you're so courageous, you get to go on an adventure," Will continued. "My two friends are going to take you somewhere that the guardsmen's fires won't ever find you. Does that sound like something you and your sister can manage?"

The child nodded, and at Will's encouraging words, she stifled her sobs to silent tears. Her sister, several years younger than her, remained silent, eyes wide with fright. Even from a distance, Joshua could hardly look at the shocked emptiness in the child's gaze.

"Master Will, we've got to stay with you this evening," one of the rebels spoke quickly. "Gabe's on the south end of towne now, and we're supposed to meet him before the next patrol comes round. We can't watch these two kids and keep at your back."

"I can handle myself. I'll find Gabe alone," Will interrupted and rose. His voice shifted to the one Joshua knew his mother had instantly disliked, though the men responded immediately. "Look at them. We barely managed to pull them out before the home collapsed."

"Damn that lieutenant!" the rebel beside Will growled. "The bastard didn't even show his face tonight, just sent Officer Barton and his men to lock the doors and throw the fires in."

The younger child burst into fresh sobs and collapsed against her sister. The older one held her up, though she struggled. She glanced up at Will, trying to hold back her own tears. Will gave his companion a harsh, reprimanding glare.

"Listen, dear, do you know the woods on the edge of towne?" Will spoke softly, almost a whisper.

The older child nodded. "Mum said to never go near the trees, or the old Armellan's curse would give us horrible luck till the day we die."

Will pinched the little girl's cheek. "Now that's just silly, don't you think?"

The girl did not smile back, only wiped at the side of her face. Soot streaked all the way to her hairline.

"You're smarter than those rumors, I can tell," Will said. "Now, my friends here are going to help you find a secret place where you will be taken care of." He glanced at the men standing on either side of him. "Take the road around the wood's edge through Morely, then head east once you reach Patten. Master

Colwell will put them with the other children. Do *not* cut through the trees before you reach Morely. It should take you less than two days. I'm sure Miss McKinlee won't mind if you borrow a couple horses. Understand?"

Joshua glanced up at his mother and saw her expression tighten. He could see fear in her dark, blue eyes, but he thought he detected something else. Did his mother want to help these children? Joshua knew well enough that if something happened to him, she would do whatever she needed to keep him safe. He watched her expression falter, and almost thought she meant to take a step forward and show herself, but . . . no. She shrank back against the Hamond's wall and remained silent.

"Yes, Master Will," both of the rebels spoke, though they sounded as if they wanted to stay here in Kaylyn, where the action was.

When the men offered their hands to the children, Joshua was stunned to see both girls shrink back and grab at Will's coat.

"Do you want to know something, little ones?" Will said. He knelt before the girls once more and took one of their hands in his. "You will not see your family anymore, and I am sorry for that, but you don't need to worry about them. They aren't in pain, and they aren't anywhere those men can reach. When I was small like you, all I wanted to do was explore Rhethos. You're lucky enough to do that . . . tonight!"

He grinned at the sniffling children, and the elder girl smiled tentatively back at him. Gently, Will pulled their hands free and guided them to the waiting men. The rebels seemed eager to move, and Joshua did not blame them. Even if many of the lieutenant's guardsmen were enjoying their celebration at the fading flames down the road, fresh patrols were no doubt leaving Towne Centre and heading down the High Street.

"Move quickly and quietly," Will ordered as the rebels each picked up a child and headed toward the stables behind the Hamond. Both men nodded, and Will grabbed the shoulder of one before he left. "Keep them both *safe*, no matter what," he added, his eyes fierce with authority.

Joshua had time to catch one more glimpse of Will's face before pressing himself against the wall so the approaching rebels could not see him. Will's mouth was set in a thin, hard line, but his eyes shone with fresh determination, and an anger that frightened Joshua.

Joshua barely saw his mother wipe tears from her face. Her hair now hung heavy with the rain that fell steadily. He stepped back when Angelyn suddenly spun toward him. She put her hand on the Hamond's side door. "Do not say a word," she commanded, her voice cracking. He did not think his mother made the best authority figure right now, with tear marks on her face and her hands trembling. "Not one breath of this to anyone. Understand?"

"Yes, Mum," Joshua replied, though this time he could barely choke out the words. That fury still boiled at the top of his throat, threatening to spill into his mouth and escape past his lips. Even as they stepped inside, and Ada fussed over his mother's soaked clothes, Joshua could not get two images out of his head. One of uncontrollable roaring flames, the other of Will's face as he spoke to the two little girls.

CHAPTER TWELVE

TREASON FOR HEARTH AND HOME

As the clock ticked closer to curfew, Angelyn's worries started to get the better of her. Inside the common hall, she saw many new faces that were conversing quietly with one another. Before she knew it, small groups started to gravitate to the closed parlor on the east wall, all of them glancing at the clock on the way as if their leader should already be there.

Angelyn wanted to speak up, especially after her trip to the market at sunset, to demand that the whole damn group just move on to another location in another towne, for the Lord's sake. But the words Will had said last night resonated in her mind: "So you'll turn your friends and workers, as well as yourself and your son, over to a slow death of torture and public execution?"

Their leader had taken the time to speak with her, and explain himself and his motives in such a calm, logical manner. Will's eyes had been kind that night they spoke, and persuasive when anyone defied him, and so caring when he'd helped those children not long ago.

But, despite all of this that seemed jumbled constantly in her head, all Angelyn could focus on clearly was the expression on Joshua's face when the officer's torch left his unwilling hand an hour ago. She decided, resolutely, she could not stand to be silent any longer.

"You know what?" Angelyn said suddenly, "I've had enough of this."

She and Ada stood in the kitchen, washing dishes in tubs of cold water, trying to get a head start on the mess she knew would come once all the plates and mugs from dinner were cleared. The younger woman glanced at her sharply, then behind her shoulder. Joshua sat sullenly in the corner on an old stool, opening and closing the brass lid on his new compass. The carving on its back glowed weakly when he touched it, and he ignored Angelyn when she told him to stop and put it away.

Joshua had not spoken since coming back from the market, and Angelyn found it odd that he wasn't in his usual spot behind the bar in the common hall. Instead, he quietly examined every inch of his newest possession, polishing the compass' surface with the sleeve of his tunic, taking care to run the cloth over the tiny, unreadable runes on the back. He kept his head down, as if he hadn't heard his mother over the clanking of dishes and mugs.

"Please don't do this, Miss McKinlee," Ada whispered hastily. Angelyn could hear the caution in her barmaid's voice as she anticipated trouble. "We're all very sorry for not speaking to you before Josh's birthday, but we had no other choice. If you get rid of Master Will and the men now, all we've worked for—"

"That's not what I meant," Angelyn said. "I've had enough of the sneaking around and all this happening without me being in the middle of it. I want to be in that parlor tonight."

Angelyn didn't have to look at Ada to know the young woman's face had lit up at her last statement. She seemed to have gotten Joshua's attention now as well.

"Are you really joining their meeting, Mum?" he asked, rising from his stool and staring at her with wide eyes.

"That is wonderful to hear, Miss McKinlee," Ada started happily. "Master Will should be here any minute. You can sit with me and Lynn, and you'll finally know what we stand for. You won't be disappointed."

"We'll see, Ada," Angelyn sighed. Even though she didn't feel any excitement at the idea, she carefully tried to tame a bit of fear that rose in her as she set the clean dish she had in her hands down on the counter. She glanced at a small clock sitting on the back corner of the kitchen's long expanse and saw the time was a quarter to curfew.

"Oh," Ada gasped when she followed Angelyn's gaze. "He should already be here."

Angelyn and Ada glanced at each other, then strained their ears. Nothing beyond the typical sounds echoed in from the main room. Angelyn suspected that Will wouldn't be late for any good reason. An image of the rebel leader kneeling before the children he'd saved bloomed in her mind, then was pushed away by a wall of flames. Was she worried about him?

She shot a questioning look at Ada, who shook her head, as if to say, "This can't be good." The barmaid went to the kitchen door, glancing through its small window at the patrons in the main hall. No one seemed to be panicking but, as Angelyn joined her, she could see some folk pacing and glancing at the doors and windows.

"So. . . whoever he wants to meet with filters into the parlor?" Angelyn asked quietly, scanning the faces she could see through the thin pane of glass. "There's no chance that someone your lot doesn't know slips in, or someone you do know betrays your location once you start talking?"

"Some of our folk stay in the main hall, Miss," Ada confirmed. "They watch who comes in and out carefully, and right now we should be—"

Suddenly, the kitchen door swung open from the main hall, and, before Angelyn could react, Ada pushed Angelyn back. The barmaid stuck her boot out to stop the door from swinging inward any further, and it snapped back to strike Gabriel in the forehead instead. The old man let out a groan and gingerly stepped into the kitchen. Ada folded her arms over her chest disapprovingly.

"Miss McKinlee!" he started, ignoring the bump forming on his face. "You need to come out here quickly!"

Angelyn stared, barely catching her breath. Did Ada always have such amazing reflexes, and she'd never noticed it before? She looked to Gabriel, who was soaked and breathing hard, as if he'd just run through the storm and hadn't paused till he'd tried to slam open the kitchen door.

"What is it?" she asked him. Joshua stood expectantly behind her.

"Come on, you three," Gabriel panted weakly, leaning on the door now that it had swung shut. "It's Master Will."

Angelyn rushed forward, but Gabriel stopped her with a raised hand. "Careful, now," he whispered, his pale blue eyes darting to the staff members moving about the kitchen doing their jobs. "You don't want the regular folk seeing you all upset. Follow me quietly."

Swallowing a sudden lump in her throat, Angelyn nodded. They left the kitchen and followed Gabriel down the length of the bar to the parlor's door on the far side. It hung open, but as soon as she stepped inside, Ada shut it behind them. Past a dozen or so men and women, Angelyn saw Will seated at the table, slumped forward with his hat over his eyes.

"What's the matter with him?" she asked Gabriel. "Please tell me he came in through the back door here."

"Yes, but he's hurt," Gabriel said. "Someone stabbed him from behind as we were headed this way. He's supposed to have two men with him at all times to make sure he's safe, but they weren't at his back as tonight. I don't know why."

Angelyn swallowed dryly, and she saw Joshua's face go pale.

"He'd just found me at our meeting point, but before I could react, a man came out of nowhere with a knife aimed at his heart. Will turned just in time, but the man caught him right there on his left arm. It's a deep wound, and he's lost a lot of blood. He passed out once I brought him in."

Joshua shouldered past the group of rebels to the chair where Will had collapsed. When Angelyn was close enough to inspect him more clearly, she noticed his black clothes hung wet with rain, though she could make out that the sleeve of his left arm was discolored dark red. There was a large bump on his hairline.

"Joshua. . ." Angelyn began. Her voice was muffled in her own ears, as if the sudden stress made it hard for her to understand her own thoughts before they came out of her mouth. She noticed how quiet it had become since she had entered the small room.

What could she do with the most wanted man in Rhethos unconscious and bleeding in their midst? Everyone was staring expectantly at her, as if not knowing if she would help or take advantage of their leader's injury and raise the alarm instead.

Inexplicably, a memory of the night Joshua was born burst to the forefront of her mind. She herself had bled under this same roof, and, though no one knew it, Gabriel had used forbidden magic to keep Josh safe before his Touch was discovered.

The same people who would have slaughtered her innocent baby for having magic would kill the rebel leader in her midst right now for trying to stop those who believed Joshua was "cursed". That, to Angelyn, seemed to help her come to the decision she had to make.

"We need to keep calm and make sure nothing looks out of place, understand?" Angelyn voiced the first idea in her head, then paused. Joshua nodded encouragingly. When none of the rebels protested, she continued: "We should move him somewhere safe, down in the cellar, since the patrols will be by soon. I've got to close in a few minutes. Wait till I clear the common hall, then we'll hide him, dead or alive."

She turned in a circle, making sure to keep eye contact with each person as her voice steadied. "All of you go out there with the other folk. Ada, step out onto the porch with a few other girls for a moment, back and front, and check for the closest group of guardsmen. Those in the front relight the flooded lanterns, and those in back check the latches on the stables. Slowly, mind you. If the lieutenant's men are nearby, time their distances for me, please."

Ada gave her a strong nod, unable to hide a brazen smile on her face. She touched Angelyn's arm before making her way toward the back door, beckoning for several other girls in aprons to follow.

Angelyn glanced at Joshua again and added, "Darling, you get some hot water and cloths from the kitchen."

Her son stared blankly at her, mouth agape. Angelyn knew what he was thinking, but pointed to the kitchen again, and Joshua quickly obeyed.

"Can we even help him?" she whispered breathlessly to Gabriel. "I don't know much about healing wounds like that, but he can't stay up here."

"It'll be fine, Angel," he replied, touching her forearm. "You've always thought fast on your feet. Bertram and I will move Will down to the cellar. Let us know when you're ready."

At the old man's words, everyone seemed to notice the dire need for some sense of normalcy and started to move about. The rebel group left the parlor and made their way throughout the common hall, grabbing their cloaks and heading toward either the main front or back doors. Chairs scraped across the floor as the Hamond's normal patrons did the same, and conversation slowly died down.

Angelyn watched with a trained eye, ready to step in if there were any protests, but everyone obeyed readily and made their way home.

We really are as well-trained as he says, she found herself thinking, reflecting back to Will's words on how subdued Kaylyn folk were. *Not a foot out of line, not a question asked, like obedient, fearful dogs . . . it's always been normal and necessary for survival, but why do I suddenly feel like it's wrong?*

"Get him up," Angelyn said aloud, turning from the door to speak to Gabriel and her head cook. "Let's move him quickly."

Several rushed seconds later, Angelyn had her keys out and the door to the cellar open, with Gabriel and Bertram close behind. She lit the candles in their sconces lining the dark, musty staircase that descended at a sharp angle.

As Gabriel and Bertram moved down the stairs, Joshua met her at the top. He bore a large pitcher full of steaming water and carried several clean dishrags over his arm. Angelyn smiled and touched his hand to find her fingers shaking. She quickly clamped both her hands behind her back.

"Mum, let's go help Will." Joshua nudged her with his free hand. Angelyn nodded, shook herself from her thoughts, and started down the cellar stairs. She made sure to shut the door behind her.

CHAPTER THIRTEEN

ALONE AMONGST FAMILY

Just after sunset, Devaki thought of packing, but realized she had nothing to take with her. When she looked around her small room, she didn't see anything she couldn't live without, and, oddly, that didn't upset her. The entire Tarran family lived within the Silk Palace, not far from the Valsara Temple. The spiraled sandstone structure was dressed in innumerable ribbons of silk, held in place by magic created hundreds of years ago. The spells from a dead language were crumbling now, and with no way to cast them again, plenty of the silks were becoming ragged, nailed into the castle for support. From far away, the appeal was still there.

Devaki had dozens of royal aunts and uncles, hundreds of cousins, and innumerable servants around her. There were always large groups headed to meals, walking reverently to daily prayers, or skipping excitedly to the market. The air was constantly full of happy chatter, sweet prayers, and bright magic.

But no one ever spoke to her.

She had the same living quarters as every other family member, situated on the same floor as many popular, upstanding Tarrans, yet, since she had left the royal nursery, no one bothered to say good morning or good night whenever she entered or left. It was a lovely curse: to be outwardly treated with all the blessings due to a member of the royal family, but always looked upon with a degree of difference that held hidden scorn behind every fake smile.

Devaki sat on the edge of her bed and glanced out the thick cut, square window above it. The small room had the appearance of a typical Armellan lodging; sandstone walls, finely carved wooden furniture, silk drapes, beaded upholstery, and a standard little shrine to Cybarys.

But you only have to look a little closer to see the truth, Devaki thought, and let her eyes drift over her space as dusk fell outside. *That beautiful chest is only full of second-hand clothes, not keepsakes or love letters. The silks are several years out of style, and the beads are cheap glass instead of gemstones. The prayer bracelets on my arms are ones I bought myself. Everyone else gets them as gifts from family, friends, and lovers.*

They smiled at her when they had to, yes, and they followed the decorum necessary to include her in daily events and special occasions, but . . .

Devaki rose, cleared her head, and left her room. The only things that mattered were what Will had said in his last letter, and what the Goddess had told her in her last vision. Devaki had waited until the sun went down to go speak with her cousin, the Armellan Temple Leader, when he wouldn't have any official appointments. Will's friend Master Rowlann would arrive tomorrow, and when she delivered Sehran's official response, she intended to leave Armelle with the Rhethosian rebel Master.

The hallways were deserted but warm, lit by many painted lanterns. Almost all the outer walkways in the Silk Palace spiraled either up or downward, leading to the living quarters of all the royal family members. Every so often, certain pathways would branch inward to official meeting rooms, grand common halls, and ornate prayer settings. Devices in the open turrets above caught and spun the night air down into the castle walls, cooling the structure significantly.

Devaki headed upward, walking along the wide hallway with her eyes cast downward. She barely noticed the intricate, colorful mosaics placed into the tiles that brushed by beneath her silk slippers. Devaki always looked at her feet when she walked, even when she was alone. It was easier to avoid the fake smiles and tune out the whispers of disdain if she didn't look at anyone.

When she reached the top of the spiraled structure, Devaki raised her head to see a set of gigantic double doors. Upon their ancient wood was a carving of Cybarys, her red-lined arms extended over a detailed map of Valsara. The doors were bound in polished copper and shone in the lantern light that bathed their frames from either side.

Will knows Armelle can't support him in his battles, but there has to be something we can do. I don't know a thing about war, but Brother Sehran might know a way to help them. For Cybarys' sake. For the sake of all the people in Rhethos. I have to ask once more, no matter what the consequences.

Devaki took a deep breath and glanced away from the doors to the guards that stood to the left and right. "Guards" was a rather generous term, since they wore neither weapons nor armor but only the blood-red robes of Armellan monks. Along the edges of their robes were hand-painted runes representing prayers of safety, order, and obedience.

Both of the men stared straight ahead, ignoring her with trained precision.

"Excuse me?" Devaki asked, her voice polite. "Is Brother Sehran inside?"

Of course, there was no response. Devaki felt her hands clench into tight fists. What did they expect her to do? Jump in front of them and wave her arms? Break down, cry, and beg? Scream in fury, tearing at her hair until they had an excuse to escort her back to her room and lock the door? It was the subtle, passive-aggressive ways of showing her she was allowed general courtesy but no real respect that hurt the most.

It would be easier if they taunted or insulted me instead of this.

Devaki felt her resolve weaken and clenched her jaw shut. What would she even say to Sehran if they let her into the reception chamber? Like Will had written, they both knew his answer: Sehran would not help Rhethos gain her freedom.

And who am I to ask for anything from anyone? Devaki thought. *I'm not important in Armelle, let alone Rhethos. This is what they've taught me, so it must be true: I'm only a shadow.*

"You must always be aware and be calm, dear girl."

An echo of the Goddess' voice entered Devaki's mind, steadying her heart and her breath.

"Weather this life's pains for me: you are the one who can help guide the world to true freedom."

Devaki drew herself up tall and relaxed her fists. She smiled and shook her wrists so her bracelets sang happily at her sides. This caused both monks to glance down at her suspiciously. She stepped forward, knotted her fingers together, placed them against her forehead, and bowed respectfully.

As she rose, Devaki grabbed one of the door handles and pulled. Her slippers almost slid out from underneath her on the tiled floor. Before either could react, Devaki yanked with all her might and slipped inside.

The reception chamber was a grand room, built at the top of the Silk Palace over five hundred years ago. The ceiling was a dome of blue glass framed in old metal, and it sparkled despite the black sky outside. As Devaki walked across the expansive floor, she glanced sideways at the high, curved walls. Artwork covered the sandstone depicting historical events long past. She knew the paints would have faded hundreds of years ago if not for the Protection Runes keeping them bright and sharp. The brushstrokes glowed with faded red light.

At the end of the circular room stood a dais, supporting a gorgeous chair. The rune for "leader" was carved in the high back. Devaki swallowed, looking beyond the throne to a long table that stood behind it. Bent over the table, which was covered in high piles of parchment, stood her cousin and several other men. They spoke quietly, their backs to her, unaware of her presence.

"I'd like a word with you, cousin."

Armelle's Temple Leader turned sharply, along with his three advisors. The three men only glanced at Devaki briefly, then looked away, as if dismissing an errant, insignificant sound that had most likely come from their imaginations.

That was the rule: only exclude her enough so she knew her place, but not harshly enough that the public could notice or listen to her if she ever dared publicly speak against them.

"It's important, Brother Sehran," Devaki continued. "And I promise not to take much of your time."

Sehran hesitated for a moment, then motioned for the other men to leave, and they all bowed before exiting through a side door. Devaki heard them begin to mutter to one another before the door shut.

She kept her attention on her cousin, someone who evoked both fear and nausea in her stomach. When she was eight, he'd made it clear that his seat of power was not to be threatened by her. Whenever she thought of that night, her memory went black, as if her mind was trying to protect her from something best left forgotten, though the impression was still clear: do not challenge the Temple Leader.

He was a young man, though still twice Devaki's age. His thin frame was enclosed in several layers of woven silk, dyed in meticulous patterns of red, purple, and gold. He raised his dark eyebrows so high when he looked at her that they almost disappeared into the black curls of his hair.

"What can I do for you?" His voice was kind enough, but there was that distrustful undertone that Devaki could pick out clearly because she was used to hearing it. He looked away from her after asking the question, lighting several fresh sticks of incense on the missive table, trailing musky smoke into the air.

"I'm only going to ask you once more," Devaki began, but before she could continue Sehran waved a dismissive hand. He shook his head sadly, as if her few words were a great disappointment to him, and turned away.

"Please!" Devaki said, and she bowed as low as she could. "I'm not here for myself. The Goddess spoke to me. She wants to bring Rhethos' people back to her faith, and we cannot stand by."

Sehran stepped close to her, and from her bent position, Devaki could only see the hem of his silk robe and the tops of his bare feet. He grabbed one of her ears, forcing her to look up at him at a severe angle.

"This is a vain attempt for my sympathy, you know," he whispered. "Cybarys didn't speak to you. She hasn't spoken directly to anyone for over a decade."

Devaki swallowed, burying the response that tried to escape her throat. *She doesn't speak to you because you don't live by her laws. You treat others with harsh judgment instead of forgiveness, and shun those that need blessings. That's not what our Mother teaches us.*

Sehran let her go, then strode past her and ascended the dais. He rested one hand, covered in gemstone-studded rings, on the arm of the throne.

"When I was blessed with this position sixteen years ago, I was shocked," Sehran began. "It was a task I was never supposed to have, yet, because of the tragedy that took place that day, here I am. The Goddess has been displeased with us for a long time now. She chose *me* to lead us all back into her arms."

Devaki straightened and took a step back so she stood before her cousin. They had had this conversation before, and from the stony look on his face, he did not plan for this time to be any different.

"You must have visions, too," she said carefully. "Cybarys isn't angry with us; she just wants us to guide those she's lost back to her. She comes to me and tells me these things, and I can't help but come before you again, and ask for the empathy Armellans are known for. There are many across the sea who need our help."

Sehran shook his head, his black curls brushing against his smooth forehead. Devaki noticed his grip on the arm of the throne tighten, turning his dark skin a dangerous shade of white. The air in the reception chamber seemed to contract, as if Devaki's words were offensive to the empty space around them.

"Those you speak of do not deserve our help." When Sehran spoke, his voice was low and cold, and Devaki had a hard time meeting his dark, brown eyes. "Rhethos exiled our Mother and her children many years ago, and replaced the Goddess' kindness with the greed of powerful men like The Bradford."

"But things are changing," Devaki insisted. She subconsciously twisted her bracelets against her wrists. "They are getting better—"

"The man who leads them is a murderer!" Sehran objected. His voice echoed around the chamber, clashing against the blue glass ceiling above. "He and his 'people' are no different than The Bradford who rules them. Rhethosians only lie, conspire, and kill." He spat the last word, as if it should stick like a barb in Devaki's heart. "I refuse to believe Cybarys gives you, a bastard child, visions of redemption for a lost kingdom. This is a personal matter for you, nothing more. I've had enough of you bringing it up. Leave."

"No." Devaki spoke the word before she was aware of it. The next thing she knew, she was on her knees before her cousin's throne, reaching desperately toward his feet. It hurt her pride and stung more than his words, but she did it anyway. She wanted to tell Sehran the details of her vision, of the ancient Goddess' Woods in Rhethos up in flames, but it would do no good.

"Please listen," she began calmly. "I am treated like nothing here. Nothing but a shadow. You must help—"

"You *are* a shadow!" Sehran snapped. He stepped back, away from Devaki's outreached arms. "It is your existence, your conception, that brought on the worst tragedy in Armellan history! You are blessed to live here with us, by the Goddess' mercy. I tell everyone to give you common courtesy due to your family name. And then you expect me to help that man, to go against all the laws of our kingdom and our Goddess? We cannot help him fight. We cannot send him supplies."

"But," Devaki began weakly, "there must be something—"

"Your child's mind has no understanding of rebellion or war. You truly have none of Isaka's sense, only your father's selfishness."

"Then write it down!" Devaki demanded. She stood abruptly after saying the words, but kept her head lowered and stared at the dais' steps. Tears were overwhelming her vision and words of hatred rose in her throat, but she kept her jaw from trembling and blinked rapidly.

"What?" Sehran snapped.

Devaki exhaled shakily, and when she looked up to meet her cousin's dark eyes, tears unwantedly fell down her cheeks. "I'll do as you say, and never mention Rhethos or the rebellion again, if you put your final decision in an official letter."

Sehran eyed her suspiciously for a moment, then stepped down from the dais. He stood before her, arms crossed over his silk-covered chest. Devaki held his gaze and tried her best to show him that she was being genuine. In fact, she didn't think she could be anything else, but that had never gotten her very far. She thought on the Goddess' words, and that image of a blazing forest flashed before her eyes.

The Armellan Temple Leader sighed exasperatedly and marched over to the missive table behind the dais. With his back to her, he sifted through many organized stacks of parchment till he found a spare piece that was slightly crumpled. Devaki waited as he scrawled across it for a brief moment. When he melted a stick of wax to seal the note, Sehran cut the tip of his finger and let his blood drip into the mixture.

Before Devaki could react, he flung the note at her feet. "Do not come to this room again," he said. "I've tolerated enough of your behavior, and it is not appropriate for you to be here at night, nor during the day when your presence may offend my guests." He paused, gave her a cold smile, then added, "I don't need to give you another *physical* reminder of your place as I did years before, do I?"

Devaki blanched, then ground her teeth, refusing to show shame to her cousin's face. Instead, she picked up the note and tucked it safely within her leather bodice. She shook her head wordlessly.

"I will pray for you, Devaki," Sehran said, his politically correct demeanor back in place. "I know it must be difficult to live with your String of Fate. But be grateful for what you have and know that Cybarys loves you despite everything."

CHAPTER FOURTEEN

ONE VITAL MISTAKE

Angelyn let the familiar chill of her cellar surround her. The bit of light that now shone in sparse bunches along the stairs only reached so far, but Angelyn was used to navigating the musty expanse of the Hamond's storeroom. Sharp smells of old moisture and spices met her nose, and she sneezed as the damp enfolded her like a wet cloak.

The narrow stairs led to a large rectangular room whose ancient floorboards were covered with shelves, each of which reached to the ceiling. Every unit was stocked full with wooden crates, all marked in black ink as to their contents.

Spare tables, chairs, and barstools were stacked along the walls, and Angelyn motioned for Joshua to help her clear off one table where they could set Will. She noticed Josh was shivering from the sharp chill and reached to pull him close. For once, he didn't seem to mind.

A puff of dust billowed around her as Gabriel and Bertram lay Will's body on the old table, but she swallowed and blinked without coughing. The thump of his heavy form hitting the wood sounded all too dead.

"Let's take a look at the wound," Gabriel said, out of breath. With Bertram's help, they first pulled Will's coat off, then his torn shirt to reveal a deep gash in the middle of Will's left arm, the bone visible through torn layers of muscle.

Angelyn covered her mouth. She couldn't help but notice multiple sets of rough, deep scars that ran along the middle of Will's exposed torso. The patterns of the old injuries were odd and ragged, and she wondered what weapon could have inflicted such unique, expansive lines of damage.

She made to put her hands over Joshua's eyes to stop him from gazing at the grisly display, but he had already stepped forward next to Gabriel, ready to offer whatever assistance needed. Unsure what to do, she watched Gabriel's face, shadowed and darkened by the little light, as he examined the injury.

In the damp air, she could see her friend's breath in small, uneven clouds. Angelyn had known him long enough to read his body language, and right now Gabriel appeared genuinely frightened.

Does this rebel leader mean so much to him? Can't he be replaced by another rash fool who wants to uproot and destroy everything?

"Angel, make strips of those rags, please, and soak them in that water," Gabriel instructed. His voice was almost a whisper, as though they could be overheard by Lord Bradford himself in the cellar. Angelyn did as he asked, the sound of weak, tearing fabric filling the dark room. Joshua fell silent as she worked, holding the hot pitcher of water out toward her.

Her fingers trembled, but not from the cold. She brought one warm, soaked bit of rag over Will's wound, wiping tentatively at the blood around the gaping hole. He let out a groan when the cloth touched a flap of skin, and Angelyn flinched. Fresh blood spurted from the open wound and her stomach violently twisted.

Gabriel stepped in next to her, took a warm strip of cloth, and started to bind it around Will's arm tightly. Will jerked and twitched, but he did not wake. When the binding immediately stained red, Joshua handed the old man another bandage, which he cinched forcefully into place. They ran out of rags quickly, but when the last layer was added, it remained a faded white.

"Shouldn't he wake up by now?" Joshua spoke, and his voice cracked as he asked the question. Under other circumstances, Angelyn would have smiled at the expression on her son's face when he heard his uneven tone, but right now she could only look at Will, wondering what the answer could be.

"He will soon," Gabriel replied, straightening from his bent position over Will's chair. He placed both his hands on his lower back, grimacing. "He lost a lot of blood, and it will take time for that gash in his arm to heal. He's a strong man, though, Josh, so don't worry. This is not the first time someone has tried to kill him."

The next ten minutes were silent torture as the four of them stood around Will's unconscious body, waiting for any sign or movement. She jumped when Will finally opened his eyes. He made for his closest weapon, and Gabriel stayed his hand as Will blinked and focused.

"Gabe. . . Miss McKinlee. . ." Will started slowly. "Where is the man who—?"

"We're in the Hamond's cellar. W-we couldn't catch him," Gabriel cut in. "Sarrett must have changed the patrols because no one should have been on those streets at that time. With the wind and the rain, I couldn't see a damn thing. My back was turned when—"

"Did they see me come here?" Will snapped. He tried to sit up, then stand, and both Gabriel and Bertram caught him as he stumbled back onto the dusty table. His shirt and coat fell back into place, concealing his scarred chest.

"I'm not sure," Gabriel replied uneasily. "But—"

"Damn it, Gabe!" Will swore, his hand testing the bump on his forehead. "You're not sure? After Ross, not to mention the burning tonight, do you realize?"

"Gabe saved your life bringing you here!" Angelyn snapped.

Will ignored her, glaring at Gabriel. His voice was hot with anger, his tone urgent: "You know we can't afford mistakes at this stage."

"I know. It's just possible—"

"No!" Will said. "I can't lose Kaylyn because of one injury and your carelessness!"

"I don't see how—"

"They will suspect this inn of conspiracy, Gabe. These people will be strung up from the rafters! Haven't you noticed that the lieutenant will shower any building with flames if he suspects a thing and has the urge to see smoke, regardless of who is inside?"

Gabriel made an indistinguishable sound and peered down at his feet. Angelyn had never seen him so shaken, nor ashamed. She took a step forward, grasping his forearm gently. He patted her hand without looking up. Will sat up on the table, breathing hard, still grasping his head wound.

"I'm sorry, Master Will," Gabriel murmured.

"I know," Will growled in a low tone. He shifted his grip to his arm, pain showing clearly on his face. "But that doesn't mean much right now."

Silence fell in the cellar, hanging in the air with the clouds of their chilled breath. Angelyn could think of nothing to say, nothing she could do; this kind of situation was completely, shockingly new to her and she was at a loss for words.

"I'll go back out on the streets," Gabriel said after a moment, and Angelyn snapped her attention to him. "Let me take a few men, and we'll make it right—"

"No!" Angelyn insisted. She tightened her grip on Gabriel's forearm. "The curfew's already past. There are guardsmen all over towne, and I'm sure there will be more than usual if they just failed to kill Will and collect his body for Sarrett."

"She's right," Will said. "If you go out there now, I'll lose you, and the Hamond will be the first place they'll search."

Angelyn watched her son look from Gabriel to Will and back again, his brow knit with concentration. She was a bit confused as well; she did not expect Will to agree with her in that moment.

"With some help, I think we could still find your attacker, before he goes back to Sarrett," Gabriel insisted. He took a step toward Will, away from Angelyn's touch, till he stood right before the rebel leader. Gabriel collected himself, and Angelyn watched as her friend shifted from a frightened old man into the demure, proper gentleman she'd known most of her life.

"I'll cut a Blessing Rune," Gabriel whispered. His pale blue eyes stared plainly at Will. "The Goddess will keep me safe."

Will shook his head. "We both know you're of no age to bleed for Cybarys."

"Let me try," Gabriel pleaded.

"What are you talking about?" Joshua asked. "Is it magic? Can *you* use Armellan magic?"

Angelyn glanced sharply at him and he was silent. Now was not the time or place to discuss her friend's past.

"I have to do something," Gabriel said. "She's shown me more than you know."

Will sighed and ran a hand through his hair. "I'm sorry, Gabe. I could care less what the damned Goddess wants. Stay here, until morning when I feel well again, and we will fix this together."

Gabriel looked at Angelyn, then took a step toward the cellar stairs. He motioned for Bertram to follow him. "Keep him safe, Angelyn," Gabriel said. "He's worth more than you know."

Angelyn threw her arms around his neck before he could leave. "Don't," she whispered. "Listen to him. Don't go."

The old man shuffled away from her, however, and she tried to ignore the steady tremble she had felt. She could never recall a time when Gabriel would not hug her back.

In fact, now that she thought about it, since Travok left, she'd never let any man touch her without thinking fearfully of her husband's fist. She used her minuscule authority as a business owner to keep rough men in line under her roof, but Gabe was the only one she truly trusted, physically and emotionally.

But Gabriel said nothing more as he and Bertram left.

Angelyn peered at Will. He looked like he wanted to rise, but the way he was leaning against the table and how pale his face was told her he wasn't going anywhere. "What's going to happen now?" she asked.

"I don't know," Will admitted. "This is not how I wanted this evening to go. I hope I did not endanger you or your people when they brought me here."

"It wasn't easy," Angelyn replied. "Ada is still timing the patrols, and we moved you down here so no one would see your condition and panic if it . . . went badly." Her words sounded sure, yet her heart had lodged itself seemingly permanently in her throat, beating against her skin like a booming drum.

"Well, look at you," Will muttered with a hint of approval. He made to stand up again but swayed violently. Angelyn caught his arm, steadying him. Joshua's face lit with surprise, and Will merely grimaced.

"Where do you plan on going?" she demanded, ignoring both of their reactions to her help. "After Gabe?"

"It's not safe to stay here, even in the cellar," Will said. He pulled away from Angelyn's touch and used the edge of the table to stand straight. "Especially with what's happened tonight."

"But Gabriel said you lost a lot of blood and you hurt your head!" Joshua protested, stepping forward. He set the pitcher of water down on the dusty floor. "And you can't even stand up! Where will you go?"

"Anywhere but here, Josh," Will insisted. "Whoever attacked me on the streets tonight seems to know my face, so staying here endangers all of you. I need to leave, now. Gabriel can't do this alone."

Joshua strained his neck to look up at the tall man. "But . . . no one will find you down here. I used to play in this room all the time when I was younger, and Mum could never find me. We have spaces below the floors for when the rains flood the ground in winter, if you need to hide."

"I . . ." Will began, then faded off.

Angelyn glanced at the injured fugitive. She crossed her arms indecisively over her chest, debating what to do. Throwing Will out into the rain after Gabriel wasn't a bad idea. She could be rid of him for good if he was captured far enough away from The Hamond. Then again . . . she glanced at her son, unable to ignore the concern that she saw in his eyes.

"This is different from games you played when you were smaller, darling," she managed.

"No, it's not!" Joshua said, though his eyes were locked on Will. "We have to take care of him, Mum, till he's well enough to go. It's the right thing to do."

Will glanced at Josh and gave him a weak smile. Angelyn half expected Will to push past them and disappear again, but instead he spoke grudgingly, "I will stay till an hour before dawn, then."

Joshua let out an audible sigh of relief, but Angelyn still wasn't sure how to feel. She reached down to pick up the pitcher of tepid water off the floor, and Joshua reluctantly followed her to the stairs. As she ascended, she listened hard in case there was anything wrong. She heard nothing beyond the crackles of the fires.

When she and Josh entered, Ada approached her and grasped Angelyn's hands in hers. The girl's eyes flicked over Angelyn's shoulders to the door down to the cellar, and Angelyn freed herself from her barmaid's grip to shut and lock it. The snap of the old, sturdy wood made gave her courage.

"Is he. . .?" Ada whispered.

Angelyn gave her a reassuring smile. "He's fine. He'll rest, hidden, till dawn."

CHAPTER FIFTEEN

AN ATTEMPTED INTERROGATION

Angelyn wanted to leave Will locked in her cellar without food or warmth all night. In fact, after cleaning up and double-checking the locks on every door, she had marched up the stairs and was halfway to her bedroom when she stopped in her tracks. How was she supposed to sleep with a man like that in her cellar?

She cursed, yanked out her ring of keys, and strode back to the storeroom door. Her eyes adjusted again to the gloom and her breath formed in a weak cloud. *I have no idea what I'm going to say to him,* she thought as she descended, *but I want some answers, and he's going to give them to me.*

Will sat on the edge of the table he'd lain unconscious on not long ago, trying his best to tighten the bindings around his bicep with one hand. He glanced at her only when she stood in front of him.

"How does someone in Kaylyn know who you are?" she demanded. "You told us this towne wasn't hard to stay hidden in, that your men would protect you."

"I'm doing just fine, thank you for asking, Miss McKinlee," Will said bitterly. "You helped me earlier, didn't you?" He wrapped his arms around himself in the chill, despite the heavy weight of his leather coat.

"Well . . ." she said, "I did some, but it was mostly Gabriel."

"I thought you didn't like me, Miss McKinlee."

"I don't *trust* you."

"I see," Will replied. "I still don't think I should stay here."

"Just stay the night and then you can go wherever you please. I don't care."

Will raised his eyebrows at her. The shadows darkened his face in the pale, flickering light of the cellar's torches. "You don't?"

Angelyn deliberately glanced down at her boots, dusted with the dirt of the cellar floor. "I'll get you something to make it comfortably through the night," she muttered, and turned back toward the stairs.

"If there's no one else about, I'd prefer a drink," Will said. He rose, wavered, and swore nastily. "Besides, I can see on your face how much I've inconvenienced you."

"I can't argue with that," Angelyn admitted. "But I'm not risking you leaving this cellar."

She blocked the first step on the set of stairs. Will gave her a bemused look and walked forward till he stood right before her. Angelyn swallowed, realizing the situation she'd placed herself in. She took a couple steps backward, up the staircase, and he matched her move for move.

A spasm of pain passed over Will's face, and he reached out to grab the banister for support. Angelyn, without thinking, put a hand under his arm to help him stand.

"I don't think you could make it up these steps without my help," she said quietly. She clutched a handful of the leather of his sleeve in a fist, and she could feel the weight of him.

"Let me go," Will grunted. Despite the poor light, she could see his darkened face contorted with pain. "I'll make it up myself, if you'd only move aside."

"You're a selfish bastard, you know that?" Angelyn challenged. She let go of his arm, and enjoyed watching him waver, just one step below her on the staircase. Seeing this tall, broad stranger in pain helped her clear her head a little, too, which was swimming with the nearness of him, and that look in his eyes when they met hers.

"Fall and break your neck!" she continued. "You—"

Will cut her short with a deep kiss. He only had to lean forward a few inches, but it still filled her with shock. His good arm ran gently along the curve of her hip to rest on her lower back. Part of her wanted to shove him backward and run up the stairs to lock the door behind her, but a warmth enveloped her so strongly she forgot to move, let alone flee.

For a few seconds, there was nothing but the smell of his hair, still damp with rain, the deep scent of leather, and the powerful musk of him as a man. Angelyn felt her arms wrap around Will's neck, forcing him to hold onto the railing with his injured arm.

He flinched against her parted lips, and the movement seemed to awaken them both to their senses.

"Miss McKinlee," Will said, eyes still smoldering. "We shouldn't . . ."

Angelyn shook herself. "Shouldn't what?"

"You'll be in more trouble than I am if we do that again," he said. "That was my mistake." Will tried to head up the stairs, but Angelyn continued to block his way.

"You kissed me," she said. Her entire body trembled. She had not let a man touch her, let alone kiss her since her husband had left, and Angelyn found herself having to stop her fingertips from going up to her lips. How was it this man could get under her skin so easily? Others had tried to kiss her in the past. Tried and failed.

"You were saying some very mean things," he smiled. Then his voice changed: "Let me go by, Miss McKinlee."

She still didn't move out of his path, but lowered her head, ashamed at how she embraced his kiss. Instead of getting out of his way, Angelyn decided to play a card she'd been holding since the first time they'd met:

"You know, your people may trust you more, *I* might trust you more, if you told us your real name."

Will offered a confused frown. "What do you mean?"

Angelyn sighed. "Have you noticed that I've never called you what everyone else does?" She smiled at the expression on his face. "'Will,'" she said with contempt, "is not your name."

"Really?" he scoffed, staring at her. "Are you sure?"

"Yes! And don't expect me to ever say it again." She tried her best to ignore the way his grin was growing. "That's one reason why I don't trust you."

"Hush," he muttered suddenly, his attention snapping up the staircase to the dimly lit common hall. "What was—?"

"Don't you try and scare me," Angelyn said. "You just don't want to talk about yourself. You've had plenty of questions about me, you know, and then you have the nerve to—"

"I don't share much about myself, Miss McKinlee," he said quietly, peering above and beyond her.

"Why not?" she insisted. For some reason another image of this man kneeling in front of those two bloodied, soot-covered children became clear in her mind. He'd been hurt tonight, risking his entire cause, to save those newly made orphans. What kind of bloodthirsty rebel leader did that?

Will ascended one more stair closer to her, once more eliminating the distance between them, and clamped a hand over her mouth.

"Do you hear that?" he whispered. Angelyn nodded when he didn't move his hand: even from halfway up the cellar stairs, she could make out voices outside on the street.

"Damn the Goddess," Will swore.

Angelyn pulled his hand away so she could speak. "What?" She heard muffled voices and thumps outside.

"Kaylyn guardsmen!" he snapped, wincing at the pain in his arm. "I have to go."

Angelyn jumped when someone banged hard on the bolted front door. "It's too late." She quickly climbed the stairs, keys in hand. "They'll be around back, too."

A new idea came to her, one she did not like one bit but spoke aloud anyway. "I'll send Joshua down here and he'll help you hide. I can handle these men, I promise—"

Outside, a sharp voice shouted, "Open this door!"

Angelyn craned her neck toward the front of the inn and replied, "We're closed! It's after curfew!"

"Your Lord commands you open this door *now*!"

CHAPTER SIXTEEN

ENDING A THREAD OF FATE

Joshua raced down the stairs before his mother could call his name. He'd been wondering why she was down in the cellar talking with Will when the banging started. When he saw the look on her face and the way she had her hands clasped tightly in front of her, Joshua felt the rage in his stomach rise and claw back up his dry throat. If those guardsmen from the Luwenn home were now knocking on their front door . . .

"Listen fast," Angelyn hissed. "Find him somewhere to hide, then come back up to me. Be careful!"

Joshua flew down the cellar stairs to find Will trying to lift one of the trap doors at the back of the room. With his injured arm bent uselessly against his chest, he could not manage to haul the heavy piece upward.

"Let me," Joshua said, and he rushed to grasp the thick iron handle and pull with all his strength. The old smells of stale air and root vegetables met his nose immediately.

Joshua glanced at Will, and saw that, behind the strands of long hair that hung in his eyes, his face was calm. He was white from blood loss, could not move his arm, and was seconds away from being discovered by the men who had hunted him since his arrival in Kaylyn, but Joshua could sense no fear in Will.

How does he do that? Joshua wondered as he struggled to hold the door up as Will climbed into the crawl space beneath. Will had to hunch down to fit in the pitch-black hole.

"Stay quiet," Joshua muttered. "No one will find you here."

He was about to ease the door back down when the banging upstairs abruptly stopped. The familiar sound of the Hamond's main door opening echoed in Joshua's ears. Angelyn's voice drifted down the cellar stairs, even and calm, followed by the heavy footfalls of several sets of boots.

Joshua froze and stared down at Will, unsure what to do. He knew he couldn't go back upstairs now, or he'd give away Will's hiding place.

"Jump down," Will said quietly.

"But I can't leave my mum alone—"

"Now, Josh!"

Joshua swallowed and hunched down next to the trap door. When he landed in the cramped space partially on top of Will, a brief clash of deep red sparks flashed in the air and Joshua stifled a scream.

* * *

Angelyn straightened her back and relaxed her shoulders when she walked to the front door. The common hall was only lit by the lamps along the main staircase with the large hearths now dark and cold, and the climbing shadows made her feel like she was shrinking with each step.

She glanced back at the open cellar door, but Joshua hadn't come back up yet. The next bang on the Hamond's entrance made the wood shudder in the frame. She knew she couldn't wait any longer, and took her keys out of her apron to open the front door.

Three uniformed men immediately pushed their way inside. Rainwater ran down their heavy wool coats and puddled on the floor at their feet. They all stood at least a foot taller than her, their faces stern, solid forms of authority.

The two guardsmen in front bore lit torches in their hands and held a semi-conscious, dirty body between them, while a third man waited behind. Angelyn squinted to see who the bedraggled person was and had to hold back a cry: Gabriel.

She almost lost herself in that moment. Angelyn could see everything spiraling away from the control she had managed to keep within the safety of her home: her best friend, her trusted confidant, arrested, the kingdom's most wanted man in her cellar, and her son's whereabouts unknown.

What can I do? she thought desperately. *How can I hold this together?*

"Good evening, Masters," Angelyn said, her tone well-guarded. "Lord, is Gabriel all right? I can find him a room, or walk him home. It's not far—"

"That's not necessary," one guardsman cut in sharply. "He'll be leaving with us momentarily, under arrest for conspiracy."

Angelyn recognized the big man as the one who had offered her son a lit torch and forced him to throw it at the Luwenn home several hours ago. Now, however, there was no recognition in the officer's cold gaze.

It's as if we'd never met now that there's trouble, she thought.

"Conspiracy?" Angelyn repeated.

"Against Rhethos and her people," the officer clarified slowly, as if Angelyn wasn't intelligent enough to know what the word itself meant. "We've been getting rebels more often these days, as I'm sure you've noticed. The rest of this man's friends are dead, and now we're here to speak with you."

Angelyn felt her hands begin to tremble, and a fresh chill spread across her entire body. It was all she could do to keep her eyes from Gabriel's face, because if she looked at him one more time, she knew her resolve would break.

Suddenly the third man stepped forward, the only one in the group that had a clear air of authority, one that could not be ignored.

"It's Miss Angelyn McKinlee, correct?"

He took off his heavy overcoat, much finer than those that his companions wore, and folded it with perfect precision over his arm. Polished rows of gemstones lined this man's collar and chest.

Angelyn's heart skipped several beats in terrified recognition. *That's him: Lieutenant Jonathan Sarrett.*

Sarrett studied Angelyn with sharp, calculative eyes. The torchlight from the open flames his guardsmen held spread in deep shadows across his face. He was almost as tall as Will, with typical Rhethosian features: a sharp jaw and bright, Rhethosian Blue eyes, that treasured hereditary color.

The lieutenant paused for one breath, and when Angelyn opened her mouth to reply, he easily continued over her, as if he had been waiting only to interrupt her. "One of the rebel rats we just dispatched mentioned this location under interrogation. You understand what this implication means for you, don't you?"

From his hunched position between the lieutenant's guardsmen, Gabriel raised his head slowly. "Leave her alone . . ." he slurred, his voice barely audible. There was blood on his forehead, and the flesh around his left eye was quickly turning a sickening violet.

Barton struck the old man hard in the gut. Angelyn's hands tightened into fists, and she resisted the urge to fall on her knees next to Gabriel. She forced her gaze upward, meeting Sarrett's eyes.

"We are here to search the Hamond, to see if there is any truth to these accusations," Sarrett announced. He extended one hand, covered in an expensive leather glove, toward Angelyn. "Your keys, Miss. *Now.*"

Angelyn fumbled for a moment, then the lieutenant ripped the key ring from her grasp and tossed it to Barton. The two guardsmen roughly kicked past Gabriel and began to check behind the bar and back in the kitchen. One man climbed the stairs and banged on every door, demanding each room be opened and searched.

The lieutenant sauntered over to the dead fireplace closest to the door, as if he could will the embers back to life with his very presence. He cleared his throat, sounding bored. When he glanced back at her, Sarrett seemed surprised at the fear on her face.

"Oh, I'm sure there's nothing to worry about," he said. "My men love your tavern, Miss, and there's never a speck of flour out of place. Though . . . it really would be a shame to put an old Kaylyn family establishment to the torch." He ruffled the ends of his curled hair at the base of his neck casually as he spoke, as if the topic were the weather and not kindling her home.

"Thank you for your consideration," Angelyn said carefully. Her eyes wanted to drift to the open cellar door. Why hadn't Joshua come back upstairs? She felt her throat go dry with guilt; what had possessed her to think it was a good idea to tell her son to hide Will?

Sarrett gave her a small, cold smile and came to stand directly in front of her. Angelyn held her ground, but the lieutenant's eyes were scanning the empty common hall piece by piece. "Why haven't I been to your little business before?" he murmured. "This place is . . . lovely."

Angelyn choked back her pride when she heard the slightly mocking tone in his voice and remained silent. When Barton and the second guardsman returned empty-handed, she watched the lieutenant's gaze go to the cellar door that sat ajar.

"Well, then. It seems there's only one last place to visit," Sarrett said, and he swept a hand toward the door. "Just to be thorough."

Sarrett stepped close to Angelyn and pressed one hand firmly against her lower back. She recalled Will's arm wrapped gently in that same spot not long ago, and the difference between the two gestures made her shiver. Sarrett's grip told her that he was used to pushing women around.

"You can lead the way, Miss McKinlee," Sarrett said next to her ear, then commanded more loudly over his shoulder, "You there, stay up here and keep watch. Barton, bring him with us."

The guardsman jerked Gabriel up to his feet, and Angelyn swallowed steadily as she stepped down the cellar stairs.

* * *

Joshua held still and tried to keep breathing. It felt as if there was no air in the tiny crawl space beneath the cellar's floor, and what he did manage to draw into his lungs was pure dust and mildew. He clapped a hand over his mouth every time he wanted to cough or gag.

His heart froze when feet crashed down the cellar's steps and onto the floorboards above them. Will tensed and tried to work his good arm down to one of the weapons on his legs, but there wasn't enough room for either of them to move much. Bulky bags of carrots and sacks of potatoes crunched under their combined weight.

Joshua caught Will's eyes, and the rebel leader pressed a single finger against his lips, then pointed it upward. A moment later, he held up four fingers, barely visible to Joshua in the cellar's darkness. Joshua nodded even though he couldn't tell who each person was just by the sound of their footfalls.

"You're very well organized, Miss McKinlee," spoke a male voice. "Now, this is what bothers me: why would one of these rebel troublemakers tell me to come to your home tonight?"

Joshua craned his neck in a desperate attempt to see something, anything, despite his current immobilized position. One set of boots marched forward, while another shuffled back as if with fear.

"You're wasting your time! Let her be."

Gabriel! Joshua thought, recognizing the old man's voice immediately. There was pain and defiance in his words. The floorboards shook when Gabriel hit the ground. Anger blossomed in Joshua's chest, and he ground his teeth in desperation. He felt Will pull a dagger loose from his leg and deftly turn it so the point faced upward.

"Here, sir!" another man's voice exclaimed, and Joshua saw the shadow of his boots almost directly above them. "A door down to storage."

"Ah. Open it, then, Barton," spoke the first voice, intrigue clear in his tone.

No, Joshua thought desperately. *Please! Someone stop him!*

Will grabbed Joshua's arm and pulled back his tunic's sleeve. Joshua tried to squirm away from his touch when he brought the knife close to his forearm. Above them, he vaguely heard his mother trying to make excuses.

"Trust me," Will whispered. "You want to know how to use your magic? Give blood, and the Goddess will answer your prayer."

Joshua stifled a cry with the back of his free hand when Will slashed four weaving lines of a foreign rune into his skin, just deep enough to make him bleed. An instant red glow leaked from the symbol along with lines of blood. Above them, a faint touch of deep maroon echoed along the edges of the trap door. Despite his shock, Joshua felt a warmth blossom in the air around him that reminded him of his mother's arms hugging him close.

The guardsman above fumbled back and forth, sweeping away dust and scraping against the floorboard. *Why aren't they opening it?* Joshua wondered. *The handle is right there!*

"Wait. There's nothing here . . . not even a hinge," Barton said slowly, as if he didn't believe the words he spoke. "Just a moment ago . . ."

"Idiot," snapped the first voice from the other end of the cellar, the one Joshua now assumed was in charge. "Nothing out of order, then, as usual, Miss McKinlee, save for some dust. But you would do best to stay away from senile rebels like this one in the future."

"Gabriel is neither senile nor a rebel," Angelyn retorted. "You know my family name and business well enough, so this entire ordeal has been an insulting waste of time. I've done nothing wrong."

Joshua was stunned. All the shock of the glowing rune on his arm and the disappearing door fell away when he heard his mother argue. He knew right after he heard the uncharacteristically defiant words that Angelyn had made a huge mistake.

No one spoke back to a military figure in Rhethos.

"Ah," began the man's voice, its tone strained with thinned patience. "I think I understand now. This old traitor is a family friend, isn't he? If I remember Kaylyn politics correctly, as juvenile as they are, the Chapman family has been close with the McKinlees for decades, investing gold in their trade and upkeep? That's one of the reasons why you've scraped by after your husband abandoned you, sixteen years ago?"

"I . . .Yes, Lieutenant," Angelyn replied, and Joshua heard all the fire from her previous statements had been extinguished.

"Get him," the man commanded sharply.

Joshua tried to stand when he heard Gabriel being roughly handled by the guardsman, but Will gripped the back of his neck with a gloved hand and held him still.

"You say nothing 'wrong' has been done here," Sarrett's voice continued, "yet we found this man with rebels, one of them denoting The Hamond as a place to look for more of their kind. And you . . ." He paused, and his boots turned sharply in place. ". . .you don't *support* these conspirators, do you?"

"No, Lieutenant Sarrett," Angelyn replied assuredly. "Nor will I ever."

"Good," he shot back. He cleared his throat. "Master Barton, kill him."

Joshua tried to scream, and Will dropped his dagger to clamp a hand over his mouth. The sound of another blade being drawn met Joshua's ears, as well as the thump of Gabriel being forced to his knees. *We can't just hide here! Will, do something! Use magic to save him!*

"Goddess, guide me to your arms." Gabriel's dying whisper barely reached Joshua's ears.

Liquid spilled in a rush and began to leak down between the floorboards. Will pressed his arms upward to try and stop the blood from dripping onto Joshua. Joshua shook all over, staring blindly at the foreign rune starting to clot on his pale skin. As the blood flow above them ebbed, Joshua held his trembling jaw shut and forced back the tears in his eyes.

"I am sure it is a shock to learn a friend turned against our Lord, so we will dispose of the old rebel's body for you," the lieutenant announced with unneeded volume. "Since I *know* the McKinlees and their establishment well enough, I don't mind doing you this small, undeserved favor. You may thank me, Miss McKinlee."

Joshua cringed at the dull sound of a heavy weight being dragged up the cellar steps. He choked back the bile in his throat when he heard his mother say:

". . . Th-thank you, Lieutenant."

"Any time, Miss," Sarrett responded. "Have a good night. Remember, your Lord loves you."

CHAPTER SEVENTEEN

LIVING WITH THE FIRE

Angelyn stared at the pool of blood on her cellar floor. She wrapped her arms around herself and trembled so badly that locks of her hair fell shakily in front of her pale face. When the trap door opened a moment later, she nearly screamed.

"Mum," Joshua said, and Angelyn finally found herself able to move when she saw Will help her son out of the crawl space. One of Joshua's boots splashed in the gore before he reached her and hugged her tightly.

Angelyn pulled Joshua back from her so she could examine him. Her fingertips shook against his cheeks. His clothes were covered in dust and the top of his head was spattered with red dots. When she glanced at Will, her stomach churned: rivulets of blood were drying along the tops of his arms and shoulders.

"What did you do?" she demanded, though her voice was weak. "How . . .?" Her hands tightened into fists when she noticed the Blessing Rune cut into her son's skin.

"Did *I* do that?" Joshua questioned, stepping away from Angelyn to stare wide-eyed at Will. "Was that magic from my blood? And what does this say?"

"It means Protection," Will said, almost distractedly. "One of three Armellan runes that can create a magical effect, if you are Touched by Cybarys. I'm sure you've been taught that such magic will bring the slaves of the Goddess back to Rhethos, despite the 'safety' your Lord provides."

"Wait, I just asked for protection and cut the shape and she gave it to me?" Joshua interrupted.

"Will," Angelyn began. "Don't—"

"It's not that simple," Will addressed Josh, ignoring his mother for the moment. "The Bradford may tell you the Goddess is an evil slave driver of humanity. That is *not* true, but your Lord is not wrong in saying Cybarys has her own designs. She gave you protection because it suited her needs. Not because she actually cares."

"So tell me," Joshua began.

"Later," Will insisted. "Now is not the time." He looked to Angelyn, then jerked his head upward. "Your guests don't sound happy that they've been disturbed in their rooms. It would be best to keep them quiet."

Angelyn listened and heard movement up on the main floor. Steadying herself, she glared at Will. "Stay here. I don't want them seeing you." When she marched up the steps and shut the cellar door behind her, Joshua was at her side.

People descended the stairs from the Hamond's upper level in small groups. Frightened and angry expressions were displayed on all their faces as they clutched blankets over their night shirts.

"What happened, Miss McKinlee?" someone asked.

"Why did they storm into our rooms like that?"

Several men glanced warily at Joshua. "Is that blood on you?"

"There isn't a problem," Angelyn managed.

"Someone's broken the lieutenant's laws, that's clear enough!" one man protested. He stood halfway up the main staircase, and dozens of heads turned to look at him. "I've got to get my family and leave this damned towne. Why we even came here is—"

"I don't know who told the guardsmen about this place," Angelyn said. "But you can rest easy tonight; they found the traitor they were looking for. Our . . ." Her voice caught in her throat, but she cleared it quickly. "Our Lord's lieutenant has taken care of the danger and we are all safe again. If you love Kaylyn, or at least value its peace, stay indoors till morning."

Angelyn took a couple of even breaths, raising her chin high so all those gathered on the balcony and at the foot of the main staircase could see her expression. She crossed her arms over her chest, hoping she could send the strong message that no more outbursts would be tolerated.

Many of those with angrier expressions sobered. A woman standing next to the man who had spoken out touched his arm, and they both nodded at

Angelyn with strained expressions. Everyone headed back to their rooms, murmurs of fear and disapproval fading behind closed doors. The common room was empty again of everyone but Angelyn and Joshua.

Angelyn sat shakily in a chair by the dead fireplace. She wasn't aware that Josh had gone off to the kitchen until he came back some time later with a hot mug of tea. Holding it loosely, she tried to get a hold of her emotions, but it seemed impossible; her insides ranged from numbness to rage and nothing in between.

"Do you want to go upstairs?" Joshua asked quietly.

"In a minute," she muttered. But more than minutes went by. Silence filled the inn and Joshua stood next to her, collapsing into his own chair after a while. The heavy hours that lay between the middle of the night and early morning arrived with her tea cold in her hands.

The door to the cellar opened, and Angelyn grabbed Joshua's arm as Will emerged. He clutched the knob for support, the bandages on his arm soaked through with fresh blood.

"Miss McKinlee . . ." he began.

Without hesitating, Angelyn set down her tea and strode up to Will. She drew her fist back and punched him across the jaw. A small grunt of surprise escaped his lips.

"You monster!" she cried, voice crackling. "He's dead because of you!"

Angelyn grabbed a handful of Will's trench coat and drew back for another blow, but he caught her fist. She struggled, her long hair flying about her face, but her anger burned out quickly. She reduced to sobs, which she stifled with the back of her hand. Angelyn wrenched away from Will's grip and fell into an empty chair, her head down.

Will rubbed his jaw, his gaze on the floor. "I told him not to go back out there," he said.

"I don't care," she snapped bitterly.

"Miss McKinlee," Will tried.

"Mum," Joshua added, almost at the same moment. "How did?"

"Quiet, both of you!" Angelyn snapped. She stood, blinking back furious tears. She did not want to hear Will's well-phrased excuses or Joshua's questions. Magic didn't matter to her, the rebellion didn't matter to her, *nothing* mattered right now except the fact that all that was left of her closest friend was a puddle of blood in her cellar.

"You," Angelyn said, directing her gaze to Joshua. "Get in your room and stay there. You," she added to Will, "get back down in that cellar. I have the only key to the only door. I'll figure out what's next in the morning."

To her relief, neither of them argued. Joshua ascended the main stairs, and Will descended the cellar steps. After she locked the door behind Will, Angelyn made her way to her own bedroom. She didn't think she could sleep, but, once all the tears were gone, she closed her eyes and fell into many dark dreams.

* * *

It made him feel awful, but Joshua disobeyed his mother yet again. She told him to stay put, to not go anywhere near the cellar where Will was hiding, but something inside of him would not let him sleep. Every time he closed his eyes, Joshua saw images of blood falling down on his head, and that rune burning on his arm. His heart ached and he felt like he was going to be sick.

Resolutely, Joshua extinguished the lamp by his bedside and pulled a pillow and several blankets off his bed. He carefully made his way to his mother's room next door. She was asleep when he entered, but her rest was uneasy; she twitched and moaned, curled in a ball on her thin mattress. Knotted clumps of her hair clung to the tear stains on her cheeks.

Joshua felt that fire rise in his chest again, the one that had started when he threw that torch, the one that blazed into his throat when he saw the orphaned children. He quickly grabbed his mother's keys out of her apron that hung by the door and shoved them against his blanket to keep quiet.

Joshua made his way down the hall, down the stairs, and to the cellar door. After unlocking it, he reached out his free hand to open the door, but it suddenly swung out toward him. He had to jump back to avoid being smacked in the nose.

"It's Josh," he whispered. Will held a burned down candle in one hand and a blade in the other, though he lowered the latter when he saw Joshua.

"What's wrong?" Will's face looked even more ragged than before.

"There's no way I'm going to sleep tonight," Joshua said. He tried to smile but failed miserably. "I . . . need to talk to someone."

Will eyed the boy. "Does your mother know you're here?" he asked.

"Yes," Joshua lied. "And I brought you some things to stay warm. Just let me down, okay?"

Will nodded and beckoned Josh to follow him downstairs. Joshua didn't need the pale light to not trip, even with his arms full of his blankets and pillow. Will had laid his cloak and many of his weapons out on the table where he'd been unconscious earlier. He now put the candle down amongst an array of daggers, settled himself with a groan into a nearby chair, and confronted Josh.

"What is it?"

Joshua bit his lower lip, looking at his feet. His pulse raced, a nervous sweat breaking on his brow. *I need to talk about Gabe, if I ever want to sleep again,* he thought, but couldn't muster the words. *And I need to know about that magic so I can keep Mum safe.*

Joshua raised his head, full of determination. He handed Will the blankets and his pillow while he gathered his courage.

"I needed to tell you that Master Gabriel meant a lot more than you know to my mother and me. I know that you both messed up tonight, but he died for it, and for your cause. Please remember that when you see Mum next, all right?"

Will stared coldly, then shook his head. "Do you realize many have died for Rhethos over the last decade? . . .no." He barked a laugh, one without any humor in it. "Of course, there's no way you could know that. I'm sorry, but these are facts of war you need to accept, if you want to survive."

Joshua bristled. "I'm not here to have you insult me," he replied. "I'm here to give you something to stay warm, and to . . . well, to be your friend."

"I don't need your friendship, Josh," Will sighed, though he wrapped one of the blankets around his shoulders. "But thank you."

Joshua ground his teeth, frustrated. There was too much going on in his head and his heart, and he suddenly had no idea why he thought he should come down here in the middle of the night. He wanted answers, assurance, something to help him cope with the trauma that had literally fallen on his head, but this wasn't helping.

Tears sprang in Joshua's eyes, and it was all he could do to stop them from falling in heavy streams down his face. Will was watching him, and Joshua blinked furiously. He would not cry in front of this man. He refused to do that, when he could tell his mother had already cried enough for both of them.

Will's face softened, and he motioned to the edge of the table next to where he sat. Joshua leaned against it, brushing at the edges of his eyes.

"Let me see that compass of yours."

Joshua looked up, surprised at the subject change. When he reached into his pocket, Joshua found it hurt a lot less than he thought it would. "Gabriel gave it to me," he said quietly. "For my birthday, a couple days ago. When I first met you, those red sparks flew and the compass burned in my pocket. What is it? What can it do?"

Will squinted and turned the compass over in his hands, bringing it closer to the light of his single candle. He traced the runes on the compass' back panel silently. Joshua noticed how beaten and scarred Will's fingers were. His knuckles were large and square, dotted with patches of white skin and bumps where broken bones had healed over many times. Joshua glanced down at his own hands, which were small, soft, and smooth.

"It's Armellan, isn't it?" Joshua asked, referring to the runes.

Will tilted the compass, watching the needle balance. His face was expressionless, but Joshua noticed his eyebrows scrunch together, as if he was in pain. "It's definitely not modern Armellan," he murmured. "Though some of the shapes are similar."

"You can read the language of the people across the sea?" Joshua marveled.

"Yes. I was raised there," Will replied, "by their temple monks, from the time I was eight to about sixteen."

Joshua felt his jaw drop. "But . . .Rhethosians don't live across the sea. We have to stay here, where The Bradford can keep us safe from their Blood Goddess. She used to enslave both our kingdoms, hundreds of years ago."

"Before The First Bradford set us free from Cybarys, I know," Will cut in, but raised his eyebrows as he spoke. "That's what the Lord's books teach you, right? That things here are bad under him, yes, but life enslaved to the Goddess would be utterly worse. That's *his* version of history."

Joshua didn't know how to respond to that. Instead, he looked down at the

Protection Rune beginning to heal on his arm. "How do I have their Goddess' magic? And what do I do with it?"

"Your mother doesn't want you hearing about that, Josh," Will said pointedly. "I should respect her wishes."

"But I want to learn so I can keep her safe!" Joshua insisted. "Why can't you help me do that instead of making it worse?"

Will shook his head wordlessly and handed the compass back to Joshua. Joshua stood and faced Will head on, his frustration rising once more.

"How do you deal with it?" he demanded. "The fire?"

Will tilted his head. "You mean Sarrett's love for arson? Well, it rains often in Kaylyn, so that's a—"

"No," Joshua interrupted, shaking his head. "The fire here." He paused and touched the center of his chest. "I have this awful pain, and this need to do something, to fix everything I've seen that's wrong lately. But it feels like it'll burn me to pieces. So how do you live with it?"

Joshua saw that he'd caught Will off guard, and Will waited a long time as if thinking very hard about what to say. Joshua watched his breath issue in small, labored clouds in the dark. "I don't live with it, Josh," Will finally said. He looked at Joshua, and his green eyes were lit with a serious determination Josh had last seen the night he met the man. "I *do* something about it. I know what you're describing, and it's a pain I've felt for sixteen years."

Will looked away and murmured under his breath, "It will go away once I get to meet my daughter."

"You have a daughter?" Joshua asked. "Where is she?"

Will started, as if surprised he'd spoken that aloud. "I don't talk about her. I'm not sure why I even mentioned her."

Joshua decided not to press the subject. "So where will you go in the morning?" he asked instead.

"There are some men I need to see," Will replied. "I need to fix what happened here tonight and gather what support I can, or I don't think I'll make Kaylyn change its colors any time soon."

"How will you manage all that?"

"I have ways, Josh," Will said with a dark smile. "But I don't think your mother would appreciate the details. Sarrett's the cause of all our troubles here in Northern Rhethos. If I can take care of him, there are only a few more monsters that block the path to our dream for this towne and for the entire kingdom."

CHAPTER EIGHTEEN

TRUTH BEHIND CLOSED DOORS

Devaki did not sleep well, haunted by distorted recollections of her conversation with Sehran. When the first touch of dawn's pale light kissed the gray horizon, she sat on her windowsill and watched the sun bloom over the distant desert hills.

She prayed silently, lighting several Sahma leaves and meditating until the sun hung much higher in the sky. There was nowhere, no escape from her life until the evening tide came. And even then she knew the Rhethosian rebel was only coming to safely collect Sehran's note from her.

I'm meant to stay silent, to obey and bide my time until I'm deemed "necessary".

Devaki stood from her curled position by the window, stretching her sore muscles. *I refuse to be useless,* she thought determinedly. *There is one last place I can go where I might be of some use to the rebel cause.*

She snatched a red silk scarf off its hook by her bedroom door before going out into the hallway. The mosaic tiles chilled her feet as she headed down the palace corridor, wrapping the thin scarf over her unruly expanse of curling hair that sprang out in all directions. Lines of monks with gold-trimmed robes moved silently passed her, their eyes cast to the floor.

The central spiral of the palace slowly sloped downward until it reached the main floor, where the hallway opened onto a courtyard lined with large brown stones. Combed, sandy earth sparkled brightly in the morning sun, and Devaki blinked as she took a deep breath and walked outside.

Coming here will be worth it, she told herself. *It won't be as bad as last time. I have to learn something useful . . . for Will.*

The courtyard was full of people, all of whom Devaki could at least partially recognize, though she had never spoken to any of them. Some of those waiting were Tarran family members with scheduled audiences with the Temple Leader, others commoners wishing to place a request with one of the Goddess Touched that lived in the palace.

Devaki walked silently into the organized throng of people, keeping her eyes down and her shoulders back. The air in the open courtyard was serene and welcoming, each person smiling and chatting quietly, but for some reason it felt like wading into a bloody ocean full of sharks.

Stay calm and listen.

Hanging over the oval-shaped courtyard was an intricate lattice of polished wood that provided spots of shade as the daylight moved over the sand. Tiny rock gardens surrounded by stone benches dotted the perimeter where some groups gathered to either speak quietly or meditate in silence. When she inhaled, the fresh scents of different perfumes and the musk of Sahma smoke hit her nose.

As the morning sun warmed her arms and soaked into the top of her head through her scarf, Devaki glanced back at the entrance to the palace, where a single monk and a woman stood side by side. A steady flow of people approached them in a line, each person keeping a respectful distance between themselves and the next. The monk bore heavy sheets of parchment that he referenced, and the woman next to him greeted and spoke to each person.

"You'll have to come back tomorrow," the monk was saying to the couple at the head of his line. "Brother Sehran simply doesn't have the time today . . ."

Devaki slipped past the monk and drifted down the line waiting to speak to the Goddess Touched woman. A pregnant woman about halfway up the queue murmured to her friends about having a Blessing Rune for Strength cut by a Goddess Touched to help her through labor, while a man toward the end of the line debated with those around him about whether someone would be sent to his home outside Valsara to cast a Protection Rune over his sick children.

I wonder what it would be like to wait in that line? Devaki thought. *I think Sehran's monk would tell me there was no room for me on his papers, and the Goddess Touched woman would announce no help was needed for someone who could already cast magic.*

Devaki sighed, realizing she didn't have the courage to actually confirm her suspicions. Instead, she turned her attention back to the patrons of the courtyard and opened her ears to all the conversation she slowly walked by. She was here to learn some gossip, some information that she could take to Rhethos with her.

The majority of those present that weren't filtering toward or away from the main lines were women. These groups of ladies dotted the sandy yard like bright gems, all dripping in fine silk, gold jewelry, and innumerable strands of beads.

They're not here on business, Devaki thought, subconsciously brushing at her silk sleeves and gold prayer bracelets, several years out of fashion. *They're here to do what I'm doing: listening. There is an art to palace gossip.*

Devaki kept her paces slow as she made her way around the courtyard. She didn't search the groups of patrons, nor did she glance up at the gorgeous wood-work that partially shaded the space. Those were signs of someone who was new to this place, and attention was always drawn to newcomers. Instead, she did her best to blend in with those that looked like they were here for a reason.

"And your crop is better this season?"

"Yes, though a lot of good it'll do me with trade cut off with northern Rhethos."

Devaki slowed even further when she heard this exchange. Without turn-ing her head toward the two male voices, she stepped into the nearest bit of shade, fanning herself as if she needed relief from the sun's rays.

"I don't expect that to change any time soon. Rebellion is more than just a rumor across the sea now."

"I know. And just after I had a Goddess Touched lad come out to my farm. He cut a Blessing Rune for us, and it's made an incredible difference with the pepper plant's health. Now I have nowhere to ship them!"

"Looks like I'll tell my wife we'll be buying more peppers than usual, yes?"

Devaki smiled as the two laughed, though this was knowledge she had heard before. In Rhethos, The Bradford was punishing his northern townes by cutting off all trade, both foreign and domestic. Instead of complaining in anger, though, the Armellan people laughed at their troubles and supported one another.

"It's awful, I'm telling you. Clancy is such a beautiful towne, but the people . . . they are lifeless."

"What do you mean?"

"They have no will, no happiness. And no matter how good the money used to be, I'm almost glad to not sail there anymore. It saddened my soul every time."

Devaki grimaced, wishing the men had something more important to speak about; this was old news, facts about the kingdom across the sea that everyone knew.

"I heard women can't walk alone down their streets, and that they turn their children over to the military at a certain age. Is that true?"

"That and more. And the rebels only spill more blood. The public executions are terrifying, Goddess help them. Their guardsmen take people, sometimes entire families, and—"

Devaki drifted away from the conversation now, not wanting to hear these details. She stepped out of her patch of shade too quickly, however, and stumbled into a group of young women.

"I'm sorry," Devaki said, adjusting the scarf around her head and blushing at her own misstep. "That was my fault."

"It's no trouble," one woman began, the oldest in the bunch. She looked down at Devaki with a forgiving smile, then stopped. "Ah. You have a lot to be sorry for, though, don't you?"

Devaki said nothing, trying to keep her apologetic smile in place. This was what she was afraid of, what happened every time she ventured into a social situation. The older woman merely beamed at her, the sunlight setting harsh shadows across the lines in her skin and the curls in her graying hair.

"Mother, leave her be," spoke up a younger girl in the group. She stepped forward and put a gentle hand on the older lady's arm. "She's just a child."

"She's not much younger than you, Priya," the mother crooned, a sardonic edge to her voice despite the politeness painted on her face. "That's no excuse. Shouldn't you be at the temple, praying to be forgiven?"

"Come now, this girl has so much to be thankful for," another girl corrected, stepping forward and joining in with a pleasant nod.

"I . . ." Devaki began, wanting to turn away but found herself unable. A quick glance to either side showed that the people nearby noticed what was happening, saw who the women were bullying, then casually looked away.

"True. Your cousin is so tolerant of your existence," the mother said. "And you are fortunate enough to be blessed with the Goddess' Touch. Will Cybarys' wonders never cease?"

"I suppose we could only hope to be as happy as you, Devaki."

Devaki couldn't help but stare at the daughter after she said that. At first the girl spoke up to defend her, but now the two had their arms around each other's waists and stared down at Devaki with wide grins. The entire group burst into nasty giggles, satisfied with their backhanded jokes.

"Excuse me," Devaki said, and she spun back toward the palace. She brushed past groups of traders and Tarran family members on her way, earning several looks of concern. When she ducked into the cool hallway, she turned into the first alcove she could find and put a hand over her mouth. The sob that tried to escape only came out as a small moan. She shook her head, chastising herself for feeling ashamed.

This happened all the time, year after year, and she knew how to cope. Why did it bother her so much today? *Dear Goddess,* Devaki thought, using the edge of her scarf to wipe sweat from her brow. *You've shown me where my destiny lies, but let me first see the path before me, and let me walk true.*

She shut her eyes and rotated the ring she wore on the first finger of her right hand. Its sharp edge was honed for the purpose of cutting Blessing Runes, and she turned the artistic silver point toward the scar of a Guidance Rune on the outside of her left forearm. It took little, practiced effort to just break her skin and offer blood to her Mother.

Comforting warmth brushed against her cheek, like the hot, dry air she'd just escaped in the courtyard. That unseen, magical touch ran down her back and came to rest between her shoulder blades. Devaki felt the urge to step forward. She let her feet move, out of the alcove, up the main hallway, and down a side corridor.

Instead of questioning her destination or letting her thoughts dwell on what had happened in the courtyard, Devaki trusted in her Goddess. The corridor was narrow, curving sharply with the spiral of the palace, and she had to hug the far wall to avoid any of the potential doors opening out toward her.

She kept the rune-shaped cut on her arm open as she went, ensuring her connection to Cybarys through her magic. A Goddess Touched could create more magical energy if their faith was strong, and Devaki did not ever doubt her Mother. When another branch in the staircase appeared, this one cutting upward into a higher section she'd never been to before, Devaki let her feet slowly lead her up the steep stairs.

". . .a generous amount of gold. Much more than usual."

Devaki halted at the top of the steps when she heard these words. They came from behind the closed door across the hall from her, and though muffled, they were clearly defined in this silent section of the palace.

I know that voice, she thought, bewildered. Devaki could not imagine why Sehran would be speaking with something in such an out-of-the-way room. This place was private, secret, even. Armelle's Temple Leader should have no privacy or secrecy; he served the people and had nothing to hide.

Nevertheless, Devaki stepped out of the stairwell and across the hall to the door, where she pressed her cheek against its cool surface. The Goddess had led her here for a reason, but now she found uneasiness in her throat.

". . .wants to help recover some of your losses from the last search." This was another voice, one Devaki did not know, but it had a foreign accent.

"It is appreciated, after we found nothing of consequence." Sehran's tone had an edge to it, bordering on irritation. "With several townes flying rebel colors, your Lord should be more pressed than ever to find a key that will turn the tide in our favor."

Devaki stopped breathing. That heat of magic had disappeared from her body, leaving her chilled. Fresh sweat broke out on her neck and palms. *Dear Goddess, what are they talking about?*

She didn't hear the response of the other man, her head too full of shock. Focusing, Devaki heard Sehran say: "Of course. Now, you must excuse me. Those damned prayer bells are about to ring, and I cannot be missed from the midday ceremony."

Devaki backed away from the door, stumbling when she found her fingers and toes were numb. She half ran back down the stairway and crouched down, out of sight. When the door opened, Devaki watched the shadows of two men flood onto the first few steps of the staircase. The dark shapes shook hands, then went separate directions, one left and the other right, leaving Devaki stunned and confused in her hiding place.

Who was Sehran meeting with in there? she wondered, confounded by the pit of fear growing in her stomach. *Cybarys wouldn't allow him to conspire in such a way, would she? It just can't be true.*

CHAPTER NINETEEN

TRADING BLOWS

Angelyn stared at Will, eyebrows raised, arms crossed loosely over her chest. The sun had recently risen, her common hall was full of the usual patrons, and she stood here in her cellar looking disbelievingly at the leader of her kingdom's rebellion.

"Say that again," Angelyn spoke through the silence.

"I need your help," Will replied.

"You need *me*," she repeated patiently, very aware of the way Will watched her. He stood at a respectful distance, one arm across his body so he could grip his healing wound.

She knew he was gauging her mental state based on her outward appearance: the way she'd hastily knotted her dirty hair in a braid, the dark circles under her sleepless eyes, the tremble in her arms as she tried to hold a strong posture.

"I made a mistake last night, and I am sorry for what happened," Will said, and there was enough sincerity in his tone that Angelyn almost believed him. "Sarrett may not have found anything, but now I need to turn his attention somewhere else."

"Why don't you just kill him?" Angelyn asked. She said the words softly, as if the dozens of people moving around upstairs could hear her treasonous question. "You have armed men who would love to slaughter that lieutenant, especially after what happened to you . . .and Gabriel."

Will grimaced and turned to sit in an old chair next to the table where he'd spent the night. His long sigh came out in a faint cloud in the cellar's damp air. "Miss McKinlee, if I marched down the street cutting down any opposition until Jonathan Sarrett hung from a noose or the end of my sword, that makes me as much of a monster as him and his masters. You and your people need change, a new beginning. I haven't forced a towne to change its colors in the last ten years. That isn't my message."

Angelyn tried to digest these statements, but her head began to ache with conflicting emotions and ideals. She crossed her arms more tightly over her stomach. "So, why do you need me?"

"Did you smell Sarrett last night?"

She frowned and cocked her head. "What?"

"Just think about it."

Against her better judgment, Angelyn recalled standing in almost the same spot, and remembered how close the lieutenant had been, how he'd brushed his hand across her lower back and whispered in her ear. She shivered. "Do you mean the wine?"

"Yes," Will said, and he stood from his seat to take a step toward her. Angelyn backed up, aware of the cellar wall not far behind her. "It wasn't just the Armellan wine; it's the Sahma extract infused in the alcohol you could smell. Across the sea, the smoke of the herb is used for prayer and meditation. But Sarrett, thanks to your neighbors, enjoys a lot of that special wine."

"I'm well aware of what Harling makes in his store's cellar," Angelyn said. "But why does it matter?"

"It's a weakness," Will replied, a small smile touching his lips. "And we're going to use it to our advantage."

"'We'? Do you know you're a manipulative bastard?"

Will stepped back as if she'd slapped him. "I know you're just being hurtful now."

Angelyn scoffed bitterly. "No, I'm being honest! You know I don't have a choice but to help you."

"Yes, and I already apologized," Will said, inclining his head. "Now, there will be people here from every corner of Kaylyn by sunset, and it's too risky to cancel my meeting. If Sarrett and his men stay away from here tonight and I have a chance to speak to my people, this towne will change its color without any further bloodshed."

"How?" She couldn't stop herself from asking the question.

Will grinned. "You'll have to meet with us and find out for yourself."

A burst of laughter erupted upstairs, and several crashes of dishes hitting the floor echoed amidst the noise. Angelyn glanced up the steps, wanting more than anything to forget about the man across from her and go back to what she knew best: running her business. "Tell me what I have to do," she said shortly.

"Harling is Sarrett's supplier, and he's also your business competition," Will began. "But not by much, it seems, since the locals only go to his place to buy that wine and come back here to drink it. Sarrett needs Harling, but he wouldn't be very pleased if Harling's special product was being sent out of Kaylyn, to a northern towne flying rebel colors."

Angelyn snapped her attention back to Will, eyeing him cautiously. "But that's not true, is it?"

"It will be true enough, once you alter his shipment records to show it. Write up your own version of what's being sent where and tuck it in his books. Maybe tie a few violet ribbons around his outgoing casks just for effect. You're free to get creative, Miss McKinlee, as long as you make sure one of Sarrett's guardsmen checks Harling's papers today and finds out the Trade Master is doing business with the enemy behind the lieutenant's back."

"No." It was the only word she could manage with some conviction.

"No? I don't think you can say no."

"You want me to frame my neighbor? Do you know what Sarrett will do to him because of me?"

"He won't kill Harling!" Will said exasperatedly. "But it will stall and redirect Sarrett, and that's what we need."

Angelyn shook her head. Was life and death so simple for him? "Do you know Harling has a family?" she demanded. "Two daughters. And innocent people work for him. You have no idea what the lieutenant will do to anyone connected to the Harlings."

"Do you want to keep your son safe? Don't you?"

"This isn't right!" she cut in. "And if you can't think of another way, I'll just close early tonight. Your people won't be able to meet if my doors are locked."

"Angelyn, please listen."

"No!" She could not believe she was having this argument. "You don't understand where I'm coming from at all, do you? You bring danger into my home, force me to lose my best friend, cast illegal magic in front of my son, and want me to commit crimes for you? I've had enough."

She turned to march back up the cellar steps, but Will blocked her way. He held the railing casually, barring her path with his broad chest. Angelyn looked up at him, unafraid. Another memory flashed across her mind, one of Will holding her and kissing her. She stepped forward, closing the bit of space between them, daring him to do something, anything.

The silence held, then Will glanced away and stepped aside. It took Angelyn all of her self-control not to run up the stairs. When she bolted the door shut behind her, she found Joshua stumbling out of her way.

"What are you doing?" she asked. He held his compass in his hands and turned it over and over across his palm. That foreign thing made Angelyn inexplicably nervous.

"Nothing," he said. "I was just . . ."

"Put that away," Angelyn said when he trailed off. "Come help me in the kitchen. We've got a long day ahead of us."

* * *

Joshua noticed something odd in the common hall that morning, and the peculiar feeling held solidly in the air into the afternoon. The day itself was normal, with the usual folk coming and going and the sea traders arriving when the ship bells rang out on the docks. The guardsmen that sat at the bar didn't harass anyone, but maybe that was because no one had spoken more than a few words.

"What's wrong?" Joshua asked Ada quietly. They stood in the kitchen where they'd both just set down heavy piles of plates and mugs. Even the lively group of cooks moving about them preparing the midday meal were silent, something Joshua didn't think possible.

Ada wiped a sweaty lock of hair off her forehead. "What do you mean?"

"Mum hasn't said a word to me, and everything just feels . . . weird." He immediately felt stupid for explaining himself so poorly, but relief spread over him when Ada nodded.

"They're all afraid," she said. "The whole towne knows what happened to Master Chapman. It's awful. I wish we could do something, but I don't even know if we can meet here tonight."

Joshua took a deep breath and said what he'd been thinking of all morning. "I can help."

"What? How?"

"I heard my mum talking to Will in the cellar this morning. He's got a plan to keep us safe so the rebels can meet again tonight, but she won't do what he wants."

Ada hooked her arm in his and pulled him over to a quiet corner of the room. "Josh, tell me what he wants," she whispered. "We can't live like this, afraid to even speak."

"I . . ." Joshua faded off, unsure what to do from here. He'd held onto the knowledge he'd gained from eavesdropping for hours. There was no way he could talk to Will and volunteer himself when his mother held the only cellar key, and he couldn't just go out onto the streets without Angelyn noticing he was gone.

Joshua held Ada's gaze, something he had more difficulty with nowadays, and suddenly realized how she and the rest of the rebels were different from everyone else; she was scared of The Bradford and his military, but she wasn't afraid to do something about it.

Last night I did nothing. I hid like a child while Sarrett harassed my mother and killed Gabriel. I have to do this. Not just because Mum won't but because I want to.

"Ada, I can do this myself," Joshua started, and rushed on when she began to protest. "You have to keep things normal. Smile like you always do. Keep my mum busy, too, or she'll notice I'm not here. I won't be gone long."

"All right," Ada agreed reluctantly. "But whatever it is, please be careful."

Joshua nodded and went to the back door before he could lose his nerve. He pulled a cloak off the wall and swung it around his shoulders.

"That Rhethosian Blue looks awful on you, you know," Ada said, and Joshua glanced back at her. "You should be wearing rebel violet."

"Can I have your necklace, then?" Joshua asked, suddenly remembering a detail Will had mentioned to his mother. "That one you hide in your dress?"

Ada gave him an odd look, then smiled and reached down the front of her bodice. She slipped the braided violet cloth from her neck and handed it to him. "Go, and hurry back."

Joshua shoved the necklace in his pocket, aware of how warm the material felt between his fingers. He stepped out into the alleyway, alone and of his own free will for the first time in his life.

He didn't turn right to head out onto Kaylyn High Street, but instead kept left and started down the alleyway between the buildings, trying his best to swallow the lump of fear and excitement clogging his throat.

Towering rows of narrow homes rose to his left and blocked out the sunlight that pushed through the heavy, gray clouds. The rear entrances to the shops that sloped up the road went by, and Joshua stopped at the fifth one down.

Around the wooden door were empty wine casks, stacked half a dozen high, the top tier soaked in rainwater dripping from the eaves. Joshua peered down the alleyway, then glanced over his shoulder where he'd come. When he saw no one, he leaned against the shop's back door and listened hard.

Muffled voices met his ear, and when they faded away Joshua pressed the door open and stepped inside. The back room of the Harling's shop was so dark it took him several terrifying moments to adjust his eyes. As he blinked, Joshua was shocked at the chaotic mess that became clearer and clearer.

He had spent his childhood helping his mother organize the supplies of the Hamond, ever since he was old enough to carry a flour sack. Memories of her instruction of the importance of a well-kept, properly documented business flashed brightly in his head.

This storeroom was the exact opposite of what his mother had taught him; full and empty shipping crates cascaded in mismatched towers throughout the room, some ranging precariously to the ceiling. Bits of parchment, packaging, empty inkwells, and hundreds of bottles littered the visible sections of floor. When Joshua inhaled, the unmistakable odor of forgotten, rotted food hit his nose.

How does this man stay in business? he thought, and then answered his own question: Harling's main business wasn't the same as the McKinlees'. When Joshua thought even further, he recalled what Will had said about the wine and came to another more frightening conclusion.

I don't know where Harling keeps his shipping logs, and even if I found them, only my mum would know the right thing to change to make it look convincing. What can I do that will keep the lieutenant away from us?

Joshua thought furiously, admonishing himself for not thinking this dangerous venture all the way through. He knelt behind a pile of crates, staring at the old, black shipment markings on their sides. Armellan script cascaded over the boxes that made him think of the inscription on his compass. Touching the brass object in his pocket gave him a bit more courage.

Pushing aside his doubts, Joshua leaned forward across the filthy floor, smearing thick layers of dust with his sweaty palms. He grasped a nearby pile of parchment and rifled through it until he found a blank sheet. He had to crawl further amongst the room's rubble to find a quill and a bit of ink. Joshua squinted hard, trying to see the empty parchment in his lap, then began to write:

Master Harling,

My co-conspirators greatly enjoyed your latest vintage, and they are eager for more. Please send the same number of casks as last month, and my servant will meet you with payment outside Morely. Enclosed is a gift from my daughter to yours. The rebellion thanks you for your continued support!

Joshua dug Ada's necklace out of his pocket, balled it up, and placed it in the center of the drying ink. He folded the note into a tight square, careful to make sure one end of the violet braid hung loosely from a creased corner. When he rose from his spot on the floor, bright light suddenly flooded the room.

"I don't care how old his family was," came a man's voice from the front of the storeroom. "He's dead now. Just as dead as the Luwenns, and the Ross', too."

Joshua flattened himself against the wall, pressing back into the remaining shadows. A part of him knew Harling's employee was talking about Gabriel, but he ignored the sorrow that tried to cloud his thoughts and focused on staying still and quiet.

"We best keep Sarrett's glass full, then, eh?" replied someone else, his words muffled by the sounds of shifting crates.

"Couldn't have said it better."

Joshua waited till the patch of light began to fade and peeked out from his hiding place. He could make out the doorway leading into the Harling's common hall, and when he stood on his tiptoes, he caught a glimpse of the bar that stretched along the room before the storeroom door shut and darkness fell again.

I can do this, he thought, and started forward.

Once Joshua worked his way around and between the jumbled mess of the storeroom, he pushed the common hall door open and had to immediately stop behind dozens of people waiting for a place at the bar.

The Harling's common hall was much smaller and narrower than the Hamond's, shaped in a long rectangle that ranged fifty feet from where Joshua stood to the main entrance. From the amount of food Joshua could see and smell, he assumed it was time for the midday meal, which explained the crowd.

He side stepped around the men before him, holding his note tightly in one hand while he casually scanned the heads and shoulders of the folk milling about the room. Joshua spotted a tall man in a Rhethosian Blue uniform forcibly shoving his way toward the bar. Maneuvering his shoulders into the small gaps between people, Joshua followed the guardsman up without much resistance.

When the guardsman pulled another man out of his chair and took his seat, Joshua stopped just behind him. He glanced over his shoulder, gauging the distance between himself and the door back to the storeroom. There were at least two dozen people crowded in his escape route, all looking for a place to sit. *I can make it back,* he told himself. *I just have to stay calm.*

Joshua pushed up to the bar, reached his arm out, and caught the barkeep's eye. "Urgent message for Master Harling," he said, and he tossed the note forward onto the bar between the barkeep and the guardsman. The barkeep barely glanced at it, and that was all Joshua had the nerve to watch; he turned quickly, squirmed back into the crowd, and began to work his way toward the storeroom door.

When a cry of distress broke out behind him, Joshua forced himself not to spin back around. He kept his paces small and even, which became easier as the crowd pressed forward to see what was happening at the bar.

"That's rebel violet!" someone shouted just as Joshua opened the back door and slipped into the storeroom's darkness. He remembered to breathe, then coughed at the stench of mold that berated his nostrils. But that didn't matter; he had succeeded. He did what his mother could not. Now Will could set them free.

Joshua stumbled out of the storeroom and into the alleyway, where he gasped huge breaths of fresh, salty air. He almost ran back toward his home, barely glancing around him. He could hear raised voices from the High Road just a block away, and when he turned his head toward them, someone reached out from the nearest alcove and grabbed his cloak.

"Joshua!"

"Mum?" He spun and found his mother next to him, her fingers clutching tightly enough to his shoulder to make him cry out.

"Have you lost your mind?" she snapped. "What are you doing out here?"

"It doesn't matter," Joshua said, wincing as she pulled him into the center of the narrow walkway. "We have to get back"

"You were eavesdropping, weren't you?" Angelyn demanded. Joshua didn't think he'd ever seen her so scared and angry at the same time. "This morning, at the cellar door. What have you done?"

"What you wouldn't do!" Joshua said before he could stop himself. He tried to get free from his mother's grip, or at least pull them back into the cover of the nearest building's eaves, but Angelyn held him still.

She glared at him, her cheeks fuming bright red in the chilled air. He could feel her fingers shaking on his shoulder. "How could you?"

"What are you two doing down there?"

The interrogation shot down the alleyway to where Angelyn and Joshua stood, and both of them froze. Joshua stopped trying to pull himself out of his mother's grip. A quick look to either side told him there was nowhere to go, and when several guardsmen advanced toward them, he still fought every instinct to break free and run.

"I'm so sorry, Masters," Angelyn began when the men stopped in front of them. "We were just going home."

"Where have you been?" one guardsman demanded. He stepped close to Angelyn, putting a hand down to his sword hilt. "Why aren't you on the main road?"

"It's just faster back to my inn this way," Angelyn explained. Joshua noticed she kept her eyes on her feet when she spoke.

"You're the McKinlee woman, yes?" The guardsman sneered when he came to the realization. "You had a problem at your place last night. Now you're causing trouble again. Not the smartest idea."

When the man started to unsheathe his sword, Joshua stepped in front of his mother. The guardsman swung his elbow at Joshua's chest and connected hard. Joshua stumbled back several paces and clenched his hands into fists at his sides. The guardsman and his companions laughed.

"I'm the reason we're out here," Joshua insisted suddenly. "I snuck out The Hamond's back door to look at what's left of the latest fire."

The guardsman stared at him, disbelief in his dark eyes. "Why?"

"I thought there might be bodies. I like admiring the lieutenant's work." Joshua shrugged shamelessly when he said the words, but swallowed bile that rose in the back of his throat.

The guardsman grinned at him. "Bloodthirsty boy you've got here, Miss McKinlee," he said, and the men behind him nodded appreciatively. "How old are you, son?"

"Just turned sixteen," Joshua said excitedly. "And I'm ready to serve The Bradford. I wish Mum could send me south to train at The Academy."

He added that last bit for effect, not really understanding much about the elite place far away from his home where they made future Rhethosian military monsters. He only knew that was where the most powerful Loyal teenagers would be sent to have the honor to potentially become the kingdom's next Bradford.

"You certainly won't stay home and work like I want," Angelyn added weakly.

"That's the last thing an eager boy like him should be doing," the guardsman admonished, rolling his eyes at Angelyn's words. "Take your poor mum home, McKinlee. If you go up to Towne Centre, you know, and tell Master Barton how old you are, he'll have a uniform on you in no time."

Joshua clenched his jaw unwillingly, then forced himself to stay calm. "I'll do that first thing in the morning, Master. Thank you!"

The guardsman nodded, and as he and his companions left, Angelyn dug her fingers into Joshua's shoulder once more. He grimaced but let her drag him back toward the Hamond.

"Mum, I—"

"Don't talk, Joshua!" she hissed, and he heard pure fury in her tone.

He held his tongue, biting it to control his protests. Fog slipped down the alleyway from the nearby docks, and rain began to smack the top of Joshua's head. When they reached the Hamond's back door, Angelyn threw it open and shoved Joshua inside.

"Do you know what you've done?" she began, instantly rounding on him. Joshua noticed every cook in the kitchen stopped and stared at his mother. "Get out!" she barked, and they retreated hastily.

"I did the right thing," Joshua insisted. "And I would have made it back without anyone noticing if you hadn't drawn attention to—"

Angelyn stepped forward and slapped him. Her palm raked across his cheek and bright pain exploded under his right eye. Despite the numbness that soon followed, Joshua still felt a tear fall as he stared at his mother.

"I have never been this upset with you," she whispered. Even though they were alone, she stood close to him and kept her voice low. "I've been angry, yes. And you've tested me over the years, more lately than ever before, but this . . . I don't even know what to say."

"Mum," Joshua started, guilt rising in his chest as he put a hand to his throbbing cheek. "I'm sorry."

"Get upstairs," Angelyn said. Her jaw trembled as she spoke. "And for the Lord's sake, stay put." She turned away, facing the kitchen's back door, but Joshua had already seen the tears in her eyes.

All the excitement Joshua had felt, the sense of purpose and accomplishment that had surrounded him for a few blissful moments, shriveled and died in his heart. He swallowed the rest of his arguments and his judgements and did as he was told.

CHAPTER TWENTY

INTOLERABLE HEAT

"Mum?"

When Angelyn heard the tone in her son's voice, she knew he wanted something she wouldn't let him have.

They had been sitting down at Joshua's favorite corner behind the bar, eating dinner silently amid the bustle of an evening at The Hamond. This was also the first time he'd spoken since their confrontation in the kitchen earlier.

"What is it?" Angelyn asked, keeping her eyes on her plate.

"Look," Joshua muttered, and jerked his head back toward the private parlor. Several men had moved to stand by the door, and, through its glass panel, Angelyn could make out the shadowed movements of many people already inside who had no doubt entered through the back door. It was time.

"I already know what you're going to say," Joshua continued, "but I want to be in there when—"

"No," Angelyn cut in firmly. "After what you did this afternoon?"

"But I want to learn," Joshua insisted, leaning fervently toward his mother. "I have to! Right now the lieutenant is paying attention to Harling because of me."

"I can't have you in there," Angelyn hissed, not wanting everyone around to hear her. "I'm sorry, but—"

"I thought you and Will talked," Joshua interrupted, that new defiant edge creeping into his voice, one she heard more and more often. "This morning, when you two were alone in the cellar. Didn't he tell you that we have no choice?"

"Hush!" she snapped, trying not to blush. "Go upstairs," she added as the men near the parlor door shut it and blocked its entry.

Joshua rose with an upset "Yes, Mum" and headed toward the stairs. Angelyn scanned the common hall as she made her way to the private parlor.

The local musicians continued to play a happy tune, two women playing flutes while the rest drummed a beat that had dozens dancing. A few drunks sang along, girls giggled at the bar while pouring and serving drinks, while others stayed at their respective tables and ate their meals.

To a foreigner, it must have looked like a regular evening full of locals enjoying the warm building away from the cold weather of a dying seaside towne. What did it matter if some of them were spending their evening in the closed parlor?

Angelyn was surprised to find there was little to no space for her in the room. The last time she'd been here, there had been less than thirty waiting for Will, with room to spare at the long table and along the walls. Now, nearly fifty people were crammed into the rectangular room, most standing shoulder to shoulder along the walls while others sat at and on the table itself. Will was seated at the table's head, speaking quietly with those nearby him.

She noticed that when Will addressed his "fellow conspirators", he knew every man and woman's name and where they came from. Despite his dark demeanor and overwhelming sense of authority, Will appreciated and thanked every person with direct, respectful eye contact. A sharp, burning knife sliced through her brain at a thought of Gabriel agreeing to go out past curfew for Will's sake, but Angelyn pushed it back, burying the ache.

Angelyn shouldered her way to Ada and Lynn, who sat in two chairs near the parlor's back door that led out toward the stables. Ada adjusted herself in her seat to offer Angelyn half of it, the only place left in the room unless she wished to stand. Angelyn sat on the edge of the chair, and Ada grasped her hand briefly, giving her a smile.

Angelyn returned it wanly; the bargirl had no idea that Angelyn was there to find a way to shut these meetings down, once and for all. She would wait till the right moment, then do her best, by threat or blackmail or whatever means necessary, to make sure Will and his conspirators never set foot in The Hamond again.

Or . . . she thought, not sure if she really meant it, *I need to see if these rebels can find a way to keep Josh out of Sarrett's ranks. Thanks to what he just said to those guardsmen, they'll be expecting him to be in a damned uniform tomorrow.*

"Dedric," Will said, "you and Belmont go outside tonight."

The two men nodded and shuffled through the crowd to the back door after grabbing their heavy cloaks, loosely rolled tobacco leaves in their gloved hands. The bit of cool air and droplets of rain that rushed in as they left were a brief reprieve from the parlor's growing heat.

"So," Will began, his voice easy. "The effects of last night's events aren't positive, but we cannot let fear stop us from gathering.

"Let me explain. I've spent the last twelve years of my life sorting and overcoming the logistics of rebellion in the northern townes. Everyone in those places has supported me of their own free will after hearing me speak. I wish to do the same with Kaylyn, but that will not work if people talk to the lieutenant and his men."

Angelyn cocked her head to the side, intrigued. *Twelve years?* she thought. *How could someone spend over a decade of their life on such an unrealistic dream? Does it take that long to coordinate an entire kingdom's rebellion without just resorting to slaughtering people like Sarrett?*

"Many of you know that Armelle has played a large role in my upbringing," Will continued, and Angelyn straightened herself, paying closer attention when Will actually started to speak about himself. "But I always begin by making something clear: I do not hold the support of Armelle, nor do I expect a response to the missives I've sent through a special source to their Temple Leader. They worship their Goddess, a mother-figure who demands devotions of blood from her children in exchange for her blessings, and I know for a fact Cybarys and her people will not approve of my methods."

A gasp rose from some at the mention of the pagan faith across the sea, but Will ignored them.

"Those who wear Rhethosian Blue are forced to comply with The Bradford in the south as if he were a God. I do not uphold any faith, only the dream that Rhethosians may choose whatever path they desire toward salvation without hindrance.

"Now," he continued, rubbing his hands together, "onto the subject I'm sure you want to hear about: I suspected certain disloyalties, so I sent out a few men to take care of the folk who had eyes on The Hamond, as well as anyone connected to the person who mentioned this place's name. Unfortunately, all were killed, including Master Gabriel, whom almost all here knew. To Miss Ada," Will inclined his head to the woman sitting next to Angelyn, "I say sorry myself, for your loss of your betrothed, Darren."

Ada nodded shakily, eyes on her feet, and Angelyn could see the grim expression on her face. Shocked, Angelyn numbly pulled a handkerchief out of her dress pocket and offered it.

"Ada!" she whispered, at a loss for words. "You didn't say anything, all day! I had no idea he went out with Gabriel's group last night."

"Don't, Miss McKinlee," her barmaid said gently, pushing Angelyn's hand away with a reassuring smile. "I lost Darren to something we both believed in. You knew he wasn't strong, but he was upset Master Will had been injured and insisted on going out. I meant to say something to you this morning, but with Master Gabriel . . ."

How can she be smiling? Angelyn wondered, even as she nodded at the girl. *What exactly did that young man die for?* Angelyn found herself fighting tears, for both Ada's loss and her own. She would not let herself cry. *The poor girl worked all day, her sweet attitude in place without a flaw. By the Lord, she is so much stronger than me, a real rebel, a fighter. The type of woman that Will needs.*

"Yesterday," Will continued smoothly, "had other faults as well. You all know the inn was searched, mainly for me. Luckily, no one spoke of where I was, and this morning, Sarrett's attention was directed elsewhere."

"We wouldn't tell those bastards where you are, Master Will!" one man exclaimed. Will smiled wryly.

"That's not true, though," he said. "Someone told those Kaylyn guardsmen about this location."

A few people gasped, and others shook their heads angrily.

"The person 'was' from here?" Lynn asked cautiously.

"Well, she isn't anymore," Will snapped. "You all know what happens when we are betrayed." The entire room glanced fearfully at each other.

This is why Josh is upstairs, Angelyn thought resolutely. *How is Will different from the lieutenant right now? Can no one else see it?*

"W-who was it?" one man asked nervously.

"That isn't what we're here to discuss!" Will replied swiftly. "Do you really want to know? Just check the closest gutter you can find!"

"Will!" Angelyn gasped before she could stop herself.

There you go, she thought, extremely embarrassed. *You said his "name."*

Many heads turned to her, but Will's was the last.

"Yes, Miss McKinlee?" he asked. But Angelyn couldn't reply. "Is there something wrong?"

Angelyn shook her head swiftly, clenching her hands into fists to hold back many retorts. *Don't say anything. You'll only make it worse.*

Will continued speaking, but Angelyn didn't hear the words. She couldn't comprehend the fact that a woman, possibly someone she knew, someone like her, was killed for betraying a cause that wasn't yet rooted deeply in Kaylyn Towne. She couldn't even imagine such a brutal, heartless thing coming from Will; she could recall his reassuring embrace, warm lips, and encouraging words, proving even more how little she really knew about the rebel leader.

". . . and it may be time to move," Will concluded. This caught Angelyn's attention.

"Move?" she whispered in Ada's ear. "What does he mean?"

"Master Will said it's become unsafe here and, so no one else gets hurt, it would be better to rally with his other rebel groups and meet Rhethos directly when we're ready. The lieutenant suspects too much and we can't take the towne under such circumstances."

"We do need more people," Regdar, one of the bar patrons, spoke up. He was a tall, young gentleman who lived only several houses north of the Hamond. He had a kind smile and soft, gray eyes. Angelyn remembered him for his polite attitude toward the stricter curfews, where most younger men were upset at the lieutenant's changes.

"It is difficult to do much but plot here without more men," Regdar continued. "Kaylyn has no walls, only old watchtowers, so there isn't much of a defensive stance we could make here even if we wanted to. It may be easier to take than, say . . . Lorington, just down the coast, but Kaylyn would be very hard to hold." Many voices sounded in approval, Ada and Lynn's included. Angelyn didn't trust herself to speak.

"Where will you go?"

Everyone turned around, looking for the source of the unfamiliar voice. All heads turned to the parlor door, and the boy who stood holding it open.

"Joshua!" Angelyn gasped, standing. He ignored his mother's objection, however, and stepped inside, waiting for Will to respond.

"Well," Will started with a smile that made Angelyn even angrier, "We have somewhere close by that I've made safe over the years. The northern townes nearby have already turned to my cause."

"That sounds like a good plan," Joshua replied. A few of the men standing near him in the tight space nodded with approval, showing they also trusted Will's words.

"I appreciate your confidence, Joshua," Will said, his smile still in place.

"Master Will," one man said, as though this was an interruption to their meeting.

"But you say we need to move?" Joshua cut in, eyes still on Will.

"We?" Angelyn retorted suddenly, snapping to her senses and finding her voice. "*We* aren't going anywhere." She'd barely mustered the bravery to try and confront Will at some point during this meeting, but now her heart was conflicted after hearing his inspiring words. Yet to be counted as one of these rebels? That was out of the question.

"Mum, please just,"

"No, Joshua. That's enough."

"No!" he cried. "That's enough from you!"

"What did you say to me?" Angelyn gasped. Never in his life had her son spoken to her in such a way. Many folk shifted uncomfortably, looking for her reaction.

"Gabriel just died in our cellar," Joshua said heatedly, "but you say no to moving to a safer place?"

"This is *your* home, too!" Angelyn argued. "Our family's land and business, for more generations than I can count. What would you expect me to do?"

"Why can't I choose what I feel is—?" her son began.

"Go back upstairs and stay there," Angelyn snapped, barely controlling her temper.

"No!" Joshua retorted.

"*Now!*" Angelyn hissed.

Will had his eyes on Joshua, a mild expression of admiration on his face, which made Angelyn furious. Joshua must have decided that continuing to argue wouldn't do any good, especially in front of everyone. Turning to open the door into the common hall once more, he held his gaze on Will as long as possible, but Will said nothing in his favor.

"Miss McKinlee, perhaps you should let him stay," Ada suggested cautiously when Joshua had shut the door behind him. "After all, he—"

"You're not helping," Angelyn cut in strongly, and the young girl lowered her head.

A few seconds later, Will glanced in Angelyn's direction. "Is he all right?"

"Let him alone," Angelyn stated poisonously. "Just leave him be."

Will nodded, ready to address the group again. Everyone listened for his continuation. . .

But it never came.

Suddenly a harsh shout came from the inn's front door, one they could all hear above the noise in the common hall. Before anyone else could act, Angelyn rose from her chair and cracked the parlor door open. One of Will's men stood at the entrance to the main hall, and Angelyn watched as he placed all his weight on the door to hold it shut. Her heart jumped when someone pounded against the door from the outside.

Many of the folk in the main hall were glancing at one another, confused looks on their faces. When a fist struck the Hamond's front door again, even louder this time, the musician's tune faltered and silence fell.

Angelyn felt many of the people behind her in the parlor press forward to try and see past her toward the entrance. If she strained her neck to see around the heads of those gathered, she could make out the front windows that flanked the doors. The streetlamps still echoed a persistent glow despite the light rain. Suddenly a dark mass was violently pinned to the glass, which reverberated inside the silent common hall. The shape slid down, leaving a dark, bloody trail behind on the pane. A few of Will's rebels cried out, and others drew weapons.

There was taut, deadly silence for one heartbeat, then two, and a voice resounded through the front door:

"We've killed your watchmen!" it declared. Two women in the room burst into tears, but Will silently bid them to stay still. "Exit out the front entrance for execution, rebels, or stay and burn!"

"I told you we needed to move!" Will hissed. "Out the back door, now."

Angelyn's eyes darted to the door inside the parlor that led back to the stables. When several men tried to push it open, it wouldn't budge. The old, sturdy wood met sharp opposition from the other side, and Angelyn swallowed a fresh wave of fear when she realized that her keys would do no good.

"It won't open!" someone announced.

"They'll have all the doors barred and guarded," Will snapped, as if explaining wasn't worth the time or effort. "But we may be able to fight our way out the back."

At that, everyone rose and started to push out of the parlor into the main hall. Angelyn found herself shoved forward and out of the way as panic began to rise.

"Joshua!" Angelyn screamed, all anger she felt toward the boy now forgotten, and he ran down the stairs as if he'd been waiting just around the corner.

Will stepped over next to the McKinlees as people frantically fought to get to the back door. With everyone standing, it was hard to move around in the common hall. Folk shoved tables abruptly out of the way, chairs overturned, glasses shattered, and liquid sprayed, but the noise level wasn't great, the fearful tension in the air stopping most men and women from speaking at all.

"We need to move fast," Will hurriedly told Angelyn. "We'll cut out back, scatter, and head toward the woods."

"We can't go in there!" Joshua objected fearfully, his eyes wide. "Those trees are cursed! We'll die if we walk under their branches!"

Abruptly, an eerie hiss permeated the tense room. Everyone stopped in their tracks to listen, and Angelyn suddenly gasped. Flaming holes burst through the top of the ceiling, and hot fire flew in through the windows as they shattered. Within seconds, the barroom was alight, the parlor behind them beginning to smoke violently.

"*No!*" Angelyn screamed.

She didn't know how many times she cried the word as Joshua pulled her toward the back door. She shoved away from his grip, not wanting to believe any of it. Regular patrons she knew by name barreled past her and her son, almost knocking them over in the desperate scramble to escape the building.

Shrieks and cries started outside the inn's back exit, and Angelyn vaguely heard several clashes of weapons, a foreign sound in her ears.

There were guardsmen at the back door waiting for them to try and escape, and, through the haze and rising flames, Angelyn saw Ada confidently take a drawn blade from the man next to her. Thanks to the bargirl and several other rebels, they were able to clear a path through the guardsmen for the rest. A memory of Ada's fast reflexes the other night suddenly made sense to Angelyn when she saw the young lady cut down an officer with a dark beard barring their exit.

No! Angelyn thought desperately, trying to think of a way to stop the fires, to plead with the lieutenant to save her home. *Not this. My home, my life, everything!*

But the fires were not quenched; in fact, it almost seemed as if they burned higher and faster, eating anything in their path. Jugs of oil were thrown in through the shattered windows after the torches, and thick, black smoke stung her eyes and nose. Angelyn would not move, could not force her shocked muscles to respond.

"Angelyn."

She turned when she heard Will say her name. Angelyn could still see the sympathy in his eyes.

"Please." The way Will said that one word should have meant something in any other circumstance, but now, with her home burning, Angelyn shook her head numbly.

"Mum, let's *go!*" Joshua cried as the ceiling above them screamed dangerously. "We have to!"

Will seemed to have had enough: handing Joshua a dagger Angelyn never saw him draw, he grabbed her around the waist with his good arm and lifted her toward the door. Angelyn could barely struggle, finding nothing to grasp that wasn't aflame. Incredible heat and smoke met her eyes everywhere she looked, stinging her vision into a harsh blur. She could still see the remnants of the staircase, her bedroom and all her belongings just around the corner at the end of the hall.

In her mind's eye, she could see her family portrait that hung above her bed, the one image of her ancestry she had left. If she fought his grip hard enough, she could make it up the stairs and save it. What would her father say if she didn't even try? Angelyn frantically reached out for the doorknob when Will tried to pull her out the back, and cried out in agony: the knob was blazing hot, searing her palm and fingers.

She sank to the floor, despite Will's grip, taking him to his knees. Angelyn held her hand to her stomach, the pain making white spots appear in front of her eyes as her head spun.

"Get up, Mum," she heard Joshua say, tears in his voice, but Angelyn closed her eyes.

Will picked her up, carrying her one-armed out of the blazing Hamond Inn. Angelyn could hear other terrified voices around her, more jarring smacks of blades, but she kept her eyes shut. Maybe if she didn't look at what was happening, she could open her eyes later and find it was all just a horrible nightmare.

"*MUM!*"

The high, panicked cry was different than any other Angelyn could hear. Her eyes flew open wildly, and she saw Will's head turn as well.

The inn was a smoking, blinding ball of fire, spitting sparks and chunks of wood in every direction. Cracked, old stone collapsed heavily to the ground in bursts of dust and debris. In the midst of the chaos, many of the rebels were racing from the condemned building with guardsmen in dark shades of blue chasing after them, determined to take live prisoners. To Angelyn's horror, she saw that many of the rebels were being dragged back to the main road, their arms restrained, knives at their throats.

One of them was Joshua.

CHAPTER TWENTY-ONE

UP IN FLAMES

Joshua had his eyes on his mother up ahead when two arms in rich Rhethosian Blue wrapped around his shoulders. He cried out and clumsily brandished the dagger Will had handed him. The guardsman behind him was pinning his upper arms in place with a well-practiced grip, and Joshua fought back panic as the overwhelming heat of the burning inn blew in his face.

The world was a blur of movement and bright flames, but Joshua could only focus on the arms constricting him. Not the rebels fleeing across the dark field to the waiting trees in the distance, not the explosions that rained debris down from his dying home, not the men he'd seen sitting with Will in the common hall five minutes ago who were being hauled away toward the main road, not the shrieks of agony that echoed out from inside the Hamond, and definitely not the fear inside him.

Will said not to be afraid.

Joshua twisted his right shoulder violently, gaining an inch of give from his captor's lock so he could slash backward with Will's blade. The guardsman rotated out of his reach, then leaned forward to smash Joshua in the back of the head. Dazed, Joshua felt Will's weapon smacked from his hand and, before he could breathe, a knife came to his throat.

"Hold still, you little shit," barked a hoarse voice from behind him. "I don't wanna kill you."

Joshua still struggled despite the sharp iron digging into the flesh beneath his chin. He vaguely saw, through the haze of smoke, Ada hauling his mother toward the woods. *Good,* he thought. *She's safe.*

The guardsman tried to force him backward, toward the High Street that led to Towne Centre and its jail, where Joshua knew he'd die. He gathered all his spite to snap a nasty retort, full of curse words he'd only heard spoken by drunks in the bar, when he heard Will's voice.

"Stop!"

His captor's pace slowed as he took a moment to look at the tall, dark figure advancing toward them with only a knife drawn.

"Lieutenant!" the guardsman screamed in recognition over his shoulder. Joshua kicked back wildly at the man's legs, but stopped when the blade at his throat cut a nasty slash under his chin. "You!" the guardsman continued, staring at Will. "You're the rebel leader—!"

Will ignored the blabbering guardsman and grabbed the hand holding the blade at Joshua's throat. Joshua flinched when he saw the cold look on Will's face, and shut his eyes when Will twisted the guardsman's wrist until it snapped. The weapon fell to the grass as the guardsman cried out, clutching his hand to his chest.

Joshua stumbled back, finally getting a look at the man who'd been holding him still. The guardsman was young and bulky, and his dark eyes were furious when he glared at Will. Will put an arm out defensively, pushing Joshua several steps behind him.

"Go find your mother," Will muttered, his eyes on the guardsman. "Keep her safe."

"But you—"

Will shoved him back another step, cutting off Joshua's protest.

Joshua watched the young guardsman's gaze look over Will, searching for a place to attack, and his eyes landed on Will's bandaged arm. Will swung his dagger forward with one hand, forcing the guardsman's initial punch to come up short. But the guardsman was quick; he came up out of his dodge and connected his fist onto the bloody bandage on Will's bicep. Will hunched over and cried out at the impact.

"*Lieutenant! Here!*" the guardsman shrieked over his shoulder, holding his broken wrist against his stomach.

Without thinking, Joshua rushed forward and punched the shouting guardsman in the gut. And damn, it hurt! He'd never hit anyone before, and all his fingers burst with blinding pain. As the guardsman staggered backward in surprise, Will grabbed him and pulled his head back at a sharp angle. Will sliced a deep gash along the guardsman's throat before pitching him forward to the ground.

The guardsman choked and sputtered, clawing at the toes of Joshua's boots. His cries turned into gurgled whimpers as black liquid pooled around him. Joshua felt his knees weaken. Lord, there was so much blood, he'd never seen so much blood, pouring in thick currents all around his feet. . .

Will caught Joshua under the arm before he fell, then sheathed his knife on the outside of his leg in the same movement. Joshua tried his best to steady his breath and glanced at the terrible scene around him and the rebel leader.

Many guardsmen were pulling back toward the main road, holding captives whose hands were bound in irons. Thankfully, the cries of men and women trapped inside the inn were overcome by the roar of the fire.

There were a few other stragglers still fighting guardsmen behind Joshua and Will on the dark slope that led to the woods, but it seemed the majority of the fleeing rebel group had run into the cover of the trees. Somehow, the idea of following them and moving away from the enormous conflagration terrified Joshua the most.

Nevertheless, he let Will turn him on his still-wobbly legs and start retreating toward the Goddess' Woods. "Next time, rotate the hilt in your palm. Don't just twist your wrist," Will said beside him.

"I should do what?" Joshua asked, raising his voice to be heard over the roar of the flames. He had to tear his gaze from the remains of the Hamond to move with Will toward the cover of the trees. His legs felt like water and his gut churned uneasily. Will had killed that guardsman so efficiently, and Joshua could barely keep his stomach from retching up its contents.

"If you've got someone grabbing you from behind, you'll never reach them by stabbing backward like that," Will clarified. "Instead, let the hilt slip in your hand, with the weight of the blade, till the tip is turned behind you. Then you can slash blindly all you want, and you'll almost always open their gut."

Joshua's stomach flipped again at the mention of spilling blood, but he swallowed bile and nodded as confidently as he could. "Right. Was part of your plan, all along, to go into these cursed trees if everything . . . went up in flames? Because of your connection to the Goddess?"

"Of course not," Will said with a shake of his head. "I don't have a connection with that bitch."

"Bullshit!" Joshua scoffed, then swallowed dryly. He had no idea where that sudden burst of cold laughter came from.

Will actually chuckled under his breath and gripped Joshua's shoulder. "Here." He unbuckled one of the straps that held a dagger around his waist and handed it to Josh. "You're going to need this in the future."

Joshua swallowed, unable to deny the fact. He fit the belt around his slim waist, tightening it to the smallest loop. His fingers, which had been shaking like his mother's earlier, were steady now.

He wanted to tell Will that one bit of advice about the dagger didn't mean he could use it, that he had no idea what to do with a weapon since all arms were outlawed within Kaylyn's towne limits, but that seemed pointless.

Because Kaylyn isn't my home anymore. That part of my life is over.

With Will's arm around his shoulder, they hurried toward the black blanket of trees with the last few rebels.

"Why didn't you use your magic against that man?" Joshua asked. "Wouldn't it have been easier to make a . . . I mean, carve a rune to help me?"

"It's not that simple," Will replied. "If I don't follow her rules I can't—"

Will grabbed the back of Joshua's tunic and forced them both to duck. Several arrows streaked over their heads and into the trees just ahead of them. When Joshua glanced behind him, he saw several new groups of guardsmen charging after them, struggling to restring their bows mid-stride.

"I thought you said the lieutenant's men wouldn't follow us in here!" Joshua protested as they rushed under the cover of the trees.

Will's face was set in a hard grimace as he pulled them both behind the thick trunk of an ancient oak. "I was wrong."

CHAPTER TWENTY-TWO

NOWHERE ELSE TO GO

"You're going to have to learn fast," Will said as he drew his bow from his back and notched an arrow in place without looking.

"Learn what?" Joshua asked, then flinched. The trunk of the oak at their backs vibrated as several enemy arrows thumped into it.

"Magic," Will snapped, and Joshua thought he felt his compass in his pocket flare with unnatural heat.

Rebels rushed past Joshua and Will, though their steps were unsure as they looked for cover. Joshua could tell none of them had set foot inside The Goddess' Woods despite its proximity to towne, and from the terrified looks on their faces, they were debating which option was worse: fighting the lieutenant's men inside Kaylyn, or battling an unknown force from an outlawed religion among the trees.

"Stay together!" Will shouted, and swung out from behind the tree to fire his shot back in the direction they had come from. Joshua couldn't tell if he'd hit anyone. Many of the rebels' turned at the sound of Will's voice. "We need to travel through the trees to find safety!"

"We won't reach the other side!" one frightened man spoke. Both his legs were covered in blood, and he held onto two others, smoke still rising off their singed clothing. "We don't worship Cybarys! She'll keep us trapped in these woods till we starve!"

Will didn't have time to reply; the Rhethosian guardsmen were rushing into the outskirts of the forest, cutting down everyone they saw. Joshua could only make out black figures with blades drawn, their forms darkened into menacing silhouettes by the brightness of the fire that was his home.

Will steered Joshua deeper into the trees, and they dodged several clumps of oaks, ducking under ancient vines that burst with dry moss as they were disturbed. The undergrowth was thick and the air was tight, as if there wasn't enough room for all the life already here to accommodate for people.

Joshua's heart strained in fear and exhaustion as he tried to see in front of him past the first few feet of black trunks. He stumbled on a slick root and careered forward, trying to keep his balance as they ran. Will's grip on his shoulder steadied him, but Joshua brushed his hand across the nearest oak to avoid falling to his knees.

Bright red sparks of magic burst in front of his eyes, cascading from his palm and fingertips that had made contact with the rotting bark. His hand felt incredibly hot for an instant, as if he'd thrust it close to a roaring fire.

"*That's* what you need to learn," Will explained hurriedly. "Those sparks are only contact magic, showing you that you're connecting with something else that's been blessed by the Goddess."

"But why am I—?"

"I'll tell you everything later." Will brought them to an abrupt halt and crouched low on the ground, pulling Joshua with him. "Right now we need to keep everyone alive, and I can't cast the magic we need to find the right path. Can you help me, Josh?"

Joshua swallowed and nodded. Will reached over to draw Joshua's dagger. He wrapped the boy's hands around the hilt, placed his fingers on top of Joshua's, and put the tip of the blade against Joshua's forearm. He cut a small rune across the width of Joshua's arm just underneath the other foreign shape that was healing. Joshua did his best not to cry out.

"What is that one supposed to do?"

"It means Guidance," Will said. "Twist the cut to keep the Blessing Rune open and ask Cybarys which way to go. I'm going to stay behind and make sure all my people make it. *You* are going to lead."

Joshua stopped staring at the rune-shaped cut on his arm to glance up at Will, his eyes wide. Will's face was shadowed by the bit of moonlight sliding through the branches above them, casting his features in dull shades of gray and silver.

"But I don't know where to go." Panic clawed at Joshua's throat. "This place, it's—"

"You're Goddess Touched, Josh," Will said, and when he put a reassuring hand over the freshly cut rune, intense heat stung up and down Joshua's arm. "She won't let you get lost in here. You can do this."

Joshua couldn't say anything; his tongue refused to move within his dry mouth. He glanced nervously around him. Despite their terrifying run through the darkness, this part of the woods seemed exactly the same as the rest. He could hear men shouting behind them, their curses and shrieks pounding against his ears. Those men had met in his mother's private parlor an hour ago to plan their fight for freedom, and now, they were dying for it.

Joshua took one last look at Will, then rose and started forward into the trees once more, jogging slowly at first, then increasing his speed. Joshua heard Will's voice behind him, fading fast, assuring the rebels that they would stay alive if they followed Josh. Shouts of confusion and denial from the rebels reached Joshua's ears loud and clear.

"Face Sarrett's men or follow the boy!" Will's command sounded after him. "Josh! Touch the trees!"

Joshua didn't understand at first, his mind too focused on not losing his footing again. Then he took a deep breath and grazed his fingertips along the clump of oaks to his right. The blackness around him erupted in a shower of blood red light, bathing the condensed woods in a brief moment of clarity.

He didn't dare look backward to make sure the rebels were following his lead; he kept moving as fast as he could, dodging and ducking and jumping around obstacles he could only see clearly at the last minute. He kept one hand on the Blessing Rune, squeezing his forearm so his palm remained sticky, and the other out to the side for balance. Every so often he lit up the night with a cascade of sparks he could scarcely believe were real.

Joshua ran as straight and long as he could until his legs screamed in resistance. How much farther could he go? Will hadn't told him how far away his rebel camp was, nor how long he thought the Kaylyn guardsmen would pursue them. His fingers played with the cut on his arm, and the shape of the rune gave him the confidence to keep moving. Intuition told him to veer right, and he did.

Please, Joshua thought desperately, listening to the cacophony of footsteps crashing at a steady speed right behind him. *Cybarys, whoever you are, help me. Help Will find everyone and lead them forward. Please just—*

A bulking force crashed into Joshua from his left side, sending him sprawling across the forest floor. He cried out and scrambled blindly among the molding leaves and soupy mud. Arms reached out and tore viciously at his shirt, reaching for his throat, but Joshua twisted and spun away. He was vaguely aware that his attacker wore Rhethosian Blue cloth.

When he found his feet, his head crashed into a low overhead branch, snapping sharp twigs and a shower of leaves in his face. Joshua instinctively put an arm up to shield his face, and blood flew from his skin to the forest floor.

He glanced down at the other Blessing Rune on his arm, the one that Will had told him meant "Protection". Without thinking further, Joshua drew Will's dagger and clumsily broke open the scabbed shape on his skin. *Keep that man away from me!* Joshua thought, stumbling away from the guardsman in the mud.

Fresh heat flared around him along with a red glow, and when the man grabbing for Joshua tried to stand, he couldn't. Joshua glanced down and saw the Rhethosian guardsman's knees were stuck in the thick mud, which had taken on a reddish sparkle. No matter how hard he tried, he could not pull himself free of the sticky earth.

The dozens of rebels following Joshua skirted to a halt next to and past the guardsman, squinting in the wood's gloom to see what had stopped their progress. One muttered something about outlawed magic and glared at Joshua, while several others rounded on the guardsman and put him out of his misery.

Joshua swallowed and looked at the people gathering around him. In the forest's gloom, he recognized some from The Hamond, regulars that had seen him grow up over the years, as well as their wives and friends. They supported the injured and watched the back of their group with sharp eyes for more guardsmen, but they all eventually looked to Josh for what to do next.

"I don't know how much farther it is," Joshua confessed, suddenly realizing how out of breath he was. "I'm sorry."

"Well, how'd you get us this far?" one man demanded.

"And what're those cuts on your arm?"

"He's one of the pagans! You saw the sparks!"

"No, that's Miss McKinlee's boy."

"Will's going to keep us safe, we just have to reach the far side of the trees where his people are," Joshua tried to assure them. He motioned with his arm for them to move forward again, but, now that there wasn't a Kaylyn guardsman in sight, the rebels were suddenly wary.

"Don't panic," came Will's voice from the back of the gathered group. Additional approaching footfalls echoed and then halted as the last of the fleeing rebel group met with the rest. Their leader made his way forward. "We're all here, and alive."

"Not all of us," someone spoke up darkly. "Many didn't make it out of the inn." An angry chorus of approval echoed through the woods.

Will glanced down at the dead guardsman in the mud at Joshua's feet, then raised his eyebrows. It was almost impossible for Joshua to see his minute change in expression in the dark.

He could tell Will wanted more of an explanation, but Joshua wasn't sure how to give him one. The mud around the guardsmen's limbs still held a warm red glow, as if bits of rubies were buried just below the surface of the muck. "Magic" seemed like a weak, foreign way of justifying why Joshua was still alive, yet he could see remnants of the Blessing Rune's power right in front of him.

"Thank you, Joshua," Will said when the boy didn't speak, "for leading us this far." He made his voice loud enough for everyone to hear. "I think I can—"

"*Joshua?*"

He heard his mother call out his name seconds before the gathered rebels were shoved aside. Angelyn collided with him, nearly knocking both of them to the ground. Joshua held her close, wrinkling his nose against the bombardment of her long hair that smelled like harsh smoke.

Joshua found, in that moment, that he hadn't thought about his mother since Will had saved him in the middle of Kaylyn Field. Yes, he had seen Angelyn and Ada run into the woods together, so he knew she was alive, but never had he been more than just a room's length away from his mother till this day. The realization was both terrifying and liberating.

"Mum, I'm fine," Joshua insisted, and pulled her away from him. "Will saved my life. I'm here because of him."

Angelyn drew back from Joshua and turned her examining stare toward the rebel leader. Joshua felt a chill pass over him when he understood and realized he related to all the emotions he saw in his mother's face: anger at the loss of their home, fear for their current predicament, and confusion as to what they should do next.

"Thank you," she murmured, barely audible. Joshua could make out a cold edge in her voice, and he understood why: their home, his mother's entire life, was gone.

Will gave Angelyn a silent nod. His green eyes flashed across the gathered crowd, and Joshua guessed he was trying to count them all. "It will take most of the night to reach the edge of the trees, where we will find shelter and the means to retaliate against the lieutenant." He seemed to get his bearings, somehow, and his words gained confidence as he spoke. "Stay together, and, despite your beliefs, don't be afraid of this place."

The men and women that Joshua could see looked doubtful, but nonetheless were ready to move when Will stepped forward. "Joshua," Will began, and put his arm around his shoulder, "I'll still need your help for some of the way."

"Because the Goddess took away your gift?" Joshua asked, trying to understand these new concepts and rules. "Because you break her laws and kill people?"

Will glanced at Angelyn briefly, and Joshua saw his mother's face was both stern and afraid. He thought maybe that was why Will refused to answer him or explain further, but it only multiplied the curiosities in Joshua's mind.

CHAPTER TWENTY-THREE

LOST PATHWAYS IN THE WOODS

"How much longer are you planning on using my son?" Angelyn demanded.

She marched through the wet underbrush at Will's side, Joshua on his opposite. Hours had gone by, and every damned tree that they passed looked the same to her. The long, narrow stretch of woods weren't large, but with no known safe roads, injured rebels, and frightened townsfolk, they moved very slowly.

"I'm just trying to help," Joshua said.

"But you shouldn't have to bleed like that—"

"Just look!" Joshua interrupted. He swung his bloody forearm around over his head. Bright sparks of red magic remnants cascaded onto his shoulders. "Magic, Mum! And it's coming from *me*."

Angelyn swallowed dryly and wrapped her arms around herself. Her hands were shaking, but not from the cold. Joshua was ecstatic that he was leading and helping everyone, and usually his smile made her forget every stress in her day. But right now, all Angelyn could do was hold her tongue against a tirade of curses and tears that, if released, she felt would never end.

Will put a hand on Joshua's shoulder and subtly shook his head. Joshua's face sobered quickly. "Sorry," he muttered. "Don't worry, Mum. It's going to be all right. It doesn't even really hurt."

Angelyn nodded, not trusting herself to speak. Her son felt important now, yes, but later, when they were safe, he'd have questions . . . ones she had hoped would never come up in his life.

"It won't be long now, Miss McKinlee," Will added. "We'll reach the other side before the sun rises." He did not look at her when he spoke. Did he feel guilty for what had happened in Kaylyn, or was she just a loose end that he didn't want to fully acknowledge?

The line of ragged rebels following behind was somber and mute, as if speaking would upset whatever curse lingered in these trees. Will had insisted countless times that someone with the Goddess' Touch could travel through without getting lost or hurt, but that only kept the group close together.

Angelyn understood their fears and could not share in Joshua's wonderment and enthusiasm. Every time she watched him touch a tree or trace his fingers along the two shapes on his arm, bits of stories her grandmother had told her as a child flitted through her mind. She couldn't focus on the details even if she wanted to, and glancing back at the faces of the survivors walking behind her confirmed her mistrust.

Many chose to stay behind in Kaylyn Field and face the lieutenant's guardsmen, she thought grimly. *They preferred torture and death to what could befall them if they got lost in these woods. And I have no idea what lies ahead of me.*

She glanced nervously into the dark trees on either side of her, looking for some sort of sign that they should turn back, some proof that this trek was madness. Her son couldn't be the only one capable of guiding these people properly, just because their real leader had upset some unseen deity who took away her gifts at whim.

Magic? Faith? Prayers? They were all childish, outdated lies Angelyn refused to accept as part of her life.

All she could find was doubt in the shadows that poured between the ancient branches; tendrils of unease clung to her soot-stained dress and grabbed at her damp, tangled hair. Her entire life was gone, up in smoke in mere moments, and uncertainty of her beliefs, her kingdom, and herself plagued her every aching step.

Angelyn glared at Will, who was doing an infuriatingly good job at ignoring her. All of her problems were right here, presented perfectly, mockingly, in one, impossible man. "Damn you," she hissed suddenly.

Will started, and, finally, met her eyes. "What?"

Angelyn cut in front of Will, forcing him to stand still. Joshua halted as well, staring back at her unsurely. "My son and I were supposed to live and die at The Hamond," she began, and all the angry, despairing vomit of words at the back of her throat crept up behind her teeth. "Do you even know what that place stood for? 'Hamond' McKinlee was my great-great-great-grandfather, and he and his wife built that inn from the ground up with their own hands."

"Miss McKinlee, I am sorry. I'm doing everything I can right now to—"

"'Hamond' means 'home' in old Rhethosian, you heartless bastard!" Angelyn snapped. She felt dozens of eyes on her and grumbles of concern echoing back through the rebel group, but she didn't care. Taking a step forward, her boots sinking into the forest's muddy floor, Angelyn shoved hard against Will's chest. He stumbled back several paces.

"You don't even realize what you've destroyed," she continued. "Or maybe you do, and that's why you won't look at me. Is your idiotic, idealistic dream worth what you've done? This mess you've created for everyone is—"

"Careful," Will said quietly, and Angelyn lowered her clenched fists. "I'm giving these people voices, their children futures. You questioning my cause will get you nowhere but more upset."

"Your *cause*?" Angelyn repeated, unable to stop herself despite the edge in Will's voice. "That phrase sounds so noble, but you commit murder, you ruin lives, you destroy safety. You leave as much fear and terror in your path as Lord Bradford—"

"Well, damn me, Angelyn, for doing what's right in a way you don't approve of!" Will shouted.

Angelyn held her breath and stepped back. Everyone stood silently, looking between her and the rebel leader. What was *right*? She found that, in this moment, she had no idea what the definition of that word really was.

"What a pleasant surprise, Master Will!"

Angelyn jumped at the new, strange voice that broke the palpable tension in the air. All around her gasps issued and weapons were drawn. A man stood a few yards away, leaning lightly against one of the ancient oaks. He smiled at Will as though he knew the rebel leader well.

"Are we really that close, Master Colwell?" Will asked, and Angelyn glanced at him, confused by the familiarity.

"Colwell?" Angelyn repeated. "That's an old Rhethosian family name. From Patten Towne, up north." On the Lord's Road that avoided these trees, that place was several days away from Kaylyn. Did this man somehow know a way through the cursed woods?

The newcomer glanced at her curiously, the smile on his thin face faltering. "You *are* up north now, darling. Knowledgeable, but not a great sense of direction, it seems." Angelyn opened her mouth to retort, but the man spoke over her: "We could see the smoke from Kaylyn. It took all my brilliant reasoning skills to stop Orton and his men from charging straight down the tree line to make sure you were alive. What happened?"

"Sarrett," Will said shortly.

"Who are *you*?" Joshua asked. Angelyn noticed he had a hand on the hilt of the dagger Will had given him.

"Angelyn, Joshua," Will began. "This is Irvin Colwell, an old friend of mine. Irvin, this is Angelyn McKinlee and her son. She is—was the owner of the Hamond Inn in Kaylyn."

"Is that what was burning?" Irvin inquired. Angelyn nodded as a fresh lump formed in her throat. "Famous place, that building, even 'up north' where I come from. Sorry to hear that. We'll get the piece-of-shit lieutenant who did it, trust me."

"That's very reassuring," Angelyn said, unable to keep some bitterness from her voice. She didn't flinch as Irvin's pale blue eyes took their time drifting over her from head to foot. She noticed the sharp angles of his long face were handsome enough, despite how thin his bright blond hair was. The tunic he wore was dyed a faded rebel violet, as if he'd been bearing the color proudly for many years.

"And I'll have to apologize once more for interrupting whatever conversation was going on before I arrived," Irvin spoke, breaking his attention from Angelyn and returning it to Will. "But I really hate this place. Makes my skin crawl and the bit of hair I have left stand straight up." He paused and shivered, glancing at the dark canopy above them. "You're going to have to lead on quickly, Will, because I can barely see straight in here."

"He can't figure out the right path," Joshua said before Angelyn could say anything. "I can."

Irvin glanced at Joshua and snorted, then frowned when his gaze rested on the Blessing Runes on Josh's arm. "Really now?" he asked. "Interesting. Then I definitely need to talk more with you later, little man."

"How much farther is it, Master Colwell?" Angelyn asked, stepping forward and putting her arm around Joshua, who tried to squirm away.

"An hour at the most," Irvin said, giving her a bright grin. "Come along, and we can, quoting Master Will here, 'conspire.'"

CHAPTER TWENTY-FOUR

PURSUING DESTINY'S LINE

Devaki ran faster than she ever had before. In fact, there was no way she could keep up this pace for long. But she was late because she had been hesitating too much. *The man named Master Rowlann should be at the docks now. Why am I suddenly afraid to go on an adventure?*

She pulled her silk scarf tighter around her mouth and nose. Such a wrapping was commonly worn for fashion and protection against the sandy winds, but at the speed she was sprinting through the streets of Valsara, the thin piece of fabric was useless. Her eyes turned a scathed red, and sharp tears ran down her cheeks.

Her run took her through the vast marketplace, and she felt a bittersweet smile touch her lips at the familiar sights. She might not come this way ever again. Somewhere above, high on the spiraled surface of the temple, a bell tolled a hollow moan.

Evening prayers. But I can't go. I can't miss meeting Will's men!

Blinking several drops of sweat out of her eyes, Devaki focused on the swift beat of her feet. Her head felt so heavy, and she let her neck rest for just one moment. When she glanced back up, the broad curve of a barrel balanced on someone's shoulder headed straight for her face.

Without thinking, Devaki touched the scar of a Protection Rune carved into the skin just below her collarbone. A burst of magical heat ran down the left side of her body as she dropped her leg to the ground and collapsed in a neat, sideways slide beneath the obstacle. A shower of magic remnants exploded around her in a sheen of dust.

Merchants in cramped wooden stalls that lined the narrow street stopped their activities to stare at her, not to mention the man staggering with a full wine barrel on his back. Devaki shook her head to clear it, and for a moment could only make out blurs of bright colored silks, the jingle of women's ornate jewelry, and the solid slap of hand-cut leather meeting the planks of tables. She heard a few murmurs about the Goddess' Touch, and saw several women pointing at the dissipating sparks around Devaki.

She glanced down at her pants and tunic when she rose and found the silk of her shirt shredded and the cotton fabric of her pants torn badly from her slide. No damage was done to her skin. She sighed, aware that this common outfit was really the only thing she was bringing with her. Patting her bodice, she found that Sehran's sealed note was still safe.

Devaki said a silent prayer to Cybarys and a louder apology to the wine merchant before launching forward once more. She took an immediate side path and darted down an alley lit by musty streaks of sun that shone through holes in the cloth overhangs. This was the right way to the west docks, wasn't it? Rhethosians weren't known for their patience.

Devaki swallowed her fear and pushed forward, hugging the narrow bend in the alley before her. When she rounded the corner, her feet slipped out from under her. A hard hand grabbed her forearm before she fell. Devaki cried out and struggled, then stopped when she saw the hand that steadied her was white. The man's grip was insanely strong, and Devaki had to blink when sunlight glared off his iron gauntlet and armored chest. Underneath a dark hood, she could make out a pale face with a thick beard.

"Easy, girl!" the man laughed lightly. "Why are you running so damned fast? You're not that late."

Devaki opened her mouth to reply but found she didn't know what to say. She had never seen a Rhethosian man, let alone spoken to one. Will had been sending her letters over the years, yes, and even the way he wrote was odd to her. Though she spoke common Rhethosian, she couldn't find what to say.

The man took a step back from her, as if assuming she was frightened by his presence, and raised both hands in complacency. He motioned to the doorway behind him that led into a dark shack, many of which lined this street for storage of goods to be shipped.

"Will's spoken a lot about you," he continued when she stayed silent. "And I'm sure he told you that my men and I aren't exactly welcome here. Can we talk for a minute inside?"

Devaki nodded and stepped through the doorway. The bright, hot world turned abruptly dark and she blinked her sand-stung eyes to focus. The little room was full of boxes and barrels, stacked high against the walls. The sharp stink of wine filled the cramped space, and Devaki knew instantly what was in the containers and where they were going. Rhethos, it seemed, always needed more wine, and Sehran did not mind trading with the current Bradford despite the bloody history between their kingdoms.

The Rhethosian rebel shut the door tightly behind her and stood in the circle of space that had been cleared in the center of the floor. Four men in similar attire stood to either side of him.

Devaki found herself, for the first time, feeling resentful toward these foreign men. Weapons went against every peace law in Armelle, and Devaki had to stop herself from glaring. She had been raised to fear people from across the sea; they were violent, blasphemous monsters that hated her Goddess and her people.

"Miss Tarran?" the stranger asked, folding his arms over his broad chest. His voice was light and soft. Hearing the Rhethosian title before her name was odd, but the way he said it made her smile a bit. "You're a quiet one, then?" the man continued. "But I suppose you really don't need to say anything. I just wanted to meet you myself, and let you know Master Will sends his regards. He looks forward to meeting you one day. Now, if you'll hand over that note he's expecting. . ."

"Let me see your face, Master," Devaki spoke up. She stood strongly, resisting the urge to put a hand to her bodice where Sehran's note rested. "And tell me your name, at least."

The stranger shrugged and pulled back his heavy hood. His pale, square face and head were covered in coarse, patchy black hair. The bright blue eyes beneath his thick brows were his only soft feature. "Master Rowlann, Miss," he said without any trepidation. "And you are Devaki Tarran. The royal family is still famous enough across the sea, even you with your . . . special circumstances."

That last comment stung a bit, but Devaki held her head high. "Show me your colors, Master Rowlann. Please."

"No immediate trust from you?" he said, raising those bushy brows. "Odd for an Armellan." He nodded to the men on either side of him, and they moved their cloaks on their right arms. In the curve of each of their elbows, between the plates of mail, were ties of violet cloth.

Devaki let out a sigh and pulled out her cousin's note. When Rowlann grabbed it, however, she held on tight and met his eyes.

"This bears Armelle's Temple Leader's royal seal," she said, "just as Will requested. But I think I'll give it to your rebel leader myself."

Rowlann frowned. "You want to travel to Rhethos now?" he asked, then scoffed at the determined look on Devaki's face. "There's no place for you in the middle of a rebellion. You should stay here, where you're free."

"You and your people won't be free unless you take me with you."

The line came out of her mouth before she was aware of how truthful the words really were. Hearing them in her own voice gave her more courage to stand her ground. Her hand tightened in a fist around Sehran's note. She could feel the uneasy eyes of the Rhethosian rebels on her, but she kept her attention on Rowlann.

"I know things that will help your leader, that will give him the keys he needs to succeed."

"We don't need pagan assistance," one of Rowlann's men scoffed, but a quick glare from his leader silenced him.

"Then why was one of *your* people meeting with *my* Temple Leader?" Devaki demanded. She hadn't planned on bringing up what she had heard in secret the other day, but it spilled from her lips nonetheless.

Rowlann raised his eyebrows. "There are no meetings between Rhethosians and Armellans, save this one," he said pointedly. "You must have misheard whatever was spoken."

Devaki ground her teeth in frustration. "My Goddess has shown the truth. And she'll continue to do so because she wants to free your people. Now, please . . . take me with you."

Rowlann shook his head, and, before she could move, he tore the note from her hand. "I'm sorry, Princess. But this is all I need, not your fortunes or your prayers."

Devaki opened her mouth, but Rowlann had already turned away from her. He motioned for his men to follow him out of the storage shack and back into the sunlit streets. She thought she had been brave, straightforward, demanding, even, yet it made no difference to them.

She stepped forward, ready to cry out to Rowlann and his men, then stopped herself. Devaki glanced around, aware of how small the storage room was, about the same size as her bedroom in the Silk Palace, and suddenly she felt very small herself. The only person who listened to her in her room, in the palace, in the temple, in this entire kingdom was the Goddess.

Will told me to wait. Sehran told me to stay silent. Rowlann told me I'm not needed. But Cybarys . . . she told me I'm important. I will not be left behind.

Devaki left the storage shack and turned back the way she'd come. She could smell the ocean and followed the scent through the tiny spaces between buildings until she found the open water. The dockside was brimming with traders, many unloading shipments, others guiding galleys into port, while the largest groups milled about the foreman's shack at the end where coin was constantly being exchanged.

The water was calm, and the docks were full of every sea trader taking advantage of the high tide and good weather. Devaki did not come here often; in fact, she could not remember the last time she came to the docks. As she realized this, a cart towering high with crates trundled down the main seaside road and forced her back against the shack she'd been standing in front of. The tail of the horse pulling the cart flicked against her cheek, and the cart's wheels barely missed rolling over her toes.

Think fast, she told herself, focusing her gaze along the stretch of the dock. *No matter how busy it is here, they took the main road, and when they arrive, they're going to stick out. But which ship is theirs?*

There were at least half a dozen trading galleys within sight that bore Rhethosian Blue flags. Devaki traced one of the Guidance Runes on her right arm and felt a familiar flare of heat along her body. She let her feet take her forward until she stood on the edge of a dock where a small ship bobbed. It looked as though its cargo had recently been unloaded because the deck was empty, and only a couple crewmen stood at the helm, talking quietly with their backs to her.

She did not hesitate; Devaki stepped off the slick planks of the dock and onto the deck, and she felt a wave of unexpected relief hit her heart. She hadn't left her home, no, but for the first time in her life she didn't have Armellan sand under her feet. It was so

"You! Stop right there, if you would."

Devaki whirled to find where the voice had come from. A group of monks stood in front of the plank that led up onto the galley next to her. One of the monks was pointing at a cluster of men in cloaks that had approached, and even as Devaki ducked against the railing to hide, she knew who they were.

The sound around the immediate area on the docks lowered to a steady murmur, and many turned to watch the monks that blocked Rowlann and his men from boarding the ship. Devaki noticed, as Rowlann stepped forward to speak to one of the monks, that if she had tried to board the correct ship, she would have been stopped just as easily. She said a silent prayer of thanks.

There was a large gap between her galley and the one next to it. The ocean bubbled peacefully in rhythmic waves when she glanced down between the hulls of the ships. Above her head dangled several sets of halyards, wound up neatly next to the lowered sails. A few dock lines stretched back to land, but these ropes were tied tightly to keep the ship in place.

The monks didn't seem very upset at the rebel Master speaking to them, and Rowlann's men were taking small steps forward impatiently. Devaki turned the sharp edge of her rune ring toward the skin on her upper arm.

She winced as she cut swiftly into the scar tissue formed in the shape of a Protection Rune. The freshly carved symbol dripped red lines down her arm, and she said a quiet, fervent prayer: *Keep me hidden, Mother. I do this for you, to follow the String of Fate you've shown me.*

It took all her courage and faith to stand from her crouched spot against the galley's railing. But she forced herself to straighten her back. When Devaki turned to look toward the crewmen standing at the helm, her heart settled a little; neither man seemed to notice her, even though she stood close by.

She smiled, then reached for one of the ropes above her, uncoiled it, and stepped up onto the railing. Her silk slippers wavered on the polished wood. Devaki leaned back, then swung forward across the gap between the decks. She landed smoothly on the galley just as Rowlann got an approving nod from the monks at the bottom of the gangplank.

The noise attracted several stares in her direction, and she froze. Some of the rebels pointed at the rope swinging oddly between the two ships. Devaki glanced down at the fresh rune cut on her arm and twisted the skin to keep the wound bleeding; she needed to be ignored for a while longer, and the Goddess would only continue to help her if she kept offering blood.

One quick glance back to the dockside told her that Rowlann wasn't going to have much more of a delay, probably because his men were leaving and not arriving. The Armellan monks were forgiving and wouldn't detain a Rhethosian man if he said the right thing in a contrite manner. Something told her that Will knew his men could get away with carrying weapons here, but she didn't have time to dwell on these details. Devaki went below deck before anyone could pay her more attention.

The hull was shadowed and quiet, but mostly empty. Only a few stacks of old crates were piled in the back corner, and when she heard heavy footfalls on the deck above, Devaki ducked behind them.

"What did he say?" one of Rowlann's men asked.

"Nothing important," returned another voice, and Devaki recognized it as Rowlann's. "Just a friendly reminder not to bear arms in their city."

Several of the rebels laughed, and Devaki chose to try to ignore the rude comments that followed. She put a hand over the rune on her upper arm, feeling her skin clot over. That had been a leap of faith, quite literally; a prayer could be answered, yes, but in what way one was never sure. Devaki murmured thanks to her Goddess.

She stayed huddled in the corner of the ship's hull for a long time after they set sail, listening to the chatter of the men above and the pound of the open ocean below. Part of her wanted to think through what to do when they landed, and she found the idea of speaking to and helping Will suddenly terrified her. She closed her eyes, many hours later, and prayed.

A loud crack brought her out of her reverie, and Devaki snapped her eyes open. The sound of the Rhethosian rebels above her had changed; their footfalls were frantic and their voices were full of anger and fear. Another crack issued, then the inside of the hull lit up with a sharp, brief flash of light.

A storm, Devaki thought, and got to her feet. The ship swayed violently, and she fell back down to her hands and knees. *Will we even make it to Rhethos?*

CHAPTER TWENTY-FIVE

A LIE OF A LIFETIME

Joshua stumbled through the forest, avoiding as many tree roots as he could. He noticed that the trunks around them were starting to thin, and the undergrowth wasn't as thick as it was a half hour ago. His mother walked next to him, her hand on his shoulder, and Will and his friend Irvin kept back several paces, talking quietly.

"Look at that!" one man just behind Joshua exclaimed, and he looked up from his boots to see he stood at the edge of a clearing.

Steep mountains rose at a harsh, unforgivable incline, and Joshua marveled at their height and closeness. He'd seen these peaks beyond the Goddess' Woods from outside his bedroom window his entire life, but their sheer size had never been real until now.

Murmurs of awe and a few of recognition ranged amongst the rebels as they emerged from the trees, but Joshua knew they weren't staring at the mountainside; throughout the clearing, scattered in the narrow stretch of open land between the forest's edge and the mountain's feet, were hundreds of rickety buildings that stood on formidable wooden stilts.

Rising before them, like lanky wooden giants, were structures unlike anything Joshua had ever seen. Most of the structures were held up above the ground by thick oak trunks, banded together in old iron. Below were haphazardly spaced shacks and poorly constructed buildings.

"Good Lord," Angelyn whispered beside him, and Joshua glanced at his mother to see awe shining in her eyes. She reached down and grabbed his hand, and Joshua let her squeeze his fingers.

"Look at those!" Joshua said, pointing upward. Connecting the bottom layer of shacks to the raised buildings was a complicated system of ladders, planks, ropes, and pulleys. As he watched, Joshua could barely make out several cloaked figures running down one set of boards, swinging across thick ropes, and landing amongst the shacks on the ground. Lit torches amongst the sea of cabins and stilts flickered little light and innumerable shadows.

Standing prominently before them was a watchtower, its rough edifice reinforced with stone from the surrounding mountainside. One ladder ascended to its single opening at the top.

"Watch your step, little man!" Irvin said, and elbowed Joshua in the middle of his back. Joshua, his neck strained back so he could stare up, stumbled forward. Irvin chuckled, caught Joshua's collar, and pulled him away from the edge of a deep ditch.

The trench at the tree line was filled with sharp rocks and stakes and ran from the woods along the exposed eastern side of the rebel camp. Joshua looked away from the hole and back at Irvin.

"Thanks," he muttered, though he glared at the stranger while he said it. Irvin only winked and grinned.

"Is Orton up there?" Will asked, jerking his head up at the looming watchtower.

"Yes," Irvin said. "Though he certainly doesn't like watch duty very much. I'll bet you tomorrow's meal rations that's the first thing he says to you!"

Will gave Irvin an exasperated look, then waved one hand up at the watchtower. Joshua had no idea how the person all the way up there could see them down below, but a moment later a shout echoed from the perch. Several men came out from the first row of raised buildings, carrying a heavy plank that they lowered across the trench.

"Why do you live out here?" Joshua asked Will. Out of all the questions squirming in his head, this was the first he chose. "Don't folk travel this way? Doesn't the Rhethosian government know anything about what happened here up north?"

"So he's Goddess Touched *and* he asks questions?" Irvin scoffed, running a hand dramatically over his lean cheeks. "Brilliant."

"No one else lives up here, Josh," Will explained easily. "Most townes in northern Rhethos range along the coast, just like Kaylyn, because of the bad weather and the harsh shape of the land up here. Do you see those mountains? They range as far as possible, so, with them to the north and the Goddess'

Woods to the south, this little niche of land is a logical choice if you do not want to be found."

"It's far from the southern capital, but still in the middle of Rhethos," Angelyn pondered, and when Joshua glanced over at his mother, he saw her nodding at the brilliance of this new place.

"It might be like our old home," he added.

"I'm sure it will be nothing like home," Angelyn murmured, then fell silent as they walked under the shade of the watchtower. Joshua heard a voice shout down in recognition when Master Irvin and several dozen men rushed forward across the little bridge. Even in the poor lighting, Joshua saw grins on the rebels' faces.

A thought hit him hard in that moment as he waited with the rest to cross into the rebel stronghold. *This rebellion is real, and it is large. It must have taken years of quiet work to build a place like this. This war is much bigger than me and my mum. And everyone here has been waiting for their leader to return, the man who gives them hope for victory.*

"Just this way," Joshua heard Irvin beckon. The skinny man stood on the other side of the trench with open arms, waving for everyone to move forward and follow the wave of newcomers under the shadow of the first layer of connected buildings. Many faces were upturned, gazing at the wooden structures that held up these buildings shadowed by the night. Joshua, still toward the front of the group, had to duck under suspended planks and brush back tangles of hanging ropes.

"Where are you taking us?" Angelyn asked Will. Joshua could hear a demanding edge in his mother's voice, but when he looked at her, her face was pale and haggard. He didn't need to glance down at her hands to know her fingers were shaking.

"We only have one decent building in this place big enough to hold this new group," Will explained. "I want to speak with everyone for a moment. This is it."

They approached the front of a large, square two-story building, the most prominent and fortified structure in sight. Windows showed that inside was empty save for vacant chairs, tables, and a makeshift bar.

Angelyn grabbed his hand again as they filtered into the main hall, and Joshua noticed that she was trying to keep her eye on those from Kaylyn she knew and trusted. Once everyone had taken a seat or had situated themselves by a table, the group quieted.

All eyes turned to Will. He changed his entire demeanor when he was addressing his people, and Joshua found himself picking up on the subtle changes. Will straightened his shoulders and back, instantly gaining a couple inches in height. His strides to the center of the room were deliberate, the confidence in his gait hiding his fatigue from their journey.

"Now, before you get too eager," Will said loudly, "I'll try to answer a few questions." He paused to survey the new rebels, taking his time to cast his gaze on every tired face. "I can see a lot of anger in here. Revenge for your losses tonight will come, but know this: we can't take action until our numbers are greater. In the meantime, there is more than enough work to be done here.

"This is your new home, but it is unlike any place in Rhethos. Here, you may do as you please. The work will be hard, practical, but rewarding because you are not sweating for a Lord who does not care for your well-being. You are here to create a future that has only been a dream for centuries."

Irvin said loudly from the door, "And that means hacking down trees and digging shit holes." He chuckled, and many laughed with him.

Will's smile stretched thin, but Joshua had a feeling that he was used to Irvin's sense of humor. Joshua liked the fact that Will was always honest and readily shared information with his fellow conspirators, treating everyone as his equal.

But something tells me that being so open isn't the best idea. What if everyone isn't as loyal as he thinks?

"Those who are wounded may be seen to immediately," Will continued after the laughs had died, and Joshua cleared his head to pay attention. "Irvin and I will find you all a place to rest, with your families, and tomorrow each of you will be given a responsibility, no matter how small. You are safe now."

Silent approval filled the room. Joshua's fingers settled on the hilt of the dagger at his waist, an unfamiliar weight he knew he could get used to.

Was my home a turning point, the final burning that made them want to stop hiding? Joshua wondered. *I think Will just promised these people they'll have blood in the future, and from the looks of it, they want it badly.*

He glanced at the others and saw many nods of approval. Now that everyone seemed satisfied, Will motioned for several men to begin splitting up and directing the new rebels to where they would spend the night. The space in the hall filled with tired voices and the shuffling of many weary feet.

Irvin worked his way to Will and put an arm around Will's shoulders. Joshua watched with curiosity as Irvin whispered in Will's ear, but Will shook his head, his face expressionless. Irvin jerked his head in the direction of both McKinlees, and Joshua's brows narrowed. Will glanced at Joshua and saw that he was watching. A strained smile grew on his lips as he walked over to them.

"It seems my friend wants to have a word with you, Miss McKinlee," Will said. "And you, Josh."

"Why?" Joshua asked. "What did we do?"

"Nothing, he talks to many of the newcomers."

"Fine. I can handle your friend," Angelyn said.

"Watch what you say," Will returned shortly, and moved on to assist with coordinating arrangements for the new arrivals. Not a second after he'd left, Irvin appeared next to Angelyn, beaming.

"I was wondering if I could have a word with you, my dear," he said politely. "In private, though. It's rather chaotic in here. And you too, Joshua."

"What do you need to say to us?" Joshua asked warily.

Irvin waved a carefree hand through the air, though, in the tight space, he accidentally backhanded someone standing beside him. He ignored the shout of protest and kept his attention on Josh. "Just the same things I say to everyone when they first get here, of course," he said. "So stop looking at me like I've got a knife at your throat, little man. You've got a lot of mistrust in those eyes of yours. Shall we?"

He made to wrap his arm around Angelyn's shoulders, but Joshua stepped forward and blocked his reach. Irvin instead gestured toward a door that stood open on the far east wall.

"Let me handle this," Angelyn whispered to Josh as they entered the room and Irvin shut the door behind them.

The small space was mostly filled with a rectangular table in the center and a fireplace to the right. The furnishings were well-worn, and none matched, as if they had been taken from many different townes and families to complete the set.

This seemed like a room that wasn't open to the general population of the rebel camp, but a private place where important matters were discussed, and, apparently, where certain newcomers were questioned by those in charge.

Joshua felt grateful for the warmth that came from the open flame of the hearth and stepped closer with his fingers outstretched. His mother, however, turned to the rebel with her arms crossed over her chest in a defensive stance. Suddenly Joshua pitied Irvin; there was no point in arguing with her when she stood like that.

"Well," Irvin sighed pleasantly. "Now that we can hear each other . . . It's always nice to get to know another loyal Rhethosian family turning to the cause. Drink?" He indicated a dark bottle near the end of the long table, but Angelyn shook her head. Irvin shrugged and helped himself, pouring a generous portion of whiskey into a scratched cup.

"Colwell is a much more prominent name than McKinlee," Angelyn answered. "You must have been offered more than a drink to break away from a comfortable life in Patten. How long ago did that happen?"

Irvin raised his pale eyebrows over the rim of his glass as he took a sip. "Clever woman, asking almost as many questions as your son. The loss of your home, though, is such a shame," Irvin continued, "and you must be angry, furious, even, that you have nothing thanks to Will and his people."

"What is your point, Master?" Angelyn snapped, and Joshua cringed at her tone.

"There's no point in bullshitting you, love, so I'll get right to it," Irvin came back. "Will has told me you agreed to support his cause, but under strenuous circumstances." His tone was not angry, nowhere near accusatory, but his light blue eyes showed distaste as Angelyn nodded.

"That is true," Angelyn replied. Joshua opened his mouth to protest, but his mother continued: "Since we're not bullshitting each other, Master Colwell, I'll happily tell you my real feelings. Joshua and I had no choice in this situation. If admitting that makes you lock me up because you don't trust me, please do. Show me what you rebels are really like."

Joshua heard the contempt in her voice. He wanted to say something, to insist there was much more than what his mother's disdainful words suggested, but Irvin spoke instead.

"Miss McKinlee, honestly! We're just chatting here. Please, relax." Joshua could see no offense in his face, yet the way Irvin stared at his mother made it clear he was trying to make her uncomfortable, as if he was used to intimidating women. "Would you sit down, dear? I'm sure you're exhausted."

He gestured at the chairs by the table, and Angelyn sat in the one nearest the fire while Joshua stood next to her. Joshua felt tempted to sit as well, especially with the way he saw his mother practically collapse against the worn wood of the chair, but he fought the urge and remained upright.

"What else do you need to ask me?" Angelyn asked, meeting Irvin's eyes. "We're both tired, and I don't see you eager to interrogate any other newcomers."

"Well, I'd think the big question would be obvious," Irvin replied with a grin. His gaze drifted to Joshua. "You're the real treasure here, Josh! A Rhethosian boy Blessed by the Blood Goddess with magic you probably don't even understand. So how is it you grew up in Kaylyn without being executed for your 'gift'?"

"What?" Joshua asked, taken aback by Irvin's sudden inquiry. "What's he talking about, Mum?"

But Angelyn didn't look at Joshua. One of her shaking hands gripped the edge of the table before her, and she sat up with her back rigid. "He doesn't know anything about that. I've done a good job at keeping Armelle's religion and its curses out of his life, no thanks to your rebel leader."

Irvin stared disbelievingly at Joshua's mother. "I can't believe you've lived your whole life with that damned forest at your back door, but you never told your son about its history and its power."

"Will told me that the Armellan Goddess only gives magic to some people, and that you need to follow her rules to be able to use the runes and . . . you give her blood, to make things happen." Joshua found the explanation sounded weak when it left his mouth, and he blushed when Irvin laughed at him.

"You don't know how special you are, little man!" Irvin continued. "I'm sorry, Miss McKinlee, I don't mean to be rude, truly. But when I saw Josh here guiding everyone through those trees instead of Will, I had to wonder! He must be sixteen, because the last Blood Moon was sixteen years ago."

"Blood Moon?" Joshua repeated. At first he'd been defensive as this rebel questioned his and his mother's loyalty, but now he was confused enough that he didn't know what to think.

"I don't believe in that pagan deity, now," Irvin said, holding up his hands as if they'd both accused him of something. "Still, everyone knows only children born during the night of the Blood Moon have the possibility of being Goddess Touched, and that moon only appears in the sky every twenty-five years. In Armelle, blessed babies are celebrated and honored. Here in Rhethos, where all this religious shit has been outlawed for centuries, Cybarys' Touch isn't so welcome."

"Stop," Angelyn said, and she stood abruptly from her chair. The fireplace behind her lit her loose blonde hair in shades of white and gold. Joshua knew his mother kept things from him, but this was unlike anything he'd ever heard. If what Irvin was saying was true, he'd had this magic in him his entire life, but he'd only been aware of it after meeting Will.

"I just want to know how you hid it," Irvin said innocently. He moved to stand beside Angelyn and put one hand on the arm of the chair she stood in front of. "When the guardsmen came to test Josh's blood as an infant, how did you hide his magic from them?"

"I'm not telling you anything," Angelyn snapped, and took a step backward, bumping into Joshua.

"Tell me, then," Joshua said suddenly, and caught his mother's eye. "I deserve to know!"

"Joshua, it doesn't matter," Angelyn insisted.

"We just made it through those trees tonight because of me!" Joshua insisted. "You've known something about this . . . this Touch my whole life and never said anything! You lied to me for sixteen years!"

"It's illegal, Joshua!" Angelyn said and reached out to grab his hands. He thought of pulling away from her grip, too confused to want any contact with her right now, but he could feel the desperation in her fingertips. "I had no choice but to never speak about it. Like everyone else, I tried to avoid the possibility of giving birth during the night of the Armellan Blood Moon, but your father . . . he didn't care. Gabriel helped me."

"Gabriel? How?" Joshua felt every muscle in his body tense at the mention of the man. It felt like he had died in the Hamond's cellar years ago.

"I'm sorry, I can't do this," Angelyn insisted and yanked her hands away from Joshua. She turned toward the door, but Irvin made his way around the corner of the table faster than Joshua thought possible. He placed himself between Angelyn and the exit, crossing his arms over his violet tunic, mimicking her stubborn stance from earlier.

"I don't think we're done here," he said calmly.

"Move, Master Colwell."

"You owe your son the truth, don't you think?"

"It's not your place to tell me what to do with my child!"

"Child? Look at him, he's a man now! You want to shelter him, lie to him, treat him like The Bradford's treated you your whole—"

Joshua flinched when Angelyn drew back to slap Irvin. The rebel caught his mother's hand, and she cried out in pain; his tight grip clenched around the fresh burns on her palm. Tears sprang in her eyes, and Irvin let go immediately.

"Don't touch her!" Joshua demanded. He yanked his new dagger from its sheath and pointed the tip at Irvin's chest. "You don't know anything about my mother or our lives. Leave us alone."

"Of course, my mistake," Irvin replied smoothly.

Joshua clumsily shoved his blade back home, then guided his mother to the door.

The main hall had cleared out more quickly than Joshua had expected. After surveying the nearly empty room, he saw Will sitting with four other men, his boots up on a nearby chair, drinks and food covering their table. He turned and saw Joshua and Angelyn.

"Something wrong?" Will asked, rising to walk to them. He held up a dismissive hand to the men that were sitting with him.

"It's nothing," Joshua's mother insisted. "We're fine."

Will stopped in front of her, clearly searching her face. Joshua glanced behind Will at the men at the table, who began whispering. Will ignored them, his attention focused on Joshua's mother.

"I told Irvin to let it be," Will murmured disapprovingly. "What did he say?"

"He was rude to her," Joshua started heatedly. "And he hurt her hand!" He found his fingers wrapped again around his dagger's hilt.

"Stay, my boy," Will said, pulling Josh's hand from the blade.

"It's nothing," Angelyn insisted. Joshua could feel her body trembling, her words coming out in whispers.

"Irvin told me my mum has been lying to me about being Goddess Touched my whole life," Joshua said, unable to stop himself. He stepped away from his mother, staring pointedly at Will. "He was trying to explain it to me, but she wouldn't let him. Why won't anyone tell me the truth?"

"Josh, please . . . stop!" Angelyn stuttered. "That's not right. I . . . I can't do all of this . . ."

Will stepped forward and caught Angelyn the moment her legs gave out under her and her eyes rolled back in her head. Her long, golden locks cascaded around her pale face, and her lips moved as if she were trying to speak but no words came.

"Mum?" Joshua started uncertainly. "What's wrong with her?" he demanded as Will gathered Angelyn in his arms.

"I don't know," Will answered. "But she—"

The rest of his sentence fell away when Angelyn suddenly stirred and shoved herself away from Will's grasp. She pushed back from him so violently that she stumbled several steps as she brushed her hair back from her face with trembling hands.

"Mum, are you—?"

"Leave me be," Angelyn insisted. "I was only dizzy for a moment. Do not touch me, please!" She held out a warning hand toward Will, who kept his distance. Joshua swallowed and did the same.

Joshua was about to speak but decided to shut his mouth. No matter what he asked, his mother wouldn't tell him anything new. Irvin was an ass, yes, but he shared something about Joshua's life that he'd never known before tonight. Will always answered Joshua's questions no matter what, yet the look on the rebel leader's face told Joshua he wouldn't learn anything more tonight.

"Fine," Joshua said. "You want me to leave you alone? I will." He marched to the front of the rebel's main hall and stepped out into the night.

CHAPTER TWENTY-SIX

NOT AMONG DECENT FOLK

After finding Angelyn a place to rest, part of Will wanted to stay and make sure she was indeed all right. The idea of someone as strong and stubborn as her almost falling unconscious in his arms was troubling. But he pushed aside his guilt; there were other matters he needed to see to, and after being awake through nearly every night in Kaylyn, sleep seemed a distant aspect right now.

He stood alone in the central building of his camp, the place he thought could be called a common hall, resembling the room of Angelyn's former home, but in truth, it was a sad comparison. Though attached to a makeshift kitchen and a private room Irvin had claimed as his own, the main hall was shabby at best.

The dirt floor created a constant cloud when walked upon in the height of the day, and what tables and chairs could be put together were always a risk to sit on. Though the walls were donated pieces of nearby townes that had turned to his cause, this place held a certain hope for Will.

I've been on the road scrounging and persuading the ignorant for too long, he thought as he made his way across the quiet hall to Irvin's quarters. *This is as close to a home as I allow for myself.*

"Well, this room hasn't changed much," Will said as he shut the door behind him. Irvin turned from the fireplace and grinned. His friend looked older, his hairline receding farther back on his pale skull. The violet of his tunic reflected in his blue eyes, still full of youth and fire. Irvin immediately offered Will a drink as he took the chair nearest the heat.

"Your girlfriend was sitting right there not long ago," Irvin said, indicating Will's chair.

"How are supplies?" Will asked immediately, ignoring the comment. He took the glass of red wine and admired its color.

"Let's put it this way," Irvin sighed, settling atop the table with his boots facing the flames. "Enjoy that good Armellan red because after your trouble in Kaylyn, I don't see any more barrels getting up here in the middle of nowhere."

Will brought a mouthful of the rich spirits to the edge of his throat, savoring the smooth, almost nutty taste before swallowing. "I'm not worried about liquor," he replied, looking at Irvin over the rim of his glass. "We've kept people comfortable up here for years, thanks to the cooperation of Patten and Morely. But those townes are running dry and their people are terrified of the coming winter. The time for ease and secrecy has passed, I think."

"I agree. The snows will take as many lives as they always do," Irvin said morosely. Will caught the flicker of a shadow as it clouded his friend's eyes, and knew very well why this time of year was challenging for him. But Irvin covered the expression with a fresh smirk and gulp of wine.

After more than a decade of hiding and planning and massing, we can begin to form an offensive move soon, Will thought. A bit of excitement rose in the pit of his stomach, directly under the pleasant heat of the Armellan wine. *I should feel as bloodthirsty as Irvin right now, but instead I'm thinking about Angelyn and her son. . .*

He let out a frustrated sigh and ran a hand through his hair.

"There it is!" Irvin pointed out dramatically, nodding his head at Will's movement. "That nervous twitch of yours. What are you worried about, brother?"

"You shouldn't have spoken to her like that," Will said. "She's been through a lot the last few days."

"Thanks to *you*, remember," Irvin pointed out. "Some of the men who returned with you have mentioned the way you've taken a liking to this McKinlee woman. You were even close enough to Sarrett in the confusion of the fire to have killed that little prick, but you went back for her son instead."

"I thought you were a man above rumors," Will said calmly. "Besides, the boy needed my help. You know what they do to the children of rebels."

Irvin nodded reluctantly. His eyes were still critical, but Will knew the scrutiny was rooted in concern. "So," Irvin said, "if it were anyone's son or daughter, not just Miss McKinlee's, not one that's somehow Goddess Touched, you would have stopped to save his or her life?"

"Yes." Will gave Irvin a smile. "Down beneath all your bitchy bravado is a heart that would have done the same."

"Bitchy bravado?" Irvin cackled. "The men of Rhethos have said many things about me over the years, have labeled my kind person with every insult, but that . . . that's truly lovely, Will."

The two toasted each other, then drank in silence. Will wanted to reprimand Irvin, to tell him that he couldn't harshly interrogate those that just joined them and had suffered great losses, but what was the point?

He had learned long ago that working with those willing to break from their Lord's rule was a harsh task: the men who followed him were not kind, nor polite, nor easy to deal with. They knew each other well, so well that Will was not surprised by Irvin's next question.

"So what is special about Angelyn? She's a beautiful woman, I'll give you that, but you need to explain why you're caring for her so intimately."

An image came to mind that startled Will, one of a moment long ago that he hadn't pondered for decades: hot sands in his eyes, blinding sun at his back, cool black marble under his feet, and . . . pressure on a slim cut along his thumb. And those soft, dark, beautiful fingers steadying his own. . . When was the last time he'd thought about Isaka Tarran? Even more, when was the last time he'd even tried to compare someone to the Armellan girl he'd loved so long ago?

Will cleared his throat without letting the emotion show on his face.

"Did you notice my arm?" Will asked.

Irvin glanced at the dirty, bloodstained bandage and nodded curtly. "A lot of good that nice sword I gave you is doing," Irvin muttered, jerking his head at the blade on Will's hip.

"Sarrett switched the patrol schedule one night, and his man's blade bit to the bone before I could react," Will explained. "I lost a lot of blood fast and went straight to The Hamond for fear of falling unconscious on the streets. I know, going there wasn't the best decision, but I had a feeling she could keep me safe."

"Well, you're here now and alive, mostly. What's your point?"

Will drained the wine from his glass and Irvin refilled it. "When I came to, I kept my eyes shut as if I were still unconscious. Her voice had changed; before she always sounded terrified, submissive, but when she realized how close the danger was to her home and her son, Angelyn . . . solidified, as if she had woken up for the first time in her life. She didn't notice it, but *I did*. I don't know how else to explain it."

Will paused, but Irvin only stared at him, eyebrows raised, waiting for him to continue. This worried Will because Irvin always had something to declare, yet right now his mouth was sealed shut.

"Irvin, she lied to Sarrett's face for me," Will continued after clearing his throat. He shifted in his chair, turning his legs away from the fireplace for a moment. "That was something I never expected. You may blame me for the McKinlee's misfortunes, but I helped Angelyn use her energy for something good, something worth a damn."

"By getting yourself stabbed," Irvin chuckled humorlessly. "All right. I've never heard you talk about anyone like that before." He studied Will critically. "Shit, just . . . be careful with her. She's defiant and she doesn't want to be here. I don't trust anyone in that state of mind. We have enough at risk."

"I can handle it." Will stood, grabbed his wine glass, and stretched his sore muscles.

"Let me guess," Irvin said with a grin, "you want to see her again. I'm sure she's sleeping, just like every other decent soul in Rhethos. But you and I aren't among the decent folk, Will. We've still got work to do."

". . . just be kinder to her and Josh next time you speak with either of them. Please?"

"You've got it, brother," Irvin acquiesced. "Where *are* you going?"

"To walk. If there are still people out, restless as I am, maybe I can ease their minds."

Will left Irvin to the last of the wine, still shaking those images of the Armellan desert and that young girl from his mind.

CHAPTER TWENTY-SEVEN

DANGEROUS COMMANDS AND SIDE EFFECTS

Lieutenant Sarrett stood on the dock's wet planks with two of his guardsmen. Hopefully, when a ship appeared on the gray horizon, his mistress and his children would be onboard. Just because Mayra hadn't replied to his letters for nearly a month didn't mean she wouldn't come.

Either she's abandoned me or Captain Caldrell is intercepting my notes, he thought, shivering against the dawn's sharp chill. *To keep me focused on my goal. But I have this towne. Despite what happened last night, Kaylyn is still mine.*

Thinking about The Hamond Inn made him turn his head and glance down the road to the remains of the famous building. Everyone was terrified enough of Sarrett's presence that no one dared place a toe out of line, let alone step near the inn's ruins. That was how this had to work: fear, above all else, commanded order.

"Lieutenant, news from the Captain."

Sarrett felt his throat go dry when he heard this. Barton pushed his way through the crowd of local tradesmen who also waited for the morning ships' arrival at a respectful distance. At this point, the guardsman was a well-trained dog and knew from the scowl on the lieutenant's face that it was best not to speak any further.

The missive that Barton handed over was warped with rain drops and bound in a Rhethosian Blue ribbon. The contents would be at least a week old, but every letter from Caldrell was getting more and more dangerous; there was a reason people called him the Insane Captain.

Sarrett shrugged his heavy wool cloak closer about his person and rotated to face the gray waves once more, turning his back to his guardsmen and the townsfolk. His gloved fingers rested on the seal with Rhethos' sigil, then, holding his breath, Sarrett broke the wax and opened the note.

Sarrett:

Rumors of rebellion continue to reach The Bradford. Punish the traitors more severely. Cut off all trade routes to the northern townes flying violet banners. Burn Kaylyn's winter supplies. Publicly execute any suspicious persons.

Sarrett had to stop himself from trembling as he tucked the letter inside his sleeve. The Rhethosian Captain had chosen him for this position because he could emulate his leader's strong, heartless methods without flinching. But this made no sense to him. Why, if The Bradford was such a perfect, powerful force, would he allow his military leader to demand such insane verdicts?

His eyes went to the horizon once more, trying to find just one set of white sails. *Think of Mayra,* he told himself resolutely. *Think of the end goal and don't question the methods.*

All he had to do was follow orders. Then, he could marry Mayra. Then his children wouldn't be bastards. Then everyone, including his newly mended little family, would have respect for him. But right now, it wasn't enough.

The lieutenant touched the flask in his pocket, yanked it loose, and swallowed half its contents in several swift gulps. A steady, familiar euphoria swept over his shaking limbs, and he had to stop himself from drinking the rest of the wine. He could stop himself, though his heart ached for the rest of the sweet drink.

Swearing under his breath in frustration, Sarrett spun, damp cloak whirling about him, to turn his attention to Master Harling. The wine tradesman stood back on the main road, fresh sweat coating his thick chins despite the freezing morning air. He met Sarrett's eyes nervously.

"Harling," Sarrett snapped, enjoying the way the man practically buckled under the mere barking of his name. "I'm sure you're greatly anticipating the new shipment of Armellan wine."

"Yes, lieutenant," the Master replied hastily, making an awkward bow. "Thanks to your insightful business advice, my daughters and I are happier than ever."

Sarrett knew that in the last week many of the tradesman's bottles had been emptied in his own rooms, but dismissed the idea that, maybe, just maybe, he'd taken too much of a liking to the stuff. It was too useful, too powerful to let go of yet.

Right now, with a slight buzz resonating through his body, the lieutenant knew Rhethos was meant to be seen this way: minute sounds rang with precision in his ears, and every person's movement was painted in golden clarity in his vision. If this was what those monks across the sea used to "connect" with their so-called Goddess, maybe the Armellans weren't as stupid as he thought.

Sarrett swallowed a laugh, and Barton glanced at him out of the corner of his eye. The lieutenant sighed and pressed the flask against his lips once more, savoring the heavy, dark flavor of the liquid as it slid down his throat. Before he knew it, the container was empty and stowed back in his pocket.

He found his gaze drawn again toward the remains of The Hamond, its husk shimmering and waving in shades of blue and violet. His breath caught in his throat.

In the midst of the inn's rubble stood a figure, cloaked in fog and silver light.

Sarrett blinked profusely, sure he was imagining it, but . . . no. There, between the remains of a doorframe and a pile of shattered china, was a slim girl. Her face shifted and melted, the palest shade of milk. The girl's body faded and then grew whole as an icy feeling of recognition formed in the pit of his stomach and the back of his mind: he knew this girl. Her name was Lily, his little sister.

But she could not be here; she had died in his arms ten years ago.

Slowly, the hallucination started to glare at him, malice clear in her gaze. Though Sarrett could see through the shining figure, the look she gave him past her dark sheets of hair struck him to the core. She opened her bloated blue lips to speak, and the words her mouth formed resonated with deadly force in his head:

"*Liar. Abuser. Murderer.*"

"A sail!"

This cry drew Sarrett back, and he suddenly realized he needed to breathe. He gasped, steadying himself on the dock, unconsciously reaching out to

Barton's arm. The officer eyed him curiously, then peered out at the horizon with the rest, where a clear bunch of white canvas had appeared. The trade ships were close now, and the crowd on the docks stirred thankfully as rain came down even harder.

"Everything all right, sir?" Barton asked discreetly.

Sarrett shook himself, then nodded. "I hate this damned weather," he growled, and snapped the hood of his cloak over his head. Not long after the ships had docked, Sarrett was not surprised that only sea traders and crew members were on board. No, one of the captains told him, there were no passengers, and no, there were no messages from the south.

Mayra wasn't coming.

The lieutenant's fingers danced over the empty flask in his pocket, this time as if he were daring to touch a dangerous animal.

CHAPTER TWENTY-EIGHT

A FIRST TASTE OF FREEDOM

Joshua made his way out of the room where he'd spent the night and down the uneven, rickety stairs of the rebel camp's main structure. He observed a familiar sight of Ada serving hot tea to the few present in the room, which was bustling with people who all seemed in a hurry to get somewhere. Every table was full of dirty cups and plates, as well as dozens of rebels who had recently emptied them of their contents.

"What are you grinning about before the sun's even up, little Josh?" Ada asked.

Joshua blushed when she used his mother's favorite nickname for him. "Really?" he snapped. "Even now, that's what you're calling me?"

"Habit, I guess," she replied, then added a bit more seriously, "I know you're not little anymore."

Joshua nodded. "So you're just going to keep serving drinks?" Don't you want to do something else?"

"Well, we've only just arrived," Ada explained with a wink. "I wanted to stay close to Miss McKinlee and make sure she's all right after what happened to The Hamond. Later, though . . ."

Her blue eyes brightened and Joshua couldn't help but grin tentatively back at her. She was beautiful when she smiled.

Ada stepped closer to Joshua and lowered her voice. "I meant it when I told Will I want to fight for Rhethos, with my own two hands."

Joshua blinked, then took a step back. For some reason being so close to Ada made him nervous. "That's great," he replied, "I guess I just never thought of you as a fighter."

"Well, that's why we're here; to change the way people think," Ada countered. "This is a war camp, Josh. Everyone here is preparing to fight in one way or another."

She filled several clay cups with hot water and transferred them to a dented tray. Her gaze fell on his forearm, where his two rune-shaped scabs had formed on his skin.

"And I know Will's a great man and all, but you shouldn't involve yourself with that pagan faith. You'll end up cursed and unhappy, Josh."

Joshua frowned, surprised at this. "But all I've done with it so far is help people. Didn't you see what I did last night?"

"Oh, I saw," Ada said seriously. "I just think it's wrong."

He looked away, suddenly thinking it was best to not discuss his new-found Goddess Touch with Ada, or anyone else, for that matter. It made him remember how furious he was with his mother, too, and his hands curled into tight fists.

"Well," Joshua began after clearing his throat, "I'm going outside. I want to see what this place looks like when the sun's up. It'd be great to meet the weapon's Master."

"Rowlann, the arms expert, isn't here, though some of his men are," a man spoke up. He sat at a table nearest the stairs with several other rebels, all looking weathered and solemn. "Off running an errand for Master Will, from what I heard. Things aren't the same here without Rowlann."

"So who does his job when he's gone?" Joshua asked.

"Why?" the man smirked. "You're a tiny thing. Probably sooner shit your-self than use that dagger. Maybe you'd be better off sorting supplies with the women." His companions laughed, shaking their heads. Ada glared, and when one of the men raised his empty glass at her, she gave him a rude gesture Joshua had seen her use often in his old home.

"Where did you come from anyway, boy?"

"Why are you even asking? We've got to get moving. Irvin hates us sitting idle for too long in the mornings."

The first rebel brushed this off and stared pointedly at Joshua.

"Kaylyn," Joshua answered. He supposed there should have been some pride in that answer, but found none in his voice.

The rebels sobered a little. "Sorry for that, then. Sarrett is a slightly saner version of the Rhethosian Captain, if that's possible," said the first rebel, spitting viciously on the floor. "I have a brother in Kaylyn, but he was too scared of that lieutenant to stand with me. Useless coward."

The man eyed Joshua knowingly. "I'm sure you want to see the weapon's Master with the lieutenant's face in mind, eh? Tell you what: find Master Orton and make nice with him. He's in charge of our defenses here in Middle o' Nowhere, Northern Rhethos. Big man, can't miss him, but if you aren't as scared as you look, he'll get friendly."

"Or he may just decide he doesn't like your face and cut you clean through with that huge ax of his," smirked another rebel. The rest burst into laughter, and Joshua stared, unsure if this was a joke.

"Where can I find him?" Joshua asked, keenly aware of Ada's silent presence behind him. Orton's description brought up an unwanted vision of the Kaylyn officer, Barton, who'd pressed a torch into his hand. Joshua suppressed a shudder.

"Look around, why don't you?" replied the rebel, shaking his head. "I ain't your father."

"For all I know you could be, you rude bastard," Joshua retorted.

Ada gasped, but didn't say anything. In fact, Joshua thought he saw a hint of a smile on her face when she sidestepped a group of rebels making their way to the door. An odd sense of pride hit him in the chest, and Joshua decided he didn't want to delay any longer.

He stepped out into the open air, waving at Ada when she wished him luck. He could hear the rebels roaring with laughter as the flimsy door shut. He forgot all about them in the next breath, however, and could only stare:

Even though it was dawn, the pathway was full of activity. Men and women hurried back and forth, some carrying buckets of water, some hauling carts full of weapons. Running along the top of the hall he'd just exited was a towering system of walkways and ladders that joined at the center of the makeshift fortress in a tall arc.

The rebels Joshua saw looked dirty and tired, but when they passed by, they gave him full grins. Joshua could feel a tension in the air similar to Kaylyn, one full of a military presence almost as tangible as the dagger on his hip, but no one with a sword had ever *smiled* at him before.

The realization that he could go anywhere without consequence suddenly terrified him. He found he could not take a step beyond the entryway where he stood.

A thunder of many feet descended, and Joshua flinched, covering his head. A group of children jumped down from the planks overhead. All six were shrieking happily. Joshua couldn't guess how old they were, especially since he'd been around few other children, but judging by the fact that they were half his height, he thought they may be at least a few years younger.

"Who're *you*?" one boy demanded. He wiped his sweaty cheeks with grimy hands, smudging dirt across his face.

"He must be new, from the group that came in last night," another spoke up before Joshua could reply. This boy stood only a few feet above the ground, with sandy blond hair that unevenly hung past his shoulders.

Though his cloth was poor, he sported a belt of braided violet leather with several ribbons of the same color woven in his boots. The little boy's eyes shone with fierce determination as he looked Joshua up and down.

"Yes, I'm Josh," he replied in the silence.

"Wanna run with us?" another child asked. He practically shouted the question, bouncing up and down.

"I'll beat you this time, Auden! You got here first 'cause you can make that gap between my place and where the fortune lady lives!" taunted the first boy, and shoved the second. The rest cheered as the two boys grappled, till the smaller one broke free and fell into a mud puddle.

The children gazed expectantly at Joshua, who was trying not to let his mouth fall open. Everything these kids were doing was so undisciplined, and . . . free. He wasn't sure how to respond.

"Actually, I . . ." Joshua started. He cleared his throat awkwardly. "I'm looking for a man named Master Orton."

The six boys exchanged wide-eyed glances. "Uh," the sandy-haired boy started, "he's up the watchtower, I'm sure. Usually he takes the watch when Master Will or big Rowlann aren't here."

"But Orton is *scary*," muttered one boy.

"And that nasty ax he carries . . ." began another.

"Do you know what he used it for in the south? I heard he used to execute prisoners for The Br—"

"Quiet!" snapped the blond boy, who seemed to be the leader of this little band. He turned to Joshua, craning his neck to look him in the eye. "Look, Josh, Orton likes food. If you want him to talk to you, bring him something from the bakery ladies across the way. Then he won't chop your head off before asking questions."

The boy pointed vaguely around the curve of the raised platforms and the thick beams that served as supports. His dirty finger hovered over the roofs of the makeshift homes, then the rest of the group became impatient and started shoving one another again.

"Come race with us later, Josh!" shouted the blond boy as they ran off.

"If you've still got a *head*!" cried another.

Joshua felt a lump of fear form in his throat as he watched several of the children grab the sides of the pseudo common hall and hoist themselves up to the planks. Was he really going to run toward a violent stranger after spending most of entire life sheltered indoors away from such people?

What would Mum say?

He cut off the thought, realizing he no longer cared what the answer to that question might be. It was time to embrace all the change that had been barreling at chaotic speeds into his life, no matter what others thought or said.

Joshua noticed that, at the end of the platform the boy had just run up, stood a heavy counterweight. It dropped to allow the boys to scramble upward. Ropes swung and wood creaked dangerously as they disappeared.

Joshua, having no real idea where he was headed, started walking in the general direction the boy had pointed. The roads between the homes around him were awkwardly dug, as if each building was added at different times as the rebels' numbers grew. With how worried his mother had sounded, Joshua had been sure the rebels would be living under rocks, starving each morning and freezing each night.

But the more he saw of the rebels' camp, despite its misshapen design, it was clearly made by those who were dedicated to change in Rhethos. Joshua gained a bit of confidence with each step, the fear receding from his heart. Every place he passed looked dirty and worn, but all the shacks were lived in and well-loved. Doors were left wide open, violet strings hung from crooked poles, and livestock grazed happily across the lumpy, weed-ridden earth.

The sun finally rose above the looming mountain tops, casting the ground in a sultry orange glow. Only minutes later, he stopped shivering. Around the next bend, he saw a rising pillar of smoke and smelled the faint yet familiar scent of yeast. As he approached a small brown hut with one window and a rusted flat roof, Joshua thought of how this time of the morning he was usually helping make bread in The Hamond's kitchen.

"You seem lost, sweetheart. Are you hungry?"

Joshua saw an elderly woman in an apron standing at the side of the cook house, gnarled hands coated in flour. She gave Joshua a smile with her few remaining teeth. He stumbled, staring in awe; the woman was an Armellan. Underneath a cascade of white, rope-like braids, Joshua saw that her skin was deep brown. Even more startling, when she blinked, he saw a milky film over her old eyes.

She's blind . . . and a foreigner. How did she even know I was here?

"My mum and I just arrived last night, so I don't really know where I am," Joshua confessed, collecting himself. "But some children told me this was the best place to go if I needed an early breakfast."

"Well, aren't you brave, coming out here by yourself?" the old woman beamed, wrinkles expanding and cracking across her dark face. Now that she spoke more, Joshua could hear an accent in her voice, one that morphed certain pieces of the common Rhethosian.

"I'll get you something," she added, "but come under here before you soak up those raindrops."

"What rain—?" Joshua said, then he felt a sharp patter across his head and shoulders. He stepped under the awning as the woman craned her neck through the single window. She hollered at those inside with surprising volume, then reached through, patted her shaking, brown hands around for a moment, and brought out four steaming rolls.

"I always know right before it starts. Now, those have freshly beaten eggs in the center, so don't let them sit long."

Joshua gratefully took the food. The rolls were bulbous and velvety, sticking to his hands because of the fresh coat of butter across their tops.

"In Kaylyn, we never put anything inside our bread," Joshua mused as his stomach spoke loudly in agreement. He'd forgotten how little he'd eaten in the last two days as soon as the aromatic steam bathed his face.

"I brought a few recipes with me from across the sea," the old woman said. "If the men can do more work because they can hold their entire meal in one hand without being distracted, so be it. Same goes for the girls; everyone helps the cause in one way or another."

"Everyone helps?" Joshua asked.

"Of course," she replied calmly.

Joshua took a bite of a roll, reveling at the rich taste. "If you don't mind me asking, why are you here? I've never met someone . . . like you."

The old Armellan woman grinned. She reached out to pat his shoulder, and her fingers left a soft dusting of flour on his tunic. "I'll tell you something, young man: I've been here baking bread and keeping my own little coop of chickens around back for five years. This is where I belong."

"Really?" Joshua asked a little too strongly, then remembered his manners and took another bite of his roll to hide his shock.

"Ever since Irvin and Will set up the first four walls with their own hands, people up north have heard of them, and the townes have turned their color slowly but surely. The Bradford has cut off trade to rebel townes, but this place filters supplies up to the north through the Lady Marselle. The women run and organize the supplies while the men train for the fight when Will says to march south."

Joshua tried his best to take in the information casually, but he was in awe of how things worked here. "I don't mean to be rude asking so many questions," Joshua added hastily in the silence. "I'd ask Will myself, but I'm sure he's busy."

She brushed a stray rope of hair from her face and tucked it behind her ear. "It's no bother. You know, five years ago, a kind man came up to me and promised me that future generations of my people and yours would be able to be free, to live where we wanted, and to speak without being executed for our beliefs. And I knew he was telling me the truth."

"And that 'kind' man was Will, yes?" Joshua asked quietly.

She nodded, her unseeing watery eyes full of nostalgia. "You and your mother made the right choice coming here. Bring her by, if she's any good with kneading dough. My hands aren't what they were."

Joshua smiled weakly, then stuffed the rest of the roll in his mouth. "I will," he replied. "What was your name?"

"Mistress Merheene," the woman replied.

Once he finished chewing, the old woman grabbed Joshua's arm and hauled him down close, so her chapped lips hovered next to his ear. "Know this, though," she whispered, her voice a fragile whisper. "All those here are truly rebels, and are ready to die in this place no matter what the outcome. I'm sure you feel the same way."

Joshua swallowed and broke free as a chill ran down his spine. He straightened before the hot bread in his arms tumbled to the wet ground.

"For Rhethos, right?" he stated proudly, and her face broke into that wrinkled mass of a smile once more. She echoed the phrase before retreating into the cook house.

CHAPTER TWENTY-NINE

RACING THE WALKWAYS

Joshua tilted his head to look up at the sky. It was full of swollen gray clouds, but the rain was light and a mild temperature thanks to the rising sun. He squinted to the south, where the tips of countless trees stretched, and found the top of the tower they had entered under last night.

I think I can make it all the way back over there before these rolls get soaked. Maybe if I run . . .

But a quick glance at the surrounding path told him he couldn't manage more than a brisk walk with the large groups of rebels moving about. Joshua glanced over at the nearest set of planks and noticed that those who needed to move amongst the buildings more quickly used the overhead system for efficient travel.

If those kids can sprint up those wet boards and swing on those ropes between the gaps, I can do it, too. Even if I've never done anything more dangerous than pull a cart down a road full of puddles.

Joshua stuffed the remaining rolls in his pockets, crushing the hard surface of his compass against the side of his leg. That gave Joshua a sudden idea. He glanced at the two Blessing Runes on his forearm and remembered that the one closer to his elbow translated as Protection. Wrapping his hand around the sealed wound, he twisted and squeezed. He grimaced as fresh blood dripped down his arm.

Let's see if this works, he thought. *Goddess, please help me get this food over there before it gets wet. Oh, and I don't want to fall and break my neck, either.*

Joshua wasn't entirely sure if that counted as a prayer, but Will had said he had to put out an intention with his blood offering to make the magic work. A frightening yet increasingly familiar surge of heat passed over his body, warmer than the morning sun, and Joshua smiled; it was a comforting sensation, like Bertram's hot soup on a freezing winter day.

After making sure the buttons on his pockets were done properly, Joshua gave his arms a good shake to let go of some of his nerves. Instead of thinking about what his mother would say, or worrying about a troop of guardsmen around the corner, or even contemplating how hard a fall would be, Joshua *ran*.

His first step on the thick wood was steady with the platform rooted deep in the earth, and his feet carried him easily up five, ten, fifteen feet. To his left was the top level of the stilted buildings, to his right the sheer drop back to the ground with only a few weaves of rope to protect him. A fine mist of rain coated his face, and as Joshua blinked away the drops gathering on his eyelashes, his boots slipped.

He faltered, letting out a cry of distress, and grabbed at the nearest rope that hung from the corner of a roof. Joshua let his weight swing with it, and his right foot danced over the ledge before setting back on the slick wood. He laughed uneasily as he gained speed again. Someone from the ground shouted up at him.

As the walkway took a sharp bend with the structures below it, a rough gap emerged before him. A large portion of the walkway had broken off, leaving a splintered space. His breath issuing in a fluffy cloud, Joshua glanced around, but found no rope to grab to hoist himself across. He tried to slow his speed and he realized his boots only slid faster forward.

Jump, Josh. He suddenly heard Will's voice in his head, deep and calm. *You'll be fine. Jump across.*

Joshua held his breath, narrowed his eyes, and leapt. For one terrifying heartbeat, the entirety of Rhethos hung still, suspended on the air beneath his feet, then he landed hard on the opposite side. He let out a shout of triumph, pumping his fist in the air. Joshua took hold of the nearest rope and yanked himself to a halt to catch his breath.

"Watch out behind ya!" shouted a voice. Joshua glanced over his shoulder to see the six boys from earlier barreling down the rain-soaked planks at top speed. The one in front launched over the gap Joshua had just cleared. Josh flattened himself against the tin wall behind him and it creaked in protest.

"Hey, Josh wants to *race*!" declared the next boy as he jumped, shoulder-length blond hair damp with rain and sweat. He slapped Joshua's shoulder as he skidded by, desperate to catch the child in the lead.

Three more boys flew past Joshua before he could even think of something to say. The only one left was the smallest of the group. His face was contorted with concentration, his footing unsure as he slipped toward the jagged gap in the walkway.

Joshua somehow knew before the little boy's feet left the surface that he wouldn't make it. Without thinking, he wrapped his hand around the closest rope and reached forward. The boy extended his arm as he began to fall, and barely entwined his fingers with Josh's. The rope pulled taut and bit into his knuckles.

"Thank—" he started, then the wood beneath Joshua's feet let out a moist shriek and splintered into pieces. The little boy screamed as they fell in a tangle of ropes and wood. Joshua could see nothing but a blur of harsh color. He kept hold of the rope in his left hand and yanked the boy tight to his chest with the other. A rough piece of canvas partially broke their fall, and then all the air was torn from his body.

Mud soaked into his aching back while an array of debris covered his chest. The boy coughed and wiggled free, peeling tangles of rope from his hair. As Joshua rose, shaking his head to clear it, he saw that many rebels had gathered to stare disapprovingly at the children and the bigger mess they'd made.

The rest of the group of children surrounded them. The sandy-haired boy extended a hand to help Joshua up, and he took it happily. His entire body was shaking and he couldn't seem to catch his breath, but when the half dozen boys grinned admiringly at him, Joshua beamed back. He didn't know if his newfound magic had kept him safe, but right now he didn't think it mattered.

"By the Goddess, Auden, you *know* you can't make that jump! Now you destroyed the run!" The leader admonished the child, ruffling his hair and giving him a gentle shove.

"Josh made it worse before I did," Auden said, then lifted his chin stubbornly.

"When Father finds out, he'll make us help rebuild it," muttered the first boy.

Joshua rubbed the back of his head self-consciously. The boys roared at his alarmed expression when his palm came back with a coat of mud and fresh blood.

"I'm glad you're all right, Auden," Josh said. "That was the craziest thing I've ever . . ."

He faded off when the smiles suddenly drained from the children's faces. Joshua turned and found himself face to face with the biggest man he'd ever seen.

Blocking out the morning sun along with most of the sky itself, he was covered in a full set of mismatched iron armor. Though most of the plates were rusted and dented from use, it added to the bulk of his broad chest and the huge expanse of his shoulders. His square jaw was covered in an unkempt nest of a beard, his head topped with short, curly brown hair. A huge ax hung through the belt on his hip, gleaming dangerously as the man put a hand on it. He glared at the children, who scrambled to hide behind Joshua.

"Master Orton?" Joshua questioned, wiping his sweaty, bloodied hands on the sides of his trousers. This made him remember the rolls, and he cringed when he felt the condition of the food.

The towering man grunted and ran his hand along his ax, adjusting its weight. Before Joshua could draw another breath, Auden let out a squeak of fright behind him and the six boys scattered.

"I'm Joshua McKinlee," Joshua continued, and stood up straight. He tried not to stare at the perfectly honed curve of the Master's blade, even though the weapon seemed to demand his full attention. Instead, he strained his already sore neck up to look the man in the eye. "I'm new here, and I was told to find you if I wanted to help."

Orton raised a pair of thick, dark eyebrows, then barked out one single laugh. When he turned to go, Joshua placed himself in his path and dug in his pocket. He pulled out two lopsided rolls that weren't quite mush.

"I need a weapon so I can learn to fight. And I'm not scared of you like those little kids are, so at least talk to me."

His heart hammered against his ribs, and he stopped himself from stepping backward when Orton leaned down and took the rolls from his hands. Joshua stood silently while the Master shoved what was left of them in his mouth.

"How old are you?" Orton inquired.

"Sixteen," Joshua said. He took out the third roll intended for his mother and offered it to the Master. "I know I'm small for my age, but—"

"So go get in line and learn with all the other new arrivals," Orton interrupted. His voice was uninterested, but Joshua saw his black eyes drift to the Blessing Rune on his arm. "Last I checked, believers of the Blood Goddess don't take up arms."

Joshua covered the bleeding rune self-consciously. "I'm not a . . ." he started weakly, then stood his ground. "I'm Goddess Touched."

Orton paused after he took the last of the food Joshua offered. Joshua jumped when Orton clapped an iron-gloved hand on his shoulder. His boots sunk into the mud another few inches at the mere weight of the man's hand. "You're not lying to me, are you?"

Joshua shook his head, very aware of how hard it was to keep himself steady instead of shaking.

"Interesting," Orton rumbled quietly. Joshua thought he saw intrigue gleam across the man's dark gaze. "You think you can handle using a blade and those pagan marks?"

"Yes, Master," Joshua said immediately.

"You know Will can't even do that?"

"I know I'm not going to quit until someone around here helps me."

Orton grunted at that, then straightened. "You see that tower?" He pointed and Joshua saw that his run along the raised platforms had actually taken him almost to his destination: the nearest of the two watchtowers was close enough that he could see the uneven rungs of the ladder that led up to its top. Joshua nodded.

"With Rowlann out on an errand, I'm up there most of the time making sure nothing bearing Rhethosian colors gets close. The latch on the trap door is always unlocked."

Without explaining further, Orton turned and walked toward the tower. Joshua couldn't help but smile at the tall man's back. He had a feeling Orton would never chop off a child's head for no good reason, but decided to keep this theory to himself lest he ruin the man's obviously terrifying reputation.

"Bring more of those rolls with you, if you have the guts," Orton added over his shoulder.

After patting his pocket to make sure his compass still sat in its spot, Joshua spotted the group of boys hiding just around the corner before they gasped and disappeared from view in a flurry of giggles. Suddenly Auden's small face reappeared around the bend, and he waved both his little arms at Joshua to come join him.

CHAPTER THIRTY

MAGIC FROM LEGENDS

The storm ripped through the ocean, tearing apart the waters that lay between Armelle and Rhethos. Devaki, however, refused to let fear command her actions. She ignored the tremor in her legs when she finally found her feet and steadied herself, despite the intense swaying of the ship.

Making her way over to the ladder that rose out of the ship's hull was easier, she found, if she just kept her eyes focused on the sea-sprayed rungs. When she popped her head above deck, lightning snapped through the air and lit *The Blue Memory* for an instant.

Rhethosian men stumbled across the slick planks, motioning for those in the rigging to work the sails down faster. The creak of groaning wood echoed dangerously, and Devaki instinctively ducked. The white froth of waves roiled from the dark horizon to the top of the ship's railings, and from her position at the top of the hull's ladder, Devaki could not see any sign of land.

The entire ship rolled toward the churning water, almost succumbing to one of the largest waves that beat against the starboard side. Devaki felt her head smack against the soaked decking. Several screams tore through the air, and she barely made out the forms of three Rhethosian men careening overboard. The rest of the sailors hardly seemed to notice as they clung to whatever they could find as the ship barely righted itself.

Devaki felt her jaw drop in horror as she watched men throw buckets of water back into the ocean, not one moment after those same waves had taken the lives of their friends.

Her gaze went to the helm, where she could make out two men arguing as rain lashed across their pale faces. One clung desperately to the wheel while the other had several halyards wrapped around his arm to hold him steady.

Pitch black clouds glared down, and, despite being soaked to the bone on the outside, Devaki's throat was suddenly dry.

She clambered up onto the deck, and several men rushing past her stumbled backward to do a double-take. They looked stunned and confused to suddenly find an Armellan girl in the middle of the bucking ship. Beyond that, though, Devaki saw fear reigning in all of their eyes; did none of them think they would survive this devastating storm?

Devaki took a deep breath and ignored the stares. She knew there was only one thing she could do to try to help them reach the shore, and it all came down to faith.

She made her way to the bow of the ship, holding her arms out at awkward angles to keep her balance. The air felt pregnant with thunder, bursting full of sound and overwhelming water. The smell of salt and fear clung to her nose as Devaki stopped between the main mast and the captain's wheel. She let the next swell take her to her knees.

"Mother," she began, and could barely hear her own voice over the wind and rain. "I'm here following my Fate's String. Show me what you want me to do. Tell me how I can—"

"What are *you* doing here?"

The question slapped across Devaki harder than any gust from the storm. A harsh hand gripped her shoulder and hauled her to her feet. Glancing up, she cringed when she saw Rowlann glaring at her.

"I told you why I need to—"

"And I told you it isn't safe!" Rowlann snapped. "Get below deck and stay put."

"No!" Devaki retorted, and shrunk back when fresh thunder slammed down against the ship. The sound reverberated in her rib cage. Men were shouting and cursing at one another from every direction, their voices strained. Rowlann tried to pull her away from the front of the ship, but Devaki held her ground.

She used her free hand to break open the healing Guidance Rune on her opposite shoulder. The symbol flared to life on her skin and emitted red sparks of magic into the rainy air between her and the Rhethosian man. Rowlann started backward in surprise but kept his hold on her.

The shimmer of ethereal, maroon light hung around them for a moment, then dissipated slowly. Devaki felt a dry heat blossom inside her head, on the edge of her subconscious. That familiar feeling, the comfort of a mother she had never met, told her what she needed to do.

"This is a test from her!" Devaki shouted, and this time she didn't stumble when the ship's deck thrashed beneath her soaked feet. "Let me help us get to shore!"

Devaki wrenched herself free of Rowlann's grip and knelt on the ship's deck. She knotted her fingers together, faced her palms outward, and pressed the backs of her hands to her forehead. The rain bore down on her head and the wind tore at her silk tunic with fresh gusto. Around her swirled the worried voices of men, the creaking of wood, and the lashing of wet ropes. Beyond that, the ocean screamed and thrust in mighty heaves toward the black horizon.

She focused on nothing but her breath, and that Touch of the Goddess that dwelled inside her head and heart. Without looking, she unwound her fingers and turned her rune ring's sharp edge toward a Protection Rune on the inside of her wrist. Devaki grimaced as she twisted the skin to force out a heavy flow of blood. A bit of warmth ran down in rivulets to her elbow, then dripped onto the tops of her thighs.

"Get up, Princess!" Rowlann's voice was rough and steeped in worry. She felt his hand on top of her shoulder. "You cannot change the tide nor the weather!"

Devaki knew this was true but couldn't stop herself from trying. Every time she'd prayed in her life, the Goddess had always answered in some way or another. *She didn't ask me to leave just to let me drown. So what does She want from me now?*

When Devaki opened her eyes, she found that she couldn't breathe. Everything in front of her was glowing in sharp, deep red lines. The surface of the deck was woven with the color of blood, and beyond the bow, the waves shimmered with maroon vibrancy. These lines moved and pulsed in every direction, and when Devaki traced them with her gaze, she followed them back to the blood coming from the cut on her arm.

She stared up at Rowlann, wide-eyed, but the Rhethosian man showed no sign of seeing what she could see. This was something she'd never experienced before when making an offering to Cybarys. The sparkling lines around her felt warm when they touched her body, and fresh shimmers of magic danced off her skin with the spatter of the rain. She noticed one of the strings that met her body stretched out toward Rowlann and met with his chest. *Our Strings of Fate . . .*

"Do you dare follow? Give more blood."

When the powerful, feminine voice echoed in her head, Devaki winced. There was something different about that tone, one that held a darker echo than the one she was used to. The Protection Rune on her arm suddenly flared up in pain, and Devaki cried out. The blood leaking from her cut amplified and flowed more rapidly. She bit back tears as a wave of fatigue rolled over her, as if the Goddess was sapping energy directly from the cut on her body.

Was this the price she had to pay to see such miraculous things? A macabre sense of wonder gripped her, dulling her awareness that she only had so much blood to give.

"Please," Devaki prayed aloud, and her teeth chattered against each other. "If it's your will to bring this ship to shore, Mother, tell me what to do."

Several men ran up to Rowlann, and Devaki could see their soaked boots out of the corner of her vision. Their arrival disturbed many of the magic lines along the ship's deck, and Devaki watched with fascination as the strings wavered, blurred, and changed direction to continue on their paths.

"The winds are letting up slightly," one sailor reported to Rowlann. "But we can't risk full sails."

"What's she doing here?" the other man demanded.

Rowlann began to bark a reply, but Devaki did not hear him. The rune on her arm magically split further, and she hunched forward in pain. Her fingertips began to shake and lose their feeling. She clenched her eyes shut and tried to focus.

Tell me what to do, Cybarys. Guide us. Help us.

"Blood, child. Give blood, and receive your blessing."

The voice that trailed through her head spoke with sharp, ancient power. Devaki shuddered.

"But are you prepared for this task that waits on the shores of Rhethos? The prices for the challenges before you are steep, the rewards more than you can imagine. Can you stand true, Devaki?"

Yes. I can.

A great agony sprang to life on the skin above her heart. Devaki glanced down at the spot and felt her mouth fall open when she saw a freshly cut rune appear. An invisible edge carved a new symbol onto her chest, and a burst of gold sparks and blood flew into the air. The force of the cut took the breath from her lungs and she collapsed on her hands and knees.

Rowlann knelt next to her immediately, his hands on either of her shoulders. He was speaking, but Devaki couldn't hear him. It took all her energy to hold herself up; all she could do was breathe through the hot agony in her chest and watch the blood pooling on the deck. *Gold magic remnants? Impossible.*

When she had the strength to look up again, her eyes went to the horizon. Ahead of the ship's bow, beyond the stretch of the immediate rolling waves, she saw gray sky. Not thick, black clouds, but clear, gray sky. The water underneath it was a calm, steady roll. A small set of red, glowing lines sailed forward across the water to that clear patch of weather.

Her vision wavered violently and Devaki felt darkness clawing at the edge of her resolve. Never in her life had she felt so exhausted, so drained of . . . everything. Vaguely, Devaki wondered if she was dying, and if that were true, what was she dying for?

She asked me if I was strong enough to do what needs to be done. And I am. I can do this.

Devaki put a hand to the mysterious rune bleeding over her heart, and, despite the dizziness that pressed on her from every side, she opened the wound further. Glancing over at Rowlann, she saw his gaze focused on the bit of gray sky ahead.

"Help me!" Devaki demanded, and reached out one, shaking, bloody hand toward him. "If you want to reach your kingdom in one piece, use that blade of yours for something good. Make an offering to your Mother."

Rowlann stared blankly at her for a moment, then back at the sky ahead. Many of the men aboard *The Blue Memory* were pointing in that direction, and renewed vigor filled their voices when they shouted at one another. Devaki felt her right arm begin to go numb and fall out from underneath her. Rowlann grabbed her elbow and kept her upright.

Devaki swallowed and clenched her jaw shut to keep it from trembling. Blood continued to flow over her fingers that pressed against her chest. Before her eyes, she watched as the waves around the ship's hull crashed heavily but didn't rise up again. The pound of rain lightened to a steady, weaker pour.

"Your Goddess doesn't want my foreign blood," Rowlann said. "I can't help you."

"Yes, you can!" Devaki insisted. "Anyone can bleed for her. Or do you want us all to drown?"

Rowlann muttered something nastily under his breath. With one practiced motion, he removed one of his iron gauntlets. He reached for the hilt of the sword on his hip. When Rowlann drew several inches of iron, he placed his wrist against the edge, and pulled downward. Fresh blood hit the wet planks, and Devaki knew Rowlann could see the bright flash of magic when his eyes widened. He twisted his forearm and a puddle of blood started to form between them.

Her vision began to solidify again, and Devaki looked up to see the men raising the mainsail once more. The Rhethosian at the helm let out a relieved cry as he steered the ship more steadily toward the calm waters. Devaki began to feel the tips of her fingers. Her breath steadied, and she let out a huge sigh.

"How did you do that?" Rowlann demanded. From his spot kneeling next to her on the deck, he turned her shoulder so she was facing him. "Tell me how in Cybarys' name you did that!"

"I . . ." Devaki began, and found she didn't know what to say. "I don't . . ."

Rowlann's features hardened, and Devaki realized she saw both awe and fear in his pale blue eyes. When she glanced beyond him, she saw many of the sailors stepping as far away from her as possible.

"You just asked your Goddess to clear a storm for you." The words left Rowlann's lips in an uneasy whisper. "That kind of magic only happens in legends, Princess."

"I'm not a princess," Devaki replied. She had no idea why this clarification was what she chose to say. "Not anymore."

Rowlann shook his head, obviously at a loss for words. He helped her stand with him, and his fearful gaze drifted to the bloodied spot above her heart. "What does that symbol mean? It just . . .blurs when I look at it."

Devaki took her eyes away from the beautiful weather before them and glanced downward. She felt a fresh wave of confusion claw at her when she studied the rune that had been magically carved into her skin. Maybe it was the blood loss, but she couldn't make out its exact shape either.

"I don't know," she stuttered.

"You don't—?"

"I've never seen it before!" Incredulously, she had to blink away tears when she looked up at the Rhethosian man. "I . . . I didn't even cut it. It just appeared, and then the clouds went away."

Rowlann stared at her harshly, then ran a hand over his beard and sighed. "I don't know what to do with you."

"You'll take me to Will, won't you?" Devaki asked. "You have no choice now."

"Trust me, Miss Tarran, I'm very aware of that."

CHAPTER THIRTY-ONE

A PLACE TO HEAL

For the first time in her life, Angelyn woke after the sun had risen. She pressed back tangled masses of her hair and tried to remember where she was before the time hit her like a blow to the center of her chest.

Before she could think on it too long, she pushed herself out of bed, laced on her boots, and marched out of the central building without speaking to a soul. She feared if she interacted too much with this new place, its people and their ideals would bleed into her thoughts unwillingly.

The mid-morning chill washed over her and reinforced her determination with its icy touch. *I have to find Joshua. That conversation with Irvin last night went all wrong. I've got to explain to Josh that this place and his new magic don't equal freedom. We're still in danger.*

"Watch your step, Miss!"

A young woman grabbed Angelyn's shoulder and made her stumble backward. Hundreds of men were making their way through the center of the dirt road where Angelyn had just been standing.

They marched in semi-organized groups toward the back of the rebel camp, their hurried footsteps matched with eager, shining faces. Angelyn stared, not used to seeing happy soldiers, let alone the pleased bystanders who waved proudly and stepped out of their way with glowing grins.

"Thank you," Angelyn said, and she turned to the young woman at her side. The girl was accompanied by a boy who had his arm around her shoulder. The couple looked to be about ten years older than Joshua, and their clothing was poor and worn, as if they spent most days outdoors, working hard, long hours.

"You look a little lost," the young woman said, brushing a piece of short, brown hair out of her eyes. "Did you need help with anything?"

"I just arrived last night," Angelyn replied, taken aback by the conversation. People didn't just talk to one another on the streets in Kaylyn; gossip started, homes were searched, and folk went missing if anything besides a simple business transaction took place during designated hours. Angelyn tried to shake her predetermined fears from her mind, but it was more difficult than she thought.

"We could tell," the boy next to her said, and Angelyn noticed that he wore a sword on his hip and a violet sash at his waist.

"You'll miss the end of the line, Drestarr," the girl said, and she pulled her companion down to kiss his cheek. "Better catch up. I'll see you soon!"

He broke out of the girl's embrace and joined the last of the men making their way through the street. Angelyn watched curiously with the rest of the bystanders, whom she noticed consisted of a few dozen women and many older men. As soon as the pathway was clear, every rebel proceeded in their own direction with haste.

"Where is everyone going?" Angelyn asked the girl, who still stood next to her, despite everyone else's movement.

"Well, we've all got a job," the young woman said. "And now that Master Will is back, we're hoping to hear news that we don't have to wait much longer."

"Wait for what?"

The girl gave her a curious look, and her smile shifted from a friendly grin to a tolerant smirk. "To fight for Rhethos, of course. Come with me." She took Angelyn's hand. "I'll show you your new home."

Angelyn was about to protest that she was only out here to find her son, but the girl pulled her down a side path carved in the space between two wooden huts. Angelyn realized something: there was no way she could find Joshua amongst all these people and these winding walkways.

And even if I found him, I couldn't force him to stay at my side, or threaten him with the fear of the law. He doesn't think he has to listen to me anymore.

"This part of the camp is where most of the clothing is made," the girl was saying, pointing at the buildings they were passing. Angelyn could hear the turning of many spinning wheels and smell the strong aroma of cloth dye.

"See back there, where all the smoke is rising?" the young woman continued, barely pausing to breathe. "Those are the bakeries and store houses, as

"Lydia hasn't spoken since we got here, Master," the older Luwenn girl explained. Her voice was small, but Angelyn could still make it out now that all movement had ceased around her. "I don't know why."

"She will," Will reassured her. A shadow of pity flickered across his features. "Lydia," he added, and tipped a finger under the brim of his hat so it sat back farther on the girl's head. "You can keep this."

Angelyn smiled when Will rose and dusted himself off. He made his way over to where they stood, and his eyebrows narrowed for a moment when he caught Angelyn's eye. She thought she saw a bit of surprise in his gaze, but any hint of it disappeared when he stopped before them.

"Lady Marselle, I really can't have you curtsey like that every time I see you," Will laughed. "You're not in Clancy anymore."

"I may have rejected my Lord and my southern family, but certainly not my manners," Marselle returned smoothly. "I think I can speak for everyone here when I say we are glad you've returned."

"Circumstances could be better, I won't lie, but yes," Will said with a sigh. His eyes drifted to Angelyn again, and Angelyn could tell Marselle was fully aware of where his attention kept going.

"I'm so sorry, Master. Miss McKinlee was not assigned here," she explained. "I was going to confirm with either yourself or someone else about where she should go."

"Angelyn can choose for herself," Will said matter-of-factly.

Angelyn tried not to smile when she saw how Belka's mouth fell open. She met Will's eyes, something she'd never had a problem with before, but found she had a hard time figuring out how she was supposed to feel toward him right now. He had saved her son's life last night, but at the cost of many others, including Gabriel. Part of her wanted to flee this place once she found Joshua, but intrigue and that smile on Will's face kept her still.

"Indeed," Marselle agreed reluctantly. "Well then, might you look at these numbers for me?" She handed the ration book over to Will, who finally glanced away from Angelyn to go over the pages. "I fear with the new arrivals and the difficulty bringing in the wagons, we'll have to split the amount of food given to the northern side of camp."

Will shook his head. "No. Keep that amount the same, and give less to those in the southeastern edge. We'll survive."

"If you insist," Marselle said, and she made notes across the current numbers. She muttered something under her breath, and Will laughed.

"Speak up, my Lady! I know it's been difficult lately, but things will change soon. I promise."

"Yes, of course," Marselle agreed, though Angelyn had a feeling the women felt anything but content.

"I can help, you know," Belka said suddenly, finally finding the courage to speak to Marselle directly. "I was hoping, now that the wagons have returned, I might be able to drive during the next route."

"Oh, Belka, darling, you're best suited for sorting, not sabotage," Marselle said with a wave of her hand. "You know that. Now," she added, and turned to look back at the women who'd brought her the ration book. "Take this, and hand it off to Miss Clara inside. You go rest, and tell the other drivers to do the same. Leave half a dozen to finish unloading. Belka, go with her and be of some use."

Both Belka and the other girl nodded, hurrying away. Angelyn noticed the look of clear disappointment on Belka's face, but she did not think it appropriate to mention anything. Her attention drifted back to Will, and she found his gaze already on her.

"Have you seen Joshua?" Angelyn asked immediately.

"No. But I imagine he's out having the best day of his life."

"Because he can go anywhere he wants, or because he's not with me?"

"Both, I assume, but his loss is my gain."

Lady Marselle cleared her throat pointedly and made her way back toward the wagons, where she began to snap orders at the women not already engaged in tasks.

Will's expression sobered once she left. "That woman is indispensable, but almost impossible to have a private conversation around."

"It seems information is part of her trade, so I don't blame her," Angelyn replied. "Do you really think I belong in a place like this?"

"Like I said, you get to make that decision." Will paused, then lowered his voice even though no one stood near them. "I have to admit, I'm surprised to see you out amongst all these rebels."

"And I was surprised to see you with the Luwenn girls again."

Angelyn said the retort before realizing its implications. Will froze, then stared at her for a moment. "You knew their family?"

"No, I . . . saw you, the night their home was set aflame," she explained, wondering why admitting the fact made her feel guilty. "You and your men rescued them."

Will watched her silently, his expression unsure. An uneven laugh escaped his lips, as if he'd been caught in some embarrassing act instead of a heroic one.

"So you were spying on me, Miss McKinlee?"

"I was on my property that night, outside my home," she said defensively. "Those girls . . . they were so afraid. They had just lost their family, and you helped them."

Will shrugged, as if to say, "of course." "Whatever you decide to do here," he said, "know that it will be a step toward something good."

"Right," Angelyn said, still unsure about everything around her, including the man next to her.

"Joshua will be safe here," Will said seriously. "If I see him, I'll tell him to be at the main hall before sundown, so you'll know where to find him."

"Thank you."

Will nodded and placed a hand briefly on her shoulder. "I'm glad you're here." He said the words and turned to leave before Angelyn had a chance to react, let alone reply.

CHAPTER THIRTY-TWO

TEMPTING TACTICS

When Will reached Irvin's rooms to meet with his Masters later that day, he found the man himself just outside the door. Irvin gave Will a wry smile.

"Where have you been this morning?"

Will stopped in front of his friend, who kept the doorway blocked with his thin body. "Helping the new arrivals find their homes and jobs to do," he replied. In truth, he'd wanted to see Angelyn and make sure she was doing well, but he wasn't about to tell Irvin that.

"We've got people to do that for you," Irvin snorted. "Everyone's here, and they're getting a bit anxious." He jerked his head at the closed door behind him. "Despite all my charm, I think all they want is you."

Will smiled and gripped his friend on the shoulder. He entered Irvin's private rooms, and found Irvin was right. All the Masters from different rebel townes sat or stood along the stretch of table that spanned most of the room, equal expressions of dour anticipation on their faces. The only woman present was Lady Marselle, speaking quietly to the man next to her about the newest goods her smugglers had brought in.

They looked up when Will entered, Irvin right behind him, and all conversation ceased. "Thank you for waiting," Will said. "I've been looking forward to this."

Irvin motioned to the empty seat at the head of the table with a dramatic bow that only elicited a few smirks. Those present were used to the previous Towne Master's theatrical attitude. Marselle sighed and Orton rolled his eyes. The towering bulk of the man took up two spots at the middle of the table, his shoulders twice as broad as the chairs he sat in.

"Now," Will said, "let's begin. Though things didn't go as planned in Kaylyn, I learned something important while I was there."

He took a cup offered to him by the man on his left, but indicated the pitcher that contained water instead of wine or ale. "Sarrett has a tight hold on that seaside towne," he began after taking a small drink. "And his behavior is increasingly erratic. Like I mentioned briefly last night, it's time to make a move with the army we've gathered. Lorington is the next towne in our path."

Several of the Masters around the table glanced sideways at one another. "Why now?" spoke up one man, his dark eyes meeting Will's. "A lot of us are pleased with the lack of bloodshed so far."

"Because we've met our first real opposition, and we cannot remain hidden up here much longer with how our numbers are growing," Will explained. "And because we can all agree Rowlann's company isn't the only group of fighters that are getting restless."

"Speaking of Rowlann," Orton began. "We need his leadership for the vanguard. Do you really want to advance south without him? He and his force of men are a key piece of the ranks we've built."

"I expect a letter from him any day now," Will said, nodding to acknowledge this fact. "Once I receive it, we will move south and meet with him as we travel toward Lorington." Orton nodded satisfactorily, as did several others at this information. "Now," Will continued, settling back into his chair and taking his time to look each person in the eye. "Tell me your news. What has changed during my time in Kaylyn?"

"The people in the brother townes of Patten and Morely are getting nervous," spoke up one man near the end of the table. Will remembered his name was Greggor, a former tanner from Morely. His thin shoulders slumped, as if the stress of speaking wore physically on his person. "Patrols of guardsmen from Kaylyn have been moving further up the trade routes than they ever have before."

"Don't worry about Sarrett attacking our rebel townes," Irvin sighed, waving his hand distractedly. Will could see Greggor wasn't convinced.

"The Rhethosian lieutenant doesn't have a lot of men," Will said. "The majority of their army is still in the south with its captain. Sarrett doesn't have the numbers to do more than patrol close to the brother townes."

Greggor shifted uneasily in his seat. "Is that what you'd like me to say to them?"

Will nodded. "Your concerns reflect the worries of our people, which I understand. Greggor, tell Patten and Morely's leaders that we will be moving forward and taking the eye of the Rhethosian military away from their homes."

"So, you do mean to take Lorington by force?" Marselle questioned. Will glanced down toward her from his end of the table and nodded. "I used to visit close friends in that towne. They have enough supplies behind their thick walls to hold out for at least a month."

"But the majority of those in Lorington aren't fighters," Orton spoke up. "We could frighten them into opening their gates. Based on our last reports, the Rhethosian army is months south of us."

Marselle's fingers tightened on the stem of her wine glass, and Will watched the knuckles on her delicate fingers go bright white. "It's quite interesting, Master Orton, how you think you have the best intelligence when my girls hear the best secrets on supply runs."

"Do you still have connections within Lorington?" Will asked, and Irvin leaned forward from his slouched position to pay better attention. "Could you learn something that could get us inside their walls without us laying siege?"

Marselle flashed a sweet smile at Will, then bit her lower lip. "You know, for you, I'd make anything happen," she said pleasantly. "But I haven't had a lot of success with that towne."

"That's what I was expecting," Orton cut in, shaking his head. When Will looked around the table, he saw conflicting emotions in many sets of eyes. "And I agree with Will that time is of the essence; with the lieutenant close by and Kaylyn well aware of our threat, we need to move."

"There are risks of an offensive advance that need to be—" Greggor began.

"Oh, enough about the risks," Irvin cut in. He stepped behind Will's chair and draped an arm over its back. "We've all risked enough, for years, and in silence. We knew this day would come, and we're ready."

"You'll need to march thousands down the coastal road, close to Kaylyn Towne, in between Sarrett's patrols," Marselle pointed out. "My women have to avoid those guardsmen when they smuggle supplies up here on a regular basis."

"Then tell us the schedule, and we'll skirt them or cut them down," Orton snapped.

"Sarrett changes when they patrol all the time," Marselle said. "It gets worse every day."

"Then what good are you?" Orton grumbled. "Wasting time, money, resources, and for what? So you can charm our leader every time you see him?"

"I feed these people!" Marselle replied, her voice rising dangerously. "I dare *you,* of all people, Orton, to go a day without what I bring here and into every northern towne above us!"

"Enough, please," Will cut in, and slammed a hand softly on the table for emphasis. He gave a weak smile to everyone present, even though he could feel Irvin fidgeting behind his chair. "I understand the need to make a stand against those who would have us in chains." He glanced at Orton and several others when he said this. "And I also see the value of peacefully turning townes to our cause. That is why I've only used this tactic so far. But the army needs to move."

"So we'll advance south to Lorington?" Irvin prompted, probing for a straight answer that Will knew everyone wanted.

Will grimaced. "Yes. We will break them, by treaty or force, before the Rhethosian Captain and his army can march up here. Lorington is an old, powerful place. All of their resources and defenses, which we desperately need, will be ours."

Marselle sighed and took a generous drink from her wine glass. "So be it. I will learn what I can before you leave."

"Thank you," Will said, giving her an appreciative smile. He looked to Orton, who was scowling heavily. "We will move by night, and in between the military patrols as best as we can," Will continued. "And I will speak to each rebel along the way to ensure their resolve. We will outlast them," Will said, emphasizing the words by standing from his chair. "I will be at the head of the column, at the gates of Lorington right at my men's sides."

"You don't need to be the tip of the spear, Will," Irvin said, raising both of his palms as if to demonstrate the obviousness of his point. "We've talked about this before. The Bradford won't lead *his* men. He won't lift a finger until we pound on his gilded front door. Sarrett and his captain will give us problems while the bastard himself sleeps soundly."

"Despite your endearing concerns, brother, I will make my point with my own two hands," Will replied. Everyone present glanced between Irvin and Will. "I'm standing for these new ideals for all of Rhethos to see, especially the Rhethosian military leaders."

"But placing yourself in front of thousands of trained southern killers isn't the right choice," Irvin insisted, rolling his eyes. "It's no way to impress your new—"

"I've made my choice," Will interrupted strongly. "Now you need to make your peace with that."

Irvin sighed and lowered his head. "Of course. But I will face Caldrell," Irvin snarled, and Will peered at his friend with concern. "It's been too long since the Insane Captain showed me his face."

"You'll lead the charge in that fight, Irvin, I promise," Will said. "And I will keep my distance."

Irvin, his face quite sober for once, nodded silently.

"Is everyone content with what we've decided?" Will asked. "We have been united so far in this endeavor, and I do not want that to change now. I am here to be a voice for the people, to make a stand that will not fail no matter what opposition we face."

"We're with you," Marselle said, raising her glass and smiling thinly. Orton and the rest nodded silently.

"Let us know when you receive word from Rowlann," Greggor said. "In the meantime, we'll keep our heads down and continue preparations."

Murmurs of agreement drifted around the room, and Will thanked everyone for their time and support. He noticed that Irvin and Orton lingered as the rest slowly filtered from the room, taking some of the fire's warmth with them.

"Good talk, Will," Irvin said, and he thumped Will on the back before taking a seat on the edge of the table. "As well-spoken and inspiring as always. Though I was kind of hoping for a fist fight for a moment there, especially with Marselle involved . . . She's feisty in all the right ways, don't you think?"

Will sat back in his chair, then tilted his head up to look at Irvin. "Something tells me you're not still here to sing my praises."

"Unfortunately not," Irvin sighed. "Orton and I had an interesting little chat earlier about something . . . well, someone you know."

"Joshua McKinlee," Orton began, and Will raised his eyebrows at the large man, who hadn't moved from his original seat. "The boy sought me out this morning, asking to be trained. Irvin here tells me that Joshua is Touched by the Blood Goddess, and that his mother hid it from the Rhethosian military for sixteen years."

"Impressive, no?" Irvin said, nodding emphatically at Orton, who in turn merely shrugged.

"What is your point?" Will asked.

"We don't have a lot of young, eager fighters," Orton explained. "Most boys his age are already sent into the Rhethosian military, and we don't have much hope of turning them to the rebel cause."

"So you agreed when he asked for your help?" Will prompted.

"No, I brushed him off," Orton replied, a hint of amusement in his deep voice. "To see how badly he really wants this." Irvin chuckled in approval, but his glee faded away at Orton's next sentence: "Master Will, I don't trust anyone related to magic."

"You trust me," Will said shortly, then continued when Orton began to speak. "But I understand what you're saying. The boy doesn't know much about his gift, and I won't be here to help him learn. If he's eager to fight, teach him to wield a blade. Forget about his Touch."

"I mentioned Josh's magic to Orton for a reason, you know," Irvin interjected.

"Most of the people here hate the Armellan faith and its magic," Will pointed out strongly. "So I can't see why you're suddenly interested in Josh's abilities."

Irvin shrugged as if this were inconsequential. "I see an opportunity here," he continued. "Will, you can't use the Touch because you don't follow the bitch's rules. But Josh is young, innocent; don't you think there's some way to use his magic for our cause?"

Will frowned, clenching his jaw. This was something he hadn't thought about, mostly because he imagined Angelyn's potential rage at the idea of her son being used even further for the rebellion's benefit.

"He's never shed blood unless it's been for her," Will murmured, almost unaware he'd stated the fact aloud.

"Exactly!" Irvin agreed. "Have Orton train with him, but let's not actually give the boy an opportunity to use a sword against an enemy. Teach him those runes, Will! 'Protection', 'Strength', 'Guidance.' Those alone are some things we really need."

Orton nodded solemnly. "I don't like it, but it could give us a huge advantage at Lorington."

Will almost shook his head, then stopped himself; it was hard to not see the opportunity Irvin and Orton were pointing out. *And Orton is right,* he thought. *Josh is eager and would most likely do anything I asked to help the cause. But for some reason, using the boy doesn't seem right. How am I better than The Bradford if I take a malleable teenage mind and mold it toward my own ends?*

"You do realize that it's pacifistic magic, brother. It's not meant to be used offensively," Will said aloud, prepared for the frustrated expression on Irvin's face. "But . . . in the meantime, Orton, teach Josh the basics of swordplay."

"Right," Orton agreed and stood to leave. Will felt Irvin staring at him intensely and waited until Orton was gone to give his attention back to his oldest friend.

"A month ago you wouldn't have blinked at the idea of using this kind of tool," Irvin said, his tone low. "What's changed?"

"He's not a tool; he's a boy," Will replied. "He deserves to learn right and wrong for himself before we force our agendas on him."

"Will, honestly—!"

"Leave it be, please," Will cut in. "We have plenty of other work to do."

CHAPTER THIRTY-THREE

SPARKS OF THE GODDESS' WISDOM

Mayra-

Please read this letter. It would be best for you to take the children on the fastest ship to Eastson as a precaution against the rebels. You have not responded for several months, which means you will more than likely burn this, but I must put my instructions to paper.

Little Nira will like all the flowers on the Eastson islands. You care for her and Keppler so well, and I cannot express my gratitude. If only you could wait for me to make a name for myself, things could be different.

Kaylyn is a miserable place, full of folk with thick skin but malleable minds. Each day my hold on them increases, but it's never enough. The captain demands more from his safe location in the south, not realizing that northern Rhethos functions very differently.

I fear it will be a long time before this war is finished. I will see you and the little ones as soon as possible.

Pray to the Lord for his blessing and my success.

Thinking of you often,

Jon

"Lieutenant Sarrett, you've received another correspondence from Captain Caldrell."

Sarrett peered up from his desk to glare at Barton, who stood in the doorway. He took his time setting down his quill, turning completely in his chair, stretching, and standing.

The rooms Sarrett had claimed as his own were high up in Kaylyn's government building. They had belonged to the previous Towne Master, whom the lieutenant wasted no time getting rid of. Heavy, double oak doors were left open most hours to allow more light into the large room, showing off its many priceless golden fixtures.

Sarrett glanced out the far window at the dark evening sky, then down at the ornate desk, its surface littered with many pieces of parchment. One note on top with the rough navy stamp of Rhethos' sigil kept catching his eye.

"Set it down," the lieutenant said, and Barton took a step into the room to carefully set the freshly sealed letter on a brass drink cart by the door. Bottles and glasses sparkled in bright candlelight, and Sarrett eyed the blue ribbon on the note with apprehension. The words from his captain that he'd received a day ago had been hard enough to swallow, and the arrival of a postscript did not please him.

"Is there anything else, Lieutenant?" Barton asked.

Sarrett sighed and tried not to yawn. Sleep kept evading him, even though he'd had the eldest Harling girl not a few hours ago and the people of Kaylyn had not made any troublesome stirrings for a full day.

No sleep, more demands from Caldrell, and no news of Mayra's whereabouts. And seeing Lily . . .

Sarrett swore in frustration under his breath. "Yes, there is something." He spun on the heel of his polished boot. "Explain to me why your men are completely incompetent."

Barton's face paled, and he shifted his weight to grip his hands behind his back. "We've been searching the remains of The Hamond Inn, and my guardsmen venture as close to the forest as they dare—"

"Venture?" Sarrett cut in, crossing his arms over his chest, pressing his thick uniform jacket against his stomach. "Ventures *require* daring. There will be nothing in the ash pit that's left of that building. *You* will personally set out at first light, in front of every other guardsman in towne, and march into those trees. The Lord help you if you do not come back with that rebel leader's head."

"The woods are cursed," the guardsman insisted, staring with wide eyes. "All of my men who followed the rebels the night of the fire haven't returned. We've tried to find a way through, but the feeling I get inside that place is . . ." He faded off, clearly troubled.

"If you are too frightened for the simple task, I will go myself," Sarrett snapped, though he glanced at the desk again and the note upon it. Captain

Caldrell's regular correspondence were turning into short demands littered with threats that left no room for excuses.

"Lieutenant, we would be honored to have you command the search," the guardsman spoke dutifully, bowing at the waist. "But I don't think you should go. The towne would be overrun with rebels without you here to defend it."

Sarrett rolled his eyes. "Go. Be sure someone informs me when my spies from the northern townes return. I swear to you," he added, not satisfied with the expression on Barton's face, "the day is coming when those rebels will meet more flames than they've ever seen."

Barton nodded, bowed again, and left, shutting the heavy double doors behind him. Running a hand over his face, Sarrett stepped to the drink cart and broke the seal on the new letter.

I am preparing to march north, and I expect to find the rebellion's leader in a cell by the time I reach Kaylyn. Lord Bradford has the knowledge to break the rebel leader once he is captured. If you cannot complete this simple task, you will not find your family in the same shape you left them.

"Family" was a loose word for what the lieutenant had managed over the years, and he doubted either of his children or their mother missed him. That did not stop him from trying to do the right thing.

Now, however, he was having trouble determining what was "right." The incorporeal illusion he'd seen in the Hamond's remains shone like a dying candle in the back of his mind. Ever since the day little Lily had died, he'd been on this path for some recognition, some purpose that would make his pain worth the effort.

Sarrett shook his head, then read the last line of his captain's note. That one sentence spoke all he needed to hear:

"Fail and Rhethos will gain a new lieutenant while you lose a head."

Sarrett undressed and tried to sleep, but every time he closed his eyes Lily's visage would swim before him in a cloud of deathly blue smoke. He tried to blink her away, to fight back the guilt, but her young, sunken face only laughed mercilessly. His head pounded, and when he thought of drinking wine to try and find rest, his stomach protested violently. He barely suppressed the overwhelming urge to vomit on the thick red carpet.

He rose from his bed and stood naked in the moon's glow. Running a hand through his rumpled hair, he forced the curls behind his ears flat against his neck. Beyond the thick windowpane, Kaylyn was dark, and he felt the urge for fire: he needed light to see by, light to root out the traitors, light to burn everything black till neither Rhethosian Blue nor rebel violet remained.

Enough, Sarrett thought. *Rumors of curses from ancient Goddesses do not frighten me. I have our Lord's fire and my own strength.*

Sarrett slipped on a pair of loose trousers, boots, and a heavy cloak before lighting a lantern and throwing open the doors to his quarters. Two guardsmen stood to either side, and one snorted awake with surprise when the lieutenant thrust the light into his face.

"Sir?" the man questioned, clearing his throat. "Where are you—?"

"Stay put," Sarrett snapped. "Obviously I don't need protection from you."

Before either guardsman could reply, he stalked down the hall, descended Towne Centre's spiraling staircase, and marched onto Kaylyn's freezing cobbled roads. He shuddered and drew his cloak tighter with his free hand. Why, in his sudden decision to leave his warm rooms, had he not put on a shirt?

Because I don't need more than the Lord's justice to guide my way and keep me warm. Besides, I can't go back and let those guardsmen see me again. It'll ruin the expression of idiotic surprise on their faces.

He barely glanced at the Hamond's remains when he strode past and down the grassy embankment of Kaylyn Field that led to the Goddess' Woods. His lantern sputtered when he faltered on the uneven ground, but Sarrett kept his eyes forward, at the trees that seemed to house deeper blackness than the open night ever could. Since arriving in Kaylyn, he hadn't set a foot under a single branch.

"Cybarys, the Blood Goddess," he murmured aloud, upset by the shaken sound of his voice despite the mocking tone he hoped to project. "Everyone in the world once knelt before you and bled for your benefit. Let's see how well your devoted followers' wounds protect you from pure heat. Your trees won't hide Will and his people for long."

The lieutenant paused at the outskirts of the woods, and his eyes fell on jumbled tracks in the dark mud. The fleeing rebels had left frenzied footprints behind, though they faded the deeper into the woods they went. Sarrett held his lantern aloft once more, took a deep breath, and stepped into the forest's embrace.

Immediately, he felt a deeper chill settle on his exposed chest, but he refused to shrink his shoulders to let his cloak fall closer to his body. His heart raced against his ribs, and his eyes strained to adjust to his surroundings. Everything was covered in leaves and moss and mushrooms. A damp smell seemed to worm its way through his pores. His free hand strayed to the spot above his heart, where, when he wore his uniform jacket, his flask of Sahma wine would have sat.

Light the damn place up, he thought and gripped his lantern. *Finish this and become the hero who stopped the rebellion without the Insane Captain's help. Do it, for your family name. For Lily.*

"Stop, brother," said a feminine voice. "This is a sacred place."

Sarrett jumped when he felt a hand touch his shoulder from behind. He could feel its weight, the definition of each finger against the heavy fabric of his cloak, but when he turned, he was staring through an image of his dead little sister. He pressed a fist to his mouth and moaned against it in frustration.

"Enough of this!" he roared at her specter. "I haven't drunk a drop of Harling's damned brew all night! Why are you here?" He backed away from the shimmering outline of the young, fair Rhethosian girl.

Lily smiled and glanced shyly down at herself as if she were embarrassed by her appearance. Her hair still hung in dripping wet curtains on either side of her thin face, and her delicate fingers clutched at the hem of her silky dress. When she shook her hands, droplets of water flew from her clothing in shining arcs and dissipated like smoke when they reached Sarrett's face. He flinched away.

Previously, the hallucinations only haunted him after he'd had a little too much wine, but here she stood. She was so solid, so clearly standing in front of him that he could not blink her away no matter how hard he tried.

It's this damned forest, Sarrett thought, glancing worriedly at the branches that wove like a thick blanket above him. *The Goddess is taunting my guilty conscience with her magic.*

Sarrett looked away from Lily and focused on the tree closest to him. When he swallowed, he found his throat was very dry, and that feeling of unease rose higher in his stomach. The local folk raved about how "cursed" this place was. Cybarys dwelled in the trees, and the faithless who did not give her prayers or blood could not dwell here long.

The lieutenant swore under his breath and removed the glass lid from his lantern. He thrust his hand forward till the open flame licked at the ancient bark of an oak. Suddenly his entire arm trembled, and cramps began to eat away at his gut. He felt Lily grip his shoulder again and spun violently, words of denial on his lips. Then her fingers were at his throat, stronger than he ever remembered in life.

Sarrett sputtered and tore at the blue hand that clenched his windpipe, but he touched nothing more than his own skin. He staggered back against the tree, unable to breathe. Though he could see through her sodden limbs, when she peered up at him from beneath her pale eyebrows, her gaze was solid and merciless.

"Liar. Murderer. Abuser."

Her words were like death bells in his head, overwhelming any other thought or sound. He felt his hand release the lantern, and, amidst a cloud of blood-red sparks, its flame went out. His nails dug into his own throat as he tried to find air, and the world darkened at the edges.

"Li—lily . . . p-please . . ." he tried, but he found that he could not move.

A new voice spoke, and even though it issued from the lips of his drowned baby sister, Sarrett knew it wasn't Lily talking. The voice belonged to an older woman, and its tone was full of ancient power, command, and prophecy.

"My poor, doomed child. How far you have sunk, and how far into the depths you may still go. Heed this prophecy, Jonathan Sarrett: your meaning in Rhethos flows from a red fount's edge."

Fresh night air filled his lungs, and Sarrett found himself collapsed against the base of the tree, gasping for his life. His vision sharpened to normal and he clutched handfuls of earth.

What is wrong with me? He was completely alone amongst the foggy oaks. Why hadn't he been able to breathe? Why couldn't he set fire to this damned place? Why was he so terrified?

"Damn it," he swore and stood on shaky knees.

It took him longer than he thought it would to find his way back to Kaylyn Field and even longer to gain his composure before heading into towne. He didn't care that his guardsmen saw him heading out for a walk alone in the middle of the night, but he did care how he looked when he returned.

He wasn't sure what had happened inside those trees, despite the lingering sense of unease that pulsed against his body like a dozen fresh bruises. Two phrases boomed over and over in his mind till sunrise:

"Fail and Rhethos will gain a new lieutenant while you lose a head."

"Your meaning in Rhethos flows from a red fount's edge."

CHAPTER THIRTY-FOUR

HIGHLY ANTICIPATED NEWS

Will must have read Rowlann's note a hundred times since the messenger on horseback had delivered it directly into his hands an hour before dawn. It was time. He walked along the line of carts that crowded the narrow road in front of the common hall, laden with gear, weapons, and food. Leaning over the edge of the nearest wagon, he inspected its meager contents.

Piled along the bottom were old, thin furs and straw for some cushion, then a layer of shields, all a faded blue stained proudly with violet dye. The blades that followed were worn and looked old despite their freshly sharpened edges.

Will placed Rowlann's note in his pocket and made his way under the watchtower, waving a hand up at Orton who kept an eye on him as he stepped over the shallow trench and under the cover of the Goddess' Woods. A comforting coolness swept over his body, caressing him like a light breeze from head to toe.

He felt a tingle itch the top of his hand, as if an ethereal fingernail was tracing the rune scar carved into his skin many years ago. He shook himself, and, after his eyes adjusted to the dim light of the forest, focused on where he was headed.

Will turned west, watching his steps through the undergrowth until he reached a tree with a wide arc of runes carved across its bark. Their shapes curved and swung in a haphazard pattern that ran from several feet above Will's head down to the forest floor. Countless prayers, cut centuries ago, held in the tree's body in hopes of reaching the Mother above.

He scoffed at the idea, then unsheathed a small knife from his sword belt.

Pride and stubbornness held him back for several breaths, then Will set aside his doubts and cut a small line on the outside of his hand, just below his little finger. He pressed the wound against the tree's bark. Even though he'd lost his Touch and he refused to pray for forgiveness to potentially gain it back, he needed to give something to make sure the Goddess heard him.

Blood trailed down in small rivulets into the prayer inscription's indentations, slowly at first, then the tree seemed to pull at the liquid and absorb it greedily. Will licked dry lips as desert heat emanated from the old oak, then he closed his eyes.

"Cybarys," he murmured, and the warmth increased in response, as if a fire was stoked inches from his body. "You know I refuse to be part of your schemes. All I ask is for you to keep Devaki safe until I can meet her one day. That's all I want; no magic, no blessings, no Lines of Destiny or Strings of Fate attached."

His hand stung against the oak's rough surface, but Will made a fist and forced more blood onto the tree. Against his eyelids, images began to form: the blur of a beautiful, womanly hand against his, pressing his fingers against her swollen belly covered in silks.

The shape of the ocean, lined by a dock that stretched along the hot sand. A man stood on the wet boards, a bloody knife clenched in his fist. Will flinched and cursed under his breath.

That's all I ever get from her: pain from the past and riddles of the future. Useless.

"Master Will?"

He turned sharply to see Joshua standing not far from him. Will whipped his hand off the ancient oak, barely noticing a shower of dark red sparks that shone through the air.

"What are you doing?" Joshua asked.

"I could ask you the same thing. It's not safe out here."

"I was up in the tower with Orton," Joshua explained. His eyes kept going to the tree behind Will, staring at the runes and drying blood. "We saw you go out here alone."

Will raised his eyebrows, mentally shaking himself to rid his mind of the images still clinging to his subconscious. "Well, you're not missing much. This place might give you peace of mind, but nothing more."

Joshua opened his mouth, then shut it as if rethinking what he would say. "I've been watching with Orton for a while, and I saw that rider meet you early this morning. Will you leave today?"

Will smiled. He liked Joshua, and the boy seemed to be adapting perfectly to his new home. His clothes were dirty, the same ones he'd worn the night his home burned, but Joshua held himself more confidently than any of the times Will had seen him in the Hamond. He never seemed to lack the courage to say what was on his mind.

"Yes."

"Let me come with you," Joshua insisted. "I know I'm not trained, but I have to do something. Isn't there some way I can help, with my magic?"

Will thought of his conversation with Irvin and Orton for only a moment; he had stayed up hours the previous evening coming to a decision between what could be easy and what was right. "You can't help, at least not yet," Will said. "I think you still have a lot to learn, about this kingdom and what it's fighting for. Orton is remaining behind to defend the camp, and I've told him to teach you whatever you want to know."

Joshua's face fell, but, surprisingly, he nodded as if he understood. "You were praying, weren't you?" Joshua asked.

Will unconsciously gripped the top of his hand where the skin began to itch once more. He nodded wordlessly.

"Can you teach me?"

"I don't have the time, Josh. But I wrote these down," Will said, and he reached into his pocket for something he'd written the previous night. He handed the paper to Joshua, who looked over the runes on it with wide eyes. "These are the three Blessing Runes that the Goddess Touched can cut to create magic. You've already got two of them on your arm, but I need you to know this: just because you ask doesn't mean you'll receive. And if you receive, it may not be how you expected."

"I . . . don't understand," Joshua said, looking up from the note.

"That's because it's very complicated," Will said. "And I don't have time to tell you more. Even if I did, I'm very bitter about the subject, if you couldn't tell." He gave Joshua a wry smile. "But you're connected to the Goddess; you can ask her for help, if this is a path you really want to walk down."

This stunned Joshua into silence, and Will gave him a sympathetic pat on his shoulder. "It's your future and you get to decide. But if you ask me, I think you may want to stick with swords and daggers instead of runes and prayer."

"Thank you," Joshua said, and Will could see all the ideas and questions warring in the boy's brown eyes.

Before Joshua could say anything else, Will glanced up at the watchtower, its peak visible just above the tree line. "You've been away for a bit now. Orton's not a man you should keep waiting."

Joshua tucked Will's note deep in his pocket. "Right. Please just be careful out there," he said, his eyes suddenly misty. He turned to go before Will could reply.

Will crossed his arms over his chest as an odd sense of calm brushed over him. *I've told myself for years that I need to get results, no matter the cost. But that may have been the first time I've done something for the sake of another person instead of myself in . . . I don't know how long.*

He felt heat grow along the edges of the cut on his hand, radiating out from the drying blood. A memory of cutting his first rune pushed itself almost forcibly to the forefront of his mind, and for a moment Will was twelve years old, standing barefoot on the black marble tiles of the temple in Valsara.

That connection to a higher, loving force had comforted him. But his older brother, all that was left of his family, had cursed the Armellan faith and its people.

They loved me because of my gift. They shunned Mitchell because he wasn't Goddess Touched, and he carried father's Rhethosian hatred. What kind of deity lets two brothers—

"Here you are! What's gotten into you?"

Will stumbled, unaware he was gripping his oldest rune-shaped scar on his left forearm tight enough to make his hands shake. Irvin stood behind him, a look of concern on his long face.

"I'm fine," Will mumbled, clearing his throat.

"Uh huh," Irvin said slowly. "The men have done everything you said; we're almost ready to go. Saw the McKinlee boy just now, climbing the watchtower ladder to see his new best friend. We're not taking him with us, are we?"

"No," Will confirmed calmly.

"Fine," Irvin sighed, shaking his head. "I won't argue it with you, then."

"Thank you," Will said.

"But," Irvin pressed on, crossing his arms over his violet tunic and grinning, "you've at least gotten his mother out of your system, yes? Was there a good reason you were up all night?"

"I wrote her a letter," Will muttered, and he pulled a folded piece of parchment from his coat's inside pocket.

Irvin scoffed and rolled his eyes, though he smiled. "A letter?" he repeated. "And I suppose you want me to give it to her so you don't have to see her face before you go? The lady truly deserves better."

Will laughed and handed the sealed note to his friend. "It's better this way."

Irvin muttered something under his breath as he took the paper from Will's hand. He ran his thumb along the thick parchment and glanced back at Will when he reached the uneven bump folded inside.

"What's in here?" he asked, shaking Will's note back and forth.

"Just get it to her," Will repeated, and for once Irvin acquiesced silently.

As Irvin left, Will tried to focus his thoughts on what mattered: his people. They had been waiting so long for this day, to make a stand, to fight for what they believed in. There were many reasons why he didn't want to speak to Angelyn, and the fact that she distracted him and confused his heart about what mattered most were the important ones.

CHAPTER THIRTY-FIVE

A REBEL'S AMETHYST

"**M**iss McKinlee? Someone's here to see you."

Angelyn set down the sack of grain in her arms and glanced up at Belka. She stood in the doorway to one of the rebel's storage buildings, silhouetted by the morning sun. They had been organizing items from the latest group of returning wagons since dawn, and Angelyn found that she was already sweating through her dress in the musty confines of the high-ceiling shack.

"Who is it?" she asked, wiping a smudge of dust off her brow. Part of her hoped it was Joshua, but something told her that her son was still happy on his own. She hadn't seen him or spoken to him in days.

Belka crossed her arms over her chest and threw a nervous look back over her shoulder. "It's, um . . ."

"Move on over, darling. I've got places to be, you know."

Angelyn recognized Irvin's voice before he shouldered Belka over and stepped into the shadows of the storeroom. The first thing she noticed was that he wore leather armor over his usual violet tunic, with a black traveling cloak clasped at his throat. He gave her a grin when he saw where she stood, in the center of the storehouse amongst the freshly organized crates that had long since been in disarray.

"Look at you, Miss McKinlee!" he said appreciatively, stepping around several towers of empty barrels to make his way to where she stood. "Glad to see you're making yourself useful."

Angelyn leaned against the supply shelf she stood next to, then stood straight again when it creaked dangerously. It was hard to remember that this place wasn't built with sturdy materials. "Shouldn't you be on the road by now?" she asked, trying to sound disinterested.

"Soon enough, yes . . ." Irvin began, then faded off. He glanced back at Belka and stared plainly at the girl until she got the hint and scurried out into the sunlit courtyard.

"I have one last errand to run," Irvin finished, and he reached into the pocket of his tunic to draw out a sealed letter. He held it out to her.

Angelyn frowned down at his fingers. Former Towne Master Irvin Colwell, famous Loyal family of the north, was delivering messages while the rebel army marched south? She thought of making several rude comments about the situation, but the serious expression on Irvin's face made her stop.

She took the letter from Irvin silently, though her curiosity rose when she felt the uneven weight inside the parchment.

"He doesn't have the balls to talk to you before leaving," Irvin muttered, lowering his voice. "That's a big deal for him, in case you weren't aware."

Angelyn didn't know what to say, her grip tightening.

"This place used to be a mess, though!" Irvin sighed, and spun back toward the door. Belka stood just beyond the entrance, waiting. Irvin gave her a stern look when he walked by. "You're lucky to have this good Kaylyn woman here to help you get this shit in line."

Irvin left before Angelyn could think of any way to respond, and Belka rushed back over to her.

"He's an intimidating man, isn't he?" she stuttered.

"Don't be scared of him," Angelyn replied, her eyes on the paper in her hands. "It's not worth the trouble."

"So who's it from?" Belka asked, leaning close.

Angelyn shooed her away as kindly as she could, unaware she was holding her breath. In the shadowed silence of the rebel storeroom, she broke the violet seal and carefully unfolded the letter.

Something heavy spilled onto her fingers, and Angelyn glanced down at a silver chain pooled in soft loops. At the center was a roughly cut amethyst, about the size of her thumb. The gem tried its best to shine in the lack of light, a powerful yet miniscule bit of violet that stood out against the pale skin of her palm.

Why? she thought. *Why would he give me this?* Her gaze drifted to the neat script on the paper, and she read as slowly as her heart would allow.

Miss McKinlee-

I cannot remember the last time I wrote a letter to anyone who didn't concern my cause. I meant to speak with you about the things written here before I departed, but I found myself incapable of doing so for many reasons.

One of the first questions you asked me was why I am doing this. The short answer is because of my mother. She influenced me and gave me a purpose, so if I die attempting to make her dream of freedom a reality, my life will not have been wasted. Enclosed is something of hers I think you should have.

Despite your protests, I hope you will recognize there is at least some nobility in what I do. When you understand, when you find your courage, wear my color for me. Word will be sent regarding my advance on Lorington no matter what the outcome may be, so be strong, Angelyn: you are a warrior of your own.

-Caulin Tarran

Angelyn lingered on those last two words, churning them over and over in her mind with increasing confusion. For some reason she recalled that conversation she'd had with Will in her inn's cellar, and how she'd told him she could never trust him if he didn't tell her his real name. *Caulin*, she thought numbly. *But why "Tarran"? Why would he sign with the Armellan royal family's name? I don't understand.*

A harsh shout echoed to her from outside, making Angelyn jump. Almost everyone had cleared out of this area of the camp, and the Lady Marselle did not let her girls raise their voices like that.

Angelyn shoved Will's letter and the necklace into the pocket of her apron. Her eyes slowly adjusted to the sunlit courtyard outside the storeroom, searching for the former southern Rhethosian Lady that everyone here admired and feared. Angelyn found in the few days she had known the woman that both her presence and her voice were not forces to be taken lightly.

The Lady Marselle stood at the peak of the arc of wagons ranged around the courtyard, wearing an emerald green dress and a scowl on her face. About two dozen of the usual women moved back and forth with armloads of bulging sacks, but Angelyn noticed everyone begin to slow and look at Marselle, who wasn't alone.

Across from the tall redhead was a large man with broad shoulders and a blade at his hip. A shiver ran down Angelyn's spine when she observed the tension between the two; she had seen it many times before at The Hamond, always right before two customers started to throw punches.

"What's going on?" Angelyn asked Belka, edging over to stand next to the girl at the edge of the courtyard.

"That's Nilus," Belka whispered, indicating the man glaring at Marselle. "He's been butting heads with Marselle for months now. I think they have a bit of a . . . history."

Angelyn glanced uncertainly between the two but couldn't see much past the initial hatred. "Why isn't he moving out with the rest of the men?"

"He's got 'bad joints,' so he gets to stay behind," Belka muttered, shaking her head. "Though I've seen him bully too many people to really believe that."

"You're selling us short, Marselle!" Nilus roared, breaking the sharp silence. "Every time your bitches come back, you send more food to the northern townes compared to what stays here."

Belka clapped one hand over her mouth and gripped Angelyn's forearm with the other. Angelyn could understand the girl's shock; no one spoke to a southern Rhethosian Lady like that, turned rebel or not.

Marselle placed one hand casually on her hip, just below the corseted curve of her waistline. She smiled coolly at Nilus, who looked ready to shout in her face once more. "Now, really," Marselle began, "I expect better of you. Let me do my job and you can go be an ass somewhere else."

Nilus's face bloomed red dangerously, and he stepped forward to eliminate the bit of space between him and Marselle. "Screw your job!" he growled, and Angelyn could practically feel the women around the courtyard bristle at this exclamation. "This is about the men going to bleed for Rhethos right now! Give us those wagons and let the northern townes wait till your next run. You know I'm right."

"I know how much those townes need to stay alive," Marselle replied, her smile now degrading into dark rage. "You're not marching south anyway, you coward, so stay out of my business!" She leaned forward, uplifted her chin, and spat into Nilus's face.

Angelyn moved just as Nilus's hands clamped onto Marselle's shoulders. Without a thought, Angelyn strode to the center of the courtyard on numb legs. She pushed Marselle out of Nilus's grip and placed herself in front of the man with her head held high.

"Who are you?" Nilus demanded viciously.

Angelyn refused to back down when Marselle tried to step in front of her. In that moment, standing her ground before this furious stranger, Angelyn remembered countless moments like this decades in her own past when she would attempt to face off against Travok. In the end she had always backed down, apologized for speaking, and flinched before her husband's blows came.

Now, however, she refused to accept that was the only option, even though Marselle was obviously more than capable of taking care of herself.

"Miss McKinlee, step aside," Marselle murmured.

"That, unfortunately, isn't going to happen," Angelyn said, keeping her eyes on Nilus's. "Now, it's Nilus, is it? It seems like you're upset, from all the shouting you're doing that's disrupting the work we're all trying to get done. But I think you're yelling at the wrong person."

Nilus glared down at her, his dark brows knitting in ugly clumps against his beady eyes. He opened his mouth to protest, but Angelyn held up a hand.

"Of course, the Lady Marselle is in charge of this operation," Angelyn continued, sure to keep her voice calm, "one that is, as I'm sure you know, vital to the rebel cause and its people. But I am the one that decides where rations are distributed."

"You?" Nilus scoffed.

Angelyn felt Marselle stiffen behind her at this lie, but she refused to look back at the woman. Instead, Angelyn nodded and crossed her arms over her chest, body language she knew every man understood no matter how thick they were.

"Yes, me," Angelyn clarified, hoping Marselle would not object further. "And I'd like you to know that there are plenty of ways to fight for the cause, but not all of them involve a blade. I'm sure, with most of the fighters well on their way south now, you still have an important place in this camp."

"Don't patronize me, little Miss," Nilus growled, his hands closing into fresh fists. "I dunno why Will puts women in charge of anything around here."

"Because we're always happy to help people like you," Angelyn insisted kindly, and she gestured back at the arc of wagons full of supplies ready to be driven up to Kerrance and beyond. "Here," she said. "Take what you feel you deserve."

"That is—" Marselle began heatedly, and Angelyn spun around to give the woman a meaningful look. The Rhethosian Lady fell silent, though her eyes glinted almost as sharply at the morning sun on her jeweled necklace.

Nilus eyed Marselle as well, as if he expected another outburst against this offering, but only silence held. The man grumbled under his breath, and let his fists fall. "I like your new woman," he said, smirking at Marselle. "She knows what's good for her."

Angelyn put a hand on Marselle's arm as Nilus strode past, favoring his right leg. She realized she was touching real Rhethosian satin when she glanced down at the emerald material flowing over Marselle's pale skin. *I don't think I've ever touched satin before,* Angelyn thought, wondering why her mind chose to notice this detail just now.

"I don't know how you ran things at your inn, McKinlee," Marselle hissed, breaking Angelyn's train of thought by wrenching her arm away. "But you've just made a mistake."

"I'm sorry, but I don't think so," Angelyn returned quietly. "This was never about the amount of food or where the supplies were going."

Marselle glanced scornfully at Nilus, who was digging through a well-organized wagon and stuffing a crate full of whatever he chose. He swung an arm at any of the women who tried to stop him, but Angelyn couldn't see any of his former aggression in his body language.

"I knew plenty of men like him in Kaylyn," Angelyn continued. "They don't know how to respect a woman with any bit of power, so they choose to try and beat her down so the world still makes sense to them. If you give them a bit of what they want, and show them you're still strong, they will respect you."

"That man doesn't know the meaning of respect," Marselle sniffed, brushing a curl of her red hair from her neck.

"Not yet, but I promise it will work," Angelyn insisted. "And he'll only take what he can carry."

Marselle sighed as Nilus limped away with a crate towered high enough to obscure his vision. She straightened her shoulders and ordered the other women to continue working in a brisk voice. Angelyn started when she felt Marselle's hand on her shoulder.

"I didn't appreciate how you gave yourself a job title all of sudden," she began, and Angelyn felt her heart sink.

"I didn't really mean anything by—"

"Hush," Marselle cut in, and a small smile formed at the corners of her mouth. "I understand your value, McKinlee, and I have appreciated it over the last few days. The storehouse has never been cleaner and my women have all told me it's because of your organization skills."

"Well, thank you," Angelyn said, surprised she wasn't being yelled at.

"But you can do much better than ration distribution," Marselle continued as if she hadn't spoken. "A lot of my team is leaving today to march south with Will, but I'm headed out tonight to ride north toward an important supply drop. I think you should drive the wagon for us."

Angelyn felt her jaw start to drop and clamped it shut. She didn't know what to say. What she had done so far at the rebel camp was familiar and safe; she could organize supplies and efficiently direct people all day long without thinking twice. But smuggling? Traveling in the dark, along roads patrolled by guardsmen?

"My son is here . . ." Angelyn began uncertainly.

"I know," Marselle said, nodding kindly. "You're not obligated, though you should know most of these women have family of some kind, either here or up north, some even in the south who consider them dead."

Angelyn nodded; she had heard such stories among the women at the storeroom and had even met some of their children. She hadn't seen or spoken to Joshua in over two days now, and she kept trying to tell herself it wasn't all because of his newfound magic.

I had no choice the night he was born, she thought, shifting uncomfortably in the center of the courtyard. She was suddenly aware of how much empty space was around her. *They would have killed him. But he resents me for lying, and now that he can do as he wishes, he doesn't want a thing to do with me.*

"I'm not asking you to die for Rhethos, you know," Marselle spoke up, squeezing Angelyn's shoulder. "You've been through a lot. So have we. But here's something most Rhethosian women don't understand until they've met Will; your happiness is just as important as your child's."

Angelyn smiled, then started when she felt sudden tears form in her eyes. This was actually her choice, her freedom to take a step in the direction she thought was right. The words from Will's letter rang in her head, then worked their way down to her heart.

"I'll go," Angelyn said. "But only if Belka does as well."

Marselle glanced back at the girl uncertainly, then shrugged. "If you insist. Now, you've got plenty to do, so go give that poor girl a hand before she hurts herself."

Angelyn nodded and turned back toward the storehouse, but Marselle asked a question that made her stop.

"So who was it?"

Angelyn glanced over her shoulder and frowned. "What?"

"Your father?" Marselle prompted, only a touch of sympathy in her gaze. "Or your husband, maybe? Who hurt you like Nilus was about to hurt me?"

Angelyn grimaced. "It doesn't matter now."

"You're damned right it doesn't," Marselle agreed. "Be ready at midnight."

CHAPTER THIRTY-SIX

NEW FLAMES AND NEW TRAITORS

Lieutenant Sarrett smiled satisfactorily at the flames that consumed the building. The pain-ridden shrieks from behind the locked doors had died not long ago, and now, just after dawn, the show of flames and bursting wood was finally beginning to calm his paranoid nerves.

His attention kept drifting to the piece of parchment in his gloved hands. It blew stiffly against the wind, and with each gust, Sarrett came closer to letting the damn thing go. Finally, Mayra had written him back for the first time in months. Her words, instead of warming his chilled, paranoid heart, felt like an undeserved noose.

He recognized the slant of her handwriting, even thought he could smell her perfume if he pressed the letter to his nose. Her response was so unexpected, he could hardly believe the words even though he'd practically memorized them.

Jon,

Rumors have reached us that things are going poorly for you. Your inability to put down these rebels without your superior's assistance is disappointing. Now you must trust in our Lord and his most faithful servant, Captain Caldrell, to set things right.

I used to care for you and your dreams, but you must know this is the last time I will write to you.

Your children don't know who you are. They are bastards of a family without Loyal status. Your advice to leave Rhethos is sound, but I will not sail east. It is best if the children and I were lost to you for good.

Now you can truly focus on what you've always wanted: military prowess. Do not look for us. May our dear Lord bless you and protect you, Jon, for I have had enough.

-Mayra

Sarrett cursed under his breath and let the letter fly from his hand. How dare she take his family from him? Mayra, as well as the image of his dead sister that seemed to constantly dwell over his shoulder, could not see how hard he was working for a greater cause. It perplexed him and tore at him, but when he touched the flask in the breast pocket of his uniform jacket, he didn't bother taking it out; he knew it was already empty.

The musk of fresh smoke and the salt of the sea mixed when Sarrett inhaled deeply, savoring the aroma. This soothing setting wouldn't last long since rain clouds were rolling in from the morning's uneasy ocean. The house in flames was an old one, the only Loyals in Kaylyn. They'd taken the bit of liberty he had given them and thrown it away.

What a pity.

Those who lived along the same block stood warily on the street, surrounding the conflagration with wide eyes. Even if they weren't aware of their underground trade and secret to success, the Harlings were known by everyone.

"Was it just the sisters in there, Lieutenant?" Master Barton asked, standing at Sarrett's right, hand on the hilt of his sword.

"Yes, Lyara and . . . whatever the other one's name was," Sarrett replied distractedly. "I suppose some of their kitchen staff may not have left before the doors were bolted, though."

"You're a monster, Lieutenant!" screamed a man to his right. "You're a traitor and a murderer!"

Sarrett let the man's accusations flow over him patiently and turned to face the guardsmen holding Master Harling back by both his arms. The man was still in his nightgown, thinning gray hair strewn over the bald spots on his skull. He fought against those holding him back from his burning home, though the attempt was comical. The fat bastard didn't have an ounce of muscle on his body.

"Monster and liar", Sarrett mused, trying to ignore the chill that brushed against his bones. *Two of the words that Lily keeps throwing at me in the middle of the night just before I find sleep.*

"Master Harling, you needn't make a fool of yourself like this," the lieutenant said quietly. "You've been spared the same fate as your lovely daughters because you are still of use to me. If I hadn't found such damning rebel evidence on their persons, I would have kept your entire family close."

"They did nothing! You just grew bored with them!" Harling bawled, his bulbous face shining bright red. "And I've done everything you asked since you arrived! Nothing you do is for Rhethos, you lying son of a—"

Sarrett punched the tradesman between the eyes, feeling the satisfying crunch of cartilage under his knuckles. Blood sprayed from Harling's broken nose, several spots staining the sleeve of the lieutenant's spotless uniform.

When the now-childless man sunk to his knees at Sarrett's feet sobbing noisily, the lieutenant felt a small stab of pity for him. *Last night when I was with the girls they did have a violet color about them,* he thought, turning on his heel to put the flaming home to his back and cast his gaze on the gray sea. *I know what I saw: they wore violet, they spoke of violet, they* glowed *bright violet, I swear it! Now they are ashes, just black, black ashes . . .*

Sarrett realized his hands were shaking and hurriedly clenched them into fists before turning back to his guardsmen and Harling, who lay crumpled on the cobblestones.

"You may insult me in front of my men if you wish," Sarrett began, "but do *not* stain our kingdom's name with your lies." Sarrett glanced down at the blood on his uniform and clenched his hands into tighter fists. "Speaking of stains, you're going to pay for ruining this jacket."

Harling blubbered obscenities through his dripping red hands, but Sarrett had had enough. He wanted the man to watch his home and his family burn, but the structure was consumed in flames now and a light rain had begun to fall.

He waved a dismissive hand at Barton, who ordered his men to get Harling up off the ground. They hauled the old merchant away to Towne Centre, and the dungeons that lay beneath.

"Lieutenant, there's a rider approaching on the main road," Barton spoke up.

"Drawn to the flames of these unfortunate traitors, no doubt."

"He's wearing violet, sir."

Sarrett stopped inspecting his soiled sleeve and spun. He had to put a hand above his brow to shield his vision from the rain, but he could see Barton was right; the rider was approaching at a steady trot. The man wore a dark cloak dyed the faintest shade of violet, its hood obscuring his face.

Well, I'll be damned, Sarrett thought, a smile touching his lips. *I didn't expect this one for another week. Intriguing.*

"No need for that, Barton," Sarrett said, and his lackey stopped unsheathing his sword. "This is one of mine."

The rider stopped in front of the lieutenant, dismounted, and shook back his hood. He had a plain square face, and a large jaw with thin lips. The flames of the Harling's home reflected back in dark brown eyes as he glanced at the building.

"Love your work, Lieutenant Sarrett," the man spoke admirably. "Awe-inspiring, as always."

"Awe is a weaker word than what I'm going for," Sarrett replied.

The rider shrugged as if intricate word choice was beyond either his care or comprehension. "Though," the man spoke, "despite roasting some Loyals, you still look upset about something. What's bothering you, Lieutenant?"

Sarrett glared, crossing his arms over his chest. An image of Mayra and his children flashed through his head, but he buried it under a fresh layer of anger. The lieutenant rolled his shoulders back and took a step toward the newcomer, standing several inches taller than before. The man's horse twitched and whinnied nervously at the advance.

"The Master of the house I've kept for now. But if your report isn't good, I'm afraid tossing you into the flames will be the only remedy I can think of for my mood."

The man's face burst into a vicious grin. "Oh, it's better than we hoped. You won't need to map those cursed woods if the rebels are planning on coming out of them and heading for Lorington."

Barton glanced sharply at the lieutenant, eyes wide. Sarrett returned the rider's grin and clapped him on the shoulder.

"Well, let's get you out of that ugly violet and this horrible rain and have a drink," Sarrett laughed. "Courtesy of Harling's private stock, though I'm afraid his girls won't come with it this time."

In the lieutenant's rooms at the top of Towne Centre's tower, Sarrett impatiently filled two crystal glasses with dark red wine to the brim. His spy sat in an ornate high-backed chair next to the fire, violet cloak and boots discarded at the hearth. The lieutenant did not like this particular man's attitude, nor the way he threw loyalty and honor around like a cheap whore.

"So, explain further," Sarrett commanded. He preferred to stay standing, elevated taller than his guest. "I haven't heard from you in a month. I want to know how you came across this information about Lorington."

Infuriatingly, his spy held up a dismissive hand and swallowed two large mouthfuls of his drink. The man glanced out the dark windows framed in heavy, ancient velvet. "Good Lord! I forgot how addicting this stuff is."

"When will they try to take Lorington?" Sarrett urged. "Master Moore has the best defenses in northern Rhethos, but it will take Caldrell nearly a month to reach us if this becomes a problem."

This was something Sarrett did not have the power to deal with on his own; if Lorington needed help, they would reach out to the closest towne with military troops: Kaylyn. And his captain had only allowed him a small force in the towne, not nearly enough to defend Lorington's fifty thousand loyal citizens.

"Will's Masters at Patten say they'll arrive in three days," the spy replied. He set his wine glass down on a table next to the fireplace and extended his thick fingers toward the roaring flames. "Though," he added, "that information was dated. They relay all their main plans through the brother townes just north of here, and it doesn't take much to get some of his people to talk."

He paused and grinned proudly up at Sarrett, as if he alone were capable of the job he performed. The lieutenant didn't bother trying to look impressed, no matter how much this news unsettled him.

"By my calculations, you now have half a day before they reach Lorington. He's got quite a few fighters collected."

"The Captain will want real numbers, not generalities," the lieutenant returned, eyes falling on the notes at his desk. *"Fail and Rhethos will gain a new lieutenant while you lose a head."*

"They're careful with numbers, Lieutenant," the spy sighed, and he paused to stretch his saddle-sore legs. "But Will has to have close to ten thousand marching at night toward Lorington, and they need at least that number to try breaking their walls. Up in Patten, all they've been talking about is bringing a bigger towne to their cause. They'll be giving their siege at Lorington everything they've got."

Sarrett resisted the urge to sit as a wave of uneasiness washed over him. Instead, he forced himself to take a deep breath and focus on the facts: he had been sent up here to stop the rebellion from becoming a big enough problem for his superiors to worry about. His captain was a month's ride away with The Bradford's army. Will was making a move in that time to do as much damage as possible before Caldrell's arrival.

What can I do to prove my value, to Caldrell and to Mayra? Sarrett thought, shifting his gaze out the window at Kaylyn's streets. His eyes danced over the smoldering remains of the Harling home. *This is my chance. A full assault isn't possible but . . .*

As an idea hit Sarrett, he gripped the glass of wine he held more appreciatively, knowing it was the drink's effects that made the brutal plan manifest in his mind.

"The rebels will be giving this advance everything they've got, yes?" Sarrett confirmed, and his spy nodded blankly. "All their supplies that they've managed to scrounge over the years will be in one place?"

"That's what I said," the man said slowly, not following Sarrett's train of thought at all.

Sarrett looked back at the man from his place at the window, and nearly shouted when he saw his dead sister sitting on the arm of his spy's chair, her long black hair framing her rotted, young face. Sarrett blinked and ran a shaking hand over his mouth. Her black eyes rippled with tears that dripped onto her pale gown as she glared straight through him.

Not now, the lieutenant thought. It took all his strength to hold still, to not cry out and make himself look insane. *Go away. Good Lord, little Lily, disappear!*

The figure beside the fire stood and shook her head sadly. Sarrett held his ground though his heart thundered. The girl opened her mouth, exposing a black tongue, and again the words she uttered boomed in his head.

"You are a monster and a murderer, Jon. Do you think cowardly sabotage will earn you fame? Is this all you are capable of?"

Sarrett swallowed dryly. How could he explain himself to her? After her untimely drowning, Sarrett had no one to fight for, nothing but the dim aspect of the indiscernible future. He knew that he could be better than his Insane Captain, and that he *liked* the horrible things he had done to get where he was today. But she knew nothing. She was nothing but a guilty projection of his mind.

"You will not sleep one minute until you turn from your twisted course, brother."

Her small round face, one that used to smile and laugh with him as a child, shifted into a blinding sneer of malice. Sarrett cringed as she reached toward him, rushed forward, and dissipated in a shower of sharp colors an inch from his nose.

"Are you well, sir?" the spy eyed the lieutenant. "Too much wine?"

"By the time Captain Caldrell arrives in Kaylyn Towne," Sarrett steadied his voice, "we will have already crippled the rebellion for him. I will hand him Will's head, and tell him it was because of your assistance that we accomplished so much with so few resources . . .if you can tell me a few more details."

"Well, now you really have my attention, Lieutenant," he replied, sitting straighter in his chair. The man took another small sip of his wine, then adjusted his damp coat closer to the fire with the side of his foot. "Though, I have a couple questions for you first."

Sarrett bristled. "Keep them short," he snapped.

"Of course," his spy said, an easy smile playing across his lips. "I know how valuable your time is. I only wanted to ask if you burned my wife and child along with The Hamond Inn."

Sarrett let the silence hold for a few breaths, then sighed as if he truly cared. He knew the man didn't feel a thing for Angelyn or Joshua McKinlee, especially after leaving them for the thrill of military work sixteen years ago.

"I hate to disappoint you, Travok," the lieutenant said, "but I didn't burn nearly as many traitors as I wanted that night. However, after you help me with this business at Lorington, we will go north into those trees. There you'll find your dear, lost family, no doubt wearing rebel violet."

CHAPTER THIRTY-SEVEN

CYBARYS' SERVANT ON RHETHOSIAN SOIL

Devaki couldn't stop staring at the color of Rhethos. Everything she could see from the moment the sailors spotted land was gray, stretching out in every direction. She had been sheltered in Armelle, yes, but northern Rhethos looked more than just foreign to her; it seemed unreal.

In the dead of night, the countryside was a bleak canvas of rocky, sodden earth, empty of any form of life save for emaciated trees and harsh shrubs. From her spot at the prow of *The Blue Memory,* she could make out the sharp, black cliffs of distant mountains that pierced into roiling clouds. But before them, along the ashy beach where the rebels were slowly guiding the ship, Devaki could only see dismal shades of green and gray.

This is the place the rebels are fighting for? she thought, pressing herself against the cool wood of the railing to avoid the sailors moving swiftly around her. *This is where the Goddess' forgotten children live?*

"You!" barked a deep voice. "Come here."

Devaki glanced over her shoulder at Rowlann, who had placed himself below the main sail. He stood centrally located so his men and the ship's crew could take orders and report to him in an efficient manner.

Even though Rowlann had spoken little to her during the remainder of their voyage, Devaki had learned a few things about him from watching carefully. Being precisely organized was something he valued. Ducking underneath the raised arms of a man guiding one of the keel lines along the ship's edge, Devaki made her way over to the Rhethosian Master.

"We'll be dropping the anchor just offshore in a few minutes," Rowlann began without preamble. His gaze was fixed on the water, and in the moonlight

Devaki noticed his pale blue eyes were washed down to silver. "We have strict orders to meet with the rest of our forces in less than twenty-four hours. I'd tell you to stay with the ship—"

"But—"

"But that's not going to happen, is it?" Rowlann finished for her, finally meeting her eye.

Devaki smiled a little. The man's hard face was almost impossible to read, but she thought she noticed a twitch of amusement at the edges of his lips. She nodded in silent agreement, crossing her arms over her chest to emphasize the fact that she wasn't staying behind.

An involuntary shiver went through her when she brushed the scab of the rune carved into the skin above her heart. Since the storm had magically dissipated, the sailors and the rebels alike had avoided Devaki with fearful precision, and, despite how hurtful that was, she didn't blame them.

Being superstitious against Armellan magic was typical for Rhethosians, but when an unseen power cut a shape from a dead language into a girl's chest to part the clouds and calm the seas, anyone would be terrified.

I'm still terrified myself, Devaki thought, but she forced herself to avoid that emotion. She had no reason to fear her Goddess or her motives, did she? Thinking on it further frightened Devaki more than anything else she could now face on this foreign soil. It was better to focus on what she did know and leave the rest to faith.

It didn't take long for the rebels to prepare to disembark from *The Blue Memory*; it seemed they all feared not following Rowlann's schedule enough that, as soon as the anchor dropped, everyone on deck fell silent and doused the few remaining lamps.

From listening to the men talk the last few days, Devaki knew why tensions were high and mouths were clamped shut: these rebels were enemies of their former Lord Bradford, traitors that would be hung or burned at the stake if the Rhethosian military were to find and catch them.

Devaki stayed quiet at Rowlann's side while the men lowered dinghies one by one into the dim, sage-green waters of the Rhethosian coastline. Their sets of plated armor were covered in thick, dark cloaks, and all shows of rebel violet that the men had displayed proudly throughout the voyage were now tucked safely away. The chilled night air seemed to take on a slightly metallic smell that overpowered the sour salt of the sea. Excitement and determination were contagious, and Devaki felt her heartbeat quicken in anticipation.

She and Rowlann boarded the last boat and followed in the wake of the rebels who had rowed toward the coast before them. Though she sat in the center of the dinghy, Devaki leaned constantly from side to side, desperate to see all that she could of this new kingdom. The rebels had chosen a remote place to discreetly land, and she was hoping that this gloomy landscape was not all Rhethos had to offer.

"Hold tight," Rowlann muttered, and he tapped her on the shoulder. The bow of the little boat smacked into sand, jarring them to a sudden stop. They had arrived. Devaki ignored Rowlann's warning and leapt to her feet, making the dinghy rock dangerously in the shallow waters. She launched herself over the side and ran up the beach to the grassy shore.

Smooth pebbles and grit stuck to the bottom of her silk slippers, but Devaki barely noticed how uneven her steps were. She brushed past the rebels that were checking their weapons and talking quietly amongst themselves until she marched over the initial rise of the beach. Before her was, unfortunately, more of the same land: bleak hills, pockmarked with ugly stones that ranged in every direction toward the distant mountains.

Devaki sighed, remembering a story the monks at the Valsara Temple had told many times in her childhood: when Rhethos still worshiped Cybarys and the world was at peace, the oldest temple to the Goddess rose out of the center of northern Rhethos' largest forest. People came from everywhere to see the incredible structure and offer blood to their Mother at this most sacred spot of land.

Closing her eyes, Devaki touched the old scar of a Guidance Rune on the curve of her shoulder and traced its shape several times. Heat bloomed down her arm all the way to her fingertips, and when she opened her eyes, Devaki felt her gaze pulled northwest.

"They must be that way," she murmured. "The temple ruins . . ."

"You need to stay close!"

Devaki heard Rowlann's voice from behind her, a low, dangerous grumble. He grabbed hold of her arm, yanking her fingers off the rune scar, and Devaki shuddered as the warm connection coursing through her body was cut off.

"Do not wander," Rowlann chided, glaring down at her from below his knitted eyebrows. "It's not safe."

"Where are the woods?" Devaki asked, brushing off his words. "After I've met Will, I want to go there."

"You're not even supposed to be here," Rowlann sighed. "You don't get to decide where we go." He let go of her arm and motioned for her to follow him back where they'd come from. She reluctantly obeyed, still feeling her attention being pulled back inland, toward a part of Rhethos she couldn't see.

Rowlann marched over to a man Devaki didn't recognize from the ship, an older fellow who was situated in the center of the group of rebels. He held the reins to half a dozen horses, which he handed to the rebels who hadn't already acquired a mount.

"Thought you'd be here hours ago," the stranger said to Rowlann. He spoke gruffly but grinned through each word. Devaki noticed that, even in the poor light, the man had few teeth left. "Your horses have been getting restless out here."

"There was a storm," Rowlann explained shortly.

The stranger glanced down at Devaki, and the wrinkled skin around his eyes blossomed with shock. "Who is that?" he asked, pointing right between Devaki's eyes. "She's a bit young for you, isn't she?"

Rowlann snorted and held a hand up when Devaki opened her mouth to retort. "Lorington is less than a day's ride inland, correct?"

The horseman nodded, though he still stared openly at Devaki. "Will should be setting camp outside the towne tonight. It'll be a sight to see when you get there. All our men gathered together, no doubt scaring the shit out of Master Moore and his people behind their walls."

"They're not hurting anyone, are they?" Devaki asked, and she instantly regretted the question when the horseman gave her a dubious look, and Rowlann clamped a warning hand a little too tightly on her shoulder.

They're talking about a siege, she reminded herself, feeling blush rise on her cheeks.

"We'll leave immediately," Rowlann said, and he took the reins to the remaining horse. When Devaki glanced around the beach, she saw that all the other rebels had mounted and were awaiting instructions, while the sailors had already made their way back down to the dinghies. Devaki stared back at *The Blue Memory*, suddenly aware of how far she'd come and where she was now headed.

"Miss Tarran," Rowlann began, and Devaki started when he put the Rhethosian title before her name; it still sounded so odd. "I need to ask you a question before we go any further."

Intrigued, Devaki met the rebel Master's gaze. She was about to give him an impatient stare and tap her foot in mock-frustration, but the ideas faded away when she saw the seriousness on his face. The rest of the men had formed neat ranks, their horses shifting their weight back and forth in the wet sand, and none of the rebels looked at her, despite the fact that she had their commander's full attention. Devaki waited, a sense of unease itching up her spine.

"There will be bloodshed where we are riding," Rowlann started plainly. "You will have to witness it and endure it because of the position you've put yourself in. Since you are here, however, there is a way you could help us and maybe save some lives."

"Really?" Devaki asked, trying to keep the hopeful note out of her voice. "What do you want?"

Rowlann placed a gloved hand on the neck of his horse, steadying it, and lowered his voice. "You did magic the likes of which only appears in legends, Princess. You say you don't understand what happened during that storm, but from what I've seen of the Goddess Touched, you have a powerful connection to your Mother. My men could benefit from that connection if you'd carve Blessing Runes on their armor."

Devaki felt her breath catch in her throat. She clenched her hands together, unconsciously running her fingers along her prayer bracelets. "You want me to keep you safe so you can murder your enemies more easily?" she asked. The words tasted like bile on her tongue.

"No," Rowlann clarified. "I want you to keep us safe so we don't have to shed as much blood. Your Goddess wouldn't object to you using magic to help those trying to free her people."

"You don't believe in her," Devaki whispered, unable, for some reason, to raise her voice beyond its meek volume. "You don't follow her." *You're just trying to manipulate me for your cause's benefit,* she thought, and the fact of it made her heart ache.

"Then don't help and stay here," Rowlann said, shrugging. The movement scraped the pauldrons he wore against the curve of his chest plate, reminding Devaki how much armor and weaponry the huge man before her wore. "Armellan refugees are usually killed on sight, especially out here all alone."

Devaki narrowed her eyes, not quite mustering the emotional strength it would take to glare at Rowlann. *I should call his bluff,* she thought. *He wouldn't just abandon me here.* But she didn't have the courage; she didn't know Rowlann, couldn't trust his motives or his integrity, yet she had seen something on board *The Blue Memory* that she did know was undoubtedly true: she and this Rhethosian rebel were connected.

When she had bled on the ship's deck, with the winds beating across her body, the Goddess had shown her Fate's Strings. Red lines of shining magic had run across the ship, from one person to another, some out across the ocean, and some back toward Armelle. The Line of Destiny from her body had stretched out to touch Rowlann's chest. *It met with his heart,* she thought as she stared down the man in front of her. *Cybarys was telling me something in that moment. Did she mean I should trust him?*

Devaki broke eye contact with Rowlann, then looked down at his chest. She slipped off the ring she wore on her left hand, turned the sharp edge away from her, and placed it against the cold metal. After tracing the Blessing Rune for Protection into the iron, she split her skin along an old scar on the top of her forearm.

Squeezing the blood into her palm, Devaki smeared the dark liquid into the grooves she'd created on Rowlann's armor, pressing hard against the smooth surface. She took several deep breaths to clear her head, then spoke quietly:

"Dear Mother, keep this man safe. Give him your protection, so he may continue to live and see the path back to your love."

Bright red sparks lit up the gray night, blossoming from the cut on Devaki's arm and down the trail of blood to her palm. Beads of coruscating maroon clung to the rune scratched into Rowlann's chest plate, glowing like soft bits of jewels in the moonlight.

"I've never done this before, you know," Devaki said, "so I am not sure how it will work. But I do know the magic will only be active if I'm offering blood."

Rowlann nodded, his gaze fixated on the bloodied carving on his chest plate. He shook his head briefly, then looked up at his men, who were staring at him with ranged expressions of disapproval and awe.

"Miss Tarran is going to give us an edge in the fight to come," Rowlann said, loudly enough for all the rebels to hear him. "I don't care what your beliefs are; we will take any advantage we can get against The Bradford and his followers. Form a line and step forward one at a time."

Despite mutterings against his words, the rebels conceded to their commander's plan. Devaki found her throat very dry; she still wasn't sure this was the right thing to do.

"Thank you," Rowlann whispered to her, and even though he sounded sincere, it didn't make Devaki feel any better. Nevertheless, she kept the rune on her arm open, twisted it so it continued to bleed, and stepped forward. It sounded like, if she wanted to help the people who served Master Will and his cause, she'd need to bleed even more when the time came.

CHAPTER THIRTY-EIGHT

A BALANCE OF BLOOD AND FAITH

"Y ou're dead, Joshua. Try again."

Joshua staggered and wiped sweat from his eyes. The tip of Orton's sword rested just above Josh's heart. Every muscle in his body ached, but he couldn't stop grinning. This was living, this was making a difference, *this* was fighting for Rhethos.

Except against Orton he couldn't land a single strike. And though Joshua brought fresh baked rolls from the blind Armellan woman to appeal to the man's better nature (his stomach), the rebel Master seemed invincible. "Dead, try again," he'd say, over and over, till Joshua was covered in bruises and soaked in sweat. They practiced at night, after Orton had taken care of all his duties and set someone else to watch in the tower.

"Do you think you could let up just a bit?" Joshua managed to ask when he'd steadied his breathing. His arms were so sore he could barely level the dulled sword Orton had given him to practice with. Despite the edges being worn down, hits from the blade still hurt like nothing Joshua had ever felt.

The towering man scowled, his blade held easily over his shoulder with one hand. Somehow, the training weapon was still as intimidating as the large ax the man usually carried everywhere with him.

"That's a funny thing for a dead boy to say," Orton barked. "If Will hadn't told me to teach you a few things, I would say this is useless. You've already eaten shit five times tonight."

A sharp breeze blew down the steep mountainside, buffeting Joshua's hair across his forehead. Usually, by now, his mother would have cut his hair to keep it from curling around his ears and into his eyes, but he refused to see her, let alone speak with her. Will was gone and Angelyn was working with the smugglers, something Joshua knew but didn't care about. He found himself alone for the first time in his life.

It was exhilarating, and, apparently, the only negative side so far was every muscle in his body screaming in exhausted agony.

"I want to try again," Joshua insisted, straightening his shoulders. "But not with this."

He set the sword down against the fence lining the cleared patch of ground and unsheathed Will's dagger. He loved this weapon and carried it with him everywhere. The weight felt right in his hand, and despite his aching arms, a fresh wave of determination rolled through him. Orton crossed his arms over his chest and gave him a disapproving scowl.

"Will told me something, the night the lieutenant set fire to the Hamond." Joshua stepped forward. He opened his palm and let the blade's hilt balance against his skin. It wavered, and he twitched his wrist just slightly to even the weight so the dagger wouldn't fall to the ground.

"With a smaller weapon like this, he said I could learn the balance of it and spin it to stab faster and more efficiently than a sword. Can you show me how to do that?"

Orton raised one brow and stared. Finally, he heaved a huge sigh and set his own sword down next to Josh's. "You are small for your age," he muttered thoughtfully. "That's not a bad choice of style for you."

"And I'm fast," Joshua added. He glanced down at the hilt resting across his palm, a solid piece of iron wrapped in old leather. The guard on the dagger was thin, allowing little room for error when it came to rotating the blade. If he could spin it just right, all his force would be concentrated along the edge of the dagger.

"Fine," Orton said, and grabbed Joshua's wrist. The dagger began to slip, but Orton tilted his hand expertly and it held still, perfectly balanced. "If you want to fight with something this small, you need to be quick. The key will be letting your enemy strike first. They'll see you as an easy target, so let them take the initial swing. Duck, dodge, sometimes parry, but not in the same fashion as a swordfight. Like this."

Joshua held his arm still as Orton spread Joshua's fingers wide, then flicked his wrist inward for him, so the hilt spun smoothly on his palm. Now Josh grasped the blade perpendicular to the ground. It felt like a good stance, his arm extended and ready to lash out. Joshua smiled to himself.

"Now spin it back," Orton commanded, and let go of Josh's hand.

Joshua flexed his fingers, getting a feel for the weapon balancing on his palm. Every time they'd practiced with dulled swords, he'd clenched the hilt and swung with every bit of strength in his shoulders, hoping to land a hit. Now, though . . . this was about steadiness, swiftness, and confidence. This he could—

"Damn it!" Joshua swore. When he flicked his wrist to rotate the dagger, the blade slipped and sliced a cut on the outward side of his little finger. The sight of the blood gave him a new idea. He reached into his pocket and pulled out the slip of paper Will had given him.

"Giving up already?" Orton asked, but Joshua ignored him and looked down at the set of runes written on the paper. He knew he couldn't shed another person's blood and cast magic; doing one would take away the use of the other.

But I bet I could use the Blessing Runes to defend myself, Joshua thought, staring at one rune in particular. *I haven't killed anyone, and I don't even know if I want to.*

"Will gave me these," Joshua said, showing the paper to Orton.

The rebel Master glared at the runes as if they had personally insulted him. "Put that shit away," he snapped. "I'm not spending my nights in this damned training yard so you can play with pagan magic."

Joshua frowned, glancing at the scars forming on his forearm, particularly the one that said Protection. Will had cut that shape into his skin, and it had helped him when he ran through the woods in the dark. *He said I have to make a choice,* Joshua thought. *But I want to find a balance instead.*

Tuning out Orton's grumbles of protest, Joshua turned the edge of his dagger toward his arm and placed the tip just below the Protection Rune, closer to his wrist. After glancing at the marking on the paper, Joshua cut the shape for Strength into his skin, wincing at the curve in the middle where he needed to rotate the blade sharply.

Now, he had all three Blessing Runes on his arm.

"Dear Goddess," Joshua murmured. "Help me stay strong." A bit of heat flared on his left arm, but otherwise Joshua noticed no change.

"Are you finished cutting yourself up?" Orton sighed impatiently, giving his sword an effortless swing in Joshua's direction.

Joshua nodded, readied his dagger in his right hand, and lowered himself into a fighting stance with his arm extended, ready to try again despite the blood dripping from his finger and forearm.

Orton took a mighty swing at Joshua's head, and Josh barely ducked in time. He could feel the air being swept aside by Orton's blade. As soon as he heard the weapon pass overhead, Joshua rose and, without looking at his hand, spun the dagger so the length of the blade faced his opponent. He slashed wide till the entire edge connected with Orton's breast plate. The sound of the blow echoed in a bright ring around the empty training ground.

Joshua stepped back and grinned. He'd finally landed one hit on the rebel Master, and for the first time he actually felt strong. Orton, however, did not appear pleased.

"I should make you buff out that scratch," he growled, examining the mark Joshua had made on his armor.

"You practically took my head off!" Joshua cried. "That wouldn't exactly 'buff out.'"

Orton snorted, the closest thing Josh had heard that resembled a genuine laugh. He came at him again, with wide, deliberate strokes, and Joshua practiced dodging out of the blade's reach, ducking under the rebel Master's outstretched arms.

Joshua kept his heels raised off the ground so he could pivot back and forth with ease, depending on how Orton chose to attack. Every time Orton took a second to line up his next strike, Joshua reminded himself to relax his grip on the dagger's hilt so he could feel the balance of the blade in case he wanted to spin it to a different position.

The next time Orton swung, Joshua clenched his left fist, forcing the new cut on his forearm to run with fresh blood. He met Orton's attack head on, clashing his dagger low against the guard of Orton's sword. As soon as their weapons made contact, Joshua reached upward to grasp Orton's gauntlet with his left hand.

Then, Joshua *pushed* with all his strength.

Orton flew backward as if struck by the force of a charging warhorse. He skidded against the soft dirt of the training ground for several feet before collapsing on his hands and knees, his sword in the earth beside him. Bits of ruby red sparks shimmered in the moonlight on Orton's arm where Joshua had touched him.

Joshua gaped, astounded at what had just happened. He thought landing a hit on Orton would be an incredible accomplishment, but knocking the giant, seasoned fighter to the ground? He stared at his bloody forearm and fingertips and found himself shaking.

"I'll be damned," Orton said, taking a moment to regain his feet and walk back over to Josh.

"I didn't know what would happen!" Joshua insisted, afraid that Orton would be furious with him. "I'm sorry."

Orton shook his head, disappointment clear on his face. "You'll be sorrier if you keep this up," he growled. "You can't have both: that dagger is meant to kill, and once you've done that, those stupid scars on your arm will mean nothing."

Joshua remained silent, unable to dispute this fact. The truth was he didn't know what he wanted yet; he was still figuring out how he fit into this rebellion, let alone whether he would dedicate himself to a religion and its magic that he was raised to hate.

"Practice that dagger rotation in your hand until you can do it blindly," Orton insisted. "Try not to cut up your fingers too much."

Joshua was about to say something when a distant rumbling started down the curve of the road. Around the bend of shacks and overhanging walkways came one large wagon, moving at a slow, steady pace. Joshua squinted in the poor light to try and see who would be leaving the rebel camp at this time of night.

"There they go again," Orton said, following Josh's gaze. "Marselle's one crazy woman."

"Where is she going?" Joshua asked.

"North," Orton shrugged. "To one of her supply drops. Before she started wearing rebel violet, that woman was part of a powerful family down in Clancy. Whatever connections she still has, she uses them to get supplies we can't find anywhere else."

Joshua didn't know much about this Lady, but he knew his mother was making friends with the women who sorted and distributed the supplies to the rebel camp and the rebel townes. He stepped forward to lean against the fence on the edge of the yard, watching the wagon go by.

Two women sat at the driver's seat, while a third was situated in the bed of the wagon. All of them wore black clothing with hoods obscuring their faces. For some reason, however, Joshua had an odd feeling in his stomach as they went past.

"Mum?" he said, not realizing he'd spoken the name aloud. One of the women at the driver's seat turned and looked at him, and Angelyn pushed back her hood. She tapped the woman next to her on the shoulder, Marselle, Joshua assumed, and the wagon came to a halt.

When his mother came over to him, Joshua thought he was looking at another person. She wore her long hair back in a tight, intricate bun, though bits of it still waved about her face. He'd never seen her wear black before, but beneath her heavy cloak, she wore a plain dress as dark as the towering mountains behind them.

She gave him a smile, but it was a cautious one, as if they were estranged acquaintances. For the first time in his life, Joshua noticed that his mother was getting older, and that she had a cold, determined energy about her that seemed to create a bigger rift between them.

"Where are you going?" Joshua asked. He had the urge to take his left hand off the fence and tuck it behind his back so she wouldn't see the fresh Blessing Rune cut into his skin.

"Lady Marselle asked me to help with a supply run," Angelyn explained.

"Oh. Were you going to say good-bye?" The words sounded childish, but Joshua still met her gaze as he said them.

Angelyn looked away now, glancing back at Orton who kept a respectful distance, then over her shoulder at the waiting wagon. "That's the last thing I thought you'd want, Josh. I've been doing my best to let you be free."

Joshua swallowed, suddenly feeling guilty. As soon as Irvin had revealed that his mother had hidden his magic from him for sixteen years, Joshua had felt so betrayed. *She sheltered me, she suffocated me, and she lied to me,* he thought. *So I've ignored her and spurned her these past few days, but she never meant to hurt me. And now I'm hurting her.*

"Just," Joshua started, then cleared his throat. "Be careful."

Angelyn nodded, and when he saw tears at the corners of her eyes, he sheathed his dagger and jumped over the low fence. Joshua put his arms around his mother's waist and hugged her tightly. She rested her cheek on his forehead, and it made Joshua aware of the fact that he was almost as tall as her; years ago, she would always put her chin down on the top of his head when he hugged her, but that wasn't possible anymore.

"It's okay," he said when he felt her shake a little.

"I'm sorry," Angelyn whispered.

That made a lump form in Joshua's throat. "Me too," he agreed.

Angelyn broke away from him and kissed his forehead before stepping back toward the wagon. "I'm proud of you, you know," she said quickly, and before Joshua could open his mouth to reply, she flipped her hood back onto her head and took her seat in the wagon next to Marselle.

Joshua watched them leave, following the north road out of the rebel camp and into the countryside beyond. Long after Orton went to sleep, Joshua stayed up in the training yard, balancing his dagger in his palm, rotating the edge back and forth until the sun rose.

CHAPTER THIRTY-NINE

UNDER THE COVER OF DARKNESS

Night fell on the outskirts of Lorington much quicker than Will expected. It seemed as if the entire day, one he spent organizing his men and sending missives for peaceful resolution to Master Moore, had taken place in a matter of moments. Right now, all he could do was force himself to rest his tired legs as he joined Irvin at the back of the columns of rebels.

"You look like shit," Irvin commented with a grin. He sat on the edge of one of the supply wagons that trailed behind the rebel forces in a black line along the countryside.

Will shrugged wordlessly, as if Irvin's comment was a fact that he didn't care to dispute. They had stayed off the main roads on their march south and arrived outside Lorington's walls in the cover of night just as Will had wanted, but he hadn't slept since leaving the rebel camp.

When Will glanced back over his shoulder, he saw the dark slopes of land covered in the troops he'd spent the last decade persuading to fight with him. Seeing them ranged openly across enemy territory made the ache in his head and the heaviness of his eyelids seem like small prices to pay.

"How long do you intend to wait for Moore to reply?" Irvin asked, adjusting his tone to a more serious one. He snatched a loaf of bread out of the arms of a rebel who was walking by, tore it apart, and tossed half at Will.

Will caught it, but he handed it right back to the rebel Irvin had grabbed it from. He knew how important their supplies were, and despite his exhaustion, he didn't feel like eating. The group of men all gave him nods of appreciation and made their way back up into the columns of fighters.

"If he doesn't send a message by nightfall tomorrow, we'll press forward." Will said the words with his eyes on the towne's walls on the other side of the field, giant gray blocks of granite that seemed impenetrable from his spot on the ground.

"Good," Irvin commented, and Will could hear the impatient edge in his voice. "In the meantime, the archers know to stay out of range, and the men know to keep their weapons sheathed?"

Will nodded, playing back the conversations he'd had with his Masters over the last day. He knew Irvin was only asking because he was trying to point out how useless missives were at this point.

Irvin doesn't approve of these niceties, but I think they set us apart from the military monsters that rule this kingdom. Lorington's Towne Master needs to be given the chance to negotiate with the army outside his walls.

"I've been waiting a lot longer than you have for this," Irvin murmured, and Will glanced up at his friend to see cold certainty in his pale blue eyes.

"I know," Will agreed. "This fight will bring us one step closer to the Rhethosian Captain. You'll get the revenge you want, I promise."

Irvin grimaced, a shadow of the past's pain flashing across his face. For once, the former Towne Master remained silent and only nodded shortly.

"Master Will," spoke up one of the rebels standing guard near the supply wagons. "You and Master Irvin can rest if you need to. We can keep watch."

Irvin snorted and spun from his perch to turn on the man before Will could speak. "Piss on that," Irvin swore. There was a critical look in his eye as he stared down at the young man, who wore cracked leather armor and a smalls-word at his hip. "*You* need rest from the looks of you. I could take a wave of a dozen Rhethosian guardsmen at this very moment and spit their blood back in their faces."

Will frowned, but he noticed that the young rebel and his companions all laughed appreciatively at Irvin's remarks. "Thank you, for your offer," Will said, and the man nodded before turning back to his friends, all of whom were gathered together to stay warm through the evening's increasing cold.

"Though, if you're making offers," Irvin added, putting on a charming smile, "we could use a drink. Fetch us a bottle of something, will you?"

The young rebel glanced between Irvin and Will, then shrugged apologet-ically. "You don't mean liquor, do you?" he asked. "Master Will made it clear none was to be brought with us."

Irvin gave Will a sidelong glance. "Of course he did," he muttered, rolling his eyes toward Will so the gathered rebels wouldn't see. "That was good of him. Very thoughtful, brother."

Will smiled briefly. He took a step forward to speak with the rebels further when a rush of intense heat flew past the side of his head. Flames blinded his vision and singed strands of his hair. That single flare of light lodged itself in the center of the young rebel's chest. Will had to blink several times to see the arrow's shaft, its fletching dark blue.

The man shrieked in pain as his friends tried to smother the flames that engulfed his neck and face. Will spun toward Irvin, his sword flying from its sheath. Irvin leapt down from his vantage point, ducking.

If Will had been standing a step to the left, the lit arrow would have struck him instead of flying into the young rebel's chest. Nevertheless, it had been a skilled shot, one that would have been made from higher ground.

"Sound a call up the ranks!" Will shouted. "The enemy is coming from behind!"

He grabbed Irvin's arm and yanked them down against the ground as a volley of fire sailed toward them through the night sky. Will shot a glance sideways, worried for his men that were gathered around the supply wagons, but most of the shots fell short of the rebels. Instead, the row of wagons closest to Will, old wood colored with violet paint and banners, burst to blazing light.

The groups of rebels scrambled for cover, but found none except for the wagons themselves. Screams of surprise rippled away from Will, all the way up to Lorington's walls. His best men were situated down there, far from the supply train and its few guards. A heat of a different kind flared in Will's chest, one of anger at this backhanded move from an unknown assailant.

He rose to his feet.

"Will," Irvin began worriedly. He stayed close behind Will as he strode forward, heedless of the flames bursting on either side of him. Will grabbed the nearest rebel by the shoulder, a friend of the young fellow who lay smoldering on the ground, unmoving. Will forced the man to look directly at him.

"Focus," Will commanded. "Run down the supply line and order everyone to pull the wagons out of their firing range. Can you do that?"

"But where's it coming from?" the man stammered, his eyes wide with fright. The flames of the wagons nearest them flickered brightly in his gaze.

"Are you blind?" Irvin snapped. He stepped forward, over the body of the young rebel. "Follow the arc of the shots with your eyes! See where the flames start?"

Will looked back over the range of hillocks they had descended to set up their camp earlier that day. The only other route in that direction besides the one they had taken was the Coastal Road, running southwest. "They're from Kaylyn," Will muttered aloud. "It's the Lieutenant."

Irvin shouted a horrific string of obscenities and waved his arms to get the attention of the nearby rebels that were still on their feet.

"Water!" Will bellowed when his men looked to him. "Get the water barrels! Don't just—"

A wagon down the line from where they stood exploded. Bright balls of fire rose into the sky as bits of wood and canvas pelted against Will's head and shoulders. He barely had time to turn as another flash caught his eye: a large bottle of dark liquid landed in a wagon full of food and blankets.

"Move!" Will shouted. The air around him grew tight, then pushed forward with enough force to send him flying several feet. His blade tumbled from his hand as he spun over and over on the hard, uneven ground. Bits of burned bread and broken glass scattered around him as he shakily raised his head.

The shadowed bodies around Will were not moving. Staying low against the ground, he crawled through the wreckage of the supply train, rolling over every body to see if he or she was still breathing. Sound and time seemed to break down into painfully slow, numb processes: the noises around him felt muffled and dull, and every movement took twice as long to complete. Regardless, Will couldn't bring himself to stand again without looking at each bloodied, burned body.

I brought them here to fight for their freedom, he thought furiously as he passed over the smoking corpse of a boy not much older than Joshua McKinlee. *For them to die like this instead . . .*

"Will, get up!"

He heard Irvin's cry, and the panic in his tone of voice suddenly brought the world back up to speed and clarity: Will's ears were bombarded with confused shouts and fiery explosions, and his heart raced back to full time in harsh beats against his ribs.

Will stood and saw Irvin silhouetted by the line of flaming wagons. His friend handed him back his sword, and Will was scarcely aware of gripping the hilt in his sweaty palm. Between the black of the night, the chaos of the flames, and the shrieks of agony around him, Will could barely focus his attention on Irvin.

"They're not firing at the men, just the wagons," Irvin said. Blood shone in spatters across his cheekbones, and Will noticed a nasty burn running up the side of his left arm. "But they're still killing plenty of us. It's got to be—"

"I know," Will spat, finally finding his voice. "But how did he know we would be here?"

"He's a low piece of shit, attacking at night," Irvin growled.

Will flinched when another explosion of flames sounded down the line, and a shard of a wagon wheel and fragments of weapons cascaded through the air. Ignoring Irvin's protests, Will marched through a fresh wave of black smoke, toward the nearest wagon. The wooden frame crackled with fire, but Will braced himself and grabbed the edges of a crate sitting on the edge. The tips of his fingers screamed with pain and the worn leather of his gloves burned away quickly.

"Don't just stand there!" Will heard Irvin shout behind him as he hauled the smoldering crate from the wagon. "Help the crazy bastard!"

Men and women approached on either side of Will, trying to save what supplies they could. Each of them looked to their leader before helping one another. When the next bunch of rebels stepped forward to smother the spreading fires, a fresh rain of arrows fell, whistling above their heads and hitting home in the already flaming wagons.

Bright pain lanced up Will's arm. He dropped the crate he was holding and batted at the flames spreading up his leather jerkin. Will felt his skin start to bubble, then water hit him from the side and he turned to see Irvin holding an empty jug.

"Damnit, throw that on the wagons!" Will snapped, glancing down at his charred shirt and burnt skin with a wave of nausea.

"You're welcome," Irvin said. His gaze went up the slope of the hill where the volleys were coming from.

Sarrett has the high ground up on top of that hill, Will thought. *But why would he make a move without Caldrell's army to back him up?*

"We've got to take care of him now," Irvin insisted, clapping a hand on Will's shoulder. "No matter how many men we lose going up there, we have to take Sarrett down."

"Without the supplies we're ruined anyway," Will said. The situation hit home harder than he thought when he said it aloud. They needed those wagons to withstand any siege Moore would put up from behind Lorington's walls.

"I know," Irvin said, and his fingers dug painfully into Will's shoulder. "I know."

When Irvin took a step forward up the hill, Will blocked his way. "Wait," he said. "Something isn't right."

He turned his attention to Lorington on the east end of the field. Even from a distance he could hear metal grinding at a steady pace in huge clicks of sound. The gates at the front of Lorington's walls were opening in minute increments, and, before Will could open his mouth to say a word, a deafening sound split through the air: a deep, raw battle horn roared through the night, drawing all attention to the gates on the far end of the field from him.

"They're attacking? Now?" Irvin asked.

"Moore must be working with the Lieutenant," Will said, watching as the attention of his men was split haphazardly between the blazing supplies on one end of their ranks and the opening gates of Lorington at the other. Will knew he couldn't reach the front lines in time to lead them before the Rhethosian fighters poured out from the towne. There were other rebel Masters up there who could handle whatever Master Moore threw at them.

"What do you want to do?" Irvin questioned.

"We stay here and take care of Sarrett," Will snapped. He spread his legs wider in a fighting stance, leveling his blade with his chest. "If you have the heart to wear rebel violet, look to me!" He raised his voice to a scream, and slowly the confused rebels around him gathered together.

Will glanced at Irvin, then to the rebels at his back. "If Sarrett is stupid enough to come here and sabotage my men, it's time for that bastard to die."

CHAPTER FORTY

BATTLE MADNESS

This was the night that would make all the difference. Tonight, thanks to his cunning, all of Rhethos would admire the Sarrett family name. *The captain will arrive in a few days and find I've already done the impossible for him.*

"At the ready!" Sarrett shouted, and he pointed toward the last few wagons in the rebel's supply train that weren't engulfed in flames. The rows of archers around him atop the hillside angled their bows in that direction. Sarrett waited until dozens of rebels rushed forward to grab the crates on the wagon before ordering his men to fire.

The land below him was a mess of debris and chaos, and it filled his heart with a sense of hope. Despite his contempt for the man, Sarrett silently thanked Travok McKinlee for the information that led to this brilliant idea of sabotage. There was nothing the scrambling rebels could do to stop what he'd started.

"Sir," Barton began, stepping up to his side. The man's plain face and dark eyes were distorted by the erratic shadows flying up the hillside. Sarrett glanced sideways at the guardsman, not wanting to take his eyes off the scene below him for long.

"What is it?"

"Your operation is a success, Lieutenant," Barton said. "But I think we should fall back before the rebels come up the rise with their superior numbers."

Sarrett sighed and brushed a hand over his breast pocket that held his empty wine flask. "We need to wait," he commanded, then raised his voice to shout down his line of archers. "Continue to fire!"

Barton looked like he wanted to speak again, but Sarrett glared at him until the guardsman shut his mouth tightly. Sarrett shielded his eyes against the glare of the flames and looked across the battlefield over the thousands of ranks of rebels. Many of them were turning from their eastward positions to head west, back toward the burning supply line.

Perfect. And now for Master Moore to do his part . . .

A grin split across Sarrett's face when Lorington's enormous gates started to open. Cries of support sounded down the line of his men, and Sarrett wished, in that moment, he could have just one more drink. He'd had plenty in the last twelve hours, possibly more than ever before, but this . . . this moment of victory deserved to be seen in the glorious, shining hues of the Sahma wine.

Nevertheless, Sarrett cleared his throat and unsheathed his sword. His men stared at him with wide, unbelieving eyes; they were a small company compared to the rebel force below and did not expect to make any kind of advance. This was a low blow of sabotage, not an open assault.

But in that moment Sarrett felt like he could do anything. He could charge down this hill with his guardsmen and destroy the distracted rebel force. He didn't need his captain or his army. This was his night. The drunken high running through his veins made that perfectly clear.

"Go down the line and prepare the men to charge!" Sarrett shouted in Barton's face, and the guardsmen ran amongst the ranks of Rhethosian fighters. The men slung their bows over their shoulders and drew short swords, ready and waiting in a trained attack formation. Sarrett let out a single cry and, without another thought, he sprinted down the hill.

Sparks of fire and tatters of canvas flew past him in brilliant flashes of color. Sarrett blinked through the smoke that drifted uphill, focusing on the lines of rebels that were forming to face him and his men. The sharp musk of burnt wood met his nose as the ground leveled out beneath him, but Sarrett refused to wince when he sprinted in between two broken, flaming wagons.

He held onto the last bit of his high, bolstering the remains of the wine's effects with fresh adrenaline. The edges of his sight buzzed with sharp clarity, the movements of the men around him defined in bright edges of ethereal light. Sarrett sprung forward toward a man wearing violet and brought his sword down with vicious speed. The rebel collapsed in a spray of blood.

The next man who stepped toward him was covered in burn marks that ranged over his arms and chest. Despite his injuries, the rebel howled for freedom with such force that the lieutenant backed up several steps in surprise. This enemy was not afraid of pain or death as he swung his weapon with all his might.

Focus, Sarrett told himself, and he blocked the wild swings of the rebel fighter once, twice, three times. When the man missed his next attempt, Sarrett pulled his arm back and drove his sword through his enemy's gut. Blood blackened his blade as he pulled it free, and Sarrett took a step back to clearer ground.

The rebel forces were growing frighteningly in number as more and more of their ranks drew back from the main force and toward the ruined supply train. Now that he stood on level ground, Sarrett could no longer see Lorington's gates or what was happening at the other end of the field.

When he looked to his men, fresh rage filled his veins when he saw that his miniscule force was slowly being outnumbered. Despite how well-trained his guardsmen were, they could not compete with the rebels' numbers.

This is my fight, Sarrett thought, readying his blade once more. *I will not let these traitors best me.*

His thoughts were cut short when he felt something bite into the side of his thigh. Swearing, Sarrett spun to see a man to his right grinning at him, his arm still extended from the knife he'd thrown. Barton stepped out of the shadows a moment later and cut clean through the rebel's arm, then dispatched the shrieking man as Sarrett looked to his injury. The cut was not deep, but each movement in his left leg pulsed with pain.

Another drink would dull that quickly. Why didn't I bring more wine?

"Press forward," Sarrett barked in Barton's direction. "Moore's men are cutting through their front lines."

"But we don't have—"

Sarrett slapped Barton across the face with the back of his hand, then threw a punch into the guardsman's gut. When Barton doubled over, Sarrett searched through the man's pockets until he found a flask. Everything flashed into familiar brilliance when he swallowed the entire container in two long, savory swigs.

This was his time, his victory; the numbers didn't matter, the supplies didn't matter, all that mattered was killing everyone between him and the rebel leader. *Find Will and take him down,* he told himself, marching past Barton and toward the clusters of rebels fighting back his guardsmen.

With fresh wine setting pleasant fires in his veins, Sarrett gathered his strength and swung at the bodies before him. His blade slashed through leather and flesh and bone, gore spraying against his uniform. As he bore into the rebels, his arms didn't feel the weight of his weapon or the impacts of his strikes.

Sarrett's thoughts were simple: *they will kill me or I will destroy them. I have to bring Caldrell Will's head, to keep my title, to earn back Mayra's love.*

The next enemy he came at was young, barely eighteen, and exhaustive sweat poured down his face. Sarrett beat back the boy's unsure advances with ease, then lowered his own defenses by dropping the tip of his sword to the dirt. Heat and fury consumed him, and Sarrett swung a fist at the boy's throat, connecting with bone-shattering accuracy. He could have easily cut the rebel down, but he was here to prove himself, to make his name famous, and he wanted to do that with his bare hands.

The boy sputtered and clutched at the side of his neck, stumbling backward in terror. He had no time to react as Sarrett ran him through, down to the hilt of his sword. Sarrett punched at his face with his free hand while the rebel coughed blood and howled in agony. Bones broke under his blows and Sarrett pulled back again and again, bruising his bloodied knuckles after six, seven, eight hits.

I will get my children back, Sarrett thought even after the boy had stopped screaming. *I will impress my captain.* He continued to beat away at the fleshy mess above the violet tunic till he could no longer draw back his fist. *I will make Rhethos remember my name.* When Sarrett forced the lifeless pulp off the length of his sword, he barely felt the cracked bones in his fingers.

Sarrett wasn't aware of his own men anymore; he scanned the battlefield, trying to find the rebel leader somewhere in the chaotic groups of men and horses. Amidst the pools of blood and twisted bodies that cluttered the ground, Sarrett started when he saw a pair of bare feet, blue and swollen with water.

They glowed an insubstantial gray, and his throat dried as he looked up at the pale form of his sister. She was lit like a deadly torch in the night, a pale flame against the flickering golds of the blazing wagons.

"No," Sarrett murmured, shaking his head in desperation. He could not see Lily right now when he was so close to his victory. But it was impossible to look away from her youthful face. Unlike every other time he'd seen her when her face had been full of contempt, Lily now bore a pitiful expression. She started to weep, her dead eyes flinching in revulsion at the corpses that covered the earth around her toes.

"Coward," she whimpered, pointing one shaking finger at him in disgust. *"You are a man without honor."*

Sarrett tried to ignore her and took several steps back, away from the illusion on the battlefield. Fear and regret started to simmer in the center of his chest, feelings he refused to acknowledge or validate. But Lily continued to cry. Her wet, silver form shimmered in violent waves as the wind blew sparks of firelight into the air and through her body.

He could taste the Sahma wine on his tongue, felt the gore covering his uniform, the broken bones in his hand, and the overwhelming stench of death around him. How could she look so real, standing there amongst the bodies? How could her judgment feel like the only brutally honest spark in his heart?

"I do this for *you*!" Sarrett shouted suddenly at the top of his lungs. "For our family! I loved you, little Lily!"

The Rhethosian guardsmen and rebel fighters around him stopped and stared. Everyone backed away slowly, as if from a crazed animal. Many glanced at the empty space where Sarrett's gaze was fixed.

Sarrett tried to swallow past the consuming lump of delirium in his throat. The wine in his stomach soured and stabs of pain lanced across his abdomen. Lily's illusion began to melt in small droplets of smoke, and her eyes pierced him with pure disappointment before disappearing.

She doesn't understand, Sarrett thought, fighting back the shaking in his arms and his jaw. *I just have to prove myself to her . . . to everyone. I have to find Will.*

His eyes tore across the battlefield in desperate arcs, searching every man on his feet. Finally, Sarrett spotted him near one of the flaming wagons, trying to rescue the smoldering crates of supplies.

Sarrett shook himself, straightened his shoulders, and marched toward the rebel leader with murder in his eyes.

CHAPTER FORTY-ONE

MAGIC IN THE CHAOS

Devaki smelled smoke before she saw the flash of fire. For the longest time she only caught the fading scent of the ocean, the aroma of wet clay, and the stench of nearby animals, but now, toward the end of their long, dark ride, there was only one clear smell:

"Smoke," she muttered, just loud enough for Rowlann to hear. She sat on the front end of his saddle, situated between the pommel and the cold, flat plate of his armored chest.

"What was that?" he asked, his voice gruff from not speaking since leaving the Rhethosian coast hours ago.

"I smell smoke!" Devaki insisted. She shifted in her seat, unfamiliar with the sore muscles that came from riding long distances. She kept her gaze on the countryside, ignoring the shadows made by Rowlann's riders on either side. They were ascending the slope of a small hill, and Rowlann pulled up on the reins to slow their horse's speed.

"I can smell it too, now," he said, and Devaki heard an edge of caution creep into his tone. He put a hand up over his shoulder, and the rest of the rebel group matched his pace. At the top of the rise, Devaki saw a glow begin to grow, first a dull orange, then a fierce gold.

Laid before them was a field covered in ranks of men. Thousands of organized rebels ranged over the wet Rhethosian countryside, all of them facing east, toward a city unlike any Devaki had ever seen. Towering stone walls surrounded homes, businesses, and a large castle at its center. The gates of the towne were halfway open, and men were pouring out from inside to face the ranks of rebels.

Devaki barely had time to take in the rebel army and the towne's troops that were assaulting them; her eyes were drawn to the source of the smoke.

Set back from the ranks of rebels was a long line of wagons, almost all of which were engulfed in flames. Devaki could see the shadows of men frantically rushing amongst the balls of fire, trying to pull charred crates from the wreckage.

"What is—?"

She had barely begun the sentence when a bright explosion of flames tore through the wagon train below. Clapping a hand to her mouth, Devaki shut her eyes when she realized the fiery debris coursing through the air wasn't just pieces of wood and canvas.

Rowlann steadied their uneasy mount and motioned for his men to ride up beside him. Devaki didn't look back over her shoulder to see his face, but she heard contempt clear in his tone. "Attacks from both sides. Those sabotaging bastards."

"Put me down," Devaki insisted. "I can't go down there."

When she glanced at him, Rowlann was shaking his head. "Those fires can spread," he explained. "And those Rhethosian fighters will cut down anyone they see, including you." Before she could argue, he raised his voice to a commanding level. "Keep a tight, narrow formation down the hill, and spread out into a full rank when we reach the field. Barrett, Jensen, you fall back toward the wagons, find someone in charge. Help them organize a counterstrike on foot."

"Yes, Master Rowlann," sounded the rebel company in unison. The horses to either side fell back and made a tight arrow formation behind Devaki and Rowlann's horse. Devaki's stomach clenched to an almost unbearable tightness, acidic fear clawing up her throat. *You put yourself in this situation,* she thought. *Maybe this wasn't the smartest idea.*

"Hold steady till we reach the front gate," Rowlann said, indicating the no-man's land between the rebel fighters and the front gates. "Then cut down anyone you see in Rhethosian Blue."

His men shifted their stances to face east instead of west. Devaki could already see more men pouring out through Lorington's open gates, filling the space between the two forces. She nearly jumped out of the saddle when she felt Rowlann roughly tap her shoulder.

"Hold tight, Princess," he said. "I will keep you safe. Let's see what your Goddess' magic can really do."

Devaki barely had time to glance back at the bloody Protection Rune scar she'd carved into his chest plate before he spurred their horse and forced it into a run downhill. Her breath caught in her throat, and, despite the brisk night air whipping her hair back from her cheeks, it took her a while to remember to inhale.

The distance between them and the front gates closed at a suicidal pace, and Devaki gripped the edges of the saddle with trembling fingers. *Dear Goddess,* she prayed. *I have faith in you so I don't ask for your protection.* She broke open the clotting skin on the Protection Rune on her forearm and let out a fresh offering of blood. *Please, keep these men safe.*

"Stay true!" Rowlann cried. Devaki looked up at the ramparts of the towne's outer wall and saw archers aiming at their approaching company. She flinched when they loosed a volley, but instead of cries of pain, she only heard shouts of astonishment, both from Rowlann's company and the ranked rebels they were riding past.

Sharp flashes of red sparked into the night, reflecting off the armor of the rebels on horseback. Devaki gaped as, every so often, cascades of blood-red light bloomed off the rebel riders and faded into the darkness.

Each time, it felt like the Goddess pulled more blood from Devaki, taking what She wanted to answer Devaki's prayer. At first, the men looked frightened, but she heard their shouts become more confident as Lorington's archers' shots bounced harmless off their armor.

"Rebel fighters!" Rowlann screamed and reached over Devaki to grab the sword on his hip. "Fall in with us!"

She shied backward as he drew the blade, the length of it running close to her face. They had reached the gate and the Lorington guardsmen that were forming ranks outside the giant double doors. Rowlann let out a battle cry and led his men straight toward the Rhethosian fighters, coming across them in a parallel line.

Devaki braced herself as their mount forced its way through dozens of men on the ground. The impact shook her as if she'd slammed into a brick wall, then broken through to the other side. Rowlann's arm worked with expert, deadly speed to their right while he twisted and jerked the reins in his left. Shrieks of agony drowned out all other sound to her right, while cheers rose in raucous waves to her left.

Devaki's head spun with the sudden chaos of it all.

This was *not* what she thought would happen tonight.

The rebels recognized Rowlann and his company and began shouting the rebel Master's name. Rowlann, however, spun their mount back around after the initial charge and reeled the horse to face the front gates. A man bearing rebel violet rode up beside him, shock and relief clear on his face.

"Master Rowlann," the rebel spoke. "We're glad to see you. We didn't expect them to open the gates tonight—"

"You didn't expect fires at the back of camp, either!" Rowlann cut in. "But we have no choice now: we have to press forward into the city."

The rebel Master nodded and raised an arm over his head to give his men a place to look to for leadership. When Devaki dared to glance around them, she saw Rowlann's company of men weren't far. Rebel fighters ran forward to fill in the spaces between Rowlann's riders, and many held shields above their heads to ward off the intermittent arrows falling from the walls above.

Rowlann raised his sword and pointed its bloody tip toward the Rhethosian guardsman before them. A thousand more were filling the field before the rebel forces, marching over the initial corpses of their comrades.

"Break their ranks!" Rowlann screamed, and a huge cacophony of blood-lust echoed around them. "Press past the gates into the towne!"

"For Rhethos!" The cry started back amongst the rebel ranks and grew in volume and passion as it was shouted by all those bearing violet. In response, the alarm horn from within Lorington's walls sounded again, burying all other noise beneath it. Devaki's ears strained, but she didn't dare take her hands off the pommel of the saddle to shield them.

Rowlann charged forward again, this time straight for the gate. His men's horses kept this pace while the rebels on foot raced behind them. This time, Devaki had to shut her eyes. The impact slammed her back against Rowlann's chest plate, and she felt a warm spray of liquid spatter across her face and neck. Horses shrieked, metal scraped incessantly from all directions, and time seemed to lose its anchor.

Breathe, she told herself. *Just—*

Her thoughts were cut off when she lost her grip on the saddle. Devaki's eyes flew open in time to see Rowlann's left arm lash around her shoulders in a tight embrace. Their horse reared and they fell from the saddle. Rowlann's shoulder took the impact, but Devaki flew from his grip. She tumbled violently, tearing her silk shirt to shreds until she landed in a puddle.

Devaki sunk her fingers into the mud, trying to get her bearings. When she glanced down, she saw the liquid beneath her was a thick gathering of gore, the source of which was a young man several feet away whose stomach had been torn open in an enormous wound. She cried out in disgust and scrambled backward on her hands and knees.

Everything around her was a rush of noise and movement, none of which she could clearly distinguish. There was no violet, no blue, nothing but bloody violence. Devaki tried to stand so she could run, but her muscles were weak and trembled beyond her control. Her ears drowned out the horrific sounds of battle raging around her and her eyes focused on the blood dripping from her hands and arms.

Someone else's blood, she thought, and she felt bile rise against her back teeth. *That's . . . someone else's . . .*

"Princess!"

She managed to gasp in a breath that tasted like copper and mud. Rowlann's deep voice met her ears and she raised her head, trying to find him. From her hunched spot on the ground, she could see innumerable corpses, dying men on their knees, and thousands of pairs of legs pressing back and forth in desperate attempts to stay alive.

"Princess! Where are you?"

Devaki turned on her hands and knees, toward the sound of Rowlann's voice, and came face to face with a boy not much older than herself. He was covered in blood, his chest torn open in a mighty ax wound that ranged from his shoulders to his hips. He stared at her with a slack jaw, as if he was trying to find something to say. When his eyes rolled back and he pitched forward into the muddled dirt, Devaki flinched sideways to avoid touching him.

That's when her stomach finally broke. The knot that had been forming at a consistent pace in her gut burst open, and Devaki vomited on the boy's corpse. Sobs tried to work their way out of her mouth, but every time she was able to gasp for air, all she could do was wretch.

With each gag that tore agony through her body, Devaki felt like she was losing more than just her stomach contents. She vomited out her innocence, her naiveté, and her faith. How could her Goddess let this happen? How could she let her children cause such carnage in the name of freedom?

An arm looped around her waist and pulled her to her feet, but Devaki couldn't feel her legs. She gagged over Rowlann's arm, her sweaty fingers slipping against his gauntlet. Rowlann dragged her backward, away from the front gate and into the ranks of the rebels that were still pressing forward. He knelt next to her, his hands on her shoulders to keep her standing.

"Are you hurt?" Rowlann demanded, his square jaw set in a harsh frown. When she didn't respond, he shook her. "Princess! Are you hurt?"

"What's . . . happening?" Devaki asked unevenly.

Rowlann rotated her from side to side, critically looking over the scrapes on her arms and shoulders. "Who's blood is that?" he asked.

Devaki felt her jaw tremble and tears welled uncontrollably in her eyes. "Not mine," she wanted to say, but the words wouldn't come out.

Rowlann opened his mouth to speak again, but he was cut off by a massive scream of metal on metal. Gigantic wheels cranked over one another from just inside the front gates. Still numb, Devaki glanced in the same direction as Rowlann. She could see the tops of the gates, and she noticed that they were beginning to close in on themselves.

"Damn it!" Rowlann swore. He kept a firm grip on her shoulder, and Devaki thought she might collapse if he decided to let go.

"Fall back!" cried one of the rebel Masters on horseback. "Fall back out of range!"

"No," Rowlann muttered. "We can't stop now." When he looked at her, Devaki saw frustration in his eyes. She also saw blood spattering his armor, some of it smeared over the Protection Rune on his chest plate, and fresh nausea attacked her stomach.

They're retreating? she thought. *All these people died tonight for nothing? I don't understand.*

"Devaki. Listen to me." When Rowlann said her name, Devaki was finally able to focus. He'd never called her by her first name, just "Princess", "Miss Tarran", or "girl."

"What?" she asked.

"You should not be here," he began, and despite the thousands of men pushing back and forth on either side of them, Devaki could still hear regret in his tone. "But your Goddess has chosen you, and I think you can help end this bloodshed. Do you want to stop these men from killing each other?"

Devaki knew the man kneeling before her was using her, manipulating her faith for his own benefit, but her heart and her mind were too numb to protest. "Yes," she muttered.

Rowlann gave her a sympathetic look, took off the gauntlet on his right arm, and offered his bare skin to her. "I need to hold that gate open," he said quickly, and when Devaki looked beyond his shoulders, she saw that the rebel forces were falling back from the closing front gates just as their Masters had commanded. "If I can keep it open, my people can break through, take the towne, and create peace. Can you help me do that?"

Devaki nodded slowly, as if in a dream, and took her ring off her finger. She turned the sharp edge toward Rowlann's skin and cut a Strength Rune on his forearm. It took seconds to cut open a scar of the same shape on her own skin and murmur a small prayer.

"Thank you." Rowlann stood and shoved aside the troops that were backing away from Lorington's gates. Everyone stared at him as he worked forward against the tide of rebels.

"Rowlann, fall back!" shouted one of the rebel Masters on horseback. "What are you doing?"

Devaki leaned from side to side, trying to see in between the shoulders of the rebels around her. Through the crowd she saw Rowlann march into the space littered with bodies, and the rebels around her gasped as arrows from Lorington's archers ricocheted from his body in deep red flashes. Both bleeding runes on her body ached and she fought back a wave of dizziness.

Rowlann gripped the edges of the thick front gate. The tips of his fingers clasped tightly to the wood wrapped in studded metal, and his boots sunk into the mud at its base. The clinks of the gate's chains slowed their progress, and Devaki winced as the strain of heavy machinery filled the air. A glow of maroon spread down Rowlann's arm and blossomed around him in a soft arc of light.

He took one slow, heavy step backward.

"Blood magic," muttered a rebel next to Devaki. "A pagan's curse!"

Dear Goddess, Devaki thought, ignoring the men around her. *Please let this work so it can be over.* She realized that, after all she'd just seen and done, she didn't know if anyone was listening to her anymore.

CHAPTER FORTY-TWO

AN INNKEEPER'S COURAGE

"I've never traveled this far north before." Angelyn pulled the hood of her cloak closer to her neck as she spoke, fresh rain sprinkling down from the night sky.

"Unless you live up here, darling," Marselle replied dryly, "there's no reason to give a damn about anything beyond Kaylyn."

Angelyn couldn't find much of a reason to dispute this, especially now that they were three hours into their ride across the dark Rhethosian coastline. The talk from southern traders in her old home was truer than she thought; the land up here was useless clay that stretched in long, thin miles between the foothills of the Rhethosian mountains and the edge of the sea.

"How much farther is it, Lady Marselle?" Belka asked from her seat in the wagon's bed. The girl had been quiet for most of the ride, but Angelyn could still sense her excitement; all she wanted was to go out on a run with Marselle, to prove herself worthy of being a driver, and Angelyn knew the question wasn't meant as a complaint.

"Not far at all," Marselle said, and she flicked the reins she held in her gloved hands for emphasis. "You can relax, girl. This should be a simple run for the both of you. We're in rebel territory. There are no Rhethosian patrols up here. Our only enemies are the tides and the rains."

"So that's why your friends can leave the supplies for us so easily?" Belka asked. She rose to her knees in the wagon bed so Angelyn could see her pale face if she turned from her spot next to Marselle in the driver's seat.

Marselle kept her eyes on the coastline, however, and when she spoke her voice was cold. "Listen closely, dear, because I'm not fond of repeating myself. I don't have 'friends' in the south anymore; most business owners and respected Loyals curse my name. But there are a select few who see the profit of working with the only person who can get them goods from northern Rhethos, and they are willing to brave these waters."

"Are the conditions really that bad?" Belka asked.

"See for yourself," Marselle said, and she lifted her chin to indicate the road before them.

They crested the small hill their wagon had been climbing, and at its peak Angelyn could see, through the sheets of misty rain, a wide cove cut into the curve of the coast. She shivered as a fresh gust of briny air hit her nose, carried from the unsettled waters up to the rise where their wagon sat.

"Miss McKinlee," Marselle began, "did your goods from northern townes come by sea or by road?"

Angelyn took a moment to answer, a bit surprised by the question. She had a feeling Marselle was testing her in more than one way on this trip. "Well, by wagon routes. Most sea traders refused to make port up here because of those rocks."

Clusters of jagged stones rose out of the surf below them, ranging along the edges of the cove and into its calmer waters. Even from the road above, the dark monoliths were intimidating, and now that she was seeing them for the first time, Angelyn truly understood why sea traders avoided this part of the kingdom.

"Your business partners are brave men," Angelyn commented as Marselle guided the horses down the slope of the countryside and toward the waters of the cove.

"Women," Marselle corrected, and Angelyn saw the corners of her full lips twitch into a smile. "Most of them are women. The money they make selling unique products down in Clancy, like salt and good lumber, makes the risk worth the reward."

Their wagon's wheels turned more slowly as the ground shifted to rough sand made thick with recent rainfall. Angelyn gripped the edge of the driver's seat when the uneven earth shifted beneath them, rocking the wagon in sudden jolts. She kept her eyes on the inward curve of the cove where the waters met the sharp decline of rocks and earth.

"It should be right over there," Marselle said, and she pointed at a spot partially obscured by the churning waves. Angelyn wiped rainwater from her eyes and squinted till she saw it: a violet cloth tied to a jutting rock just above a spot of shadows that were darker than the rest.

"The caves," Angelyn muttered, recalling what Marselle had told her about their destination. *Her southern friends are both brave and coordinated,* Angelyn thought. *They have to arrive when the waters are high to get close to the cove and fill the barrels in that cave with the supplies we need.*

"Shit!" Marselle exclaimed suddenly, and she brought the wagon to a sharp halt. Angelyn nearly fell from her seat, Belka squealed in surprise, and their two horses snorted indignantly. Marselle was a Lady of the South through and through, and Angelyn never thought she'd hear a curse pass the woman's lips.

"What's wrong?" Angelyn asked.

"The water line," Marselle hissed. "It's way too high."

Marselle tossed the reins carelessly to Angelyn and leapt down from her seat. She started forward across the small beach that lined the cove like a strip of lace. The breeze ripped back her hood, sending her dark red curls flying in every direction.

"Stay with the horses for a moment," Angelyn said to Belka, and she marched after Marselle before the young girl could protest.

"I don't understand," Marselle was murmuring when Angelyn reached her side. "The tide should be at its lowest right now, but the marker is barely above the water line."

Angelyn felt her throat go dry when she realized the implications of Marselle's words: the arc of the cave's entrance was nearly obscured by the rise and fall of the waves, the violet cloth dipping into the surf with each steady swell. Their point of entry was completely flooded.

"It must be the rains," Angelyn said suddenly.

Marselle spun toward her, sharp frustration in her gaze. Angelyn refused to look away. In Kaylyn, whenever she was presented with an unforeseen problem, she knew the easiest ways toward a solution were a calm heart and a clear mind.

"Even though the tide is low," Angelyn continued to reason, "the cove is flooded above its normal water line. Did your informants mention how bad the weather has been lately?"

Marselle sighed and shook her head, sending raindrops flying through the air. "Those lying bastards," she murmured viciously. "I bet they did this on purpose."

Angelyn seriously doubted that was possible, but she knew she had to prove it to her new companion to make her believe it. She rotated slowly in the sand, taking the time to glance over every bit of her surroundings.

The hidden inlet was obscured from the view of the countryside above thanks to the sharp drop that led down to the surf, but, as she looked a little harder, Angelyn saw something odd: fresh, uneven breaks in the cliffs above the marked cave.

"Look," Angelyn said, putting a hand on Marselle's arm. "The rains must have been worse than usual up here; parts of the cliffs have disintegrated and slid down into the surf."

"Lovely," Marselle said when she followed Angelyn's gaze. "You've got a sharp eye, McKinlee. Something tells me you were always meant for more than just innkeeping." She gave Angelyn a wry smile before returning her attention to the caves. "I don't need to tell you how important this run is, do I?"

Angelyn shook her head. Will and his fighters had taken almost all of the rebels' supplies with them to Lorington, and if she, Marselle, and Belka came back empty-handed, they wouldn't be able to feed the rebel camp, let alone trade with the brother townes of Patten and Morely on the other side of the Goddess' Woods.

"What's the matter?" Belka asked, raising her voice from where she stood with the wagon. Angelyn and Marselle both looked back at her.

"Don't say anything to her or she'll just panic," Marselle whispered sideways to Angelyn. "Let the useless girl stay where she is while I figure this out."

Angelyn frowned; she found it odd that Marselle trusted her after only knowing her for a few days, while poor Belka, who wanted Marselle's attention and approval for months, never got a task beyond sorting crates or holding a set of reins.

The night we arrived in the rebel camp, Will told everyone they would have a task, Angelyn thought. *He said we were all important in this place he created, and the same would be true when he freed Rhethos. We get to choose what we fight for.*

"I can do this," Angelyn said, her eyes on the cave's entrance.

"Do what, exactly?" Marselle asked slowly.

Angelyn ignored the rising beat of her heart and looked back at Belka. She motioned for the girl to approach. Belka led the horses and the wagon up to the edge of the waves, a worried look distorting her reddened, round face. Angelyn gave her a reassuring smile, walked around to the back of the wagon, and fished out a length of rope.

"Belka," Angelyn began, "tie the end of this to the wagon bed. When I pull on the other end three times, I want you to march those horses straight back up the beach."

Belka's mouth fell open. "What? Why?"

Angelyn unclasped her cloak, handed it to Marselle, then gave the end of the rope to Belka. "You want to be a driver, right? So, tie that off, and when I give you my signal, *drive*."

It took Angelyn a moment to unlace her boots, and a little of her anxiety calmed as she sunk her feet into the wet sand. She couldn't remember the last time she'd felt sand in between her toes.

"Are you sure you want to go in there?" Marselle asked. "The barrels are all the way at the back of the cave."

"I've lived next to the sea my entire life," Angelyn said. "I can swim." She turned her back on Marselle, then glanced back over her shoulder. "Now, help me with this dress before I lose my nerve."

Marselle laughed dryly and loosened the laces at the back of Angelyn's new, black dress with one hand. Angelyn's clothes were already soaked through with rain, but she knew she'd swim faster if she wore only her thin shift. When she shrugged out of the dress, Angelyn wrapped the rope around her waist for good measure and gripped its frayed end in her freezing fist.

She stepped into the surf, flinching as the waves crashed against her shins, then her waist, then her chest. She didn't look back, knowing Marselle and Belka would see the fear that was undoubtedly creeping up the sides of her face like a fever. Her eyes rested on the violet tie hanging over the cave's entrance, and her hand brushed across Will's necklace at the base of her throat.

By the time she reached the archway of the cave, Angelyn had to tread water. She reached out with her free hand and touched the gray rocks, rubbed smooth with the passing of endless tides. Taking a deep breath, Angelyn let herself sink beneath the foam and down into the sea.

The world became a dark mess of water and seaweed, pushing and pulling at her body in demanding currents. Angelyn blinked hard against the stinging salt in her eyes and ignored the stabs of needle-like cold piercing through her thin undergarment. She kicked forward into the dark hole of the cave, keeping herself as steady as possible with her free hand on the rock's edge.

Keep moving forward, she thought. *Don't think about anything but the supplies and the people that need them.* The narrow pathway of the cave started to expand as she swam onward, and Angelyn squinted against the dark waters, trying to see anything in front of her. Slowly, she saw a collection of barrels on the seafloor. Her heart skipped a beat, and a bubble of precious air escaped from her tight lips.

Angelyn kicked hard and felt the fabric of her shift strain against the motion as she dove a little further. Her lungs protested in dull aches against her ribs. She placed a hand on the first barrel and quickly counted eight of them in all, each one almost as tall as her.

On the sides of each barrel were iron rings meant for strapping supplies together in the hulls of ships. Her vision began to cloud at the edges as she quickly wove the end of her rope through the first barrel's ring. After surfacing two more times, Angelyn knew she only had a few more dives in her.

Just a moment longer, she thought as she wove the rope through the fourth barrel's ring. *You can do this . . . you can . . .* But her fingers slowed and cramped when she grabbed the edge of the seventh barrel, and the rope fell from her grasp into the sand.

Angelyn spread her arms wide and swam up toward the roof of the cave. Every muscle in her body fought against her command to move. Water flowed down her throat, making everything a suffocating blanket of sodden death. Her forehead slammed against the cave's roof, and Angelyn turned her cheek against it, scraping away strips of her skin.

Her mouth hit a pocket of air driven into the caves by the churning tide. She fought desperately to stay afloat, sucking quick gasps of stale life. Mere inches separated her lips from the roof of the cave. She tasted acrid stone and sludge. A small whimper escaped her mouth and panic clawed at her brain.

Breathe, focus. Angelyn sputtered salt water as she pressed her jaw onto the mossy rock. Her courage hung by a thread, quivering like the weak muscles in her legs, and then her mind conjured up something she didn't expect: the last line from the letter Will had written her before he left. "Be strong, Angelyn: you are a warrior of your own."

Angelyn took a shaky breath, pressed her hands against the roof of the cave, and pushed herself back under the surface. She paddled slowly down to the barrels, conserving her remaining strength for the rest of her task. After gathering the rope once more, she wove its length through the rings of the last two barrels. Her trembling fingers could barely work a finishing knot into the rope's end, but as soon as she pulled it taut, a final, desperate wave of energy coursed through her limbs.

Gripping the rope as hard as she could, Angelyn tugged on it three times. She felt the line strain instantly, but the barrels wouldn't move from their spots at the cave's floor. *Come on, Belka,* Angelyn thought as her vision wavered. *Just get them to float for a moment and pull us out. Please . . .*

The rope flexed again under her grip, and suddenly the water around her was filled with clouds of mud. When she felt herself being pulled back the way she came, coursing slowly through the black waters, Angelyn focused all her strength on keeping hold of the line.

Her head broke the surface and the world came back into sharp, gray resolution. She draped her arm over the rope, too exhausted to tread water any longer. Up ahead on the beach, Angelyn saw Belka in the driver's seat of the wagon, urging the horses to pull the line of barrels toward the shore.

Marselle waded up to her waist in the surf, the layers of her black silk dress billowing around her. She grabbed Angelyn's arm, and Angelyn clung to her with trembling fingers. When the sand hit the bottoms of her feet, Angelyn collapsed on her hands and knees, unable to move any further.

"Damn, McKinlee!" Marselle exclaimed, and Angelyn coughed out a weak laugh when she realized it was her fault the proper woman beside her kept swearing. "That was incredible."

Angelyn found her lips shivering too violently to respond. She glanced behind her, back into the water, and saw the eight large barrels resting in the waves. Relief spread over her, and her eyes wandered back to the cave's entrance and the violet cloth tied above it.

"Are you all right?" Marselle prompted.

Angelyn shook her head. A new feeling bloomed in her chest, and she realized she had never felt more alive than right now. There was pride in her past, for her home and her family, but this was a rush of pure, virgin excitement she had nothing to compare to. Her mind sought a comparison, trying to make sense of the emotions raging through her chest. For some reason she recalled the moment Will had kissed her on the steps of her cellar.

At the time it had been shocking, infuriating, even, but that rush was the only thing she could remember that came close to what was coursing through her veins right now. A short burst of laughter escaped her lips, and she was unaware that tears were welling in her eyes. She touched the amethyst around her neck, trying to calm her racing heart.

"I'm fine," Angelyn said, finding her voice. "In fact, I feel better than I ever have."

Marselle gave her a relieved smirk, then offered her a hand to help her stand. She gave Angelyn her cloak, which Angelyn wrapped around herself despite how wet it was. Belka was grinning at her from her seat at the front of the wagon, and Angelyn returned the girl's smile.

"You know," Marselle began, and Angelyn saw Marselle's gaze was on her necklace, on the stone that had belonged to Will's mother. "That rebel violet looks good on you."

Despite everything, Angelyn found herself nodding. "You're right, Marselle," she said. "I think it does, too."

CHAPTER FORTY-THREE

TWO KINGDOMS MEET

Fury, betrayal, and confusion were emotions Will could handle, but regret was something he truly hated. *How did this go so wrong?* he thought. *What could I have done to stop this?*

After Sarrett's men had charged down from their high ground, Will fought back the urge to slaughter every fighter he could see bearing Rhethosian Blue. Instead, he ordered his men to attack and made himself look toward the wagons and what could be saved from them. Some rebels were breaking away from the massed forces on the other side of the field to help those at the rear, and Will beckoned for them to follow him toward the supply line.

"Will!" Irvin shouted, currently occupied fighting two Rhethosian guardsmen. "Stay away from there before you get yourself killed!"

Will ignored him, focusing on the only thing that made sense: saving his supply wagons. Heat washed over him in a palpable wave, almost stopping him in his tracks. He ran toward the nearest wagon and helped two rebels who were trying to lift a heavy crate away from the flames.

A breeze swept across the battlefield, billowing up the fires in fresh clouds of destruction. Even as they stepped back from the supply line, the men gripping the sides of the box let go and fled for fear of being burned. The crate fell to the ground and Will barely got his fingers out of the way before they were crushed beneath it. He let out a cry when bright pain tore across his left side and flames blared up the length of his coat.

Fighting panic, Will tore off his outer layer of clothing just as his tunic caught fire underneath. Smoke clouded his vision as he swatted at the flames. Despite his efforts, when he glanced down at the left edge of his ribcage, he saw a bubbled layer of burnt skin that screamed the angry color of blood. *It's not that bad,* Will told himself, but his entire body trembled at the shock and severity of the burn.

"WILL!"

He spun when someone shrieked his name at an incredible volume. Across the field, his rebels were slowly picking through the Rhethosian fighters, and some of the wagons had burned down to smoldering wrecks of ash. Down at the far end of the stretch of land, Will saw Lieutenant Sarrett. The man's eyes were bloodshot and black gore caked his uniform. Will gathered his fury, pushed past the pain in his side, and drew his blade.

Sarrett came at him like a madman, and Will sidestepped the lieutenant's erratic strikes. It didn't take him long to realize that Sarrett was stumbling toward him instead of taking the smart, measured steps of a trained military fighter. Will recalled how the man had smelled strongly of Harling's special brew, but now, when Sarrett lunged at him with unbridled spite, he reeked of the Sahma wine.

What is wrong with him, drinking that foul elixir before battle? Will thought. The next swing Sarrett made was wide and low, forcing Will to lean backward to avoid being splayed open. The burn on his side stretched to a dangerous point and made his head spin with black agony. Despite his awkward gait, Sarrett pressed forward and Will barely swatted back a strike meant for his neck.

"Die, you rebel bastard!" Sarrett howled and unleashed a flurry of swift, fast strokes. It took all of Will's concentration to keep him at bay. He felt his sword arm tiring, weakened by the seething burn along his torso. The lieutenant was clearly intoxicated, possibly insane. Will gathered his remaining strength to put an end to the madness that the man opposite him had begun tonight.

Will stepped back and anchored his left heel in the dirt before pushing all his momentum into one sideways cut. He rotated his weapon halfway through the attack so he caught Sarrett's blade on a steep angle. When he pressed forward with his anchored heel, the edge of his sword slid down Sarrett's, slipped past the guard, and cut into the lieutenant's fingers.

Sarrett shouted in surprise and agony, dropping his weapon to the ground and clutching his hand to his stomach. He spat venomous threats in Will's face, but Will didn't bother listening. Despite everything that had happened, he felt an unexpected wave of pity for the blithering, staggering man before him. Beneath the hatred in the young man's Rhethosian Blue eyes, Will saw tears of fear and self-hatred form in dark clouds.

"I'm sorry, Lily," Sarrett muttered as blood dripped in heavy streams from his injured hand. He stared past Will at an empty space. "So sorry . . . Lily, please . . . I tried . . . Lily . . ."

Will stepped up to the lieutenant and kicked his legs out from underneath him in one swift motion. It didn't take much effort to get Sarrett to his knees. Sarrett ignored his sword that lay just within his reach. Will stood above him, blade ready, but something stayed his hand that went beyond the twinge of pity he'd just felt.

This was the man who had murdered Gabriel Chapman, threatened Angelyn McKinlee, burned The Hamond to the ground, and destroyed the rebels' siege in the middle of the night. He was an addict, a coward, and a monster. Killing him now should be easy; in fact, it should be justified. "Rhethosian Justice" at its finest.

And that was when the situation became clear to Will, even as he leveled the tip of his sword with Sarrett's chest. For over ten years, he had justified all his actions as necessary for his cause, because the ultimate goal of freedom was worth every sin. *Then I met her,* he thought, and his hand began to tremble. *What was it Angelyn said the night she lost her home because of me? "You commit murder, you ruin lives . . . you leave as much terror in your path as Lord Bradford."*

Is that really what I want to create?

"Will!" Irvin's voice brought him forcibly back to reality. "What are you waiting for? Kill that bastard!"

Will didn't glance at his friend, his first true supporter, despite the desperation he heard in his tone. Instead, he spun the hilt of his sword sideways in his hand and brought it down across Sarrett's forehead. The lieutenant collapsed in a spray of blood.

Irvin came up beside him, staring in dismay at Sarrett's unconscious form. It took Will a moment to realize that the skirmishes around him had died down, and the sound of ensuing battles were echoing toward them from the other end of the field.

"Tell me you did that because you want to torture him slowly," Irvin said. He was drenched in sweat, his thin hair hanging on either side of his long face, but Will could see no major injuries on his person.

Will shook his head, though not without a bit of regret. "Tie him up and throw him over the nearest horse," he said, and he put enough command behind the words that Irvin seemed to swallow a retort. Instead, Irvin motioned for the rebels behind him to come closer and uttered several quick sentences to the men.

"The Kaylyn guardsmen are defeated," Irvin said. "And I'd like to just take a moment and say I told you so. That burn looks awful."

Will glanced briefly at his left side and swallowed past a wave of nausea; the smell of the burned flesh was worse than the sight of it that showed through his damaged tunic. He waved off Irvin's concerns.

"We need to find out what's happening at the gates." Will jerked his head down the battlefield, away from the ruined supply line. "Tell the men to gather what's been saved from the wagons and form a guard around those supplies. They're all we have now."

He'd barely finished the orders when several rebels came up, pulling frightened horses by the reins. Two of the men bent to secure Sarrett with a length of rope. Will waited until the lieutenant was completely bound and unceremoniously thrown over one of the horse's saddles before climbing on top of his own mount.

As he rode toward Lorington's walls, Irvin just behind him, Will squinted through the darkness to see that the gates were still open. Was it because his men had broken through, or had Master Moore's fighters bested the rebels in the front lines and broken the siege before it had a chance to begin? Uncertainty wound through his gut as he spurred his horse viciously onward.

Will pulled up hard on the reins when he spotted something on the churned mud of the battlefield. Amongst the rocks and pools of blood were bits of red light, echoing like buried gems. They appeared in haphazard bursts, barely visible in the moon's light. Nostalgia hit him like a palpable punch to the chest, making it difficult to breathe.

Magic remnants. But that's impossible, he thought, dismounting and stepping toward the closest patch of blood-colored crystals. *How can there be a Goddess Touched here?*

Will knelt down, ignoring the sting that coursed along the left side of his body. When his fingers brushed the red sparks of solidified light, they disintegrated into gray dust. The weight of the evening's events threatened to crush him as this new development landed forcibly on his shoulders.

When Will looked up through the parted sea of rebels to the front gate, his astonishment grew further. Rowlann, whom Will had expected to arrive back from Armelle any day now, stood at Lorington's entrance. He held the massive slab of wood and metal open with his bare hands as the rebels forced their way into the towne square.

All it took was one glance at the man's bloodied chest plate and the collection of magic remnants at his feet to move the pieces slowly together in Will's mind.

Irvin matched Will's stride when the rebel leader pushed forward toward Rowlann. "Tell me you know how that's possible," Irvin whispered. "I know he's strong, but . . ."

"I have a feeling," Will said. "But I hope I'm wrong."

He marched past the front lines of rebels and up to Rowlann, who, miraculously, let go of the front gates with one hand to wave at Will and Irvin. Will glanced down at the Blessing Rune cut into Rowlann's arm and recognized the symbol for Strength.

"Good to see you, my friend! Though I have to admit," Irvin stated loudly, breaking the tension that hung in the air, "this is not the way I thought we'd gain entrance to the towne!"

A shout echoed down from the ramparts and a moment later the gate's mechanism locked into place with a perfunctory clang. The rebels around them cheered as Rowlann was finally able to let go of the entrance and step back so more men could flow through the gateway.

They had their orders if they were able to break into Lorington, and Will knew they'd follow the set plans. He turned his attention to the command of his elite forces.

"Explain," Will commanded. He ignored the men that slapped his shoulder and shouted victoriously at Rowlann as they went by.

Rowlann grimaced, rotating his arms and flexing his hands with a pained expression on his face. "The men have orders not to attack any of the citizens inside. Some of my company and several of the other Masters are taking control of the gatehouse and the barracks along the outer walls, but no one is pressing forward to the Towne Centre without your approval—"

"I meant *this*," Will cut in, and he pressed one finger briefly to the Protection Rune on Rowlann's armor. A flicker of maroon sparks blew briefly through the space between them. Irvin whistled in an impressed tone over Will's shoulder.

"She hid in the ship's cargo hold," Rowlann started, and Will noticed an unusual, uncomfortable edge creep into the man's tone. "There was a storm, so we couldn't turn back. I never meant to put her in danger."

An acidic claw gripped the bottom of Will's rib cage, peeling away layers of his life he'd hidden for sixteen years. "She"? There was only one person the man could be referring to, and the mere mention of her made Will's stomach turn sour with fear. Rowlann had to be lying to him; there was no way that one of the men he trusted most could ruin a simple mission like retrieving a message from Armelle's Temple Leader so badly.

Will clenched his hands into fists and stepped close to Rowlann, using all his remaining strength to keep his arms at his sides instead of around the rebel Master's throat. "You son of a bitch."

Irvin took a step forward, but Will didn't bother to react; his attention was drawn instead to the movement he spotted to Rowlann's left. A girl walked out from the large man's shadow and placed herself between Rowlann and Will. Everything about her sudden appearance made the rest of Rhethos fade away.

Her dark brown skin stood out against the silver flare of Rowlann's armor, and her wide auburn eyes stared up at Will with a calculating gaze. A mess of curly hair was plastered against her cheeks and her neck, and Will noticed how torn and battered her traditional Armellan clothing was. She said nothing, only staring at him as if she were measuring his soul from where she stood.

Sixteen years. He had been waiting for sixteen years to see this girl's face, to hear her voice, to know her mind. She was supposed to set foot in Rhethos for the first time after he'd set the kingdom free from The Bradford, so they could be introduced properly in a place that was free of corruption, tyranny, and fear. This was horribly wrong.

This isn't how it was supposed to happen.

Will watched as the girl opened her mouth to speak at almost the same time he did. Instead of uttering a word, he took a step back and set his bloody sword on the ground beside him as he knelt in the mud. Despite the many years that had passed, his fingers remembered the pattern easily as he wove them together, faced his palms outward, and placed the backs of his hands to his forehead.

Familiarity blossomed slowly on the girl's face, relieving some of the harsh lines of uncertainty that had sat under her eyes. The corners of her mouth twitched as if she wanted to smile, and her hands raised toward her forehead as if she were about to respond with the same greeting. Instead, tears welled in her eyes and a small sob issued from her lips.

Nothing could have prepared Will for the moment she put her arms around his neck. All he could do was hold her, amazed at how simple the action was compared to the many years that had passed between them. The meaning of everything amplified to a high frequency in his head, as if each action in the coming future would be infinitely more significant because of the girl he now held against his chest.

"I'm so sorry," she said. "Cybarys told me to come here, but . . . this isn't what I thought would happen."

Will shook his head, broke away from the girl, and stood up. Rowlann and Irvin looked at him cautiously, waiting for orders of what to do next. Everything pressed in on Will and threatened to overwhelm him; the captured Rhethosian lieutenant, the newly gained towne of Lorington, the destroyed supply train meant to feed his people, The Bradford's army less than a month's ride away . . .

He took a deep breath, forced the frustration out of his mind, and straightened his shoulders to their full height.

"Walk with me," Will said to the girl, indicating Lorington's opened gates with a turn of his head. "We're going to forget how we both got here. How we *all* got here," Will added, glancing at Rowlann, Irvin, and the rest of those around them. "We'll move forward. Together."

Rowlann nodded with wordless approval. He motioned for his company to gather around him so they could ride under the gateway first, keeping the path clear and safe for their leader. Irvin mentioned wanting to stay back with the rebels guarding Sarrett, and Will didn't miss the mistrustful glance his friend gave the Armellan girl at his side. Torches were lit by the rebels that had entered the towne first, bathing the stone walkway ahead of them in fresh light.

"Devaki," Will said, motioning for the Armellan girl to follow him. Will had waited many years to say her name aloud in her presence, and the small smile that touched her lips instantly warmed his heart. He walked into Lorington's courtyard with his daughter at his side.

THE END

ACKNOWLEDGEMENTS

When your heart and soul are inked onto paper, it is terrifying. Fortunately, I have never been alone in this author's journey. From the birth of the idea of Rhethos in a middle school classroom to the launch day of this book that holds every dark and light piece of myself, there have been people beside me. I'd like to take a moment to acknowledge as many of you as I can.

As an awkward teen, art spoke to me in both words and music. Both of my band teachers, the late Mr. Randy Tyler and the incomparable Mr. Chris Moura, taught me that I should never be afraid to authentically express myself. Mrs. Karen Waldmann (who soon became Mrs. Aragon) was one of the first teachers who just gave me permission to write and write and write. Thank you, too, for letting me recite Romeo's death speech in front of the class. My bleeding romantic heart needed that and has grown exponentially since because of our mutual love for Shakespeare.

Every woman can either sink or swim because of her parents. Thanks to my mom and dad, I have soared in ways I could never imagine. Thank you, Mommy, for letting me get every book, every journal, and every gel pen that I ever wanted. Your fierce pride has given me the confidence I desperately need. Thank you, Daddy, for letting me grow into a hobbit-loving hippy like you. Your love of classic rock, fantastic worlds, and hard work have given me my foundation for success.

There are two women who've stuck by my side as writing buddies since the day we met in a tiny kitchen next to the cat food. Betsy Snider and Cara Shaw, Rhethos would not be anywhere close to true freedom without you. Your honest, difficult, and brilliant feedback made Angelyn strong, Will merciful, Joshua adventurous, Sarrett relatable, and Devaki empowered. I hope you both continue to fight over your opinions of my writing for many years to come.

The ultimate confidence booster is when a professional in an industry you desperately wish to be part of acknowledges and praises your skills. Bridget Cook-Burch, since the moment we sat together, drinking tea and watching the sun rise over the red cliffs of St. George, I actually felt worthy of my own words. No one has ever cared so deeply for the intricate "real-ness" of my characters like you have. You knew they were parts of me and you honored them, sparking my launch into the writing and editing and publishing world. Forever, you are a star in my universe that holds extremely unique, compassionate luster. Thank you for being my business partner and my dear friend.

And, my soul mate, my Elven Sprites' father, my lifetime partner of Team Lyon. . .Montana. I know my books are not your style, but you have provided the foundation for my creativity to exist. All my adventures, my passion, and my inspiration are possible with you at my side.

Finally, I want to share some things with my girls. Terralynn and Alice, right now, you are small (in age and stature only). This fantasy world your mother has built has a hidden purpose: to show you that, no matter what challenge you face in this life, anything is possible. Never lose the spark of what gives each of you true joy. Let your hearts embrace whatever makes you feel alive (whether it be writing like this or something else). There is magic all around you, my Elven Sprites. I love you both.

ABOUT THE AUTHOR

Hannah R. Lyon is a bestselling author who has been working in the book industry for seven years. As the mother of Rhethos, she explores deep meaning within her fantasy series that span across the fiction world into the struggles and triumphs of today's reality.

As the executive editor and retreat coordinator for Your Inspired Story, Hannah has worked with hundreds of authors, helping them find their voices and own their stories across genres. She speaks about her experience in writing, publishing, and more at conferences, events, and retreats nationwide.

She lives with her husband in the Smoky Mountains of North Carolina, in an old brick house they are remodeling by hand to create their own castle. Her free time consists of indulging in story-driven video games, spinning classic rock and roll vinyl, and raising her two Elven Sprites of daughters.

You can find her on Facebook at www.facebook.com/ladylyon19, on Instagram at @LadyLyon19, and on her websites at www.hannahrlyon.com, www.freedomforrhethos.com, and www.castlelyonediting.com

REVIEWS

"A beautiful tapestry of adventure and intrigue, Lyon has the ability to create a deep passion for her characters and the world she built. Tugging at the vast human emotional spectrum, *The Rebel in Violet* is the beginning of a series that you will be caught in until the end. A debut novel that you can't put down."
–Finn O'Malley, Bestselling Author of "Keeper of the Elements" Series and More

"I couldn't put the book down! It pulled me into a world of intrigue and wonderment. This book transported me into different worlds and dimensions. It's just what people need to get out of the monotony and challenges of daily life. I would highly recommend this book to anyone who enjoyed The Davinci Code or Game of Thrones. I expect to see it on the shelves at my local bookstore, Barnes & Noble, or the next airport bookstore I pass. I look forward to reading book 2 in the series!"
–Deborah Wiener, Senior Board Member of the Quickscrews International Corporation

"This story shines brightly in the fantasy realm! Deep questions and even deeper characters swept me away and left me waiting for the next installment. Well done, Lady Lyon!"
–Woody Woodward, Author, International Speaker and Coach

"Reading *The Rebel in Violet* was like a voyage for my mind. Chapter after chapter, I felt infused with Hannah›s story, drawing me closer to her characters and their challenges. Her writing gave me the impulse to dive into my visual imagination, my emotions, and my values!"
–Sophie Roumeas, Mindful Therapist, Bestselling Anthology Author

"Not only is this book a powerful escape from reality, but its deep themes come back to this world with you afterward and leave their mark on your everyday life."
–Jacob Cooper, LCSW, CH, RMT

"I was delighted to find a combination of engrossing worldbuilding and amazing female empowerment in this book. If you'd like to be inspired by reading about a heroine navigating what it means to be 'free', this is a compelling book!"
–Nancy Mills, Energy Artist, <u>SpiritedWoman.com</u>

"*The Rebel in Violet* checks all the boxes. Suspense, magic, mystery, and rebellion? Count me in! This book gets better with every page. Full of surprising twists and turns, it kept me guessing until the very end. My favorite kind of book series!"
–Tiffani Freckleton, Bestselling Author of "My NICU Story: Written with Love" and "Letters to a Future Nurse"

"As an author who writes about personal transformation and self-discovery, I'm excited to endorse this book. It is vital for humanity today because it explores themes that are relevant to current social and political climates. The story highlights the struggle for freedom and the risks associated with challenging the status quo.

"It forces readers to question the institutions and systems that may be limiting their own personal growth and potential. Additionally, the book encourages readers to consider the consequences of their own choices and actions, and the impact they have on the people and world around them. In a time when many people are searching for meaning and purpose, it offers a powerful message of hope and inspiration.

"Lyon has created a captivating world with complex characters and an intricate plot full of twists and turns. This thought-provoking adventure explores themes of sacrifice, truth, and societal change. *The Rebel in Violet* is a must-read for fantasy fans who love deeper themes."
–Jeffery Olsen, Bestselling Author of "Knowing" and "Where Are You?"

"Fiction translates so much meaning into the real world, and you won't find a better example of that than this book. It is an epic adventure with heartfelt connection that is worth diving right into."
–Trevor Farnes, CEO and Co-Founder of MTNOPS

"Excitement, courage and magic, a battle between good and evil. Exquisitely written, Hannah Lyon is a master storyteller whose characters are complex, with binding relationships that grip the reader's attention to the very last page. Already waiting for the sequel."
–Maureen Ryan Blake, TV Host at Maureen Ryan Blake Media Productions, International Bestselling Author of "Step into Your Brilliant Purpose"